To dearest

Much L

The Imagined Child

Jauthe.

7/5/2023

## Also by Jo-Anne Richards

### My Brother's Book (2008)

'Richards has an acute sense of place, in its small town and big city guises, and a wonderful ear for South African idiom. *My Brother's Book* is her most ambitious work to date. Moving subtly between past and present, it casts a searing light on the way we reveal and conceal our truths in stories.'

– IVAN VLADISLAVIĆ

### Sad at the Edges (2003)

'After the novels of apartheid and of the state of emergency have come the novels of transition: Nadine Gordimer's *None to Accompany Me*, Ivan Vladislavić's *The Restless Supermarket*, André Brink's *Rights of Desire* and, of course, JM Coetzee's *Disgrace*. Jo-Anne Richards's third novel sits squarely in this tradition.'

– MICHIEL HEYNS, *SUNDAY INDEPENDENT*

### Touching the Lighthouse (1997)

'Her writing has the tang of authenticity, so that it seems as if she is truly remembering rather than inventing . . . The result is as engrossing as it is impressive.'

– ALLAN MASSIE, *THE SCOTSMAN*

### The Innocence of Roast Chicken (1996)

'Jo-Anne Richards has the writer's eye, that natural ability to sniff out the telling detail and the right word. She is a delight to savour – one of the freshest voices to emerge from South African literature in years.'

– PETER GODWIN

# The Imagined Child

Jo-Anne Richards

PICADOR AFRICA

First published in 2013 by Picador Africa
an imprint of Pan Macmillan South Africa
Private Bag X19, Northlands
Johannesburg, 2116

www.panmacmillan.co.za

ISBN 978-1-77010-277-4
eISBN 978-1-77010-278-1

Editing by Ashleigh Harris
Proofreading by Jane Bowman
Design and typesetting by Manoj Sookai
Cover design by K4

Printed and bound by Ultra Litho (Pty) Limited

# Part One

# Chapter 1

*I FEEL STUPID DOING this. I have no clue what I ought to be writing. It's lucky I've always been an early riser or I'd never have agreed to this, getting up at the crack of dawn to scribble the first banal thought that comes into my head.*

*I'm not even sure what good it does. That's the thing with new shrinks. I think Heather's at a loss and this is some shrinky fishing expedition – I know, let's make her scribble her innermost thoughts before her first coffee and some repressed trauma is sure to pop up.*

*My first attempts have all consisted of shopping lists . . . I'm sure I should get moving soon if I'm to meet Trudie by nine. Can't see the clock from here. Must remember to move it nearer tomorrow.*

*And now look what I'm writing. I told Heather I'm not much good at delving into my innermost at six-thirty. I'm more of a list maker. I like lists. They make sense of things. I'm sure you could deal with most heartaches and traumas that way . . . List them in the great shopping list of life. Write it down, tick it off, throw it away. Quite profound really, especially before coffee. I'll suggest Heather write it up as a journal article.*

*In Jo'burg, you can always judge the time by the cars. Here it's the roosters, then the birds, and the keening of the calf next door. Taken from its mother a bit earlier than it would have liked, poor creature. Spare a thought for its mother though. Probably deserves the rest. Doesn't make her a bad cow. Oh for heaven's sake.*

Mike's fence went off apparently. His electric fence alarm began blaring and by the time he'd got up to check things out, he was awake.

'So I thought I'd shoot down to your place, since it had to be done sometime.'

She considered asking why an alarm shrilling in his head should make him think of her. 'Well, you'd better come in,' she said. If life had taught her anything at all, it was to pick her issues.

He strode past her and found his way to the kitchen, as though it didn't cross his mind that she might object or feel uncomfortable. As though he were entitled. Unless she relished a scene, she would just have to be gracious with coffee on her breath and a face still rumpled like the fine cotton bedlinen she wondered if he still insisted on. She followed him through.

'How'd you find the place?'

He shrugged. 'GPS. Look, since I was up...I don't have an early meeting today, so it made sense. Means I don't have to come over the weekend.'

Stepping in front of her to lift a cup from its hook, he poured from her precious arabica. A draught of city air flapped from beneath his jacket – the sulphurous smell that clung to winter mornings in Johannesburg. And probably in hell, if you were inclined to be fanciful.

He sipped and his mouth turned down. She might have warned him had he not just dragged her out of bed backwards. Too strong for his taste, but watch, he wouldn't unman himself by asking for milk.

'I don't have long, though. What is this?'

'Rwandan. Don't drink it if you don't like it. Milk?'

He gave an imperceptible shake of the head. She opened the kitchen door, tugging her dressing gown tighter as a breeze carried the chill from the river. She turned to face him. 'I don't have long either actually. I've got an appointment with my new business partner...'

'Not exactly the stately country seat, is it?' He glanced about the kitchen then moved through to the lounge. A shot of fury smacked her in the gut.

She followed him to see what he was inspecting now. 'Would it suit you better if I lived in a Tuscan cluster-fuck with security booms like all your clients?'

'Don't be crude, Odette. It just demeans you.'

The trouble was, it did. She allowed him to provoke her then handed over the moral high ground, every single time.

'You can be superior, but it's my clients that paid for a good deal of... At least I have some. I have no idea what you think you'll do here.'

'I told you, I'm meeting my business partner. We've got big plans.'

'Or what you imagine you'll have in common with a bunch of Dutchmen with sheep dung on their hands.'

'Cow dung.'

'I mean, come on Odette, you've made your point. Why don't you just admit it was a mistake?'

'Cow dung.'

'What?'

'It's cows, not sheep. This is cattle country.'

'Whatever. Trouble is, it's going to end up being my problem, I can just see it. I hope you had the sense to keep...'

'Yes Mike, I've kept a foot in Jo'burg, if that's what's bothering you. I'm not an idiot. I'm still writing storylines for the soap, at least until the business takes off.'

'And this shanty? It didn't... please tell me you didn't sell up everything to buy it.'

She wouldn't let him spoil it for her. She would not. Crossing to the double doors, she flung them both open, though the breeze was biting.

'It's an original Free State cottage. They're meant to have corrugated roofs. It wasn't easy to find one this unspoilt.'

She kept her back to him. Mist hunkered in the hollows, obscuring the river across the commonage. The weeping willows and riverine bush emerged as spectres through the grey.

'Whatever.'

She turned back. He was sitting in her chair, the one she'd found in the local second-hand. Somehow he always honed in on her one special thing. It was not a thing of great beauty when you saw it through his eyes. Pink velvet with a white tasselled trim and she'd bought it on a whim – because she could do as she pleased. And because it was a buxom, generous chair that rocked gently on its heels.

It was too low for him. His knees poked skyward like a giant black locust's. Looking down on him, she noticed that he hadn't greyed these past years so much as faded. Not that he was unpleasant to look at. He'd simply grown ordinary. The blond curls, once his dominant feature, were now more mouse than fair, and trimmed to his head in a tight grizzle.

'What did you come for, Mike, besides the opportunity to criticise my new home?'

He looked up, surprised. She was usually more conciliatory, but then he had just got her out of bed on the wrong side. He pushed himself upright, tramping across the Indian rug without noticing any of it: the splash of art across rough walls, the lavish cushions, the hand-tufted wool on worn wood. Did it remind him of anything, that rug? It was the only piece of furniture she'd brought into – and then taken out of – their marriage.

She darted about, retrieving kilim cushions before he trampled over those too. It was still warm where she had lain with her book and her glass of wine the night before. The old stove still smouldered.

4

'Mandy's stuff, remember? You were meant to fetch it and Lindy wants . . . Anyway, I've been meaning to bring it.'

He glanced down as she tidied, then quickly away, as though the cushions were doing something vaguely indecent, clustered on the rug. And she saw that he did remember: she and Melissa, just back from Goa, in the Melville cottage which never got the sun. This same rug in front of the fire, how many years ago? How old was Mandy now?

She rose with an arm full of cushions and, gripping the stem with her toes, inched her wine glass to the side of the stove, behind the coal scuttle, before he could notice. Just in case he felt inclined to comment.

'I'll bring it in then, shall I? Where's her bedroom?'

Oh Lord. It was full of boxes, of course, and the sewing machine she hoped she might finally have the time to use, beside the easel she hadn't touched since she was a student. The room smelt faintly musty. The curtains squawked on their rail as she tried to open the old sash and then gave up as though she'd simply changed her mind, not wanting to ask for his help.

'I thought I'd use it as a spare room in the meantime. While she's away, I mean. In case anyone comes to stay.'

'Oh really? Who exactly? Your mother?' Then he left the room.

'Hilarious,' she yelled after him. 'Melissa said she might.'

'Melissa's in Australia, with a family to settle. How likely is it she'll come back while Mandy's still overseas?' His voice echoed through the house and her limbs felt drained.

'Do you think perhaps you could bring yourself to help?' Mike reappeared in the doorway and let a box thump to the floor. Enervated, she sank to the bed and looked up at him.

He shrugged. 'Fine. Suit yourself.'

'Why couldn't this stuff just have stayed where it was for now? You can see everything's still a mess.'

'Lindy's . . . We're clearing space for the baby, I told you. You were supposed to fetch it all weeks ago. As soon as you were settled, you said.'

She didn't feel entitled to say that yes, she knew, but perhaps, just perhaps, it might be his turn when Mandy finally came home. Even for a short while. It didn't have to be long . . . He wasn't stupid though. His determined hefting of boxes was eloquent enough.

On his third trip she heard him stop in the lounge. She found him leaning over the couch, Mandy's suitcase at his feet, riffling through the box of CDs she'd been intending to unpack for days. He scattered them over the couch.

'Been meaning to check,' he said. 'There's a few I've never been able to find.'

She crossed her arms. 'Help yourself.'

'You're going to have to clear it up, you know.' He didn't look up.

'What've my bloody CDs got . . .'

'Mandy's room. What if she comes home suddenly? This is mine, by the way. I remember buying it.'

'Her contract's for a year.'

'And this. I asked if you had my Puccini box set. You said no.'

She shrugged. 'Probably blanked it out. Why would she come back early? She wanted to go.'

He stopped scattering CDs and turned to face her. 'Come on, Odette. Don't be naïve. Would you employ her?'

'I would if I had small kids. And they did employ her.'

'Sure, through an agency.'

'It's just her manner. Anyone can see she's great with children. The kids'll love her and that'll win anyone over.'

She tugged the belt of her gown tighter, feeling unaccountably vulnerable, as though she had just become aware of her state of undress.

He turned back to the CDs. 'Anyway, it's done now. We'll just have to wait and see, won't we?'

It was too early to phone Mandy. She'd be seeing to the kids now, or still getting up. Odette never could remember whether the UK was one or two hours behind at this time of year. Anyway, she was late for Trudie. It was already a quarter past. Surely the call could wait till tonight? It was time enough.

The big farm gate, which had so delighted her, felt heavy and unwieldy. Her fingers were stiff on the metal and misted breath obscured the chain and padlock. The gate needed to be lifted before it would swing... but no, she would never wish it. Not for a moment. The remote control had tyrannised her old life, she wasn't about to give it that power again: blue for the gate, grey for the beams, red for panic. Red for panic. Hell no, she would simply get better at opening gates.

The poor old Corolla sputtered and she revved in reverse, annoyed with it because she was late. Luckily nothing in this town was any distance and a taxi gridlock was a concept so absurd as to seem otherworldly. It was clear all the way up to the main road so she gunned it up De Wet, in control again and somehow triumphant, like the feeling you got when you caught a green wave coming down one of those long stretches on Jan Smuts or Beyers.

Her tyres raised a screen of dust in the rear. She glanced back at the road just in time to swerve around a chicken. They were like pigeons – you expected them to move, but they saw it as your duty to dodge them. It tumbled in her slipstream, righted itself and flapped to the side of the road.

She focused on the road again. A tractor with an unwieldy trailer had materialised from a side street. Terrifyingly close.

Adrenalin shot her foot out. Tyres bit and crunched on gravel as the Toyota swung sideways in a slow-motion arc. She felt herself slide, pumping the brake, thinking as she did that it was the wrong thing to do, knowing it would cause her to skid. Then she stopped.

The tractor driver stared down at her. Dust billowed to the level of his seat so that he floated above her on a grubby cloud. Lucky for him it wasn't quite another cloud, she thought: the pearly, white kind. He hadn't moved. Just sat there in his blue overall, hands on the bloody wheel, like a stupid chicken who expected her to avoid him. She felt rage surge through her arms and shoulders. She threw her hands out, palm up, in the universal sign for 'Stupid, fucking prat, where'd you get your bloody licence!'

'Complete arsehole,' she yelled. 'What the hell d'you think you were doing?' The tractor driver sat frozen, eyes unnaturally round.

It was about then that the stop sign finally managed to attract her attention. It was bent sideways, admittedly, and the white line had long since worn away, along with all but the most obdurate traces of tar. She opened her door and stepped out.

'Sorry, I didn't see it was a 4-way stop.'

The man still stared, arms stiff on the steering wheel, as though she were an apparition from another world – which, of course, she was. She wanted to sit down and cry. She had walked away from all that. She had left her warrior-self back in the combat zone, and now Mike had brought her here with him.

# Chapter 2

FOR THE REST OF that year, whenever she thought of her precious new beginning, she pictured bones. White bones. Perfectly preserved by searing summers and winters that cracked the flesh and turned the soil to dust.

'*O genade*,' said Trudie, 'the poison must've got him.'

Trudie had found him as she was clearing out the old storeroom behind the home-industry.

'Oh don't . . .' said Odette.

There was something poignant about the intricate scaffolding that had once supported a whole existence. Insignificant to anyone outside of its tiny life. Ridiculous even.

'Serious? No, you're not serious. He's a rat.'

Trudie spread her legs so she could bend more easily and brushed him briskly into a plastic pan. And that, if Odette had been in the mood to see it, should probably have warned her. But she was in no mood to heed warnings.

The room was dark and smelled of hessian and cold concrete. All it had ever contained were eggs and sacks, old bottles and rolls of wire. And rats, of course. Don't forget the rats. It would be beautiful once it was fixed up, though. Mike would probably dismiss it, but then he lacked the imagination to see anything the way it could be, if you attacked it with a mop and a splash of vision.

'Hey Trudie, how's this room of yours...Can you picture it in a couple of months?'

'Of course yes. We'll be full. Over there, we'll have a couple of farmers drinking black coffees, and...'

'Yes, and over here, two tables pushed together. A birthday breakfast. With champagne maybe.'

'Why not? It'll be sophisticated. Like a Jo'burg place.'

Trudie led them back through into the home-industry. A bee buzzed listlessly along the shelves of carrot cakes and marshmallow tarts, before making its way over to the honey and preserves. One of Trudie's army of farmers' wives drew up outside, leaving her bakkie idling as she hefted a crate from the passenger seat and dumped it just inside the door. From where Odette sat, it looked like freshly picked carrots, a couple of milk tarts and six loaves of ready-to-bake rusks.

It was good to watch them exchange goods for cash, news of Kallie's leg and Klein Jan's matric, while they just expected the bakkie not to make a break for it, but to stay exactly where she told it to. When the growl of diesel faded, she sat across from Trudie at the small desk which held her calculator and her red plastic file of accounts. Trudie replaced the cash box in the bottom drawer.

'So, what was it you wanted me to sign?' Trudie asked.

'Oh shit.' Odette pressed her fingers into her eyes. 'It was my ex, Trudie. Sorry, he turned up at the crack of dawn and made me so late that I rushed out without thinking. So idiotic. It was the main reason we scheduled a meeting.'

Trudie looked at her uncomprehendingly.

'We said nine, didn't we? It was after half past...Oh, I'm being all Jo'burg again, aren't I?'

Trudie laughed. 'You shouldn't worry so much. Where would I be going? I'm always in the shop.'

It was the laugh that reassured her, and Trudie was right. Life was lived differently here. Mike had his own agenda in unsettling her. She wasn't sure why she still gave him the power.

Trudie rose and began packing the milk tarts on shelves. 'Trudie? Look, you're busy. Maybe I should run back...'

'Ag, sit a bit. Relax *maar*. I'll make us a tea. Just let me get these packed.'

Trudie reached up to make room for the rusks beside the home-baked bread. Before she had moved here, Odette hadn't known about loaves that would break apart into perfect rusks. But then, she hadn't known you could live your life without worrying about every half hour that passed unaccounted for.

Okay, she hadn't known Trudie very long, that much was true. But there were times you had to trust your gut. Stopping in this town, then meeting Trudie, had felt like more than chance. If you considered quite how many Free State towns she had trawled through to find one she liked, and at a price she could afford, it had felt like it was meant to be.

She'd been driving back to Jo'burg when her eyes had been drawn by the sun glancing off the roofs in the valley. She had half-decided not to turn off – she'd been tired from driving – but then she'd changed her mind, and fallen in love. She had stopped at the home-industry only to ask where the estate agent lived and there she'd met Trudie, with her giggle and the huge storage room behind the shop, just begging for a bit of imagination.

'Listen Trudie, I can't just sit like this, I might as well get it now. I'll be back before you're done packing, then we can both relax and have that tea.'

Trudie shrugged and laughed. 'If you think it's so important.'

Trudie had sturdy legs set on a torso that brooked no nonsense. But when she laughed, she dropped the mantle of her farmer's wifeliness. Odette imagined it to be the last remnant of the young girl who had once been passed from the farm of her father to that of her husband. It made her sad to think of that young girl lost in the folds of this floral matron. But that was ridiculous, of course. Everyone had a lost younger self tucked away somewhere.

'We should really sign it before we start breaking the wall open, and I'd like to do that soon, so I can fetch the espresso machine.'

'Are you sure you want it so very open? It'll just fade the curtains.'

Anxiety flared again. What did she really know about this woman? 'Seriously, Trudie. Why would we block this view? You'll be able to see all the way to the river.'

Trudie laughed and shook her head. 'You and your views.'

Oh Lord, it was true. As usual Mike was right and she was the fool. What on Earth did she have in common with these people? What had possessed her to think she could start a business here? The whole bloody idea was probably insane.

Trudie turned and smiled. 'What is it? What's the matter?'

'No, nothing.'

'Still think we're doing the right thing?'

'Never had a moment's doubt. You?'

She carried the handset out to the back stoep so she could watch the herdboys leading the cattle across the commonage to graze.

If she made the call now it would be done. She didn't want to be worrying all day and as Trudie had quite rightly said, she wasn't going anywhere.

She felt the heat on her face and tried to picture her awkward daughter way over there in a northern autumn. It seemed so remote, so very far from the life she was making here. She liked to imagine the phone ringing in a London house. Mandy, slimmed down and happy, skipping to the phone, telling the Hopes not to worry, she was sure it was her mom and she was dying to tell her...

'Mandy? It's me.'

'I know.'

Across the commonage, two lone poplar trees guarded the tortuous bends of the river. Cows massed at the river crossing, shuffled down into the river bed and reappeared on the other side, single file on the eroded path like a line of sugar ants.

'You're probably busy with the kids, but I haven't spoken to you in a few days.'

'Why do you always have to check up on me?'

And here Odette had been feeling guilty for letting slip two days. She wondered whether Mandy ever imagined her as a separate being, with a life that was hers alone. Perhaps it was just easier the other way around.

'I've been thinking of you, that's all. I wanted to hear your voice.'

'Well, I'm fine.'

She wondered if Mandy also dreaded these calls. It wouldn't be unnatural if she did. She was the child – it was almost obligatory. Odette did think of her though and she hoped Mandy knew that. She liked to picture her living her own life, giggling with the kids, perhaps. Playing horsey, painting suns and clouds...

It was only now and again. And only for an instant. Odette might imagine her new life, say, and in that moment she might allow herself to forget that she had a child like Mandy. It was probably because they shared no memories in this town and she was trying to find...trying to reclaim...Who was she kidding? She was a terrible mother.

'I just thought I'd phone and tell you I was thinking of you. But I'm happy you're doing so well.'

'Emily's crazy about me. She never leaves me alone. She even comes looking for me when I'm off.'

'You are taking your time off though, aren't you, Sweetpea? It's hard to find your way at first, but you must go out.'

'When I go out they both cry, even the baby.'

'You mustn't think it's only you that feels nervous of new places. And many people aren't great with maps, but you must make the effort.'

'They cry for me more than their mom even.'

'Oh dear. Mandy...'

'When she goes out, they don't cry at all.'

'Mandy, listen. You mustn't draw attention to that. Try not to let the mom see...'

'Mrs Hope says she thinks they love me more than her.'

13

'Listen to me, now. Remember when you were little, I used to show you pictures of people's faces? To teach you how they were feeling?'

'Don't treat me like a baby. She was joking, I could tell. She was smiling.'

'Yes, but sometimes when people smile . . .'

'Why do you always think I'm stupid?'

'It's got nothing to do with intelligence. It's got to do with reading face signals. Lots of people find that hard . . .'

'It's fine, Ma. You never trust me to do anything. I must go now. They're waiting. Bye.'

Odette replaced the handset on its base and wiped each of her hands against her jeans pockets. She was being ridiculous. Like Orpheus, forever glancing back when of course Mandy was capable of negotiating her way through this year. Sure, there were obstacles, but she had no cause to see disaster around every corner. No cause at all.

Beyond the commonage, the hills were visible now that the mist had lifted. Almost white on a chill spring morning, they burnt red and gold in the sunlight.

She found Trudie shaking the soil from a bunch of carrots on the grass outside. It took another ten minutes for her to pack the carrots beside the spinach and wash her hands before she could be persuaded to settle at the desk with their agreement. Even then, Trudie couldn't seem to read the bloody thing without lifting her head every three lines with another question.

It would be one thing if she wanted clarification, but would Odette miss Jo'burg? What did that have to do with anything? And how was she supposed to answer anyway? How could you ever consider Jo'burg in isolation? It was the bony structure that had contained an entire life. It had trappings.

Odette shrugged. 'I'm sure there's some things I'll miss, but it can wear you down, that place. Tell me if there's anything in there you don't understand.'

'I don't know how you lived there. All that crime.'

Odette laughed. 'You can talk, you farmers.'

'What do you mean?'

'I read somewhere that farmers have the highest murder rate of any group in the world.'

'Not around here, though. We haven't had any serious crime in the district.'

Odette laughed again. 'You should work for the tourist board, Trudie. Don't worry, you don't have to convince me. I know it's a safe town. But out on the farms now...'

She was being mischievous, but she couldn't resist. Trudie was like a hen, flustered and indignant at being shooed off the road.

'Willem lived on our farm his whole life. We've never been scared, him and I.'

'Come on. You moved into town.'

'Lots of us live in the town these days. Not for security, though. It's the convenience.'

'Okay.'

'No really!'

'Okay, okay. I'm just teasing you. You're going to have to get used to me, if we're going to work together. Anyway, finish reading that contract and I'll make us some tea. Remind me where...'

Trudie pointed. 'You have to wiggle the plug a bit.'

Odette set out the cups and inspected the shelves, so as not to catch Trudie's eye and distract her again. The smell of sugar mingled with the red soil still clumped about the carrots. Perhaps she would take a bunch of spinach for her supper, and she might even have a bash at baking rusks. As soon as she was settled, she would ask Trudie for seeds and grow her own vegetables.

What the hell did Mike know about living in the country? He was a spoiler, that's all. She carried the cups back to the table and Trudie looked up.

'Heard from your daughter? How's she enjoying herself?'

Odette shrugged. 'I wouldn't know. All she tells me is "fine".'

Trudie gave her bell-like giggle. 'All of them are like that on the phone. Sjoe, you must miss her.'

Odette felt a small burst of irritation. It was the kind of comment mothers always made at the school gate. Meaningless. It didn't require a response, so why bother to say it at all? The trouble was, the irritation ushered her anxiety back. She was entering into a kind-of marriage here, and with someone from another world who was little more than a stranger.

The tea had brought Trudie out in a faint glow and she lifted her forearm to rub at her forehead. Odette must have stared because Trudie dropped her hands quickly and spread them palm up.

'What's the matter? Are they dirty?'

'No, it's nothing.'

'What's so fascinating then? Are you a palm-reader or something?' Trudie thrust her hand across the table and Odette was obliged to take it.

'No, nothing like that. Really . . . Okay, look. You've only got one crease line across your hand, that's all. Instead of two. See? I've got two.'

Trudie retrieved her hand and studied it. 'It's a bad thing?'

'People associate it with Down Syndrome, but actually one in thirty people have it. It doesn't mean anything. Sorry I raised it.' She gulped the last of her tea and rose, wanting to get home now.

'How do you know all this?'

'Research, that's all. For the soap I write for. And no, I can't tell you any more, or it'll ruin the story for you.'

'I wouldn't care.' Trudie smiled up at her. 'People would suck up to me if I knew what was going to happen next in *Trophies*.'

Pushing her chair back, she bent to rummage in the recesses of her drawer, one curl still plastered damply to her forehead.

'If it had teeth, it would bite you.' Odette handed Trudie the pen that was lying beside her hand. 'Just make sure you're happy, hey Trudie? You'll be doing most of the day-to-day running.'

'It's only fair. You bought all the equipment. Anyway, I told you, I have to be here for the shop.'

16

'So it's settled then.' Odette brandished an imaginary cup. 'If we had our machine, we could toast in medium-roast Ethiopian. In the meantime, partner, here's to our brave new career as baristas.'

'It's a very grand name for a home-industry lady, but thank you. It's quite special for me. I've never had a proper partner before.'

Trudie rose and, for one awkward moment, the way she held her arms made Odette think she was planning to dance her around the room. Discomforted, she stepped back just as Trudie made a self-conscious attempt to embrace her. Trudie dropped her arms abruptly and Odette instantly regretted her stiff shoulders, and the rebuff they implied.

'Sorry Trudie. I just wasn't expecting...' She raised a hand, but then was unsure what to do with it, or where it could safely be placed about the person of someone she hardly knew. Trudie gave a laugh and shook her head.

'It's not important, don't worry about it...Listen, before you go, there is something...'

'Anything, Pardner. Name it.'

'No, it's just...that thing on my hand...'

'Oh hell, I knew I never should've mentioned it. It's nothing, I promise.'

'No, it's...my brother...' Trudie cleared her throat. She opened her mouth, but nothing came out and Odette saw that she'd gone and done it again. Guarded with her own innards, she'd somehow managed to put a great calloused foot on what was tender and exposed in someone else.

Granted, Odette hadn't known her very long, but Trudie's face never seemed to alter much, as though it had discovered what was expected of it and just settled there. She looked different now though. Her features clung more closely to the bone as if her flesh had drawn back from its centre.

Odette sat down again. 'You have a brother with Down's?'

'No, not that. I don't exactly know what he had. He passed when he was still young and Ma only said he was one of God's special children.'

'It's got nothing to do with the line on your hand. Really.'

'I was worried when my children came. And now my boys . . . Soon they'll be having their own and I don't know what to tell them.'

Odette hesitated, then reached across the table to lay her palm over Trudie's. She felt Trudie's hand flip and grip her own.

'I don't know why all that suddenly came out.'

'It's fine. Don't worry about it.'

They sat like that, while the breeze stirred the leaves of the lemon tree outside the home-industry. They gripped as hard as they could, both gazing at their clasped hands on the table. And for ages after, the smell of lemons would make Odette think of empathy.

# Chapter 3

ODETTE PASSED THE DAIRY and couldn't resist stopping, cheered by the thought of taking home an old Coke bottle filled with unpasteurised Jersey milk, yellow cream floating on top. To be honest, her city self had developed leaner tastes, but still. It was the idea.

She could always let it sour into curds and whey: the taste of childhood; the smell of Mabel's room with its medicinal roots and paraffin; the smell of refuge, when her ma couldn't cope. Oh come on, next she'd start believing this move to be some pathological need to reclaim a lost childhood when, of course, she'd come to terms with her childhood long ago. It was one of those things you listed on your big shopping list. Tick. Crumple. Chuck.

She hoped Mandy would learn that trick eventually. Don't hang about in the difficult parts of life. Tick them off and move right along.

She crossed De La Rey. This was the street she'd originally fallen in love with: two rows of low shops, dominated at one end by a massive silo and at the other by the sandstone slabs of the Dutch Reformed Church. It summed up the town, in many ways. It was a working agricultural town, not some theme-park village, recreated by the semi-retired with a Jo'burg aesthetic. She was glad of that.

You did see the odd bit of litter; a pothole or two. It was to be expected. A Pep Store had wriggled in beside the outfitters, with its wooden sock drawers and glass display cases. There was an Ellerines alongside the general dealer, with his tin baths and bulk bags of mealie meal. It wasn't quite as city people liked to envision a rural village. It was flawed, but it was simple. It was real and it suited her down to the ground.

She was just grateful it triggered no memories. There was no one here to remind her; no one here who would remember. It had no trappings. It was a clean, white skeleton – the superstructure within which she intended to construct a new life.

Cars and bakkies jostled along the one main street. Despite having never laid eyes on her before, most drivers lifted a hand as they crawled past, arms crooked on open windows. It was a country thing.

Oh, forget Mike. He had his own life to plan; he should just stick to that. And Mandy . . . well, her daughter might not yet have learned grace with those closest to her, but she was out there. She was really doing it, living an independent life. It was a blessing and every day she counted it.

Crossing De La Rey was like passing a border. This was the *onderdorp*, the wrong side of the tracks, where sheep grazed grassy pavements and dusty hens played chicken with bakkie wheels.

She unlocked. With one key, and no remote control. No red for panic. It was such a simple thing, yet it made you feel as though something heavy had been lifted from you. You forgot it was there, but it felt good when it was gone. Novel but nice to feel safe at last, especially after her incident.

Placing the bottle of milk in the kitchen to sour, she retrieved the long-life low fat for her coffee. It was ridiculous, but what the hell.

❖ ❖ ❖

'This is Mike Evans. I'm unable to take your call right now. Send a fax or leave a message after the tone. And leave the time and date of your call.'

'Mike? I just wanted to let you know that I spoke to Mandy and she's doing absolutely great. No problems at all and the kids are crazy for her. There's no reason for you to think she can't make it work. Oh, and I do know it's still Thursday, but I have no idea what time it is. Don't worry, it's a country thing. You wouldn't understand.'

She started to collect the CDs Mike had scattered over the couch even though . . . no, especially, since she had a deadline to meet. It was the perfect procrastination task. She felt a funny mix of purpose and curiosity, a bit like paging through someone else's diary. Perhaps she should classify them according to life stage.

There were her U2 and REM albums – from her rowdy days. If she were inclined to alphabetise, she could place them all under 'P' for 'Parties'. Melissa had the much larger collection, of course, but then Melissa's unruly days hadn't been abruptly curtailed.

What came next? Ah, the Melville house, where they had taken turns playing the Waterboys and Violent Femmes. The Waterboys had been her thing – pagan and party in equal proportions. She had fancied it suited her: rock for her wild self, Celtic for the inner romantic. (Oh, how young she'd been.)

The Violent Femmes had been Melissa's discovery. It was this particular album that had brought the neighbour over. He'd been cute and blond and they'd eyed him in the street. Then he'd popped over to ask them to turn it down. He only listened to classical, he told them, and Melissa had laughed at him. He'd stuck to his guns though, saying he couldn't abide punk, and Odette had liked him for it.

'Folk-punk,' Melissa had corrected him. 'Seminal. We'll have to educate you. What are you doing for supper?'

Odette had only the one Violent Femmes. She was content to know it was there, but she had no desire to play it now. It had been another time, and an unfamiliar girl, who had cadged off Melissa to buy it. Melissa, of course, had been desperate to lend whatever it took if it bought them more time at the headphones. Melissa had been cultivating a crush on the CD Wherehouse manager and, naturally, Odette would have done anything to help Melissa cultivate a crush on the CD Wherehouse manager. Anything for love. Who was that intemperate girl ?

It was funny to think that her whole life might have turned out differently had Melissa never set eyes on that 70s leftover with his straggly hair and fake cockney glottals; if they had never bought the album; never played it loud enough to bring the neighbour over.

There was a void where the 90s should have been. A whole decade seemed to be represented by a nostalgic 80s compilation she and Mike had bought for his twenty-fifth birthday. In the end, they hadn't felt much like a party and she wasn't sure they had ever played it.

A couple of Patrick's CDs had slipped beneath the cushions – which was probably fitting. She should send them back. It wasn't as though she would ever play them again. Too French and intellectual for her taste. And besides, she just had to hear Gainsbourg to conjure the smell and taste of Patrick. As for Air, with their *Amour, Imagination, Rêve* . . . that was all Patrick was now: *love, imagination, dream.* She hardly needed reminding.

She felt like something happy now. Something infused with a little wild, danceable delight. Somewhere here were a smattering of CDs, bought in the first flush of her Patrick year. They had dated in the old-fashioned way: held hands in the movies, then browsed through Musica for CDs and on to Exclusive Books for Patrick's *Technikart*.

Patrick had teased her for trying to be 'Indie'. She hadn't known what she was. All she knew was that she liked something with melody, but that retained its bite. She liked music you could dance to. But surely, he had asked, dancing her backwards on to the escalator so that she gasped, the slow dance was the best kind, *non?*

22

Actually no. All that wistful music had been his thing, not hers and, right now, she wanted some beat. Once upon a time, before the trappings of husbands and children, before all of their skeletons had been thrust into cupboards, she might have been tempted to dance now. Just for the hell of it; for the sheer joy of living here and having no one to please but herself. Nada Surf would almost do, but not quite. The Shins were quirky enough and at least they made her happy. But no, for now, it would have to be the Dandy Warhols. Not their psychedelic explorations, but their good, old-fashioned rock.

She opened the double doors wide. It was the first change she'd made to this house. Not quite traditional for an old Free State cottage but what a difference it made. The nights might still be icy but now, in the middle of the day, the air was heavy with birdsong and the zing of beetles. Tiny buds were forming on the apple and fig trees. Her own fruit from her own orchard, from which she could make jam, or eat straight off the tree if she felt like it.

She cranked it up. Somewhere deep inside she felt a click as the music rose through her feet and unlocked some last remnant of her original self. There was no one to embarrass. No one to watch her or snigger except a herdboy, way across the commonage, leading his cows over the river.

# Chapter 4

IT WASN'T THE CALF *today, it was the dogs. What would the collective noun be, I wonder – a dissonance of dogs, perhaps. A disharmony . . . oh dear, sometimes I even tire myself.*

*I think it was the Boerboel two doors down that set the others off. They drowned out everything else, even the roosters. Still, it's far better than traffic. I've been neglecting my morning writing thing, but I'm over my little hiccup now. And that's all it was, nothing to bother Heather with. Shrinks always make things bigger than they are. The trick with life is never to look back. Remember Lot's wife – and keep Mike at arm's length. That's all there is to it.*

*Anyway, it turned out to be the perfect evening, despite Mike. It was exactly how I pictured my life here.*

*In Jo'burg I was always too busy. There was always Mandy, and she always needed to be fed or chivvied or nagged or placated. When did I ever have the time to watch the sun set?*

*Last night I rocked in my chair with my glass of wine while the sun disappeared behind the hills and then the hills themselves, into the absolute blackness you get here when the moon is new. I sat so long I could feel the chill creep up from the valley and smell the loam it coaxed from my garden. Hell, if I stay here long enough, I may even learn to sleep again.*

Odette had risen so early that she had time to pass by Ou Stella's. She turned the corner and walked as far as the ruin that backed onto her orchard and had once been a historic municipal house. A corrugated iron sheet grated aside, and Ou Stella blocked the doorway in its stead. The wooden door had long ago been sold.

'*Go-oed* Miesies.' She folded her arms.

Six scab-kneed kids pushed past her to goggle up at this being who had clearly been beamed down from space.

'How're the kids?' The youngest, caterpillar of snot crawling mouthwards, reached up for the tinfoil bundle of last night's chicken and the apples that would rot if someone didn't eat them.

'Miesies?' With a slightly baffled air, Stella wrested her offerings from the child. She never smiled when Odette gave her things. Odette's obligation, Stella's right. And Stella wasn't wrong, she supposed.

'The children. Your grandkids, are they well?'

Stella shrugged impatiently. Like, dear Lord, do I have to go through these motions just to get the woman's leftovers? Odette hadn't been so naïve as to think Ou Stella and she would be fast friends. But polite exchanges over the fence perhaps? Friendly calls over the washing line? Metaphorically, she meant: her washing line had disappeared the week she moved in.

Two yellow dogs sloped behind Stella, a low rumble in their throats. Past them she glimpsed a cracked and blackened shell, glassless windows covered with cardboard. Stella cooked on a fire in the garden. Odette didn't like to consider the consequences of other missing fittings . . . Yes of course, she wasn't stupid. Why should Stella like her? Just across the fence and she didn't have to sell her toilet to survive.

'Giving stuff to the squatters?'

Her next-door neighbour was hanging over the fence when she passed. Marlise, nakedly curious about her every move, sucked her dentures back into place.

'Well, they have so little.'

'Just encourages them.' She gave a reproving shake of the head. At a glance, their cottage wasn't in much better shape than Stella's squat, but the distinction was obviously very clear to Marlise.

'I don't mind.'

'You must put a bigger fence up. They steal your fruit.'

Marlise pointed back at their littered yard. Beside her, a large girl pointed too, mimicking the gesture. Odette had seen her in the street, holding her mother's hand: a slack-jawed, fatter version of Marlise, as yet with all her teeth.

'Hi.' She held out her hand. 'I don't think we've properly met.'

'Don't bother,' said her mother, with a cackle and a flip of her hand. 'She's a retard.'

'Re-tard,' mimicked the daughter. So much for the niceties.

'No but, serious. You must be careful,' said Willie, pushing away from the wall beside his father. He and the old man sat against the east wall of the cottage each morning, absorbing the sun.

'Haven't you had stuff stolen?' He grinned, one tooth shy. 'My mate from school's a cop. Told me all the sons are in jail. Stock theft.'

'Whose? Stella's? Well I haven't had any trouble . . . except, well, my washing line.'

'Didn't you see them in your fruit trees?'

She didn't mind them shinning up her trees. One person could hardly eat all that fruit if it all ripened at once. But she swallowed her reply. No need to get prickly. Willie and his family would learn to live with the Stellas of the world in their own time. In the meantime, at least they were friendly, and their protectiveness was touching.

She forced herself to walk to Trudie's place. She had to curb her constant anxiety about time. The air held only the last brittle edge of night. Already, the chill had slipped away, leaving a day growing limp with heat.

The neighbour's dog followed her with slicked-back ears and a lip lifted derisively to show yellowed teeth. He was the kind that was very brave until you turned and faced him. Mean-spirited little fucker, in contrast to his owners. Funny that.

Everyone had dogs, even the squatters. Two doors down, old Boerbul's leonine muscles strained at a spiked fence low enough to bring panic to the throat, but just tall enough to keep him in. You hoped. Next door were more white people, with two yapping Jack Russells. The corner house was the informal shebeen. Kitchen chairs were clustered in the yard, damp still from the morning mist. This was the home of Penis Dog, the butt of all humour since a fight had given him an unretractable penis.

The black neighbours had lean dogs with fox-like ears who ran in packs. They were unknown above De La Rey, but down this end of town they were, if not yet at every other fence, at least numerous enough to sneak through holes and form gangs. In the end, some mingling of the breeds would be inevitable, of course: Lean-backed Boerboels? Jack Fox-ears? Wouldn't that be something.

'Hey Trudie?' she called, eyes blinded briefly by the darkness indoors. 'D'you think it looks like rain?'

'I'm here,' came a muffled voice. 'You can come through, as long as you don't mention that word in here. Don't even say it aloud.'

Trudie was in the storeroom, packing cobwebbed bottles into crates. 'What, "rain"? I thought you'd be longing for rain.'

'It's only August. If it rains on the bailed grass, the cows won't eat it. The new grass hasn't grown yet.'

Odette slapped a hand to her forehead for Trudie's benefit. Trudie found her agricultural ignorance endlessly amusing.

'Never mind, you'll learn.'

Actually, Odette suspected she might always be the rank outsider. She constantly hoped for rain at harvest and clear skies when it was time for growth. She wished them high mealie prices when it was time to sell calves to the feedlot and low when they gambled on the mealie market.

Trudie yawned and pressed her hands to her knees to lever herself upright. 'Klein Willem woke me at 3 a.m. Forgot the time difference or, by the sound of him, that he was in Texas at all. Sounded like he'd been partying since I don't know when.'

She moved through into the home-industry. 'Won't be a moment. I boiled it just now. I suppose yours is the same.'

'My what?' She yelled, thinking of her kettle.

'Your daughter, silly. These kids go a bit wild on gap year, 'specially if you've been a bit strict. I know farmhands party non-stop, but au pairs can't be so very different.'

'Oh that. No you're right. Like crazy.'

Sometimes she liked to pretend she had a child like other children. That in other circumstances, she might have turned out to be a mother like other mothers. It was just easier when Mandy was continents away.

She sighed, then joined Trudie in the home-industry. Trudie handed her a cup of rooibos that a teaspoon could stand up in.

She longed for her Wega to arrive.

'Do you want me to bring anything back from Jo'burg? It's my storyline meeting, when we all get together to brainstorm the soap. You look nice, by the way.'

'It was the church dance.' She patted her hair and laughed, 'That's why it still looks a bit nice.'

Trudie and she seemed to have resumed their prior style of communication, which was to trade in gentle insincerities. It suited Odette. She had grown weary of the state of the nation.

She wondered briefly if Trudie expected her to mention her revelation or, horror of horrors, reciprocate with one of her own. They had no need to labour on about it, did they? Jo'burg's brisk exchange in intimacies had never attracted her and she wasn't looking to start here. Trudie couldn't expect it, surely. They had each other's backs now, that's what mattered.

The shop darkened as a figure ducked to enter. 'Ah, and here he is. Our local engineer,' Trudie said. 'Adriaan. Remember I told you?'

'Sorry, yes. For the doors, right? Thank you.'

He stretched out a hand. 'For what?'

'I suppose for saving us untechnical damsels . . . well, not quite in distress.'

'I prefer to do my rescuing before the distress sets in, if you don't mind.'

Trudie fussed at him, asking if he was eating okay, before packing him a food parcel like a refugee. He laughed, but thanked her and took it meekly.

'See what I put up with,' he said to Odette. 'So, you're the other foreigner.' He had a tentative smile, which was funny because his laugh was anything but – a bellow that bounced off the walls.

'Didn't Trudie tell me you went to school together?'

He was in denims, not khaki shorts. And not from Pep either. He wore a white T-shirt, rather than a two-tone or khaki shirt, and he clearly hadn't bought it from the farmers' co-op. Adriaan shopped in the city.

'Let's say a returnee. Back five years. But what brought you here? Not many English-speaking types end up in Nagelaten. You're not exactly indigenous to the region.'

'It's a lovely town. And . . . there's no coffee shop.'

'Yet!' said Trudie.

'We'd better get a move on then. I've been dying for my coffee...oh, for about five years now? So where do you want these outlandish German...no, Swiss...French...'

'Oh, the French windows? Over here.' They moved through to the storeroom and he retrieved a measuring tape from a back pocket.

'So why d'you call them windows when they're doors? Hold the end. No woman, hold it still.' She glanced at him, but saw that he was grinning.

'It's a foreign custom. How could you hope to understand?'

'It's not quite decent. I feel I ought to consult the dominee.'

'The town was well-named, then. Nagelaten, for God's sake. Whoever heard of a town named "Left-behind"?'

'We don't like brazen young women pointing out our back-wardness,' Adriaan tutted, shaking his head.

He squatted, marking a point on the wall with a pencil. Odette glanced back and caught Trudie watching, hands on her hips, an unaccustomed frown lining her face. Odette turned, letting the tape go.

'You are okay with opening it up, aren't you, Trudie? It'll make it so much lighter.'

'Oh ja, ja, it's fine. Although I don't think us Nagelatens worry so much about that, it's always so hot. No, I'm sure you're right. It'll look like a real Jo'burg coffee shop.'

'See?' Adriaan nudged her with an elbow. 'Foreign. What are you doing, woman? Hold the tape or they won't just be foreign window-doors. They'll be skew.'

She laughed. She hadn't come to Nagelaten expecting to find a kindred spirit, and she was comfortable with that. She'd tried the kindred spirit thing and look where that got her. But it was nice to have someone to kid around with. (A f-f...what was that thing again? Oh yes, a friend.)

'Adriaan, leave her alone. She's got to get to Jo'burg.' Trudie still looked concerned. 'And don't you have to get back to the farm?'

'What? I thought you were the local engineer? Don't tell me we've got a farmer measuring our doors.'

He laughed and shrugged. 'Only son. Someone had to take over the farm.'

Through the interleading door, Odette saw a figure enter the home-industry. 'Trudie?' She gestured with her chin. 'She's right, though. I should be going.'

Adriaan stood, brushing off his hands. They followed Trudie and waited while she handed a chocolate cake to a young black woman, blanketed toddler on her back. It was a birthday cake, with two candles.

'*Vyftig rand*,' said Trudie.

The young woman hesitated, hand stretched towards the cake – like a goal to be achieved, Odette thought; a symbol of the life her child deserved.

'You want to put it in the book?' Trudie spoke softly.

'Ja miesies. End of the month is better.'

'Okay, you can pay then. Enjoy the party.'

It was one of the things Odette liked about this place. They might still struggle with change, especially down her end of town, but you wouldn't find a Jo'burg shop that kept a book.

'I'll walk you home, shall I? My bakkie's at the co-op. Loading fertiliser.'

'Oh you don't have to. I'm fine...'

'Of course you'll be fine, this isn't Jo'burg. But it's nice to have company, isn't it?'

'Adriaan, shouldn't you stay a bit? Finish the measuring?' Odette was puzzled by Trudie's tone.

Odette glanced at Adriaan, but he shook his head. 'I have them.' He gave an ironic bow to Trudie. Almost defiant, she thought, though chances were she'd read it wrong. She had no idea of their history.

It was while they were walking that Odette managed to put her foot in it again. Her excuse was that people...well, they didn't quite stare, but they certainly noticed. It led her to take liberties.

'This can clearly only do my reputation the world of good.'

'How d'you figure?' His laugh fell flat, as though he were trying to be a good sport. It should have warned her off.

'Oh come on. You're a single man . . .' It was an educated guess, but Trudie wouldn't have asked a married man if he was eating okay. He lacked the complacency of the local belly. '. . . and by the reaction of the good people of Nagelaten, I'd guess you were knee-deep in widows and divorcees – if the dominee even permits such a thing in the little town of Left Behind.'

'You've no idea what the dominee puts up with.'

He said it under his breath, but the comment piqued her curiosity, which is probably why it stuck in her mind later.

'What d'you mean, "what the dominee . . ."?'

'I'll leave you here, shall I? I can cut down De La Rey to the co-op. Good to meet you, Odette.'

And he was gone. Just like that, leaving her wondering what she'd said.

'So is the mayor's wife going to confess about her black bastard?' It was Marta, elbow like an undercooked leg of lamb resting on the door of her old Beetle.

Marta smelt of fried fish and bigotry. Odette stepped on to the pavement, out of range. She had been enjoying the warmth, trying to put Adriaan's odd reaction out of her head.

'I can't tell you what'll happen next, Marta. It's not allowed. You'll just have to watch the show like everyone else.'

'Poor Pieter works his backside off trying to be a strong mayor, while that commie bastard's popping out the woodwork to spoke his wheel for him.'

Two responses sprang instantly to mind. One: It's a soap opera, Marta. It's not real, for God's sake. And two: The mayor's the villain, isn't it obvious? What was she talking about: Marta's identification with him made perfect sense.

'I'll be sure to let the storyline team know. In fact, I must rush a bit. I'm about to leave for our brainstorm meeting.'

She crossed De La Rey, but Marta still didn't take the hint.

'Want a lift?'

'No, thanks. I like to walk. It's one of the joys of this town.' She waited for a tractor to pass, trailing diesel.

'Still enjoying your house?'

'I am, actually.'

'Blacks not bothering you?'

'Marta, I told you before, I don't mind a mixed neighbourhood.'

'I told you to buy above town, but you wouldn't listen.' Marta had an unpleasant laugh. She just resented that Odette had bought on auction, rather than any of the claustrophobic houses she'd tried to foist on her. Besides running a fish 'n chip shop, Marta was also the local estate agent.

She kept walking, but Marta's Beetle continued to crawl beside her. Odette's clumsiness with Adriaan still stung, largely because she had no idea how she'd offended him. But the sunshine was like a balm.

'Your other neighbours treating you okay? At least you've still got some white . . .'

'We pretty much live and let live, Marta. I really don't mind living at the wrong end of town.'

Just like Mike. She couldn't see further than Odette's scraggly yard and odd neighbours. Marta would never appreciate the glory of her orchard and vegetable garden. Or the sweep of empty plot leading all the way down to the commonage.

Marta laughed her witchy laugh. She always seemed to be lying in wait for the I-told-you-so moment. 'I see you've made a friend.'

Odette made a small detour into the road, avoiding the bow-legged pony tethered to an acacia tree. She glanced at Marta, who looked arch, and oh-so pleased with herself to be the bearer of such valuable information. No wonder she was cruising so patiently beside her.

'Adriaan? He's helping with the shop.'

'Pity you didn't come a year ago. He bought the best house in town. Pre-Boer War sandstone. A real beauty.'

She was interested – enough to be drawn into asking a question anyway. 'I thought he inherited the family farm.'

'That's a beauty too, the old farmhouse. Wraparound stoep, all the original floors.'

A group of red-billed wood hoopoes chattered in the acacia tree. Two males seemed to be courting the same female.

'So, if it's such a beauty, why doesn't he live there?' Marta looked at her oddly. 'I mean, it sounds idyllic.'

'He couldn't stay there, naturally. Not after what happened.'

'What do you mean?'

'Didn't he tell you? I'm surprised. Well, you're new in town. I suppose he didn't want to put you off.'

She paused as the hoopoes flew over their heads, red beaks spread in a raucous kak-kak-kak. Odette remembered hearing their Zulu name meant women's laughter.

'They lived there for a couple of years, him and his wife, after his mother passed on.'

'He's married?'

Marta gave her a triumphant look of superior and graphic knowledge. 'Was.'

Ah. Perhaps that was the source of his comment about the dominee...

'Murdered.'

The sound of it paralysed Odette for an instant. She stopped short and stared.

'While he was in Jo'burg getting supplies. It was a farm murder. Blacks looking for weapons and money.'

'Oh my God. But I thought there hadn't been any crime around here.'

'Shot six times she was. He found her on the lounge floor when he came home.'

# Chapter 5

THE SECONDARY ROAD WOVE through the hills before levelling out into the flat yellow landscape that people always associated with the Free State. Behind her, the road trundled off to KwaZulu-Natal, overburdened by articulated lorries avoiding the toll route.

She managed to pass a couple of trucks before she hit the first hilly stretch. She was free and clear by the time she reached the solid white line, which, if you timed it wrong, could hold you tethered to some diesel-belching beast ahead of you.

Sunlight glanced off distant windows, forming haloes of condensation around a church spire in the hollow of the hills. It was a beautiful early spring day and she wished she could just enjoy the drive, but her comment to Adriaan still brought heat to her face. She couldn't let it go. He was almost certainly still struggling to get over her death, particularly the manner of it, and here she was bringing it all back. Why was she always so clumsy? She hadn't intended any harm. But then, she never really did.

She hoped she hadn't entirely alienated Adriaan. Not that she wasn't content in her own company – no one had ever accused her of being the life and soul. But she had sensed in him the potential for conversation that ranged beyond the rain, or lack of it, and that wasn't to be sneezed at in Nagelaten.

She had just succeeded in shaking off the disquiet Mike always left in his wake, and now the day was infused with this bad feeling. Largely her own fault, of course, but it also stemmed from Marta's crassness and Trudie's . . . what? She couldn't precisely recall their conversation, but Odette was certain she had asked specifically about farm murders. What was that about?

And why could no one take her move at face value? Mike, with his insinuations of duty and desertion; Melissa with her equally annoying implications of indecent haste and fleeing a sad break-up. They were both way off the mark. It was a running to, not a running from.

She passed the mine-dumps, yellow in the morning light. Once they'd been Jo'burg's mountains, source of a certain defiant pride. Who needed a real mountain anyway? They liked them; preferred them even. And now they were being reclaimed, little by little, for the specks of gold dust they might still contain. But that was Jo'burg all over, wasn't it?

The highway swung by the grubby office blocks of the old city centre, past the glass Diamond building, once a monument to a brazen city that could take on the world. Empty now, its occupants relocated north, to a newer, higher, brasher testament to trade.

It was a city that sucked in the new and spat out what it had no more use for. It was a fast-paced, fast-talking, fast-buck town. It was exhausting. It wore you down and left you dried out and spent. Never mind what any of them said. She was right to have moved. She didn't want that any more.

There was so little traffic that she got to Heather's in a little under ninety minutes. It was so quick that she barely had time to tidy her feelings and compose what she would talk about. Nothing weird about that. It was no different from clearing up before the cleaner arrived.

'Look, it was a faux pas. I felt bad, but no doubt he'll get over it. I couldn't have known.'

Heather poured the Earl Grey and placed a crunchie on Odette's saucer. Then she sat in the other armchair and crossed her ankles.

'It didn't spark any flashbacks?'

'Oh please. Mine was hardly more than a burglary. It was nothing compared to that.'

'You had five guys in your house, Odette. You thought you might be raped. Don't minimise it.'

'But no weapons, no real violence ... I was lucky. Compared to many, it was hardly even an incident. It doesn't entitle me ...'

'Entitle? What are you saying? You got away with something? You got off easy?'

'Of course not. But at the same time, we do live here. Maybe it's just something ...'

'This isn't sociology, Odette, this is therapy. It's not the space to haul out our collective guilt. And you are not personally responsible for the root causes of crime.'

'Maybe it was just my turn, okay? Whatever. I dealt with it. The important thing is I'm fine with it now.'

Heather picked a crumb from her lap and smoothed her skirt. Come to think of it, Odette had never seen her in anything but skirts – always of a sensible length, not too long, not too short. What did that say about her? More to the point, what did it say about Odette that she found such evidence of control reassuring? Perhaps she was hoping to catch it. Like a virus.

Heather was regarding her steadily. 'You did leave Jo'burg though.'

'Not because of that. What's wrong with everyone. I told you, I've never been able to choose before. My life was always dictated by other ...'

'And last week, you particularly mentioned how safe you felt.'

'Yes and nothing's changed. Farm murders are a completely different phenomenon. There's no crime in Nagelaten itself. None at all, beyond some petty pilfering.'

When neither of them spoke, traffic noise rose between them. At first it was just a cushion that absorbed the silence, but the longer Heather contemplated her, the more it hardened, till it seemed a brutal thing; a weapon.

'I jumped, okay? I wasn't pushed. Nothing wrong with choosing a simpler life. Lots of people are looking for something more authentic.'

Heather reached over and tugged a tissue from the box on the table between them. The snarl of traffic rose again while she dabbed at her nose and tucked the tissue into the sleeve of her cardigan.

'But your business partner did conceal quite a crucial fact from you. How did you put it? She let you believe... It sounded as though you felt betrayed.'

'A bit strong, Heather. Jeez. I'm sure it was probably just kindness. Come to think of it, I'm absolutely certain of it – she didn't want me to feel scared.'

'Okay.' Heather smiled and raised her hands in surrender. 'Funny name though, isn't it, Nagelaten? Left behind. Forgotten. By what, do you think? By the world? The country? By life?'

'What, you think I chose it...? Oh Heather. Being a bit literal, aren't you? Actually, it's from the Great Trek. One brother fell in love with the other's wife and next thing, the younger brother's found dead beneath a rocky koppie.'

'Foul play?'

'Who knows. It was the Wild West back then. But when the husband trekked on, the wife stayed behind to mourn her great love. Romantic, no?'

Heather gave her mannered little laugh. 'Not sure about romantic, but I grant you it makes a good story. Funny how crimes of passion always do.'

Heather placed her cup on the table and gave her an intent look. 'But let's leave the anecdotes now, shall we?'

'But why? Why can't we just chat? Maybe I don't need conventional shrinkage. Okay, I admit I needed a bit of counselling...'

'You might have come because of the robbery, but there must be a reason you've stayed beyond your four trauma sessions.'

'Not much beyond, and maybe not for much longer, either.'

'Threatening me now?' Heather cocked her head and smiled.

Odette laughed. 'Maybe I just enjoy having the space to catch my breath. What's wrong with paying you to have tea with me?'

'Because that's not the role of your therapist. That's what... Okay, let's deal with that. Tell me about your friends.' Heather lifted her cup, and viewed her over its rim.

If you thought of the M1 as the sea, it didn't sound quite so threatening. If you imagined it as the rush of waves on the first night of a holiday, say, it wasn't bad at all.

'Here or in...?'

'Both. Don't prevaricate.'

'Sjoe Heather, you do use such big shrinky words. Okay, okay... so I'm a bit of a loner. Nothing wrong with that, is there? Everyone's different.' Odette shrugged. 'It's not that I'm unsociable or anything. As a kid I was always hanging around at Melissa's, and she had a cast of thousands.'

'Was the friendship reciprocated?'

'Yes, of course. I wasn't implying it was one-sided. We just preferred her place to mine.' Heather leant forward. Ah. Funny how transparent shrinks could be.

'Hey Heather, would you mind if I tossed this cold tea?'

'As long as you don't use it as an avoidance tactic. Go on. You preferred...?'

'All kids prefer other people's homes, don't they? Besides, Melissa had a Barbie house her uncle brought from America.'

Odette looked around, then with a flash of inspiration, treated the rubber plant to her tea.

'So this gregariousness, when did it stop?'

'How would I know. When I grew up? Perhaps it's just part of growing up. Do you think tea's good for pot plants? I read somewhere...'

She rose to pour a fresh cup. Heather waited for her to sit, then leant forward, keeping her body language very open. 'Look Odette, this is like a friendship in that I will be on your side. I do understand that you need the time to trust me, but when you're ready, I hope you know you can talk about anything, even things that are difficult to explore.'

'But I don't need that. For God's sake, it's not so hard to understand, is it? Especially since now my best friend's inconsiderately packed for Perth.'

'That must be a big loss.'

Odette dunked her crunchie, certain that Heather found it very uncouth. But the crunchie was like a sponge, sucking the moisture from her mouth.

'This is a time out for me, that's all. I thought it would be nice to have somewhere I could chat idly about myself and not worry about everyone else.'

'I said ...'

'I heard you.' Odette paused and said more quietly: 'But if Melissa's happy, I can't begrudge her.'

'And at a difficult time too, with your only child leaving. That's a massive loss. You can admit to it, Odette. It doesn't mean you're not happy for her. It's nothing to be ashamed of.'

No. It wasn't. Of course it wasn't. It was the opposite that was weird. Odette shivered. Heather practised from a stately old home built largely from stone. It was lovely, but always cold, even on a warm day.

'Enough with the empty nest, Heather. I have a very full life.'

Heather busied herself brushing Odette's crumbs from the table into the palm of her hand. Odette could just see her thinking: Yeah sure, loads of friends, a good relationship ...

'Not everyone needs a rent-a-crowd. I have a whole new venture. That's exciting. I don't need to be validated by a relationship.' Odette could hear that she sounded prissy.

'Of course not. But ... I would like to know what happened with Patrick. Did he give you a reason?'

'Assumptions are the death of good theories, Heather. You'll never get a journal article out of me at this rate.'

'You ended it? But why? I got the impression you were crazy about the man.'

'Yes, but I'm a realist. He could have anyone, practically anywhere. I wasn't going to wait for the axe to fall. Men are essentially practical beings.'

Heather's eyes followed Odette's to the clock and they both began to rise.

'Are you persevering with the Morning Journal though? I thought it might...'

'Oh yes, I meant to tell you how useful it's been.'

'...help you to open up.'

'It's an excellent way of getting my shopping lists done.'

'And that's exactly why I recommend it.' She had the grace to laugh. 'Shopping lists are such good therapy.'

'Play your cards right and you'll get a journal article out of me yet.'

Okay, here's the fantasy: hot sun and rolling sea – not too wild, no dumpers. Mandy laughing. Patrick, brows salted into spikes, throwing her into the waves. His skin would be hot from the sun, sand tangled in the patch of hair in the small of his back.

Overcast afternoon: the three of them eating ice creams, walking on the beach. Mandy laughing. She even had a rainy version: playing Monopoly, Patrick telling stories of faraway places from his peripatetic childhood. Mandy laughing without reserve.

She had a fantasy for every eventuality, except what actually happened. The charming guesthouse, chosen off the Internet, was too far from anywhere to walk. Their bedrooms smelt of damp. Salt burrowed into clothes and pasted them into a sticky semblance of family with nowhere to go except with each other. Anxiety crawled into her stomach like a centipede.

From the first day, she awoke far too early. Sensing her wakefulness, Patrick rolled over and entangled her in warm limbs. She willed herself to relax. Please let Mandy be okay. Please don't let it be spoilt. Let him love me enough. Please, please, please...

41

'What's the matter?' He rubbed at her face with his nose. His morning skin smelt like happiness; like clover on summer grass. Rough-housing her into position, he hefted her bum into the crook of his body and pinned her with an arm. 'Go back to sleep. We're on holiday.'

Wriggling from his grasp, she muttered something about coffee and disappeared to the kitchen. She waited till the kettle's exhalation was louder than the sound of Mandy's door opening.

'Morning Sweetpea. Do you want to go to the beach today?' She was aware of her tone, too full of chivvying cheer. Mandy lifted her head briefly then closed her eyes again. Odette scurried back to the bedroom with a coffee for Patrick. It would keep him happy in the meantime.

'Why are you up so early? Who were you talking to? Mandy?'

'Nothing. Don't worry. It's being at the coast I suppose.'

She scurried between the two of them, spreading joy, light and happiness. To Mandy she spoke in a half-whisper, not to alert Patrick to conflict. 'Come on, Sweetpea, we don't want to sit around till eleven. Don't you want to explore?'

'You go.'

'Patrick thought it would be nice to find a coffee shop for breakfast. You could have a milk shake...'

'I'll stay here.' Odette tugged at the curtain, sticky on its rusted rail. Face puffy with sleep and ill humour, Mandy reached up to tug it back, snapping a curtain hook.

'Then we'll have to come all the way back and fetch you. You can't walk anywhere from here.'

Odette longed to snarl, set an ultimatum, count to ten. But they were still in stand-off, which was preferable. Way preferable. The alternative was not what she had planned for their first morning: Mandy blue about the mouth, unquiet, unmoving, unnerving. Nor any morning until... what? Until he loved the two of them enough? What had she been thinking?

Mandy buried her face in the pillows. Tendrils of hair stuck to her forehead and tufted damply about her ears. It can't have been comfortable in there. Just don't set her off, Odette, whatever you do.

She bustled back to the small stoep, the only place it was light enough to read. Patrick was wrestling for possession of the local knock-n-drop against the gusts of sea air funnelling between the holiday flats that blocked their view.

'Look Patrick, do you think we could make coffee here rather? We've got the plunger...'

He pinned the paper to the concrete floor, subdued it, and folded it into a small square. Then he gave one of his shrugs. Rueful, she thought. She hadn't yet learned to interpret them all. He looked up at her and smiled. 'Come here.'

She squatted beside him, her face against his thigh. 'Look at you.' He shook his head. Dampening a finger, he smoothed the sunscreen she'd applied a little too hurriedly. 'Relax. Just relax. It's okay.'

But he didn't know. He had no notion. She had so far managed to protect him from the full force of Mandy's rage.

'Just tell her we're going. We're the adults, she must fit in.'

'I know. But it's...' What did she want to tell him? It's hell every morning, Patrick. Support me. Be my rock... No Patrick, don't blame her. Don't judge. Don't think badly of her.

'It's what?' With thumb and forefinger, he smoothed the frown lines she wasn't aware had formed. 'I hate to see what she does to you. It makes me a little angry.' His 'little' rhymed with wheedle. It made her smile.

'She's... she reacts badly to change. Some adolescents... New environments are stressful.'

'But this...' Another shrug, disbelieving.

'I know, but please be patient with her? She'll be fine, once she's settled, and got to know you a little better.'

And back to Mandy, her voice still lowered to a murmur. 'You can't stay in this dark cave all day.'

'I didn't ask to stay here.' Mandy's voice, on the other hand, was pitched to carry to the balcony.

43

She was tempted. Just the two of them, a quiet coffee overlooking the sea somewhere. It was Mandy's choice after all. But Mandy took ages to learn routes. No sense of direction. She would hide in this dingy room, too anxious to go for a walk in case she got lost. It would only make her worse later.

'What's for breakfast?'

'Well, you could have something in the coffee shop.' Bad idea. Mandy liked her routines. Anxiety made her angry. The stand-off moved to the kitchen, but it was progress, at least. Mandy was still in her nightie, diaphanous enough to make Patrick uncomfortable. She should . . . No, pick your battles, she thought. One at a time.

'There's cereal.' She thought she sounded calming, though it cost her. She pressed a fist to her gut.

'I don't like cereal.'

Patrick made a guttural noise. Odette bustled to the balcony. 'It's okay, Patrick. She'll just have breakfast and then we'll be off.'

'I can't stand the way she speaks to you.'

'I know. But she can't . . .' She shrugged. She suspected her own shrugs expressed only defeat.

Patrick's only daughter, who lived in a Parisian apartment somewhere in the Marais, left lilting messages on his answer-phone, complete with little kisses: 'Mwah mwah Papa.' Odette doubted she was dumpy and awkward. And if she'd ever had a difficult adolescence, which she doubted, it was long since expunged from his memory.

Back in the kitchen, she enumerated its many delights. 'Toast, Bovril, porridge . . . eggs. How about eggs? I'll cook you one, if you like, while you wash?'

'I hate Bovril. Eggs are my worst. Why is there never anything for me?'

'Well, if you told me what you wanted . . .' Anxiety squeezed out through her clenched teeth. 'Mandy, please don't do this.'

And so on. For the whole God-awful week, she longed to go home. She went for long cheery walks, pressing a fist into her spastic colon, commenting on the flora. Patrick, disconsolate hands in pockets, grew lined and dark-ringed with misery.

She pictured them still – on the boardwalk, on the beach, in town – Mandy hunched forward, arms rigid, hair in clumps about her face. She should have told her to wash it, Mandy never did seem to notice. But, pick your issues, she thought. Pick your bloody issues.

No matter how she grinned and pranced and mimicked excitement, her troll-like daughter showed no joy in any of it. 'A little smile, Mandy. It goes such a long way. Look Patrick in the eyes when you say good morning, can't you? Show that you notice him at least.'

Mandy was genuinely bewildered. Odette knew it made Mandy seem odd, so she tossed red herrings, rolled her eyes and said, with a laugh: 'Teenagers!' But she didn't think Patrick bought it. She threw in a few difficulties for good measure. Mandy's concentration; her fine motor skills. Lots of children had them. No big deal, except for how it made her feel about herself.

'She's being a self-absorbed leedle monster. ' He wasn't wrong. She'd said it herself a thousand times. It's what she'd longed for, wasn't it? (Be my support, Patrick. Be my rock.)

'It's only because she doesn't have friends.'

'She doesn't consider others. She treats you like dirt.'

'She's angry at the world. I'm the safest person to be angry at. Can't you be a little understanding?'

She heard the sharpness and saw the misery settle in the shadows beneath his eyes. But how dare he? He couldn't know. He hadn't given Mandy the life she seemed to despise so much. She wasn't his daughter. He had no right.

And there it was.

# Chapter 6

THE STEERING WHEEL BURNT her hands. She had parked in the irresolute shade of a syringa tree, which had been a mistake. Too close to midday to hold its ground, it must have shifted shortly after she parked, leaving a feast of overripe syringa berries and gouts of digested seeds to bake into the enamel of her roof.

Heather's gate slid aside and spilled her out into the street, wide and silent and fringed by jacarandas, whose tips were just beginning to turn green. With its gracious houses carved from the stone of the ridge, she might once have said the area suited Heather. But marooned now by the M1, and by the disorder and decay of surrounding suburbs, it was growing increasingly shabby.

Unfortunately, she probably did have time to pass by Jake and Ravi before the storyline meeting. Melissa had given her strict instructions – something about a surprise – and she couldn't honestly put it off for another week. Odette hated surprises only slightly more than she disliked receiving presents. They made her feel obligated to a degree that was entirely disproportionate to the value of the gift. Ridiculous, but there it was.

Best get it over. She cut through streets dappled by overarching trees, gratified that she hadn't lost any of her rat-running proficiency. It was one of those essential Jo'burg survival skills, avoiding the robots and taxi routes. She got there in under fifteen minutes – something of a personal record.

'Hello there, stranger.' The disembodied voice floated from the intercom. There must be a camera trained on her somewhere. 'Better bring the car in.'

Jake came out to greet her and she was surprised at how genuinely pleased he appeared, gripping her arms to look at her then enveloping her in a hug. She felt inert and slightly overwhelmed. They were Melissa's friends more than hers, shared as she had always shared her Barbies, her jeans and LPs. Odette had been toted among them like an accessory, and probably only slightly more animate.

She didn't know how to respond, so she nodded. Jake laughed. 'So just bugger off to the Free State and don't bother to visit us, why don't you. Listen, you're parked behind a client, but don't worry, you can move it later.'

'I'm just popping in. I could've left it outside.'

'No you can't. There's a Polo gang in the area. Why they can't catch them, I don't know, but they only take Polos and Toyotas – especially blue ones apparently. Crazy, hey?'

Jake had a face like a favourite flannel shirt, much slept in. He had that skill of instant familiarity, as though you had seen him only yesterday. He let her go and led her down the sloping drive, from the constrained lead-panes of the 1930s frontage to the startling sweep of glass where the house opened out on two floors at the back.

'I'm sorry I didn't warn you. I wasn't sure if I'd have time.'

'Who the hell cares. You're here now. You'll stay for sushi. We've ordered in and Ravi wouldn't forgive me. Ravi? Look who's just blown in.'

She was surprised all over again, and touched. Ravi shifted to one hip and brought an index finger to his cheek to survey her. Striding out through the open doors, he lifted her from the ground and swung her from side to side. 'Where have you been, you silly cow? We've missed you.'

47

She couldn't quite credit it. It wasn't as though she'd ever contributed much to the group. Perhaps she elicited a kind of Pavlovian response: ah, here's Odette. Melissa can't be far behind.

The glass doors opened into the studio, where an old drawing table stood against the wall, piled high with old copies of *Architecture SA* and *House and Leisure.*

'Come, we're about to eat,' said Ravi. 'Let's sit on the patio so the minions can get on with the actual work.'

A young man with trendy hair made a face at him over his computer then moved across to the plotter via the coffee machine. In the glass boardroom behind, a woman in dishevelled black leant over a plan, pointing things out to a suit. Lawyer? More likely a company director.

God, she could murder a tuna nigiri. She hadn't realised quite how much until she saw them. It was just a luxury, of course, not an essential. It was something you could easily trade for a different kind of life.

Ravi settled beside her, crossing his powerful legs. He seemed so smooth and substantial, she had a superstitious urge to reach up and rub his head, as though it might bring her luck. Melissa would have got away with it, but she wasn't given to such easy affection.

Jake came down the stairs from the house, carrying a shoebox. She felt rigid with embarrassment already. 'Oh, what have you gone and done, you two?'

'Well, him and I got it together,' Ravi gestured at Jake with his chin. 'But it was Melissa's idea.'

Ravi pulled the box onto the table between them and lifted the lid, revealing a pile of envelopes and small parcels.

'What is it?' Odette asked, unwilling to rummage and unsure where to start. Her face was already burning.

'It's a care package,' said Ravi.

'What, like for a refugee?'

They both laughed. 'Not far off,' said Jake.

This was ridiculous. Where did they think she had exiled herself? She laughed too, good-naturedly, and poured herself a glass of sparkling water. The only sparkling things you could find in Nagelaten came in tins, usually overwhelmed with sugar.

She looked out at the garden, which always reminded her of a page from *Landscaping Digest*. They had made a feature of the giant koppie boulders in front of the house, surrounding them with aloes and indigenous shrubs. At the far end, a gardener was scooping leaves from the pool in a glade formed by camphor trees.

'Well?'

'Well, what?'

'Aren't you going to open it?' Ravi handed her the note first and she skimmed it, thinking she'd rather read it slowly at home, without an audience. It was a longish note, but the gist was that Melissa wanted her to have the things she'd be missing the most out there in the bundu, and which she must not, repeat not, give up on altogether.

Ravi handed her the packages one by one. They had gone to so much trouble and she didn't know how to thank them . . . or make it up to them . . . or be the kind of person who could make it all worthwhile.

She opened each now to please them: the beautifully drawn token – by Jake, no doubt – which awarded the bearer a bedroom for the duration of the World Cup. From Melissa, a ticket to the opening match, 'which we'll be back for, don't ever doubt it, and you'll go with us, if we have to drag you out from your hidey-hole'.

Another envelope contained a movie card and the directive to 'see a bloody movie once in a while, or you'll have nothing to talk about'. There was a book token, with a note urging her to see it as an excuse to browse.

She couldn't look at it all properly now. She would open it again at home. And then she would write to them, that's what she'd do, because she couldn't talk now. Slipping a tuna nigiri into her mouth, she held it there, momentarily unwilling to let it go. And in that moment, it tasted to her like tears.

In the end she had to leave rather abruptly. The suit needed to extricate his Merc, and it seemed silly to come back in when she had to leave in a minute or two anyway.

She kissed Ravi...'Bye sweetie. I must just make nice and say bye to the client. Can you walk her out, Jay? Don't forget the beams.'

Jake carried the box, carefully placing it on the passenger seat. 'Are you sure you won't still be here tonight? There's a really great opening. Part of Kurt's Jo'burg collection. I've seen one or two. He's really perfected that light on the mine-dumps.'

She paused, considering. There would be clever chatter and art, glasses of good wine...

'You could stay over if you like. You'd be welcome.'

It wouldn't be an admission of defeat. She knew very well she'd made the right choice. There was nothing wrong with wanting this as well, now and again. She stepped forward and was instantly engulfed in a screech of sound that rocked her on her feet and battered at her so hard that she covered her ears and gasped.

'Switch the fucking alarm off, can't you?' Jake yelled. The rush of adrenalin made her light-headed, as though the blood had deserted her brain. She wasn't used to it any more. She had forgotten.

Ravi's head appeared round the corner. 'Told you to switch the fucking beams off.' The sound stopped abruptly and the phone began to ring. 'And you can answer that.'

'I'm seeing Odette off. How hard is it to pick it up?'

'You're always setting the fucking things off, then you leave me to make the excuses.'

Odette leapt into her car and started it abruptly, desperate to escape.

'Oh for fuck sake, Ravi. Sorry, Odette, I must dash. I'll just open for you...'

She reversed from the driveway as Jake began a slow jog back to the house. When she reached the corner, an ADT van raced past her and drew up in the driveway, disgorging men in helmets and bulletproof vests, carrying automatic weapons.

Grey for the gate, blue for the beams, red...

Venezia was cramped and dark, the owner creepy and the coffee not great, yet their storyline meetings were held there every bloody week without fail. It was Lex's local – and his alone, apparently, or the owner would surely not have agreed to their taking it over once a week.

She paused at the door while her eyes adjusted, Lex was scrabbling about for something he'd lost, snapping: 'Jesus Margie, find it, can't you?' Odette wondered, not for the first time, why Margie allowed him to treat her like his personal skivvy.

Chevonne looked up as Odette made for her spot. Funny how they all did that, as though they had a homing instinct for the same chair every week.

'So! How's the great escape going?' she asked Odette. There were chocolate biscuits and brownies. Just for a change.

'What do you mean?' Odette was always a little wary of Chevonne.

'Oh nothing.'

'Nothing what?' Palesa always arrived on the verge of late, but not quite late enough to draw censure. 'Don't you hate when people do that? Oh, chocolate again.'

'Well,' said Margie, 'if you're all so fed up with chocolate, then bring your own.'

'Imply something then withdraw,' Palesa glanced at Chevonne as she deposited her yellow legal pad with a crisp snap. 'It leaves you no possibility of countering whatever it is they're trying to say.'

'Well I order the biscuits,' Margie cheerfully pushed ahead on her own personal tangent. 'But Lex is the one who likes chocolate and since he's the head writer, I think he has the final say, don't you?'

'I meant her escape from real life in Africa, if you must know,' Chevonne said righteously, an attitude undermined by the fact that she was filing her nails into sharp talons. Odette laughed. Had she never seen Nagelaten?

'Since Palesa has graced us with her presence,' Lex looked up at them for the first time. 'Perhaps now we can start?'

'Thank you, thank you.' Palesa sketched little bows around the table. 'Of course,' she hissed in Odette's direction, but loud enough for everyone to hear: 'Chevonne only says that because she feels obliged to make it crystal clear...'

'Shut up, Palesa,' Chevonne said, eyes on the blur of file on nails.

'...that all evidence to the contrary, she actually is slightly tinted. Yes, it's true, people. Absolutely true. Beneath that pink exterior...'

'Come along, Palesa, settle down,' said Margie. 'Lex wants to get going.'

Palesa burst into raucous laughter – loud enough for all of them, since she was the only one who could have made the comment, let alone laughed so hard at it.

Chevonne shot her a look of pure malice, pointing her nail file across the table like a weapon. 'I said, shut up, Palesa. Lex is starting.'

'Okay, general comments?' asked Lex.

'Yes, me. I'd like to make a big jump forward.' Odette waited till Lex looked up and the hiss of the coffee machine died down.

'Look, I've written the current B story the way we discussed last time, but I'd like to propose a change. I just think there's a much better alternative.'

'Just so long as there's no baby on set,' said Lex. 'Christ, remember *Temptations?* They tried to have a fucking baby...' Lex dunked his biscuit just long enough to make his hands drip with chocolate.

'I knew you were going to hate the idea, but it makes the story so much better if Rochelle doesn't miscarry.'

'She's the coach's piece of stray, Odette. We weren't even going to keep her, remember? We want to write her out once she's fucked up his marriage.'

'Just listen, okay Lex? It makes for a much stronger B story. Which I know is important to you since it's the emotional heart of the soap.'

'We can't have a baby on set. It's too much trouble. Too expensive. Like, just no way, man. That foetus must die.' He began licking each finger in turn with horrible smacking noises.

'I know where you're going with this,' said Palesa. 'You want to keep your storyline going for nine months.'

'You dog-in-the-manger, you. You wangled the gay story, which is certainly going to drag on for months.'

'Well gay's different. You can't miscarry it, and no one minds having one on set. Unlike babies.'

'Kobus minds,' said Chevonne. 'He hates gays on set.'

'Who's Kobus again?' Palesa was doodling wild amoebic shapes that took over the page and swallowed whatever she wrote.

'Six foot something cameraman. Remember? He objected to the kissing scene.'

'It's just so predictable to miscarry the baby.' Where the hell was her rearguard? Come on, Palesa. Less concentration on single cells; a little more on the complex cell structure she was proposing.

'Don't object to my baby, or I'll object to your gay boy,' Odette muttered. 'He's not immortal, you know.'

'Ha, I just knew you were all itching to make my boy Positive. But anyway, it needn't even kill him any more, so there.'

Palesa laughed and Odette joined her a second later.

It was a slightly desperate joke. They both knew just how much each of them needed a long-runner. As far as she was aware, Palesa hadn't yet found herself a rich patron and Odette certainly needed the work: Lucky Bean wasn't even in operation yet and it would take months to build up the business.

Odette had been given the pregnancy storyline because, surprise, surprise, she was the only one to have been pregnant. Naturally, Palesa had been lumbered with the mayor's gay son. She'd taken it good-naturedly enough. It was the C story and she was good at comedy. It could also be eked out over countless blocks, each five episodes long. Good work if you could get it.

'Look man, Odette, I'm not sure we should even hear it,' Lex was saying. 'This is a daily soap. Do you know what's involved in having a baby on set?'

'Yes, but it's worth it. They can use a doll for the most part. Or it can be in the bedroom. At most there'll be a couple of calls a month.'

Palesa leant across her and whispered: 'What is this? Can't bear your empty nest, or what? Bit Freudian, don't you think, replacing your lost child with an imagined one?'

'Shut up, Palesa. Anyway, this is what I'm suggesting: I think she should have an amnio. And I think she should find out there's a problem.'

Odette caught a quick exchange between Lex and Margie, who was supposed to be his script editor, not his cheerleader, all evidence to the contrary.

'Ja, that it's going to die.' Someone should tell Lex he would make a more credible leader without the chocolate smear on his nose.

'No. No, it shouldn't. It should have Down Syndrome.'

Lex's brownie halted. She wondered if anyone would. Tell him, that is. Margie was making surreptitious gestures at her own nose, but he was oblivious.

From the street came the cacophony of Friday's shopping for the weekend, the exhortations of broom-sellers and the men who made wire sculptures, cross-street greetings and pavement reunions. 'How a-a-re you? Going away for half-term?'

'Where would you find a baby who looks . . .' Palesa trailed off, looking pensive. She tended to be preoccupied by practicalities, but she did have imagination, she'd say that for her.

'Is that the same as a Mongol?' asked Chevonne. 'My cousin's best friend had one. Her boyfriend wanted to give it to the welfare. It was a huge drama. He didn't want to pay maintenance – said it was a waste.'

'I rest my case,' said Odette. Lex and Margie still hadn't said anything. 'Don't you see? I just think the A story's a little dry. And think of the guilt, the blame, the drama.'

'What d'you mean, dry?' asked Lex, throwing perplexed glances at Margie, who was squinting as she touched the tip of her nose.

'Not everyone's wedded to your soccer corruption and shenanigans. Okay, I get that this Nowhereville town might try cashing in...'

'Christ, with the World Cup coming, what could be more natural than a small town trying to draw attention to itself? It's like...'

'It's "Full Monty" meets "Dream Team",' added Margie. 'Only in South Africa.'

'What's the matter with your nose, Margie?' asked Palesa, totally deadpan. Margie jerked her finger back to the table with an impatient shake of her head.

'I don't think it's dry,' Margie said, glancing at Lex. 'I think it's romantic.' Odette wondered if they were having an affair.

'What, small town proposes big charity match to round off the World Cup? What's romantic about trying to make lots of money and hobnob?'

'It's cute, in a naive kind of way. As though their little team could ever be good enough for a curtain-raiser.'

'But so far, except for the mayor's gay son, it's all been corruption and backhanders. Where's the real human drama?'

'But still,' said Lex. 'A baby. They'll never agree to a normal one, let alone...'

'When *Eastenders* introduced a Down's character, their audience ratings shot through the roof. That baby's still alive. Too popular to kill.'

Lex put his biscuit down. She'd mentioned the magic words. 'Well, I suppose...while she's pregnant at least, it would make it harder for the coach. I guess it does put more pressure on him to leave his wife.'

'Especially because she was so ambivalent about his transfer in the first place.'

'I suppose we could make a case,' said Lex. 'I mean, we're not tied into anything. We can always kill it at birth.'

'Lex,' said Chevonne. 'Did you know you've got chocolate all over your nose?'

'Bloody brown-nose,' said Palesa and collapsed in hysterics.

# Chapter 7

IF THERE WEREN'T TOO many trucks, she'd be home by half past. She could just make out the cattle clustered in fields, but the mealie stalks had gradually darkened to bristling silhouettes and then vanished.

Palesa had asked her to stay for a drink, but that would have made it very late to drive back. Ha, see, Heather? She did still have friends. Of course she had friends. It was just that Palesa could be a little overwhelming, especially if you'd just spent the whole afternoon together.

Someone had told her – probably Chevonne – that Palesa was sleeping with a Cabinet Minister's wife. Who knew. They didn't delve into each other's personal lives. It was tacit between them and that was fine with Odette. There was nothing she hated more than the peculiarly Jo'burg habit of exchanging instant intimacies with someone you'd met half an hour before.

She was nearly home. Another fifteen minutes or so and she could pour her glass of wine and sit in her chair by the window. Too late to watch the herdboys. And it would be cold, of course. Once the sun disappeared, the chill still inched over the hills from the Drakensberg and grabbed you by the throat. But she could treat herself to a fire if she felt like it. She could do anything she pleased.

This was the first place she had truly made her own. She'd created a real farm kitchen with a big table, where eccentric neighbours could jabber away in Italian or French (with subtitles) while she dished up wine and feasts of local delicacies. Uh oh, no filmic reference point. No one had made a romantic comedy about escaping to the Free State.

And of course, she wasn't escaping at all. Okay, she was prepared to concede that Melissa was right. She did miss the bookshops and movies and openings. She still loved all the qualities people associated with Jo'burg: its vibrancy, the urgency of its engagement; even the way people went on and on about its vibrancy, the urgency of its engagement blah blah. She was just better able to appreciate it from a distance. A bit like Mandy. But she didn't want to think about that now.

She opened the gate and parked under the peach tree, with its first hints of downy blossom. She walked through the kitchen, traversed the lounge to dump her bag in the bedroom and returned to the lounge before she realised something was wrong.

Her chair. It wasn't there. Now where could she have . . . Absurd, the thoughts that flit through your head in that moment of shock. She moved back to the bedroom. Her bedside lamp was gone, and her small stereo.

She realised why the kitchen had seemed so spacious. No fridge. The kettle was gone, and the toaster. The crockpot she got for a wedding present. The pressure cooker her mother-in-law had given her.

She opened a cupboard. Every plate was gone. Every cup, saucer and teaspoon. Everything gone. Every cupboard was bare.

*I am standing on a high building. It's old, with a flat roof. There are parapets at the edges, but these have largely crumbled away. Huge trees spread almost to the height of the roof, which is dizzyingly high.*

*I don't know what the occasion is, but it's milling with people. I'm standing apart, watching. The others are drinking and talking, whispering together, sharing confidences. They're having fun, which makes them reckless. I can see they're standing too near the edge. No one seems to notice.*

*Moving quickly, I approach a young woman who is talking intently into another's ear. I grab her arm: 'Can't you see, the bricks are crumbling. Don't go so near the edge.'*

*The woman starts with fear. I can see the whites of her eyes and she loses her balance. I watch her slow pirouette through the dappled sunlight, past the great tree with its spreading leaves.*

*With growing urgency, I turn to save the others. One by one, I clutch at them, a crazed Ancient Mariner. 'Look what happened. Don't go near the edge.' And one by one I startle them to a slow fall. A crumpled death at the foot of the old building.*

*The funny thing is, it looks as though it would be a lovely garden, if it weren't now crowded with twisted bodies, leaking blood across the grass and gravel paths. The sunlight buzzes with insect life. The flowers are larger than life, vivid with colour and scent. It's a garden of childhood.*

It had taken her ages to fall asleep. It was the shock, of course, and the informal shebeen on the corner. She had become aware of its boom-motherfucker-boom while brushing her teeth and she wasn't sure what time she had finally fallen into a drugged sleep. But then, it was the end of the month and that was what happened when neighbourhoods began mixing. It was a good thing, of course. She did know that.

It was a stupid dream, but once she was awake she regretted coming out of it. No coffee. No toast for breakfast. She couldn't bear to get out of bed. To avoid the moment, she reached for her journal and, instead of concentrating on the practicalities, which would at least have been useful, out popped the idiotic dream. Pity. She could have done with a list or two: Buy new cup to replace the one stolen because I was stupid enough to move to this God-awful town, with no electric fences and no security company.

No crime, my arse. Why this conspiracy to keep people in the dark? What was that about?

The previous evening, she had rushed from room to room with increasing urgency. And when the house could no longer contain her, she had spilled out into the darkness: a headless chicken, desperate for someone to help, to say it was a mistake, to bring it all back. Her chair, her things, her new life. Oh God.

Stella had been tending the cooking fire in her garden and she'd stumbled through the fruit trees towards the fence, stubbing a toe painfully on a rock or a root.

'Stella.' But Stella didn't appear to hear. 'Stella. Stella.' Her toe hurt like hell, but at that moment, it felt less like an abrasion than the pain of loss.

Stella couldn't continue to ignore her forever. Still gripping the stick, she moved nearer, but not close enough to make shouting unnecessary.

'Stella, did you ...?'

'*Angazi.*' She shook her head vehemently.

'Stella, I just need to ask ... I mean, did you see ...?'

'*Angazi. Angazi.*' This time she waved her arms before Odette's face. Turning her back, she poked viciously at the fire, raising a cloud of sparks.

*Angazi.* I don't know. I don't know what? She hadn't even asked. She turned and ran towards the gate, still with no plan. For the first time since she'd moved in, she felt her isolation in this new place.

The neighbour woman appeared quite suddenly, trailed by her daughter. She must have been watching through the window.

'You've been robbed.'

'Did you see them, Marlise?' A thread of hope.

'It was the squatters . . . through there. Told you to put a bigger fence up.'

*Angazi. Angazi.* Of course. And Odette had said the kids could eat her fruit. She had brought her food. Why had she ever thought they could be good neighbours?

Rage rose like a sob. That beautiful old house. In a matter of months it had been reduced to a shell – gutters, doors, all its fittings, all gone the way of her own stuff, no doubt. It was a disgrace. They should be evicted.

'Did you call the police?'

'Those police, they never have vans. They're always driving them to their girlfriends. It's how it is now.'

Marlise and the girl were joined by Willie, who shook his head at her. 'It's bad, hey. These times . . . If only I'd been here. Bastards.'

Side by side, they watched her leave for the police station. They were odd, but they all looked so sad for her that she felt comforted.

Her phone had been ringing when she got back from the police station. They hadn't stolen that. She unlocked and ran, thinking it might be the detective. There was silence at the other end. A dark silence, full of foreboding.

'Mandy?'

Silence. She waited.

'Is there . . . is something the matter?'

Don't panic. Keep perspective. What was the worst that could happen: they could send Mandy home. It would be difficult, disappointing . . . Okay, more than disappointing. But she was thinking worst case here and it still wasn't the end of the world.

'Mandy? Just tell me. It can't be that bad.'

Odette should be used to this by now. It shouldn't make her heart batter at her throat. Mandy was out there in the world, that was the main thing. Somewhere along the line, she would learn to enjoy her life, wouldn't she? She would acquire that trick, or was it the skill, of happiness. Surely she would. Somehow it was easier to imagine when the phone didn't ring.

She glanced about for the chairs that were no longer there. She sank to the floor. 'Mandy, I'm afraid this isn't the best time.'

Just breathe normally. Mandy was good at her job. She really, really was. But couldn't she try a little harder to fit in with the adults? How hard was it, for God's sake, to be a little more like everyone else?

'For goodness sake, Mandy. What is it?' She heard the faintest sound, like a mew.

'I can't hear you. Just say what it is. Whatever it is, just speak, can't you?'

Deep breaths. In and out. In and out. If she'd told Mandy once, she'd beaten it into her skull a thousand times. It was those little things that made the difference between normal enough – and odd.

'Mandy, if you don't speak, I can't do anything. I can't fight what I can't see.'

No doubt it was that bloody family too, with their dislike of the least minuscule difference. Probably made out they were so tolerant, yet when it came down to it...Okay, okay. This was ridiculous. The silence was exasperating, but it didn't warrant this...this rage. It was unreasonable.

'Mandy.'

Count quietly. Breathe from the belly, not the throat. She could control the rage. Always had. It was amorphous, without clear source or tangible target. It wasn't really Mandy she was angry at, she knew that. It was completely irrational. It didn't bear consideration. Mandy was the way she was. It was something you accepted and then came to terms with.

'Kids still love you?'

'The kids are fine.' At least she was speaking. That was a good sign.

'And... and the parents?'

Silence. Ah. 'Do the parents...?'

What could you say? Do the parents find you ever so slightly strange? Do they worry that you don't look them in the eyes and don't always get their jokes? Do they think there's something... something about you... but just can't put a finger on it?

'Did they tell you off? You mustn't take it personally. Just listen to what...'

'I know. I'm not stupid. And they didn't tell me off.' In the last resort, any parent must love someone that good with their kids, no matter how odd her manner. Surely.

'Well, that sounds okay then, doesn't it? You're just feeling down. You'll feel better tomorrow.'

Silence.

'Okay? Mandy, I've just had a really bad burglary and there's things I must deal with now. Will you be all right?'

Silence.

'Okay Mandy? I'm going then. Bye.'

'Bye.'

Oh Mum, what a terrible thing. Have you lost much? Are you feeling okay? Do you need anything? Yeah right. With life, you got what you got and you moved right along. Irrational emotions had to be suppressed, not taken out and wallowed over. If you left them alone, they would disappear of their own accord.

She should have reminded Mandy to ask if she didn't understand something. How hard was it? Speak up, for God's sake. Don't rattle on about inconsequentials or, worse, just stand there. How often did she have to go on and on? Some quick life skills for good measure. In her chivvying tone, as if she could fit Mandy for life within the span of a phonecall.

She didn't remember being quite as plagued by rage when Mandy was at school. There was something very satisfying about having battles to fight – actual ones she knew she could win.

'You're a teacher. You should know five-year-olds can't sit still for long. Get her to run round the quadrangle between periods.'

'I'm sorry you think one six-year-old can disrupt the whole class by banging her head on the floor. It's not like she's banging her classmates. Keep a cushion handy.'

'Well, if you must put all the lunch boxes on the shelf next to her desk...How much self-restraint do you expect of a seven-year-old?'

Mandy was this close to being like everyone else. This close. There were one or two things she had to catch up on, that's all. 'See Mandy? Happy face. Well done. And this? No, this is a thoughtful face. It's not cross at all.'

She could be fixed. Between them, they would fight her battles. Anything at all could be learned if you just pushed hard enough. Who could remember all those names, anyway? All those people in a new class.

'Never mind, Mandy. Here's a picture. We'll learn them. No, that one's Jason. This is James.'

All those yuppie names sounded alike anyway. It was not, absolutely not, the time for fear. It wasn't a train smash. They would fight back. Mandy would catch up. Fuck them all, with their lowered voices and meaningful glances.

'I know why no one plays with me,' Mandy told her outside the school gate one day. She must have been six at the time. She always came out alone: a potato sack among all those rangy legs and laughing faces.

'Is it something we can fix?'

'Yes. We must buy Pokémon cards. Everyone has them except me. They spend all break swapping them. If I had some, I could join in.'

'Well, what are we waiting for? Let's go buy some.'

They stopped off at the CNA and bought an album for her nascent collection. Helluva price, but some things were worth it.

'What's your favourite character?' the assistant asked, but Mandy didn't know. She rarely watched TV.

Odette bought a starter pack and then, just for good measure, a handful of booster packs. She had to be sure Mandy would have some valuable cards. But how would they know which were which?

Then she had a brainwave. Melissa, of course, whose stepson was older. 'Oh, he's outgrown that stuff. Come on over. I find those bloody cards in every drawer and stuck in every skirting board.'

Damon was reluctant to part with his (she had to say) truly magnificent collection, until she flashed indecent amounts of cash. Took after his father, that boy.

'Saving for a skateboard,' Melissa muttered, caught between pride and shame. She poured them both a coffee from Hannes's shiny espresso machine that took up half the kitchen. 'What did we collect, again? Oh yes, charms. Remember charms?'

Of course Odette remembered charms. She'd had the best collection in Standard 4. Melissa had the best bedroom. And the Barbie house, of course. Odette spent a lot of time in that bedroom, especially after Melissa was forbidden to go home with her. It was mostly, she sometimes thought, because of the currency of her fabulous charm collection. That's how things worked at that age. Well, if charms could buy her a lifelong friend, surely Pokémon could do the same for Mandy.

Part of the deal was that Damon coach them through all the funny handshakes of this latest cult. Odette began to enjoy herself. They could learn this, Mandy and she. It wasn't so hard. Pikachu wasn't strictly valuable, but he was popular because everyone liked him. A good mainstay for any collection. The shiny, holographic cards, obviously, were the most valuable.

They spent the afternoon, Melissa and she drinking countless coffees while Mandy and she memorised the three kings. She became quite light-headed. It was probably the caffeine, but it seemed like something more.

Mandy was intent, rather than giddy. She frowned, comparing Damon's cards to her memory of what the other girls had. She made deliberate decisions and she learnt her lessons well.

'Hell, this is great. You can do this, Mandy. Tomorrow you'll be able to swap with the best of them.'

'Tomorrow I'll have friends.' And Mandy smiled.

'You'll totally have the most awesome collection,' said Damon. 'Most girls aren't so hot at collecting. And this Venusaur . . . I was lucky to find him. I shouldn't really even give him up.'

'Think skateboard,' Melissa said, and they all laughed, even Mandy.

The next morning, Mandy was up and dressed before Odette. No hairbrush assault on a screaming, ducking head. They were at the school gates early. 'I need the time for swapping,' she said.

At home time, Odette was there to see her come out – in a cluster perhaps, skipping a bit, calling her byes. Wouldn't that be something.

Mandy exited last, and alone. She said nothing as she climbed in, album on her lap. Her expression was neutral. No light of triumph at a job well-executed – which it surely must have been. No one could have faulted her collection. But Mandy never did show much on her face.

'Let me see.'

She handed her album over and Odette opened to an empty page. She turned to the next, and the next. 'What happened?' she asked. 'Where's your collection? Didn't you swap?'

'I swapped and swapped. I swapped before school and then I swapped even harder at break time.'

'So what happened?'

'They laughed at me.'

'But . . .'

'They swapped from me. But no one swapped back to me.'

She thought that must be the purest hatred she had felt in her life. She often wondered what happened to those children; whether they grew up hale and hearty, with all their faculties intact. Because that day she visualised them maimed and mutilated. With exquisite clarity, she wished them dead.

# Chapter 8

PENIS DOG AND HIS bat-eared acolytes loped just behind her, like jackals, turning back only when she neared the market square. Skulking close to the gated Boerboels and Jack Russells, they flaunted their freedom as outsiders and ruffians, causing Old Boer to fling himself at his fence in an ecstasy of bloodlust.

She should have got over the burglary by now. There was nothing to be done about it so she might as well put it behind her. At least she'd forgiven Trudie who, she had to admit, had been wonderful, closing the home-industry to bustle over with a spare toaster, a couple of pots, a bowl – and assurances.

Adriaan's had been an isolated incident. Nothing more, nothing since. Why would she scare Odette for nothing, more than a year after the event? Just like this burglary now. It was bad luck, that's all. Wrong place, wrong time.

Trudie was right, it probably was. But somehow she had expected more from this town. It was illogical, but she felt it had betrayed her with its promises of a less complicated life, free from remote controls and electric fences. She wasn't sure she could forgive it.

She had always loved the market square on a Saturday, especially at month-end. This was what she had described to Melissa when she still hoped she might understand this move.

Donkey carts waited for transport customers; women spread blankets and sat with legs stretched out, selling socks or fruit, their babies crawling between them.

Now though, it was out of kilter, like a favourite song played slightly off-key. The yell of conversations across its breadth sounded raucous and forced. The braziers of shin and samp gave off the sizzle of fat, faintly rancid. A whip-like breeze had mounted a quiet offensive. A film of dust crept up bare legs and babies became as earth-coloured as the grassless square. Children rubbed grit from their eyes and wailed.

Even on De La Rey, things were skewed. In a town like Nagelaten, people greeted each other, stopping to exchange the trivia of family and friends who had known each other all their lives. But today, one figure passed through them like a phantom.

He wore a caved-in hat low over gaunt cheeks and pale, wispy hair. The townsfolk tugged at their children and parted before him as though he rang a bell to warn of his approach. Sticking to the shadows, he spoke to no one.

She leapt over the watercourse, trying to make sense of their reaction, or at least see which direction he took . . . and heard a yell. At that moment, she didn't think she had ever been quite so grateful to see another soul. He seemed so substantial and down-to-earth.

'Heard you needed help. I was on my way to your place. Lucky I saw you.'

'At this moment, Adriaan, I can actually see your wings sprouting.'

'No man. It's nothing.' He shrugged, embarrassed. 'This isn't Jo'burg. We like to help each other.'

Smiling his tentative smile, he leapt from the bakkie and walked with her. Oddly though, he hadn't seen any strange apparition. The man had brought so palpable a change to the town's usual exchanges, she would have thought him hard to miss.

Adriaan shook his head and laughed at her evident frisson.

'But then, everyone's a bit strange in Nagelaten, aren't they? Come on now. Let's get on with what needs to be done.'

She allowed herself to be led across the road. She probably was being ridiculous, letting her disquiet run away with her. They haggled over a discount for a kettle, cups and a couple of plates at the Indian shop, which smelt of spices and Basotho blankets. Rugs were piled on the concrete floor next to tin baths and teetering stacks of pots and pans.

She found herself laughing. Adriaan had a quirky view of the town's goings-on. You wouldn't take him for a local. He was more like an interested visitor who had learned its ins and outs, and described them with an irony that carried a sense of the world beyond the farm.

'Come, I'll stand you,' he said when they'd finished, and she realised she was hungry. She allowed him to buy her a boerie roll outside the general dealer, where men with bare thighs like tree trunks tended a boerewors braai.

'So how do you feel now? Are you okay?'

Acutely aware of what he'd gone through, she was more vehement than she felt. 'Of course yes. Only a burglary. It's just things. It's not like they stole my whole life or anything.'

Speaking it aloud, faking it for his sake, she realised that it had become true. She would survive this. She'd had worse. Perhaps she could forgive the town this one infraction. The wind seemed to have dropped, or perhaps they were more sheltered in the lee of the church. It didn't soar – too sturdy for that – but it did preside over the street. And right now, its sandstone walls shone golden in the sunlight.

They made their way back towards the market square and Adriaan's bakkie. A crowd had gathered outside the Rendezvous café, where a ghetto blaster pounded out slightly distorted kwaito.

Two kids in oversized sunglasses stood on milk crates and lip-synced. All around, people broke into jives, waving their hips and calling 'heh, heh' in time to the beat. Suddenly, the street had something of a carnival air.

'Oh shut up woman, it's not such a big deal. I had to be in town to see a man about a bull. Make us some coffee while I inspect these outlandish foreign doors of yours and see what security gates they need.'

'Machine's gone, I'm afraid. All I can offer is tea.'

'Fine. No wait. I'm going to need a writing implement. And while you're at it . . .' He nodded at his toolbox.

Adriaan treated her like an inept younger sister when she didn't respond, taking her by the shoulders to urge her towards the screwdrivers then rolling his eyes when she passed the pencil instead.

'No man. The Phillips. Have you never handed a man a screwdriver before?'

'What do you expect? I don't speak non-verbal.'

'What's wrong with you? You were married weren't you?'

'Never to a farmer, though.'

He smelt faintly of pine trees. It was a dependable smell. She wanted to say something about her faux pas, but it had passed. Perhaps she should just let it go.

'Adriaan?'

'Hmm? By the way, I asked Fitz to come over. Just to check things out a bit.'

'Look Adriaan, I'll just say it, okay? The other day I didn't know . . . I said stuff . . .'

'Of course you didn't. How could you. You'll like him. Fitz, I mean. He's our best detective. Something of a magician. I've never seen someone get results like him.'

'What *kak* are you talking now, jong?' A man had appeared around the side of the house, making her jump.

Adriaan made a 'relax' gesture with his hand and pursed his mouth: don't get all hysterical on me. (She was getting better at non-verbal.)

Captain Fitzpatrick had the wide gait of the large lock forward, confident on field and off and, despite the name, Afrikaans as they come.

'His great, great oupa came out to build the church,' Adriaan said. 'Ended up staying, unfortunately. Which is why we've ended up with this bugger.'

'Of course he stayed. Groot Ouma was a knockout.' He was a flirt, the Captain. Not in a serious way, but with the lazy charm of the small-town hero.

'It was a local tragedy,' Adriaan added. 'If his Groot Oupa hadn't ended up here, we'd never've lost that final game against Standerton.'

Fitz ducked his head and bulled his shoulder into Adriaan's chest. More non-verbal, not worth translating, but it was gratifying, particularly after a painful break-up. The men roughhoused, Fitz allowing himself to be gripped in a headlock, while Adriaan tried unsuccessfully to make him admit he'd been the worst first team captain in the annals of the Nagelaten Hoërskool.

When they were done showing off, Fitz got down to business inspecting the scene of the crime. Odette pointed out the poor old municipal house and sagging fence. He nodded.

'Ja, Ou Stella. Couple of her sons has been our guests at the station. Stock theft though. They didn't try burglary up to now.' He took notes and paced. Eventually he came back and said he'd be in touch.

'There's a chance we can find your stuff.' You could tell he wanted to please, though. 'If it's still in town, that is. If it's boarded the taxis for Natal then I'm afraid it's gone.'

Yes, much like her illusions.

'You all misled me, you know?' Both men looked at her. 'You Nagelatens. Everyone said there was absolutely no crime. Makes you wonder what other skeletons lie in wait for unwary newcomers.'

There was an uncomfortable pause before they both bellowed with laughter. She hadn't thought it warranted either the awkwardness or the hilarity, but perhaps they weren't quite used to her humour yet.

'Can I phone and see how you're doing with the investigation?' she asked.

'Only a pleasure. The wife's also Captain Fitz though, so make sure you say which one you want.'

She and Adriaan continued inspecting possible entry points until the midday heat of a premature spring urged them indoors.

'Now, if our outlandish coffee shop was going, I could invite you there.'

'Well, why don't I invite you for a drink and dinner instead.'

Oddly, she agreed.

# Chapter 9

*So, THIS IS THE game: if the big Captain only finds some of my things, which would I choose? If I'm honest, I'd probably take my ugly chair, because it meant something. Fridges and amplifiers can be replaced...Oh what am I doing, this will only make me feel bad all over again. Everyone knows you only fill in police forms for the insurance. I have to accept that it's gone, put it behind me and forget it ever happened.*

*Largely, I am getting there, I think. I'm quite proud of how I handled things. I've even kept up this idiotic writing thing. At least it gives me something to do in the early hours.*

*You'd have thought the country air would have given me back my ability to sleep. I always blamed Jo'burg: you're constantly alert there, even in sleep. But perhaps it just takes time to lose that. I still startle in the depths of night, thinking there are urgent things to be done. But then I can't for the life of me recall what they are.*

*I got the angry treatment again last night: What do you care how I'm doing, you wish I'd never been born, all the usual. I know where it comes from. I'm the adult, I know there's no one Mandy can be angry at except me. Just as I know there's nothing wrong with hoping she stays halfway across the world. If she copes there, she can cope with the rest of her life and if she can't . . . well it's an intimation, isn't it?*

*What would Heather know, with her romantic views on mothers and their empty nests. I'm sure most mothers feel the same, though we'd never dream of admitting it to each other.*

*There's nothing wrong with wanting a rest. Isn't it part of our natural life cycle? And is it as stupid as I think it is to write rhetorical imponderables to myself? As though some cosmic pencil will appear and write: No, it isn't natural. Mend your ways.*

'Duck, Adriaan.'

'Not on this menu, I'm afraid. The Waenhuis is not what you'd call haute cuisine.'

'No man, duck your head. Don't look now . . . uh oh, too late.'

'Ah Marta,' said Adriaan, all charm. 'How are you, my dear. Gerrie over his op?'

'Ja *dankie*, Adriaan. Thanks for asking. Everyone seems to think it's very funny. But I can tell you, piles at his age is not so very funny.'

'No Marta. I feel for him.' There was an awkward pause.

It was the waitress who broke it – the cook's mother apparently, which obviously gave her the impression she owned the place, along with their personal space.

'*Bietjie sit*, Marta? I'll bring you a chair over.'

Die Ou Waenhuis had the air and, Odette imagined, the smell, of a funeral parlour: polish, musty carpet tiles and dead flowers. Marta's presence did nothing to dispel the impression. She wore a perfume that would kill flies and a face perfectly suited to the tragic progression of Gerrie's piles.

'*Dankie*, Tannie Lettie. Well, he worked too hard, that's the thing. And for what, I wonder? Ag Tannie Lettie, you'll let me know when our take-aways are ready, nè?'

'Gerrie was the town's utilities manager,' Adriaan explained. 'Lost his job when the new council came in.'

'When the blacks took over.' Marta's cackle segued into a cough. She had the kind of cough that never cleared, like a starter motor that turned, but never caught.

Their wine arrived. It had been a choice between Chateau Libertas and . . . Chateau Libertas, but what the hell. As her oupa used to say: 'You can't go wrong with a Chat Lib.' Of course, her mother had never gone wrong with anything much at all.

'Just a *klein glasie*, Adriaan. I must get home to Gerrie.' Marta nodded first at him, then Odette, 'I see you two are getting mighty well-acquainted all of a sardine.'

Odette didn't know which was more excruciating, Marta's grotesque coyness around Adriaan, or the arch looks she threw Odette. There was no way she would gratify Marta's prurience. She turned away to ask the hovering waitress for water.

'Ag no, Lettie, they can't drink tap,' Marta added. 'Bring her a tin of soda.'

'Can't you drink the water here?' She looked at Adriaan. 'No one told me.'

Adriaan opened his mouth, but Marta rabbited on. 'No man, I wouldn't touch it. Haven't you noticed what it tastes like? Sies.'

'Well, it hasn't seemed to harm me, although I admit it tastes a bit funny sometimes, some days worse than others. I suppose you'd know all about the water, with a husband in utilities.'

'Manager. He was manager of Town Utilities.' She leaned back in her chair and took a great slurp of their Chat Lib. 'They don't know how to do it, do they?'

'Who? The new . . .'

'The water would never have had that mouldy taste in Gerrie's time.'

'Well, surely . . . I mean, if Gerrie looked after things so long, couldn't he give the new council the benefit of his experience?'

Marta raised both hands as though to negate all responsibility for the iniquities of the new council. She tucked her chin back into her dewlap: 'They wanted to take over, they must *maar* live with it.'

The waitress, who must have been eighty in the shade, brought Marta's take-aways. Thank the Lord and not a moment too soon. There was silence after she left.

'Funny how satisfied she sounds about things going wrong...' she began, at precisely the same moment that Adriaan said: 'Sorry about old Marta. But Gerrie lost a lot of his will...'

They laughed and he raised his glass. The octogenarian had filled Odette's to the brim. Short of bringing her mouth down to the glass, there seemed little chance of avoiding her new white shirt. She wasn't even sure why she'd worn the bloody thing. It wasn't as though this was a date.

He was a nice man and all that, but he wasn't Patrick. It just suited them both to have a bit of company now and again, that's all. He was obviously still grief-stricken and she certainly wasn't looking for entanglements.

'It'll be all over town by tomorrow,' he said. 'Sorry about that.'

'What? Us? Oh no, not that. Anything but that.' She clutched at her throat and Adriaan laughed. They were the only diners. The octogenarian had nothing to do but lean against the heavy dresser, fiddling with a dried arrangement of proteas. Listening for all she was worth.

At the sound of a handbell, she shuffled to the kitchen and returned with their ribs and chips, unadulterated by greenery. In Nagelaten, the onion ring was clearly considered a vegetable.

'*Dankie* Tannie Lettie.' Lettie treated Adriaan to a beneficent smile, which disappeared before it reached her. Odette placed a hand over her glass, holding the ancient one's gaze as she brandished the bottle threateningly.

'No more?' Adriaan asked gently, seemingly unaware of their silent tussle. To his credit. If he were fully conscious of his status as town's prize possession, he would be insufferable.

'No thanks, Adriaan. One's my limit.'

'Cheap date, hey.'

Odette laughed, to show that she knew he was joking. To change the subject, she asked about the bull he'd been looking at.

'Bonsmara. Good buy or I wouldn't get another bull. We mostly use artificial insemination these days.'

He seemed to find it odd that a city girl could hold her own in a cow discussion, but she explained that she'd been raised by a frustrated farmer. She knew her *uitskot* from her bearing cows.

'Well, you certainly know a good rib when you see one. Sign of a good farm girl.'

Odette laughed. She was rib-sauced to her wrists, and she felt sticky to her eyebrows. 'Very fetching, I'm sure.'

'Actually, I do find you rather fetching, Odette.' She concentrated on her ribs.

'It's okay,' he said, laughing. 'Let's forget I said anything so stupid. I've been meaning to ask, do you ...'

'What, you were lying?' She could play this game too, that's what made it so perfect. It was safe. They both understood exactly where the boundaries lay because neither of them wanted anything more.

'Very funny. No, I was going to ask about your name. It's unusual, but you still come across it in the old Huguenot families.'

'Well, unfortunately for me, my mother was the grand romantic. I'm named after some famous Resistance heroine. Could've been worse, I suppose, though it probably condemned me to be the very opposite.'

'I like it. Suits you. No heroic siblings?'

'Only briefly. Lucien, poor little mite. Named after an obscure Resistance fighter, but he never got much chance to be a hero. He was a cot death.'

'That's hard. Were you old enough to know what was going on?'

'Luckily no, especially because they suspected ... Ag never mind. You don't want to hear all that.'

'What? They suspected your mother? For the baby's death?'

Odette nodded. 'Probably because she was so highly strung. She struggled with babies. But there were never any charges, so I'm sure it was all just conjecture.'

'That must've been tough.'

'I suppose. She never got over it. Quite forgot she had a living child to look after much of the time. But hey, that's the way it goes. I never knew any different, so it didn't blight my life or anything.'

'But you and your mother...?'

She shrugged again. 'She removed herself while I was growing up. Not physically, just away with the fairies, but we weren't exactly close, so I can't really see why I should make the effort now.'

He drove her home when the octogenarian finally turfed them out. ('Don't you have to be up in the morning, Adri?') He switched off the engine outside the house.

'I hope you enjoyed that as much as I did.'

He leaned forward at the precise moment she turned to thank him. The kiss he aimed at her cheek landed somewhere between her mouth and nose. They laughed and it didn't feel quite so awkward.

'I'd better try that again.'

'I suppose you'd better.'

# Chapter 10

*Finish storyline*

*Phone Capt Fitz*

*Buy loo rolls and Handy Andy*

*That's about all I can think of now. It wasn't a bad night. I managed to get some sleep and at least there were no dreams, or no worse than the roof dream. None that would make normal people run for a straitjacket. It probably accounts for my mood. I suddenly feel there could be life beyond Patrick. And burglaries. Perhaps living in a small town is beginning to rub off on me.*

*I'm even changing my mind about this writing. It's not just something to do when I can't sleep. Once I get beyond the lists, I'm finding . . . I don't know. It's like I start to chew over the words, the taste of them, the patterns they make on the page.*

*I'm glad no one will see this but me. I spend so much of every day writing, it can seem like a chore, and those words are so cramped by the busy dialogues of life as soap opera. Or soap as life, if you like. I find myself mulling over things here. Like this morning, I*

*was thinking about this town, and how spoilt it had felt after the
burglary – which started me thinking about Johannesburg.*

*Meaning is always sieved through your experience of a place, isn't
it – like my incident, my marriage, my time with Patrick. And of
course Mandy. They all change the meaning of the word.*

*It's the same with marriage. It has such a different meaning for me
and Melissa. For me, it's like missing an absence. A void. For her,
wife probably means the clatter of getting the supper on or arguing
over the crossword. For me... For me I suppose wife means silence.*

*And mother? Where to start with that one. With my mother? With
me? That word could hold an entire lexicon. It's probably best not
to go there.*

'Captain Fitz please.'
  '*Man of vrou?*'
  'The man please.'
'Captain Fitz the man. Wait please.'
Scuffling at the other end of the line. A yell. Odette sipped her
coffee. It was a nice balanced Ethiopian blend she was trying
out for the shop. The grind was wrong for the plunger, but it was
better than nothing and at least she'd tracked a dusty Bodum
down, in the hardware shop of all places.
  'Fitz *wat praat.*'
'Hi Captain Fitz. It's Odette.'
'Ja, okay. *Hoe gaan dit,* Odette. Nice to hear you.'
This time, she wasn't phoning to bargain or beg. She had put
the burglary behind her. It hardly crossed her mind, in fact. But it
did no harm to check now and again, especially when her storyline
faltered. It gave her something useful to do.
  'Thanks Captain. Not that I want to rush you, but I was just
wondering...'

'Ja well, we have made some progress. I've interviewed Ou Stella the squatter, and I also spoke to your neighbours, since they seem to be the only witnesses.'

She stepped out on to her stoep and gazed across at the old municipal house. Deep fissures divided the walls on either side of the chimney, whose days would be numbered once the rains came. Stella was leaning over a tin bath in the yard, scrubbing viciously at its contents.

'Did Stella admit to anything?'

'I don't think it was Ou Stella's sons. Not this time at least. Stock thieves don't usually switch to burglary. Also, in my experience, a thief will always keep some small thing and we found nothing.'

'But maybe they sold everything.'

'Even then, they will always keep one thing. Like a souvenir, you know? I would say it's almost without fail.'

Stella yelled over her shoulder and one of the grandchildren appeared from the house. Pulling a blanket from the bath, she handed the end to the child and they twisted it into a dripping rope between them.

'And the neighbours? Couldn't they give you any more clues? Surely they saw something helpful?'

'They saw black people with a wheelbarrow, and they were definite they entered through Stella's ground.'

'Well, that would seem . . .'

'Ja. Even if she and her children are not involved, it's not to say she didn't allow other people through. I discount nothing.'

Stella carried the wrung blanket to the boundary between her yard and Odette's orchard. Hanging it over the fence, she looked up and saw Odette watching her. Stella stood her ground, holding her gaze. Bloody woman had no shame. It was Odette who blinked. Turning abruptly, she went back into the house.

The Captain was giving her the rundown on leads still open to him. It didn't sound hopeful. She didn't know what made her feel worse: the thought that Stella, eater of her food, pilferer of her fruit, had done the burgling, or that she'd let other people in to do it. She had to stop phoning Captain Fitz. It wouldn't change anything and it didn't speed up her storyline either.

She was still wrestling with Rochelle's pregnancy and the timing of her revelation about the amnio. For some reason, she was struggling to articulate how Rochelle was feeling, which was odd. Perhaps she'd dealt with her own feelings a little too well. Or perhaps she was just tired. Luckily Reno was a soccer coach. He wouldn't be much bothered by pesky things like emotions.

'. . . anything like that stolen?'

'Sorry Captain, line's bad. I didn't catch that?'

'I said, did you have any clothing stolen?'

'Don't think so. Or not that I've noticed, anyway. Sometimes, it's only when you're looking for that particular shirt, you know?'

'No, it's just that my contacts in the location have found a stash of stolen clothing, and I was wondering . . .'

She moved through to the bedroom and began a silent inventory of her Jo'burg clothes, most of which she'd probably never wear here.

'So you didn't have a purple-coloured sunhat?'

'Captain Fitz! I'm trying to make an impression in Nagelaten. I would definitely not make such a style error.'

'Ag, sorry man,' Fitz mumbled. Bless him. It probably wasn't very funny anyway.

'Oh, but hang on a sec.' And there, in a drawer that had remained firmly closed these past weeks, she discovered a void.

'There is something. My ex-boyfriend had a collection of caps. He was foreign, you see, so he liked to collect the local rugby and soccer caps.'

'And you definitely had them here. With you?'

'Yes, I . . .' (Go ahead, Captain Fitz. Underscore that one humiliating fact.) 'He didn't fetch them . . . I don't know. Somehow they came with me.'

Actually, she had pushed them to the back of her cupboard while he'd packed the few things he kept at her place. Like a teenager, holding on to an ex's T-shirt to wear in bed until it lost the smell of him. Pathetic.

'So these caps, what did he have?'

'Pirates, Chiefs, all the usuals. And rugby ones. I'm fairly sure he had Sharks, And definitely Blue Bulls. I remember that because he got it in Pretoria and he couldn't believe how the supporters . . .'

'Never mind the supporters. We couldn't believe the players. Bulls have just moered us in the Currie Cup. Anyway, I'd rather not go into that.'

'Yes, best we not dwell on these things, Captain Fitz. Never look back, that's what I say.'

The day was mild rather than hot. A breeze blew the scent of bluegum from the trees that huddled at the far end of the commonage. This was another form of procrastination, but she still couldn't get her head around Reno and Rochelle. It was peaceful, no sounds beyond a call of greeting from the township end and the bluegums, stirred into sibilance.

She had waved to her next-door neighbours as she passed: allies now against encircling crooks and thieves. Except for the girl, rolling in the long grass, they had all been lined up against the east wall for the sun. Willie had pushed himself up and ambled over to the wall.

'Any news?'

'Not much. Fitz is still interviewing people, but he doesn't seem to have much.'

Willie's mullet swished lugubriously behind him. 'Bad business.'

Cows bunched at the river crossing, picked at by cattle egrets. Protective of their calves, two of them began walking purposefully towards her, heads lowered. She shooed them and they trotted back.

The rains hadn't come yet. The wetland had dried into mud-tiles under sparse grass. The river was very low, a trickle moving between algaed pools. She sprawled on the flat rocks that swelled from the river bed. They were warm in the sunlight and water rippled either side of her.

Her call to the Captain had settled something else for her. If he ever found her belongings, she was determined to pack those caps up and send them back to Patrick. She didn't need them any more. She had a new life now.

A cluster of hadedas, spooked by the skitter of a very young calf, rose with an aggrieved cry. They swooped low over the river and flapped away. She tried to focus on Rochelle's regrets and Reno's horrors. Poor old Reno. Served him right, though.

She had once been late with her period. When she'd told Patrick, his face had flashed from an instant of happiness to a grimace of terror. Jesus Christ. Not that she'd ever wanted another child, but she hadn't wanted him to feel like that. Not about her. Certainly not about Mandy. No one was allowed to feel that way about Mandy. No one but her.

She had done the right thing, of course she had. And like the song said: she would survive. Striding back through the long grass, she felt the tap-tap of hoppers against her legs. Warblers chorused from the bank. She felt better.

Not better enough to greet Stella though. They passed stiffly, Stella on her way from town, bag of mealie meal on her head, a grandchild either side of her. Odette averted her eyes.

She had popped into town for loo rolls and Handy Andy when she caught a glimpse of that gaunt face and wispy hair. So he wasn't a figment of her imagination, but then neither was he some kind of spook. He was just an odd-looking guy, nothing more.

He was slightly ahead and she slowed to keep pace. She was curious, that was all. There were so many cross-cutting connections of family and church in this town, yet he seemed such an outsider. Her phone rang as they turned off De La Rey.

Mike. Oh God, now what? She hung back to take it. 'Odette? Mike. How's Nagelaten?'

'Good thanks. Jo'burg?'

'Good.'

They communicated in unsaids, she and Mike. Adept at avoidance, they were careful with each other, never saying what shouldn't be said, or naming what they hoped could no longer harm them.

The man glanced back briefly, but continued walking. She let him disappear around the corner. What was the matter with her? He was just some weird guy.

Mike breathed noisily. He did that when he found a conversation hard. He used to speak to his mother like that when they were married.

'Is something wrong? Is it Mandy?'

'No, no, nothing like that. Thanks for your message by the way. She doesn't really call and, I must say, most of the time I tend to leave well alone.'

'I try to call every couple...'

'Anyway, just thought I'd let you know that I'm going over next week. Board meeting.'

She began walking again. 'Pretty sure you told me. But that was the idea, wasn't it? That you'd look in on her periodically? It's why we let her go.'

'It's why you let her go, Odette. Let's be clear on that. I was just wondering how I let myself get conned into this. When did this become my responsibility? You're her mother, after all.'

She felt a moment of panic. 'Because you said you'd be back and forth all this year, that's why. We discussed...'

'No, you discussed it. I can't remember agreeing. This was foisted on me and now, besides a full schedule of meetings...'

She turned the corner and started. Somehow she'd expected the man to have vanished again, like the phantom he was. But he was struggling with a rubbish bag on the pavement, torn open by dogs. She nodded and smiled at him. He showed no sign of greeting.

An old stoep wall had collapsed, replaced by a structure of stones, hubcaps, an old cart wheel and beer bottles, which allowed the sun to glance darkly through them. Rising abruptly, he stepped over it onto the tiny stoep that abutted the pavement.

'Hang on a sec, Mike? Excuse me, you've left something...'

But the man had disappeared, leaving his battered hat on the pavement beside the spilled contents of the rubbish bag.

'She's fine, Mike. She might have had a shaky start in life, but she's come a long way since then. Didn't you hear Mrs Brink at final assembly? She can do anything she sets out to.'

'You just assume that I've all the time in the world though.'

'All you have to do is show your face. A bit of reassurance, that's all. We're both just being over-protective. How's Lindy, by the way?'

'Fine. Really good. Not sure if I mentioned it, but her amnio results were fine, so no worries there.'

'Oh. That's nice.'

'She really enjoys being pregnant. It's nice to experience that.'

'I'm sure it must be.'

They said their cool goodbyes and she was left alone outside the box of a house, the last in the street before the coalyard and a store selling farm machinery. She hesitated. Lifting the hat, she stepped onto the stoep just as the man reappeared in his doorway.

She started again. 'You left your hat...'

He nodded and stepped forward to take it. The house seemed to repel sunlight. The unpainted concrete appeared damp. On the stoep stood the bench seat from a 1950s car.

'*Dankie.*' He was younger than she had first supposed. His eyes were lined, but he couldn't be much beyond twenty. He reached for the hat and turned abruptly, moving back into the front room. It was sparsely furnished – an ancient armchair, a plain table and wooden chair. It was the walls that held her attention though. They were plastered or, rather, smeared, with thick clods of what looked like mud and cow dung.

She had seen it packed hard on the floors of old Voortrekker houses. On the walls though, it made the room close, claustrophobic rather than cosy. And darker than any room she had ever seen. It smelt of fire and damp.

She felt a prick of fear, not because she felt threatened by him. It was the strangeness. The rancid darkness that felt, not just forbidding, but forbidden.

Odette would have loved to enjoy her pregnancy. It wasn't as though she had refused to enjoy it, to prove her credentials as a 'new woman', or something equally banal.

Everything was different for Lindy, as Mike well knew. Odette's pregnancy had been so filled with uncertainty, for one thing. He couldn't have forgotten, though he now seemed intent upon airbrushing any part he may have had in it all.

It didn't take a genius to figure that Lindy's amnio had subconsciously sparked the idea for Rochelle's. She should just have kept her bloody mouth shut and waited for the insanity to pass. Who but a madwoman would choose to recall a time she had already dealt with and successfully packed away?

The birth itself had been nothing to write home about. Like a million other women, Odette had gestured 'begone' to the anaesthetist, muttering things like 'natural' and 'experience'.

After eight hours of torment, it was the nurses' turn to mutter: 'Too late, my dear, it's just too late', while their exchanged glances said: '*Ja, hulle wil mos.*'

The pethidine was marvellous though. Later, she felt guilty about that too. Other people's babies slept. They made serene little tableaux with their mothers while adoring husbands snapped photographs. Mike made guilty appearances, muttering that he had to make money if they were to make a go of this.

To be fair, he hadn't wanted any of it. He wouldn't have chosen the registry office nuptials at eight months, which his parents chose not to attend. 'It's not what we would have chosen for you, son,' his mother told him, as Odette shamelessly listened in on the other line. What was she, a masochist? It was that bloody hopefulness, of course, wanting to hear Sylvia say that nothing could make a mother happier since Odette clearly made her boy so happy.

'I know, Mom.' He had sounded so miserable, so trapped, that she had felt it in her heart to be sorry for him.

Not as sorry as she was for herself though. She still found that odd: the implication that she *had* chosen it. That her girlish dream was to wait beside her pacing bridegroom, cramping with Braxton Hicks, beneath a sign that declared: 'Marriages' this way; 'Mental Patients' that.

'What's the diffs?' Mike had muttered.

Her baby was the one the other mothers quietly asked the nurses to take to the nursery. 'We just can't sleep. Not very restful, is it?'

The child couldn't seem to latch on. The nurses demonstrated patiently. The mother alongside smiled encouragingly, resplendent in a maternal trousseau that was bridal in its laces and bows. Her babe nestled in plump arms, sucking greedily at a lard-white breast.

They showed her again. Then again, with patience wearing as thin as their mouths. Grabbing an aching breast in a meaty grip, they shoved it at that gaping mouth. But she just didn't seem able to hold on.

'Nonsense,' the nurses told her. 'You haven't learnt how to feed yet.' Was it possible that a baby could be born without the instinct to suck?

'Why aren't you holding her?' Mike said on one of his unhappy visits. 'The other mothers pick them up. Look how they stop crying when they cuddle them. Why can't you do that?'

'She doesn't seem to like it when I touch her.'

'That's rubbish. My mother says you may not love a baby at first sight, but as soon as you start cuddling it, you'll bond. That's how all mothers feel. Why won't you even try?'

'You try then.' Mike reached in gingerly and lifted her from the bassinette. She arched her little back and howled. Other babies clenched their hands. She stretched them out like two starfish unable to find a rock to cling to. Or as a warning not to come near.

'Well, I'm not her mother. She obviously wants you.'

Eventually, Odette couldn't stand it. She couldn't bear the rejection. She sent her away. The nurses wheeled her to the nursery. Odette lay and watched the other mothers fall in love with their babies. They laughed and drew attention to every burp and fart. They found it almost unbearable to lay them down.

Odette walked to the nursery and stared through the glass. Her baby was damp and red with screaming. Odette's arms ached. Perhaps she touched her wrongly. Perhaps she hadn't been born with a mother's touch. She had failed to learn it from her own mother, who had never been much for touching. Too close a relationship with that other love, Jack Daniels. But perhaps it was just as well, considering what happened to her brother.

Odette's arms ached, but they were useless arms, without the skill to comfort. She watched as the nurses scurried about, jiggling her, laying her down, swaddling and unswaddling her, feeding her water and leaving her be. Nothing worked and she couldn't bear it.

She couldn't bear that she shrieked and arched her body. She couldn't bear that she was so unhappy. She was angry with the nurses for not trying harder. She hated them for leaving her to cry. She wanted to rush in and snatch her away. She should be able to do it, even if they couldn't. She was her mother. What kind of mother was unable to comfort her own child?

# Chapter 11

'HERE I AM, PACKED with pathologies.'

Heather smoothed her skirt, caught between amusement and exasperation. 'If you're not careful I will write a journal article – about all your devious deflections.'

'Ah, well done Heather. We could play alliteration tennis. Maybe we could keep it going for the full hour.'

Heather struggled to retain her severity. It didn't suit her. She was pretty without being singular, Odette had always thought. Very few lines and none from frowning.

'At least I don't have to sit through your interminable heart-breaks to get a word in. With real friends, decency eventually requires you to say: "Okay, enough about my life. Let's talk about you. What do you think of me?"'

Odette would say this for her: at least she always laughed. She felt she couldn't sustain this – she still found it hard to say 'therapy' – without some semblance of mutual exchange.

'Now, if I recall, we were going to talk about your feelings of loss.'

Ah, so Heather did dunk. But naturally she managed it without fuss, mess, or biscuit debris silting up her Earl Grey. 'I was just admiring the neat way you dunk. Did you need lessons?'

'Odette, I do enjoy our chats, but you know that's not my role.'

'Thank goodness for that. I'd hate you to dread my coming . . . No seriously, Heather, I don't have any issues there.' Heather looked doubtful. 'I tried to tell you last time. Kids leaving is all part of life's natural cycle. And no, I don't feel at all guilty about that.'

'Why do you . . . ?'

'I don't believe in guilt, that's why. I think it's unhealthy. What is, just is. Deal with it and get on with your life, that's how I've always felt.'

'Interesting you should bring up guilt. I never mentioned it.'

'Oh but you shrinks always do at some stage. You infer it everywhere. I know you.'

She smiled her shrinky smile. 'Let's go back to friendships then. We'll come back to the guilt issue.'

'Ah don't labour it. I'm not the type to spill my guts to every acquaintance, but I told you, I'm spoilt for choice. This very day I'm meeting a friend for lunch. And then there's my business partner . . .'

'Yes, what happened there. Did you talk to her?'

'Yes, it was just as I thought, she didn't want me to feel nervous. Talking of which, I do actually have something real to tell you this week.'

Odette ran through the burglary with, she felt, justifiable pride. In fact, repeating the story only emphasised quite how well she'd coped. When she finished, there was silence. Not what she'd expected.

Heather leant forward. 'But why didn't you mention this immediately? You left Jo'burg partly to escape the crime, and now . . .'

'No I did not. Anyway, my burglary here . . .'

'Robbery. It was a robbery, Odette. We spoke about that.'

'Well okay, then. But this really was just a burglary. Don't make it a big thing. It hasn't destroyed my life. I actually thought you'd be proud of how I handled things.'

'You did handle things, Odette, but perhaps a little too well, considering. I'd prefer you to face your feelings, not bury them in activity.'

'Ag feelings . . . I told you. It happened, I felt bad for a while then I moved along. Singularly healthy, I should say. And I did not leave because of crime.'

'Why did you leave then?'

I left . . . I don't know. I just wanted something . . . smaller, I suppose. More manageable. Something that was mine.'

'Smaller? But why? Don't you deserve a big life?'

Odette sighed. Not even halfway through and they were already mired in shrink talk. She looked up for inspiration and, as usual, found none. Heather's rooms were powder blue, with harmonising prints. Heather had made damn sure there could never be the slightest occasion for: 'Did you find that sculpture on your last trip to Samarkand?'

'Is your life so very large? Is anyone's? It was a throwaway remark, Heather. And I'm busy talking about my burglary, if you don't mind. This is why I have to save up things to tell you.'

Heather laughed. 'So you've had no flashbacks. And you're sleeping fine, no bad dreams . . .'

'I'm sleeping like a baby and no, I never dream.'

Heather watched her. She could feel herself fidgeting. 'Well, hardly at all. Nothing to write home about, anyway.'

The sound of traffic rose between them until it seemed that, if she didn't break it, it would overwhelm them both. 'Okay, straight after the burglary I had . . . not a bad dream, exactly. More ridiculous really, so you can stop casting about for your bloody journal article.'

'Tell me this ridiculous dream then. Hopefully, it has at least a few decent pathologies. By the way, you're dripping damp short-bread on my new carpet.'

Odette gave a rapid summary of the flat roof, her attempts to warn the oblivious party-goers and their inexorable fall. Predictably, Heather asked what Odette thought her dream meant. Odette shrugged. She'd been forced to trot the bloody thing out, she wasn't going to interpret it too.

Heather smiled. Perhaps Odette was afraid of doing harm while trying to do good? Odette shrugged again.

'Maybe you fear your capacity to damage the people you care about.' Odette still wasn't buying. You could say that about anyone.

'Perhaps you suspect that all your attempts to save people are really attempts to harm.'

'Oh come on Heather.'

'So you're not trying to shrink your life smaller and smaller so you're less able to cause harm?'

'Oh for fuck sake, that's a stretch, even for a journal article. I'm sorry I raised the stupid dream. Maybe sometimes a dream is just a dream. I probably just saw something on TV.'

Heather fussed with the tissue box. She always did that, making sure one tissue was sticking out in a hopeful way. Heather caught her watching and laughed grudgingly.

'Well, you could do worse than use one now and again. It's good to cry.'

'I've nothing to cry about. I have a new beginning and . . . I even have a new friend, which ought to please you mightily.'

There were only five minutes left, so she told her about dinner with Adriaan. She timed it wrong though. She should have waited a couple more minutes. It was hard to judge, like dunking a shortbread.

'Oh.'

'What do you mean, "Oh"? Sometimes a dinner is just a dinner.'

'Yes, much like your dream. Do you like him?'

'I wouldn't have dinner with the poor man if I didn't like him.'

Heather considered her silently. Odette shouldn't allow it to get to her. 'Oh, don't go there. I've done the love-of-my-life thing. I'm not looking to repeat the exercise.'

Heather still didn't say anything. Irritating.

'It's emotionally uncomplicated. Totally. I had a nice dinner . . . and he paid. Always a plus.'

'So, he didn't kiss you goodnight then?'

It was one of those still spring days that aspire to late summer. In just a couple of weeks, winter had vanished. Baked jasmine gave the air a holiday smell. Bougainvillea massed on walls and colonised trees.

Newspaper sellers sweltered at intersections, their bundles proclaiming FIFA's confidence that the stadiums would be ready in time. The World Cup seemed to have become central to the city psyche, unlike Nagelaten, where she was hardly aware of it.

Heather's *Star*, skimmed while her earlier client took his leave, had brimmed with earth-shattering conjecture: Would the roads be ready? Would the world get lost on endless detours? Would the lights stay on or would the world stumble around blindly in the dark? Would the world like us? (Please like us. Please.) Would the world get mugged? Would the world get drunk at Ellis Park and wander off, unwary, into Hillbrow?

Beggars and hawkers had sussed the mood. Flags and makarapa helmets were replacing cardboard signs declaring when their children had last eaten, that they didn't do crime or the odd comedian's: their dog was dead and their cat in rehab.

They swarmed the red lights, making winding motions when she shook her head and failed to open her window. She had no cash. Not enough to spare, anyway. But their hand-to-mouth gestures made a liar of her and filled her with shame, making her wish the bloody robot would change.

Had there always been so very many? She wasn't used to the roads any more: the hooting, weaving chaos of them. The way the taxis cut and thrust and the Mercs jostled and bragged of their horsepower. It took her longer than she expected and she arrived at the bookshop rattled and slightly shaky. This was why people left this place. All that adrenalin couldn't be good for one.

She had arranged to meet Palesa here so that she could kill two birds, one being Melissa's book token. It was cool inside and she found herself absorbing the peace rather than seriously browsing. She missed having a bookshop to pop into, if only to hear someone ask when the new Franzen would be out, or what the name of that book was again? The one about the boy...? It made a change from the cattle auction, or the price of mealies.

Palesa managed to crack the still surface just by entering the store. Robust and shiny with vigour, she caused people to look up and smile at the sight of her. Odette ordered them each a slice of quiche and a cappuccino (which was good here). She carried them out to the courtyard where a Yesterday Today and Tomorrow overpowered even the smell of coffee.

She was unused to being in Jo'burg company. She panicked briefly about what she still had to talk about, so she rushed into an account of her burglary – the short version, because burglaries were hardly hot news – and she was relieved when Palesa lost interest and took over.

'We rode a good twenty ks. Fine once you're on the open road, but getting through Jo'burg traffic! And it doesn't help that we were two women.'

Odette was content to sip her coffee and punctuate with the odd 'uh-huh'. Palesa could make even the traffic diverting, purely through her vociferous engagement with it. It made Odette smile.

'...those snooty white women in their 4x4s are bad enough. But those Zulu men: they're not used to giving way to anyone, least of all anyone they see as weaker.'

Odette found she was enjoying herself. Heather had filled a gap, there was no doubt about that, but she wouldn't be seeing her much longer. There was something seductive about speaking entirely about yourself for an hour, but it wasn't as though she needed the therapy. What Heather had done, though, was make her realise the need to make some effort with the friends she still had. If only to avoid becoming a loony recluse who spoke only to her cats.

'I could just imagine the headlines if we'd both been flattened by that bus. We have to be a bit careful of things like that.'

'What, of dying?'

Palesa laughed. 'No, I mean . . . you do know who I'm dating, don't you?'

'I've heard talk, but you don't have to tell me.'

'Chevonne, I suppose. I told her in a weak moment, but that girl never could keep her mouth shut. No it's fine, I trust you. You don't blab.'

Odette wished she didn't. She really wished she wouldn't. No way of stopping her though, without causing insult. Odette felt like clapping her hands to her ears and breaking into raucous song. But Palesa was bursting to tell someone, anyone, about her weekend with the City Councillor's wife.

It wasn't that Odette felt strongly about the infidelity. Their indiscretions were their own responsibility, and only the City Councillor's wife knew what the City Councillor was like at home. No, it wasn't that at all.

'Funny, I heard he was a Cabinet Minister,' Odette said, largely to divert her from more detail.

'That Chevonne, she always has to make a meal of everything. It's why I should never tell her anything. I certainly haven't told her why I don't speak to my family, so don't tell her, okay?'

Odette didn't say anything. She didn't know why Palesa didn't speak to her family and she hoped against hope that Palesa wasn't going to tell her.

'I was dating this chick from varsity, see? It was last Christmas and she was pissed off that I wasn't showing her off to my family.'

Odette found she was holding her breath. Once you set them off, Palesa's confidences were like an avalanche. After a while you felt you might suffocate beneath the weight of them.

'So she goes and outs me. And right there at the Christmas table too. I'll never forgive her for that. So, what about you? Are you seeing anyone?' Odette shook her head.

'Never mind. Without a kid in the house, I'm sure it'll be easier. Not that I'm suggesting you . . .'

'What, that I've pushed her from the womb? Hell Palesa, they should be full term by Mandy's age, or at least viable. Even if I did, it's at most an elective C-section, not a sneaky abortion.'

'Shut up, you. You've got your character on the brain.' Palesa threw back her head and laughed without the least awkwardness, bringing a pause to the silent browsing and murmured discussion about them. 'Which reminds me, I've been meaning to ask. With all that stuff you're writing, your kid, she isn't . . .?'

And here it was. It wasn't the infidelities or outings that made Odette uneasy. She wasn't a prude. It was friendship itself that she found hard. She paused to form her words.

'There's not much to say really. Yes, Mandy was born with a condition . . . very manageable though.'

'Not like in the storyline?'

'No, no, nothing like Down's. Nothing to write home about really. She needed a few therapies, but only to write neatly, hit a ball, concentrate, stuff like that.'

'Far as I can see, every bloody child needs therapy these days. So was it your . . . I mean, was it from your family?'

'Pointless to speculate. The way I see it, everyone gives their kids something: bad eyesight, fat thighs, a ghastly personality . . .'

She should have known this would happen. She should just have stuck to Heather. She paid her, after all. She could leave anytime. Real friendship was so much harder to control. Sooner or later you were always called upon to do more than 'uh-huh'. Friendship wasn't free. It was a transaction. The price was paid in confidences. It was a price too high for her.

Venezia was still empty when she arrived, except for the owner, who was in full sordid argument with his daughter in the corner. They were a soap opera in themselves, those two. Odette nodded a greeting. She had never cared enough to catch his name, and now it seemed too late to ask.

Palesa followed on her bicycle a minute or two later, strong legs gleaming with effort. Odette had offered to push the bike into the back of her car, but Palesa had countered that you didn't push a racing bike anywhere, least of all into the back of a Toyota.

'Pity the burglars didn't take it. You could've claimed and bought something decent,' she added, just as Chevonne came in. Bloody hell. She hated to provide Chevonne with such a giveaway for *schadenfreude*.

'You were burgled?' Unpacking her capacious bag, Chevonne burst into gales of merry laughter. 'You left here . . . and got burgled there?'

'Why is this so funny, Sis'Chevonne?' asked Palesa.

'Oh, no reason,' she said tilting a smug glance their way. 'Except . . .'

'Except what?' Palesa shouldn't get drawn in. It was exactly what Chevonne wanted.

'Where will the poor white folks go to escape us next?'

That, however, Odette could not ignore. 'I beg your pardon? Have you ever been to Nagelaten?'

'And since when did you become so very black?' asked Palesa, hands on hips, waggling her head from side to side

Chevonne's needling always sent Odette's irritation level screaming into the red. Somehow you shifted into defensive mode and ended up furious at yourself.

'There's bloody-side more black people in my neighbourhood . . .'

'Eish. Exactly why I wouldn't move there,' said Palesa. 'What! Don't look at me like that. I've just moved to the suburbs. You think I want the whole township moving in next door?'

She and Chevonne both stared. Then the three of them packed up laughing.

'Ag come on, girlfriend.' Chevonne looped an arm over Odette's shoulder. 'Only kidding hey?'

Palesa sank into her chair, laughter tearing her eyes. 'I don't mean . . .' she said, and tried again, dabbing at her eyes. 'I don't mean because they're black.'

'I'd be worried about your self-image if I thought you meant it.' Odette was relieved to feel her anger dissolve. She took the seat beside Palesa as Lex cleared his throat.

'I just mean . . .' Palesa whispered across her to Chevonne, but Chevonne was already listening to Lex call for general comments.

'Never mind,' Odette whispered back quickly. 'Thousands wouldn't, but I know what you're trying to say.'

When they got to Odette's storyline, Lex was sucking ruminatively at a chocolate digestive, lips coated in a brown veneer. He normally gave his notes first, but today he called for comments. Probably wanted to gauge the general reaction before committing himself.

'I think it's great the way you do the pregnancy stuff,' said Chevonne, making up for her earlier goading.

'Nice taut emotion,' added Palesa. Odette gave them a surreptitious thumbs-up, for the support. 'Hey, I was surprised. You're not exactly the most emotional person.'

'Doesn't mean I can't imagine it, idiot.'

'There's just one thing I don't get,' Chevonne said. 'My cousin's best friend was really old so it was her own fault. But Rochelle's supposed to be in her twenties.

'It's no one's fault,' said Odette, probably with more asperity than it warranted. 'And Down's can occur even under the disgustingly advanced age of thirty-five.'

'Yes, you sickeningly young person,' added Margie. 'And for your information, women in their forties are still fertile and do actually still have sex.' She couldn't resist a glance at Lex.

'Ee-ooh,' said Chevonne with a grimace of distaste, but everyone ignored her. Odette made a rubbing motion over Palesa's foolscap pad, to indicate the fifty rand Palesa owed her. They were *so* having an affair. Palesa shook her head and mouthed: 'not proven'.

'What are you naughty girls discussing there amongst yourselves?' Margie asked, trying for arch. Odette judged her to be at that stage of love where she couldn't resist letting it be known, despite their sworn secrecy or Lex's unhappy little wife. All these social signals went directly over Lex's head, of course. Sometimes Odette wondered how he managed to appreciate the emotional content of her stories.

'Margie? Anything?'

'I have ... hmm, I have a couple of notes on Odette's story. Lex? Why don't you have your say first though. I don't want to muddy the waters.'

'Might as well. Lex is busy muddying his sparkling water,' Palesa muttered.

They paused while cappuccinos were served. Odette's had a fern etched in the foam, better than she could have managed. She needed more practice.

'I'm liking it, I must say,' Lex said. 'I like the way you set the poor bastard up. First he's actually quite happy about the amnio results. Like, whew, now she really has to get rid of it.'

'Exactly what I was going to say,' added Margie quickly. 'I like that you've even set the date for the abortion. Clever girl.'

Odette made another rubbing gesture in Palesa's direction, but Palesa frowned and feigned total concentration.

Lex ran through his notes quickly, always a good sign: an unmotivated comment in scene 32 (Granted. Fixable with a word or two); scene 45 sounded like it would move a bit slowly (Idiot! Emotional content can't be rushed. Worth a relook though.); and a slight contradiction in the final scene (wording could be changed – for fools).

'Should we quickly brainstorm the B story from here on out? I gather you'll have her go to the brink. Does Reno go with her?'

'Hang on a sec.' Chevonne, naturally. 'I haven't got the motivation for changing her mind. Surely she wants her life back.'

'Actually, that's true.' Lex said. 'Why the fuck?'

Odette spoke very slowly. 'Well Lex, abortion isn't easy, emotionally. Rochelle's been brought up strictly. This is likely to be very traumatic.'

'Ja ja, I get all the trauma and shit. But this is different. The child's a ...'

'Guilt, Lex. Ever heard of it?'

'Ha. Not motivated,' said Chevonne. 'You said it wasn't their fault, so why would she feel guilty?'

'God, you guys. If you're not mothers, you must at least have met one somewhere along the line. Even your own will do.'

Everyone was talking at once, Margie shaking her head and chuntering on about children being a blessing, Chevonne with another flower of wisdom from her cousin's best friend.

Odette raised her voice over the din. 'All mothers feel guilt, okay? Now, multiply that by ten when the kid has a genetic condition, irrational as that may be. Goes with the territory.'

'You don't,' said Palesa.

There was silence. Odette contemplated murder. If she hadn't already concluded as much, this should amply demonstrate why friendships were best kept at a certain level.

'Well you . . . I mean, you don't appear to.' She looked uncertain.

'I'm highly evolved.'

'Did I say the wrong thing?' Palesa muttered, staring down at her pad. 'I thought it was just a few school problems. I didn't know it was secret.'

'It's not. I just don't talk about it – mainly because it's not an issue.'

'So what the hell *is* wrong with your kid?' Lex asked with admirable sensitivity.

Stock version: Thousands of genetic conditions. Many completely unclassifiable. Still more completely random . . .

She'd lost them. There seemed to be much running on the pavement outside. A few shrieks and yells. Chevonne, being the youngest, was first to the door. Odette rose more slowly to see car guards scattering.

'What's happening, what's happening?' Lex called. 24/7 vans were screeching up in formation further down the road. It looked like one of those American crime series in which the police always have enough cars to cut off the villains' escape.

Palesa and Odette pushed past Chevonne to see. Mothers tugged children to cars. School kids and delivery men ran towards the commotion.

'What's happening?' Lex called plaintively. A young mother, frog-marching two toddlers and a pram to her car, glanced briefly in their direction. 'Robbery. Fruit shop.'

Candice from the stationery shop, who was married to the optometrist, ran by, yelling: 'Thought it was Eddie's shop. But it's Carlos. They've gone now. Five guys with AKs.'

She and Palesa made their way through the mêlée in her wake. They reached the fruit shop just as Carlos said: 'Okay folks, show's over. Still open for business.'

The 24/7 guards stood around the pavement, rifles cocked self-consciously. A parrot-grey lady, unpacking her veggies, called out: 'Well Carlos, I'm not surprised they picked on you. It's daylight robbery to shop here.'

Everyone laughed, except Carlos. Odette and Palesa wandered back down the pavement, while Carlos berated all and sundry for the injustice. There was a high state of excitement in the street. People talked urgently in clusters, comparing notes and sharing tales of robbery and anarchy.

Palesa put a hand on her arm before they reached the others. 'I'm helluva sorry, hey, Odes. I didn't mean . . . I never realised.'

'It's nothing. It's fine. I hardly think about it, that's all.' Gently, she removed Palesa's hand – with a small squeeze to show there were no hard feelings.

'Friends?'

'Nah, hate your guts. You're just too insensitive to throw off.' Palesa punched her arm.

Chevonne was shaking her head as they returned. 'So, can I come join you in your little town? I am an Afrikaner after all. I can *praat* the *taal.*'

'Brown ones don't count,' said Palesa.

'Hey, so now I'm too brown? Earlier . . .'

'Oh shut up, you two. You're both welcome to join me in the Free State, but just remember I'm a storyliner. I couldn't afford the arty Karoo town with quaint shops and galleries.'

'Bugger that,' said Palesa. All you need is two gay boys to open a restaurant and your prices will instantly soar. I'll use my influence.'

'Look you guys,' said Lex. 'We've wasted enough fucking time sight-seeing. Can we get on with this or what?'

The traffic wasn't too bad. Where it really counted was on the secondary road. You couldn't speed on the main highway – there was always at least one trap. The secondary road was a dream, as long as you missed the potholes and didn't get stuck behind a truck.

Once you'd been on the secondary road for a while, the ground undulated like waves preparing to break. The land was yellow, bleached by frost and lack of rain. Before her move, she had considered it the pallor of deprivation, but now she could see the variation in its undertones: its browns, fawns, vaals and wan yellows, even pinks.

She did end up behind a truck, sitting in his fumes for three blind rises. On the downhills, he gave the monster its head, bucking wildly over the ruts left by its countless brothers.

There were few trees, except around farmhouses and villages. She spied a cluster of bushes, but dusk played tricks. It was a gathering of cows – Drakensbergers by the look of them, though it was hard to tell how black they were in this light.

Funnily enough, she had always found cattle romantic. Maybe that was what had drawn her to Adriaan. Awful thought, but it was true to say those were probably the happiest times she could remember, after Lucien died and her dad left. Her mother had been a fabulous storyteller, although she could barely remember that now. When the task fell to Oupa, he could only rustle up stories about cows. Special breeds of Nguni who, 'like you and me,' had adapted to their harsh conditions.

'Just as beautiful as you, with those speckles on your nose.' He would break off to draw pictures of their dappled reds and flashes of white.

'You might think, because they're small, they're delicate. But, despite their beauty, they're hardy. Like you, my poppet. Your mom is not strong, but you . . . you are a true survivor.'

Poor old Oupa. He didn't have the imagination for made-up stories. It was the best he could do. That and the games he and the herdboys had played on the hills outside Ixopo, before he'd been sent to boarding school. He told her the names for different cattle markings, like Eggs of the lark, Hornbill takes to flight. He had loved them, she thought, almost as much as he'd loved her.

She managed to pass the truck, though the manoeuvre was a trifle hairy. Just as she put on a burst of speed, she had to brake and veer onto the gravel to avoid a cluster of potholes.

Oupa would have loved to sit down with his pipe and a *glasie brandewyn* to discuss the cross-breeds and variations on the old Ngunis. Or maybe he wouldn't. Adriaan might love his cows, but his farm was a business, whereas for Oupa it had been a romance, a love affair that never was.

The sky was dramatic, and vast. Cumulus, flattened beneath, rose in bulbous formations. Garlands of sunlight draped over the sides of darkened hills. Before her, the clouds grew intensely pink and bled over the sky. In her rear-view mirror, they were a deep gold, in garish contrast to the cerulean beneath.

The pink disappeared first, then the gold. Darkness dropped over the landscape as though a black-out curtain had been drawn across one of her mother's stories of wartime heroism.

Oh well, perhaps her oupa was looking down from wherever he was and feeling pleased. That she had come full circle. She had come to her own place of cows, where she was fairly sure she could grow her own sturdy, speckled strength, just as he had always hoped she would.

She pulled up in the pitch-dark, grabbed bags and Woolies packets and rustled awkwardly from the car. Scrabbling for keys, she put the bags down and took a moment just to appreciate living here rather than Jo'burg. The Milky Way was a creamy smear across the sky, the Southern Cross a beacon just beyond. Over the next hill almost.

Something moved on her front stoep. For a second, everything halted. Then the shadows clotted into a figure which advanced to where the moon dribbled light across his face. Willie, from next door.

'God, you gave me . . . Willie! What the bloody hell are you doing here?'

'Sorry man. I was waiting for you. Watching the house.'

'Did something happen?'

'No man, but they watch, you know. They can see when you're gone.'

He smelt of cheap brandy and acrid stompies left in ashtrays overnight. Gesturing in the direction of Stella's tumbledown house, he added: 'They've been checking things out.'

'Did you call the police?'

'Ag, what's the use of them. But I can help you. I'm back from Bloem for good now.'

She put her bags down again. They were digging into her fingers.

'Couldn't get a job. All they want is the blacks.'

'Okay that's . . .'

'And if you get a job, they'll chuck you out you for any-blêddy thing.'

'Okay I get it, Willie.'

She had snapped and he blinked at her, his gaze uncomprehending. She felt defeated suddenly. Oh for God's sake, he meant well. Where did she get off, going all principled on him? She had no conception of what his life was like, and a sense of grievance was probably the only legacy he could expect from old Fanie.

'I'll stay in your house. In the back room. The one down there next to the kitchen.'

Dismay rose in her throat, so sharp it burnt her tongue. Would this happen every time she travelled to Jo'burg? Would she fear Stella's sons or cousins or nephews had been . . . were still . . . inside her house? She couldn't live like that. Yet this was no alternative.

'Look, I don't . . . I work from home.' She picked up her packets and took a step.

'You're a white woman on your own. It's not going to be the last time. At least then they know there's a man around. And if I'm not here, I'll be next door with the toppies.'

'I know you're being kind, Willie and I'm grateful. But I don't think so. I'm too . . . I'm just too bloody solitary, okay?'

'You're making a big mistake.'

Well, if she was, so be it. She let herself in and poured a glass from the Chardonnay she had opened two days ago. It tasted sour. Probably just open too long.

# Chapter 12

'CAPTAIN FITZ, PLEASE.'

'*Man of vrou?*'

'Man. The husband, please.'

'Fitz *wat praat.*'

'Hi Captain, it's Odette.'

'Ja Odette, no news I'm afraid. But we are still...'

'No Captain...well, partly. But I wondered if I could ask your advice.'

'Oh, okay. Hundred per cent. I was going to *maak a draai* past you anyway. I'm going to have one more go at talking with Ou Stella. I still think she know more than she says.'

'Thanks Captain. I didn't think you'd still be interested.'

'No man. In the city, they don't care about burglaries. But me, I never let a case go. Besides, we are hospitable here on the *platteland.*'

He was busy with a stabbing in the new tavern near the church, so they made a date for the day after next, in the morning. 'As long as it's not too close to lunchtime. My wife will kill me if I'm not home for lunch.'

'The stricter of the Captain Fitzes?'

'You have no idea.'

Something had changed in De Wet Street, much as she might try to ignore it. Forcing her eyes up the road, she tried to focus on the bank on De La Rey, its dome an incongruous flourish in its row of dumpy shops, topped and tailed by the church and town silos. It was a building that spoke of important business.

Those old buildings told you stuff: they said what the town was about, what it existed for and what it had hoped to become... Or hell, what did she know. Perhaps they only spoke of the past.

De Wet was impossible to ignore. Overnight, it had become a field hospital for cars: spent hulks drooling oil; entrails of engines; carcasses leaning over fractured axles. This was not the stuff of rural fantasy.

A large black man – or, to be absolutely clear, a giant of a man – leant against an old bakkie, its hindquarters resting on bricks. He held a spanner bunched in his left hand, as though he were about to use it as a weapon rather than a tool. It took Odette a moment to realise he was speaking to her.

'I said: "You're the Corolla". I'm George.'

He had been impassive, sizing her up. But just then he broke into an abrupt grin that split his face like the Red Sea parting.

'Odette. Sorry? I'm the...?'

'The Corolla round the corner. Gauteng registration?'

'Well spotted. And you're... This is your, um...?'

'My business, yes. I'm the new neighbour.' He pushed himself upright, buttons defending their stronghold against an advancing stomach. 'Come, I'll show you. Seen you a couple of times. What mileage have you done?'

'Jeez, I don't know, George. It's like asking a woman her age. Probably more than we'd either of us care to admit.'

George laughed musically, strange in so large a man. He ushered her towards his new house, his pride a physical thing; a being who walked between them into the yard. Where a week ago, that yard had served as a dainty display to an old man's roses, it was now a riot of indecently exposed car innards. Before her eyes, she saw property values falling...whee-ker-chunk.

Two terriers, identical in their mongrel oddity, charged forward, yapping frantically. George swiped a large arm at them. 'Voetsêk.'

They voetsêked, disappearing beneath the rusted shell of a kombi from where their noses emerged, emitting aggrieved yelps. Anomalous creatures, they combined the jackal ears of the township dogs with the long nose and wiry hair of some trusty pedigree. Oh, the trouble and strife that must have caused.

'I know Toyotas. Taxis were my main business in Standerton. I'm cheaper than the white garage, because I work from home.'

'Yes, convenient. Has anyone...I mean, are you allowed to open a workshop here, in your house?'

He shrugged, a barely perceptible rise of mountainous shoulders. 'Some of the white people around here are complaining to me.'

Odette clicked her teeth and shook her head, disassociating herself from such reactionary views. He looked her over, shrugged again. 'What must I do? I'm a businessman. I must make a business.'

'And the council?' She felt uncomfortable asking, but she did wonder.

'The council has enough to worry them.'

In principle, she supposed there probably wasn't much difference between this and keeping cows or sheep. Less picturesque though.

'If I pay them what they're due, why should they trouble me? It's a business, fair and square...And you? Where do you work?'

'Oh, I work from home too. Although,' she glanced around at the mechanical carnage, 'writing doesn't take up quite so much space.'

He laughed his tuneful laugh, squinting in the sunlight. He was infectious, George the businessman. Hell, she wasn't doing too badly in the friend stakes. He might just end up being as close to a friend as any of the people she allowed only so far and no further. Something else she could tell Heather.

'Lucky you brought that baby here. Corollas are number one on the stolen car list . . .'

'. . . in Jo'burg, yes I know. And now I go and get myself burgled here. Lucky the car wasn't around at the time.'

'Eish. Bad. Very bad.' His large head swung to and fro. 'I'll speak to a few people. I've got a few contacts. See what I can find out.'

'Thanks George. Captain Fitz is apparently some kind of hot-shot, but he doesn't seem to be getting anywhere with Stella. She's the old lady squatting in that house down there.'

'The municipal house, yes, I know her. Tried to buy that place myself.'

'What happened there? Why was it standing empty? Surely the municipality could still use it?'

'Housing clerk ate the housing money. They were planning a big extension to the township then one morning he was gone, and all the funds too. Done a flit.'

He shook his head and settled the folds of his face back into a scowl. Leaning his elbows on the bakkie, he waved the spanner at her. 'I'm not sorry now. It wasn't big enough for me, but Ou Stella was quick as lightning. Squatted it before the council got through the red tape. Sorry for them.'

'And now it's falling down. What a shame. And she can burgle me anytime she feels the urge.'

'Ai, I don't know. She's not a bad old auntie, that Stella. My wife's mother's cousin.'

'Ah hell, I'm sorry.'

'Uh uh. Uh uh.' His cheeks shivered in harmonic motion. 'Every other person you look at in Nagelaten will be some family to me. Half I wouldn't give them water on a hot day.'

His terriers crept towards him. George treated each to a hind-quarter scratch with the heel of his boot. They collapsed and bared stomachs in a delirium of submission.

'Enough,' he said, throwing an arm upward. She wasn't sure if he was referring to the dogs or his relatives. The dogs scrabbled back under the bakkie, just their noses visible.

'If I can make a business . . . we had the same chances, see? Why come ask me for money, as if I owe them?' He gave a resounding click. 'But Ou Stella now. She's the only one never asks for help.'

Bloody hell, she was getting tired of this. Why did everyone defend Stella, even Fitz? And when had she become the bad guy? Turning things around, wasn't it?

'Well, I'm very sorry for her – all those kids. Look, maybe she wasn't personally involved, but she sure as hell let other people through her property.'

He gave another click, this one sliding off his front teeth. 'Ja no it's bad, man. Listen, I hope you come right with that. But Ou Stella?' He shook his head, considering, 'I don't know.'

They parted and she continued up the road. Okay, so he might cause her property value to drop but he was some kind of businessman. Cars stretched from his yard nearly as far as the Liebowitz Hardware, on the corner of De La Rey.

Dr Babu, white robes flapping, left the hardware store with a bottle of what looked like paraffin. He headed across the road to his glass-fronted shop. A row of sad faces waited beneath a sign that promised penis enlargement and powerful erection; making you liked at work; curing the sickness of the kidney; barren women; lost lovers and the bewitched. *uDokotela wesintu.*

She passed the Indian shop where mattresses jostled buckets and transistor radios across the covered pavement. Women wrapped in bright blankets called to friends on the other side of the road. White ladies, handbags in the crook of their arms, side-stepped and greeted each other with queries about children and husbands.

At the Chinese shop, two dark-eyed faces framed the doorway. Who had decreed that these solemn little girls, the smaller of the two audibly sucking a thumb, should circumnavigate the world, only to end up in a dusty town somewhere in the Free State?

A figure brushed out through the doorway, taking with it the faintest whiff of wood smoke and dank spaces. She straightened and watched the strange guy from the dark house lope across the pavement and into the street. He kept his face to the ground, hair straggling from the cap he hid beneath.

Of course, it made perfect sense that he would shop here among the sunglasses, fireworks and junk. His affinity with the owners lay in being accepted by no one, black or white. And in having no language that could ever breach that divide.

The Nagelaten Outfitters still had all its original fittings – wooden cases and shallow drawers for socks and underpants. There was something reassuring about its smells of polish and musty furnishings. Probably resonated with some childhood memory. Or perhaps it just fitted her template of a rural town.

Odette greeted the owner with a passable '*Middag*', but the woman switched instantly to English. She had a hairdo very like Trudie's. Nagelaten only had one hairdresser.

'What can I do for you?'

'I saw you had those warm flannel shirts marked down . . .'

Maybe she wouldn't have worn one in Jo'burg, but she had an image of herself tending vegetables as the weather turned again. She lifted a shirt tail and rubbed it against her cheek.

'Do they make these here?'

'What? Here?' The woman harrumphed. 'Chinese, of course. There's not a thing in my shop that's not Chinese . . . except for me and my cat.'

Odette smiled and replaced the shirt. They weren't as nice as she'd thought, but she riffled through them, searching for something other than XXL and XXXL.

'Aren't you the English from Terblanche Street?'

'Sorry? Oh, yes, that's me. The English from Terblanche Street.'

'I'm a friend of Trudie. From church. She tells me you write for *Trophies*?'

'I'm in the storyline team. We work out the story, then the script-writers fill in the scenes.' The colours were nice, but the sizes . . . 'Do you watch?'

'Every single day. On the dot of five I'm out of here. I was hoping to see you, actually. Something's been worrying me.'

'Have you got any other sizes maybe?'

'What's the matter with you people? Can't you see Reno and Rochelle are keen on each other? Even I can see that.'

She couldn't find a shirt small enough. (Or an answer, beyond a sigh.) They were sturdy people, these Nagelatens. Big-boned men who ran to fat in their middle years, and farm-bred women who became barrel-shaped before they turned forty.

'Haven't you noticed how they feel about each other?'

She no longer found this weird. After a couple of years working in soaps, she now just accepted that the existence of writers didn't necessarily preclude the reality of their characters in some parallel world.

'Well yes . . . Look I'm not allowed to tell you what happens, but just so you know, we've already written months ahead of what you're watching now.'

'You can just tell from the way they look at each other. His poor wife. You don't want that to happen, really, man. They must pull themselves together before it's too late.'

'You know? I think you shouldn't worry too much. What will be will be, I always say. Think how I feel, being able to see so far into the future.'

'That's all the stock I've got left. I'll get more next winter. But now tell me. That mayor's son, he's not really a moffie, is he?'

'But you've seen that already, haven't you? He just hasn't had the courage to come out yet.'

'No man. I don't like to see that in my home. There are ways, you know? He shouldn't give in to it. He should trust in God to help him. Will you tell him that please? From me?'

She didn't buy a fake flannel. To be honest, she found them a little disappointing.

The man turned as she entered, mid-complaint. 'I don't think it's fair, that's all.'

He was clearly at home in the home-industry, even if he did look like a parrot in a chicken coop. His shirt was brightly abstract, gathered at the cuffs. He wore it tucked into his pants.

'*Ag* Danie,' Trudie was saying, 'you know what this town's like. Oh hi, Odette.'

'Hey, the celebrity. I'm Danie.'

'Celebrity? Hardly.'

'You're a *Trophies* writer, aren't you?'

Trudie was sitting behind her table while Danie paced, lifting jams and inspecting tartlets. His lips were pursed, cheeks flushed. A plastic sheet was taped across the doorway to their coffee shop, and very satisfying sounds of banging emanated from behind it.

Odette appropriated the chair on the other side of the table. 'What's not fair by the way? Or am I butting in where I'm not wanted?'

'*Ag nee,* nothing really. Danie and I were at high school together. He went away to be an artist, but now he's come back to teach art at the high school.'

Danie was standing on tip-toe to see into the mirror Trudie kept on the shelf above her table. He rubbed at a minute imperfection on his cheek.

'I paint nudes,' he said, without turning. 'That's me. It's my expression. But now suddenly I'm not allowed.'

'Now Danie, that's not exactly true. The dominee did say they can't stop what you do in your own home.'

A farmer appeared at the door to drop off a load of milk tarts and carrot cakes. Trudie broke off for an exchange over his wife's blood pressure and next week's order. Danie waited for the man to leave.

'What's the point if you can't exhibit? Come on, Trudie. Whose side are you on?' Trudie began packing cakes on shelves. She gave a small shake of the head and bestowed an indulgent smile on him.

Odette couldn't resist: 'I'm sorry, but I don't understand what the hell it's got to do with some dominee.'

Trudie and Danie looked at each other. 'They won't let me teach if I show my nudes. Besides, he is still my dominee.'

'Are you religious?'

Trudie and he exchanged glances again. 'Look,' he said at last, 'It's not like I go to church every week. But I still have a church. Everyone has a church.'

They both glanced at her, realising she supposed, that now perhaps someone in the community may not actually have a church.

'So you'd be like an outcast, or excommunicated or something?'

They glanced at each other again. You'd swear she came from outer Mongolia, not a city some ninety minutes away. Danie seemed to be forcibly restraining his eyes from rolling. They both laughed.

'No man, it's not like that,' said Trudie.

'It's not medieval.'

'But your church is your people. It's your community. It would just make it hard...'

'Anyway, I can't afford to live here if I don't teach.'

That at least she could understand. Speaking of which: she told Trudie she'd arranged to fetch the coffee machine as soon as renovations were complete. And, she certainly wouldn't wish it away, but heavy rains were forecast and maybe they should hold thumbs for it to hold off? Just till the renovations were done?

'Can you two use your influence? And maybe for Lucky Bean's grand opening, while you're about it.'

Trudie threw a superstitious glance at the ceiling and shook her head. Danie waved a dismissive hand. 'Nothing will put people off coming. Telling you.'

'We don't like to pray for no rain,' said Trudie. 'It's not right.'

Trudie could remember drought more readily than she could rain apparently. 'Seven years to one of rain – it's about that. And then it usually rains too much and ruins the crops. Still a *misoes*, but somehow we prefer a harvest ruined by rain. Feels more like plenty.'

She started on the milk tarts. Danie whipped a small bag of fudge from a shelf, tugged at its ribbon and popped one into his mouth. Trudie slapped his hand.

'By the way you guys, I've been meaning to ask. There's this strange guy I keep seeing. Lives in a weird little house down by the coalyard.'

She didn't know what she expected to hear, but she wasn't much illuminated. 'Oh him? Ag no,' said Trudie. 'Don't worry about him. He's a bit funny, that's all.'

'Every town's got one, hey Trudie? Listen, have you seen Rentia's hair? She got it cut in Bloem when they went to the auction. Looks a total fright.'

She should get going, but something still niggled at her. She waited till they'd finished with Rentia's hair.

'So when you say everyone in Nagelaten has a church, do you mean . . . like everyone?'

'You mean Adriaan? Don't think we don't know you had a date.' How the hell did Danie know? He'd only been back five minutes. Trudie was looking anxious for some reason, twisting the hem of her blouse.

'It was not a date. Trudie? What on Earth's the matter?'

'Well Missie, it doesn't matter if you call it a date,' Danie pronounced, hands on hips. 'The whole town is calling it a date. And of course yes. Adriaan belongs to the same church as us.'

Trudie still had that look, but she nodded. 'The big NG church in De La Rey. The *moedergemeente*. That's the church we grew up in.'

'And Marta? And . . . and the Captain Fitzes?' (This was an evasive manoeuvre.)

'Marta went to the APK for a while. Afrikaans Protestantse. Same as NG. But they prefer to worship with their own.'

Odette felt very dense. 'Like . . . what? You mean with other APKs? Other Christians?'

'No man, it's like the NG used to be. They still make rules about who can come in. Like the old days.'

Odette felt like laughing hysterically. The old days seemed so remote now that it hadn't crossed her mind. 'You're not serious. Isn't that illegal? But I suppose it figures where she's concerned.'

'They did come back, though. It's where she grew up – even if it has changed. Anyone can come in our church now, as long as they worship same as us.'

'And the Captain Fitzes?'

'Hervormd.' Trudie seemed more comfortable again, discussing churches. 'Your neighbours are with the PPK – the drums and hallelujah church near the police station.'

'Are they all so strict? About nudes and stuff?'

'Our church is the least strict of everyone,' said Trudie. 'You know what they say: *Een mens mag nie dans nie, een mens mag nie drink nie. Die NG mag beide doen. Maar die dominee moenie sien nie.*'

Danie gave small shrieks of laughter and Odette joined in. It was ridiculous, but somehow infectious, imagining the whole congregation dancing and drinking – but only when the dominee wasn't watching.

'But the woman from the outfitters goes to your church, doesn't she? And you won't believe what she just told me. She thinks the mayor's son in *Trophies* should pray for deliverance.'

They exchanged glances again. Then they both regarded her silently. 'But surely...' She appealed to Danie. He stared back woodenly.

Early on in the series, Odette had suggested that Lex advise the actor to calm down on the mayor's son. She thought he lacked subtlety, that his mannerisms approached stereotype. And here was Danie, who could give him a serious run for his money. Oh well, what did she know? Perhaps Danie had prayed.

She wondered what Palesa would make of them all. Probably laugh her head off. She wasn't one to miss an absurdity, or take it too seriously either.

'Look,' said Trudie, 'we're not old-fashioned, but we just believe . . . this town's seen enough tragedy, especially from that sort of thing.'

'What kind of thing?'

'There's just legacy here, that's all. I don't want to burden you with it now. It's gone and past so it doesn't matter any more. We just don't talk about it.'

'And neither should you,' said Danie. 'Especially with . . . other people. It's okay with us, but just . . .' He made a dousing gesture with his hand. 'It's best forgotten.'

The church spire dwarfed the dome of the bank, if not the silos. For the first time, she noticed that it was topped not by a cross, but a weather vane. A subtle reminder to God, perhaps? (Hey, remember us? Any rain going spare? When you have a moment.)

Adriaan pulled up in his bakkie as she reached Terblanche Street. He was wearing work denims. She liked them better than his going-out clothes.

'Brought your security gates . . .'

'Apparently the whole town is talking . . .'

They both laughed. 'Great minds,' he said.

'It's only great minds if we say the same thing.'

Her neighbours were still lined up against the wall, catching the last of the morning sun. Their mutt raised a lip and snarled.

'So we don't have great minds?' He had a nice twinkle, which always made you happy to see him. That's all it was though, and luckily they were both okay with that. 'What were you saying?'

She followed him around the back, ineptly holding the corner of a security gate. 'Apparently the whole town's talking about us.'

He laid it down and took out his measuring tape. For a moment, she thought he wasn't going to reply at all. Then he turned to face her. 'Do you care?'

'Shouldn't I? They care about you. I'm the interloper, it seems. I don't even have a church, while you, I'm told, have your own little pew.'

'Ah, so that's what's bothering you.'

'Not really. I just wondered, that's all.'

'It's nice they still regard me as one of them. Truth be told, I haven't been to church since my wife died. Probably infected by all that city-agnosticism in my years away.'

'It wasn't so much that. I suppose it's what the Dutch Reformed used to stand for.'

He shrugged. Taking a pencil from his shirt pocket, he began marking the position of the door.

'We grew up in that church. There wasn't much choice in those days. It's why I stayed abroad so long. The church has changed though. Had to, same as the town . . . Just going to fetch my drill.'

She unlocked the house and returned to find a fine layer of brick dust spraying into the slight breeze. The drill had set the squatter dogs going.

'Talking about things changing, I had a couple of funny experiences this morning. Not so much experiences as . . . well, attitudes I suppose. I was surprised, that's all.'

He stopped drilling. 'You hit some old-style attitudes? Come on, Odette. You don't strike me as naive. Things are changing so fast, give them a chance to catch up, won't you? Hey, tell you what, how about I cook you a meal sometime. We can discuss religion, politics too if you like?'

'It wasn't politics actually.'

Adriaan was drilling again She waited for him to pause, so she could ask what tragedies the town had seen, and what the big issue was about homosexuality, anyway.

She watched him place the drill down and wipe the brick dust from his forehead. He turned to face her, yet still she didn't speak. She couldn't have said why. Something about his set face, or perhaps life had taught her to be wary of asking questions she wasn't sure she wanted to hear the answers to.

'One thing about coming back though,' Adriaan said. 'I do get tired of the constant bloody gossip. People making up stories to make their own lives seem more interesting.'

Oh, for goodness sake, she was being stupid. Of course she could ask him. He was a man of the world. She would never have considered him a friend were she the least bit unsure of his attitudes. But by then, of course, the moment had passed.

# Chapter 13

THE PHONE RANG WHILE she was planting her beans and tomatoes. She nearly ignored it but changed her mind, scattering spots of soil as she sprinted inside – and then instantly regretted it.

'I thought I was just meant to look in on her, wasn't that the idea? That I would just check in now and again?'

'Hello Mike, nice to hear you too.'

'Did you know there were issues? Is that why you sent me?'

'Why, what's the matter? What happened? Is it the parents...?'

'No, I just don't have time for dramas, that's all. I think I made that clear. Look, Amelia and John seem nice in their way, but I walked into a bit of a to-do and I felt completely unprepared. If you'd just told me...'

'What happened? Was it the child's attachment to Mandy? Because I told her...'

'No, much more basic, I'm afraid. They'd just had a go at her about washing her clothes. And I must say I feel vindicated, Odette. The level of personal hygiene that's acceptable in your house...'

She leant against the wall, momentarily unable to reply. When Mandy was away, she always hoped... she imagined... well, she pictured something different, that's all.

'It was embarrassing, Odette. And I simply don't have time for this. I told you this was an important trip for the business.'

Odette tried to speak, then cleared her throat and tried again. 'You know very well she only forgets to wash her clothes when she's stressed. If they relax, then so will she. What the hell were they doing in her room, anyway? That's her private space.'

'The trouble is, she goes blank when they try to speak to her and they think she's being obstinate. And then she won't meet their eyes. Even while I was there...'

She stepped outside and watched Stella's grandchildren play. A little girl roared like a lion, hands raised into claws, while her brothers and sisters and cousins ran from her with high-pitched shrieks. Odette turned back inside. It was too hot there anyway.

'Ok, so she sometimes does that, but it's just her manner, you know that. Why is it such a big deal?'

'Because it makes people think she's shifty, that's why. I just wish you'd told her that. Anyway, let's not start on recriminations. Bit late now, I suppose.'

Odette clamped her teeth down on her fury. Outside, the children erupted into laughter. Two herdboys held a lilting conversation which carried across the commonage. She longed to be planting again – something simple that she couldn't be blamed for.

'Anyway, we sat down to a glass eventually – big fans of South African wine, by the way...'

'I hope you told them shy people often struggle when people yell. And they find it hard to look people in the eyes too. It's not so very strange.'

'Luckily they did put a lot down to different cultures. Apparently they had friends over and she dominated the conversation, but then there are times they can hardly drag a word out of her.'

'Well, that's actually true. It is different. How do they expect her to pick up the cues when they deign to show half an emotion?'

A crescendo of shrieks rose from outside. Odette stepped through the door to see Stella flapping a towel and advancing on the children. She made a lumbering attempt at a run and the children scattered, all except for the littlest girl, who was lassoed by the towel and gathered, giggling, to Stella's stout side.

'Look, they do say Mandy's terrific with the older kid. She's good with the baby too, but a little nervous. I said they shouldn't worry at all. It was natural to feel anxious with such a young baby, but she was more than capable.'

'Of course she is. We couldn't exactly keep her home because she doesn't meet people's eyes, could we?'

'I just hope I did the right thing.'

The first time she wished her baby dead was at 3 a.m. one very cold morning. Ah hell, was that so very shocking? Surely she couldn't be the only one.

When she took her brand-new baby home from the hospital, Sylvia impressed upon her the importance of allowing her husband to sleep if she wished him to get ahead.

'Michael didn't expect to be saddled with a wife and baby at this crucial stage of his career, my dear, so you do need to make some sacrifices.'

It was achingly cold, yet the baby seemed to hate all her jerseys. Odette asked if Sylvia thought they scratched, but she said it was her imagination. They were the finest quality, how could they?

She was a funny little soul. It was hard to absorb that this baby was hers. Sometimes it seemed a small alien had been foisted on her, while her perfect, nuzzling baby had been given to other, more deserving people.

Dummy? No, that didn't work. Okay, one more humiliating attempt at breastfeeding. No? Well, perhaps she wasn't hungry. She tugged on the string of the mobile. And back, by popular demand: 'Wish Upon a Star'. It wasn't the best rendition, but the small body went rigid. She shrieked till her upper lip turned blue and foam appeared at the corner of her mouth.

'Can't sleep with that racket,' Mike's voice emerged from the bedroom, muffled by warm duvet.

Odette carried her outside, swaddling her in a blanket, the softest she owned; the one thing she'd kept from her mother. It was the only blanket the baby seemed able to bear. They were house-sitting for Sylvia's friends, who were spending six months in Europe. Odette never felt quite at home, never wanting to sit in the patio chairs in case the baby puked, or worse.

She walked slowly around the pool, so tired she thought she might pitch forward into watery oblivion. Oh the relief. You feel sorry for yourself at 3 a.m. You can't help it. They were lucky to have the house. It was a favour, as long as they fed the dogs and the stupid bonsais. Another way for Mike to get ahead, while she and this . . . this succubus, pulled him back.

Her eyes burned with tears she was too tired and too angry to shed. Her throat felt rough and parched. Hell, her whole body felt rough and parched. The baby shrieked when she pulled her close, and screamed when she held her away. Briefly, Odette laid her on the concrete beside the pool. She seemed to cry more quietly, but she looked so neglected and abandoned that she lifted her again.

That scream could cut through your brain. It could slice through flesh like a red-hot knife. Was this her life now? Was this it? Her fucking lot to stand by this swimming pool in the freezing cold?

If she just dropped her arms . . . If she tripped for a minute, felt light-headed, fainted perhaps . . . it would only take a minute or two. There were two of her that night. She was possessed by two forces. One rasped in her ear: drop it, let it go, let it all go. Make it shut up, just make it, and listen to the blessed, blessed silence.

There was another though, who spoke of sins and mothers; who defended her baby fiercely, saying: You are not your mother. You are not.

Odette gave the baby a little shake. She knew it was dangerous. She did it anyway. Then she clutched her convulsively: 'Sorry. I'm so sorry.'

That night she saw what she was capable of. She knew. And deep down, she knew that this child knew it too.

Fitz shook his head. Nothing. No more from Stella. No more news at all. She was starting to lose hope. If the burglary had sparked an old fear, then Willie had rekindled it. She realised just how much she'd been relying on the Captain to find the culprits for her.

Time had run away with her this morning. She was dressed, but only just. The house was a wreck – the curse of working at home. Fortunately, he seemed perfectly comfortable leaning on the big farm gate. They talked about Stella and what she might or might not know.

Marlise and her daughter returned from town with shopping bags. Their dog skulked out to greet them, turning to squint at Odette from under flattened ears. Old man Fanie was sunning himself against the wall, tortoise head bobbing as he chewed – on what, she couldn't tell. Perhaps just his dentures.

Marlise yelled at Fanie for not taking the washing in. They must have bought themselves a washing line. She hadn't replaced the one that had vanished. It would probably just end up at Stella's like the last one.

Willie appeared from around the corner, trailing behind with more bags. He hunched and bobbed just like his old man. He looked different somehow... she couldn't quite put her finger on it.

The Captain hadn't seen him yet. She wanted to tell him what Willie had said, to ask for reassurance. She waited for him to finish what he was saying about Stella not having any souvenirs and not making any slips at all, which was unusual.

'But I still get the feeling she knows something. I'm just not sure what. Can't seem to break her story.'

'So Captain, this is what I wanted to tell you. Willie from next door...'

She gestured with her chin as he passed behind Fitz. She was still trying to work out what was different about him.

The rest happened really fast. The Captain half-turned and Willie threw them a self-conscious wave. As Fitz's head began its return, it froze. He turned his head again, this time extremely slowly, to stare after Willie. Then he began to run.

Fitz was a bulky man, with hefty thighs and large hands. He wasn't made for quick take-offs, but when he picked up speed he looked like a runaway tank.

He barrelled into Willie, knocking him clean off his feet. Willie's shopping bags went flying. Tins of pilchards clanked in the road and a bottle burst and glugged milk into the gutter.

The two men sprawled on the grass verge. Willie had no hope against the big Captain. He was whipped over onto his stomach and pulled upright by the scruff of his neck.

It was then that she realised what was different about Willie. He was normally bare-headed. Today he wore a cap over his mullet head. It was a Blue Bulls cap, remarkably like the one from Patrick's collection.

Willie was pushed unceremoniously into the back of the police van parked at the verge. Captain Fitz brushed off his knees and elbows. A big grin formed and, hard as it was for so large a man to swagger, she would have to say that he made a remarkable attempt. He thrust a big hand at her, clutching in his other the Blue Bulls cap.

'Shake on that, *Mejuffrow*. I've caught your burglar, just like I said I would.'

'But ... how can you possibly ...?'

'This is Cheetahs country, Odette. No one would be seen dead in a Blue Bulls cap. In fact, I don't think I'd be wrong to say that this here ... is the only Blue Bulls cap in town.'

# Chapter 14

'YOU COULD TRY THE patience of the Dalai Lama, really you could.' Heather re-crossed her ankles and continued staring at her. Odette sighed.

'Well, how do you think it makes me feel? Jeez, if ever there was an irritating, shrink-like question. I feel fury. I feel murderous rage. I could kill those bastards.'

'Because they're your neighbours?'

She wasn't stupid, Heather. Odette rose and poured herself another cup. Tea, I ask you. If she came here much longer, she would have to buy Heather a plunger.

'Yes, of course because they're my neighbours.'

Heather waited for her to set her cup down, shifting the tissues to make room. Come to think of it . . . Odette grabbed the box and dropped it decisively on the floor.

'Does that make you feel better?'

Odette had to laugh. 'Actually yes, it does. And I know, Stella is also a neighbour, but that's different.'

'Because . . .'

'Because she's a squatter with lots of children to feed. I was angry with her, but not as bloody angry . . . They were drunk, you know? That's why they did it.'

'It is okay to feel fury at them. There was a huge breach of trust. They offered to help you, to protect you even. And they misled you into believing it was Stella.'

'But I believed them, didn't I? I accepted their word.'

'We all carry assumptions.'

'Okay Heather. Thank you for pointing that out. I just don't like to think of myself carrying quite so many. And quite so . . . I don't like to think of myself that way. Leave it alone now, can't you? I don't want to talk about Stella any more.'

Heather nibbled the corner of her damp crunchie with sharp mouse bites. Odette watched, then shook her head in admiration.

'If you must know,' Heather said, trying not to laugh, 'I've been perfecting the dunk since birth.'

'Oh there you are then. Clearly I had a wasted childhood.'

'Tell me a bit about that wasted childhood.'

Oh Lord, only twenty minutes gone and they were rummaging about in her childhood. She shrugged. 'It was all perfectly ordinary, Heather. Nothing to write in Morning Journal about. I had my slight traumas, like a million others.'

'What kind of traumas?'

'I wasn't chosen as Mary, and all the angels were stupid-looking girls with blonde hair. Must you always be so overwhelmingly shrinky? You just can't bear it that I've come to terms with my stuff and got on with my life.'

Heather didn't say anything, but Odette could see it inscribed across her forehead: Yes, but what kind of life?

Through the open window came the ocean roar of the M1. 'Before you say it, there is absolutely nothing wrong with my life. I specifically chose it.'

'I didn't say anything, Odette. But since you raised it: are you sure you're not accepting less? The way you describe the town, you could be moving into the TV-sized world of your soap.'

Odette stared at the powder-blue walls and carefully matched prints, all with touches of the same blue. Oh for God's sake, she must've chosen the pictures to match the colour scheme.

'What are you saying? That I'm trying to move into some kind of *Truman Show*?'

'I'm just asking if you're realistically moving into a new phase of life. Or is this some mythical time out in which you don't have to examine your real self?'

'That's just rubbish, Heather. There's nothing mythical about starting a business.'

'And this new relationship...?'

'He's a friend, okay? Adriaan is a friend. Not some lesser replacement for Patrick. He's company, that's all.'

'That wasn't what I was going to ask you.'

'But I can see what you're thinking. That I'm choosing him because he can't disappoint me. It's a completely different situation though. Patrick...'

'...was your great love, yes I know. And he did disappoint you, although I'm still not sure exactly how. It wasn't he who chose to end it.'

'I told you. He would've left anyway.'

'So you say. Because you don't believe you deserve him. I wonder why that is, Odette.'

The M1 swelled again, filling the room with the dark sound of seabeds. She wasn't going to mention George when Heather was in this mood. She would just make it into a bad thing – another friend from a different world whom she wouldn't have to get close to.

'Don't you think it's healthier just to step over things? No, I suppose you don't, or you'd be out of a job.'

'Yet you keep coming.'

'Not for long at this rate. You were company after my friend left, that's all. Doesn't mean I need all the deep-shrinkage.'

Heather gave her small laugh. 'Perhaps you'd like to use one of my spurned tissues for your fingers?'

Heather must've seen the look on her face. It would be so delicious to sully the powder-blue perfection of that couch with a bit of soggy crunchie.

'Talking of leaving, is there anything you'd like to say about your empty nest?' Odette raised her eyes ceilingwards, and Heather smiled. 'Okay, okay. How's she getting on, though?'

'Great thanks. Mike's there. My ex. Oh, there're the standard teething problems, of course: new family, new culture, all the usual stuff.'

'Go on. What...?'

'No, nothing. That's all I was going to say. She's getting on really well and she's apparently very good with the kids. She's got a talent for that. Time's up, Heather, much as I'd love to stay and keep you company.'

'We still have three minutes by the clock.'

'It's slow. I checked my watch with the phone. I have to get way over the other side of town for my brainstorm and I can't be late.'

'Then we'll take up there next time, shall we?'

She was way too early, of course. Not even Margie was there. She asked for a cappuccino and stood at the counter to watch. The owner let it gush a bit fast – she considered telling him, but let it be.

He was excellent at leaf patterns, but you could taste the grind was off. Patrick would've... oh, never mind Patrick. At least he'd got her into coffee, so something good did come out of the relationship. He'd even encouraged her to do the barista course.

It would make such a difference to have a proper coffee shop in Nagelaten. And she was doing that. She was making that difference. Okay, it wasn't like curing cancer or eradicating poverty, but some people were only intended to make the small differences. Some people... Wasn't this shrink business supposed to make you feel better, not worse?

She ordered a haloumi salad and settled at one of the pavement tables to watch the world go by. Nagelaten didn't go in for pavement tables. Acknowledging the Zimbabwean woman who sold crocheted garments, she scratched around for change, but avoided asking how she was. The woman had lost most of her family in the last floods. What could you possibly say after that?

A toddler whizzed by on a plastic motorbike, followed by his mother, who stowed the bike, the toddler, a box from the fruit shop and paid the car guard without having to scrabble for coins or keys. Odette was impressed. Three schoolgirls in uniform sauntered by, comparing texts, each with a sprig of jasmine tucked behind an ear. Bringing their faces close – two dark and one fair – they paused while they brought hands to mouths and giggled. It still did her heart good to see.

It was a decent salad, she would grant him that, the creepy owner, and she was starving. Rocket and sprouts and good olives – it made a change from burgers and chips with barbecue sauce. If she and Trudie served salads, would the locals eat them? Perhaps they could acclimatise them by deep-frying the rocket.

To start with though, they wouldn't be doing any cooking. It would be coffee from the machine and eats from the home-industry. The most they might do is warm the odd muffin.

A man wandered by with wire sculptures. She shook her head, but he thrust a crocodile on to her table, where it bared its beaded teeth and regarded her with beady eyes. She stopped eating. It didn't feel right to be stuffing her face.

A woman followed, unfurling exquisitely embroidered bed-spreads. She put her fork down again. Yes, they were beautiful, but she didn't have the money right now.

'But it is a lot of work.'

'I know. I wasn't saying they're expensive. I just don't have that much right now.' She could see the woman didn't believe her, but she really did have to be careful until Lucky Bean became viable.

A dreadlocked pavement artist stopped and made a small display of multimedia street scenes against a pillar for her edification. She pushed her salad aside and agreed that they were beautiful. Yes, they really, really were. But . . .

'Maybe later, okay? Let me just see what I've got . . . no, you don't need to wait. No, I'll find you in your usual place. Yes, up the street. No. Not now okay?'

The rains hadn't come yet and it was so dry that her lips were chapped and her fingertips snagged on her top, yet a beading of moisture had formed on her upper lip. She had forgotten quite how tense you became when you had to refuse and refuse, and refuse again. She wished she had endless money. She wished she could just hand out to whoever asked. She wished she didn't have to say no all the fucking time.

It was when the broom-sellers arrived that she grabbed her salad and made for the door. 'I bought one last time, remember? From you.'

'Just another one. Please Mummy. I haven't sold anything for two days. I'm hungry Mummy.'

Handing her salad to the owner, she stepped back out to scrabble in her purse. 'I'll give you something, but I can't buy another one, really. How many brooms can a woman own?'

'Feather duster, then? I've got all colours – pink, green . . . a purple one then. How about red?'

She escaped into Venezia just in time to see the owner disappear into the kitchen with her salad. It hardly mattered. She had lost her appetite anyway.

There was a flurry and a commotion as everyone started arriving – Palesa wheeling her bike right in, since her lock had been tampered with. Chevonne was showing off a new hair colour; Palesa had gone three whole weeks without biting and would soon have to invest in a nail file; Margie was red-eyed over a cat that might have to be put down . . . And Odette's burglars had been caught.

'It was the white people that burgled you?' Trust Chevonne to hone right in on what everyone else delicately chose not to mention.

Palesa slapped her legal pad down and placed her hands on her hips. 'White people do commit crimes, you know Chevonne.'

'Yes but it is kind of funny, the whole thing, isn't it.'

'I'm delighted to have brought you so much amusement,' said Odette, caught between irritation and a grudging laugh.

'It's just that her kidneys are shot,' Margie murmured, untangling a balled-up tissue from her sleeve. Lex came in and began organising his pens, failing to notice Margie hiccupping gently alongside him.

'I just don't know if it's crueller to keep her alive,' Margie said, a little louder.

Having finally discovered a working pen, Lex looked up. 'So where the hell are the biscuits?'

Margie burst into tears. Lex looked completely bewildered. 'What? What did I say?'

Chevonne leapt up and offered her a tissue, carefully holding her nails clear. 'Her cat died, Lex,' Palesa said accusingly.

'Well fuck me. I mean, why didn't anyone tell me?'

'She's not dead,' Margie sobbed into her tissue. 'She's not dead yet.'

Odette chose the ensuing mêlée to slip off to the loo, passing behind Margie to give her shoulder a quick squeeze. It was easier than speaking – she generally said the wrong thing and made things worse.

Eventually everybody calmed down, Margie still sniffing and dabbing with her balled-up tissue. Lex had a few notes on Odette's storylines, mainly editing issues. Chevonne got the brunt of it. All her characters seemed bent on unmotivated acts, and no one (read: Lex) could understand what the hell her dramatic imperative was.

They decided that Reno would drive Rochelle to Jo'burg for the abortion. She would seem resolved, but a little too quiet. Then she would see something . . . a sign of some kind. Odette couldn't think what it should be. She couldn't bear Chevonne's idea of a weeping Jesus. It was so on-the-nose. Not to mention unlikely in the Marie Stopes.

Finally, they settled on a bird. It would come in through the window and batter itself against the walls. When it finally slid to the floor, nearly spent, Rochelle would raise it to the window...Anyway, that was the idea.

Palesa had the mayor's son (finally) coming out to his mother, and she taking him in her arms, saying he was her only son blah blah blah.

'I don't think he'd tell his mother like that.' Chevonne spoke decisively. 'He wouldn't suddenly say: "Hey Mom, I'm gay".'

Lex didn't say anything. Margie nudged him. 'Well, how the hell do these things usually happen? Palesa, how did you...?'

'I've got an idea.' Odette didn't, but it took the heat off Palesa. And then suddenly she did. Straight from the horse's mouth too, but no one would know that but her. That trade in intimacies might still come in handy after all.

'Well, I think he dates this guy, who gets in a knot about being kept a secret from the family, so he outs him at the dinner table.'

Without shifting her hand or looking at Palesa, she flipped her pen to the side and tapped Palesa's fingers. (It's okay, I won't let on.) Palesa nudged her with a knee. (I get it, thanks.)

'Totally humiliating for the boy. Shocking for the parents, of course, but you could also quite easily play it out in a comic way.'

'That outing thing...in this day and age?' asked Margie, sucking in small breaths between words. 'Does that still happen? Palesa?'

'Maybe in your culture,' said Chevonne. 'Maybe in the township. But I'm not sure...'

'Oh and your community is so much more enlightened?' Palesa didn't look up from her doodling.

'I didn't say that.'

'Last I heard, corrective rape wasn't entirely unknown in the coloured community.' Palesa was starting to sound a bit too upset for this to be entirely academic.

'Well, it's extremely likely someone would be outed like that in Nagelaten,' said Odette. 'Which means it's very likely in our Piss-willie-dorp too. I think we should settle on it.'

Palesa nudged her again. She gave a small nudge back. It felt quite good.

'So how will the old bitch react?' Lex ploughed ahead. 'She's hardly going to lovingly take the boy in her arms.'

'No,' said Odette. 'Naturally she'll drag him off to church.'

'Are you sure? Why church?'

'They'll pray over him, of course. They'll ask God to cure him.'

Everyone laughed at the absurdity, but they liked the idea.

If she had read it in a book, or watched it in *Trophies,* it would have strained her credibility. That was the thing about life. The sky was darkening to the east, but glowing to her rear, the stubbled fields golden. The air was dense with mousebirds, weaving across the fields, long tails rippling. They wheeled again and again in their involved rituals of coquetry and courtship.

It happened too fast for evasive action. There was nothing she could do but watch it happen. One of the birds miscalculated. She didn't think the car actually hit it – no ominous thud – but its force-field certainly did. She slammed on brakes and watched in her rear-view as it was thrown clear, tumbling through the air in a parody of earlier grace.

She slid to a halt on the gravel, heart pounding. She had to run quite some distance, but there it was, long tail draped over a clump of *rooigras*. One wing was slightly spread.

It seemed so frail and damaged that she reached out. It was warm. A bubble formed in her throat. She lifted and cradled it, trying to infuse it with a little of her own life. Suddenly she imagined ... no, she did. She could just feel the flutter of heartbeat.

She began to run, tucking the bird inside her shirt. She could still save it. She would drive like the wind ... then the futility struck. The Nagelaten vet would be closed; that's assuming the bird even lasted the journey.

In this soap opera, there was no high window to which she could hold that small beating heart. Curtains of dark fell either side of her, but she didn't move. She held the bird while its heart hovered between life and death. She held it while the small flutter of life faltered, and finally faded altogether.

# Chapter 15

THE KITCHEN WAS WARM with the steam and fragrance from her slow cooker. She opened and stirred. The beef was falling from the bone, infused with raisins and dried peaches, thickened by carrots and baby gems – all the vegetables she could find in the house last night.

She found a large ice-cream container, hesitated, then spooned just two scoops into a bowl. Her supper. The rest overflowed the plastic container and half-filled a second. She placed them in a packet with the rest of the dried peaches, some apples and a loaf of bread.

Catching a glimpse of Marlise through her open door, she averted her eyes. Tried to call the police, my arse. She turned the corner, passed the side of their house and stepped onto Stella's small stoep. All the windows had now been replaced by cardboard and plastic packets. She hammered at the corrugated iron that covered the door.

There was a scuffle of voices and movement. Someone screeched the metal across the concrete from the inside and three children appeared, dressed for school. Through the open back doorway, a tin bath stood next to a metal-legged chair in the backyard. Blankets hung to air over the fence between her yard and Odette's orchard. In the middle of the central shell of the house was a metal sheet upon which was laid the acrid remains of a fire.

'Is your *gogo* here?' The children goggled at her. 'Your *gogo?* Stella?' Stella appeared behind the children and Odette handed her the packet. She nodded.

'Stella? If you knew . . . I mean, if you saw those people burgling my house, why didn't you say something?'

She shrugged. The children clustered about her legs, clutching her skirt. She slapped a hand either side of her, as though swatting flies.

'Did you see them?'

She shrugged, then nodded. Odette waited, but she had no more to say. 'Okay then,' said Odette. 'I'll see you around.'

The tall grass catapulted dew as she pushed it aside, soaking her legs and shoes. The sun was coming over the rocky koppie to the east. From a cluster of bluegums, horses surged across the commonage, flanks shining, manes sweeping behind them.

They were from the stud at the end of town, but they appeared untamed, part of the wilderness. Veering towards the river, they startled a heron from a weeping willow, its long neck thrusting above the trees.

As she reached the corner she heard a bakkie idling. Mr Hassim, from Liebowitz Hardware. Leaving the engine running and the car door open, he manoeuvred his stomach from the driver's seat.

'No, no,' he said when she greeted him. 'Call me Mohamed.' He gave a small laugh, then added: 'It's not my real name, but everyone calls me that.'

'Well, wouldn't you rather . . .?'

'Hardly remember it myself, now my mother's passed on. Mohamed's fine.'

She gave a start. The strange man from the dark house was behind her, approaching so silently she hadn't noticed him. He was recognisable only by his lope, blackened head to foot by coal dust. Acknowledging neither of them, he approached the bakkie, heaved a load on either shoulder and set off down the road. Laden by sacks that wisped black dust with every step, he looked like a chimney sweep in a story.

'Coal deliveries,' said Mohamed. 'I give him odd jobs.'

'What's his background though? Do you know?'

He shrugged. 'I don't ask and he doesn't say.'

'I suppose he was here before you got here. When was that? 94?'

Mohamed opened the passenger door so he could place a foot on the frame and lean a beefy arm across the roof. 'Strange story actually. I was made a partner while old man Liebowitz was still here. Early 90s already. He helped me get special dispensation to live in the municipality.'

'So is he still a partner? Liebowitz?'

He smiled and shook his head. 'Followed the kids to America. I bought him out. Gave me my start though, before they even allowed us coolies to live in the Free State.'

They watched the strange man lope back. Tom the chimney sweep waiting to be freed by the water babies. 'What's his name?'

'His? Wolfie.' He gestured with his chin. 'That's why I try to help him, I suppose. He's pretty much an outcast. Also why I kept the name of the shop too. Because he was a good Jew.'

She could hear her cellphone ringing as she unlocked, but it had stopped by the time she reached it. Mike. She held it for a moment, then set it down. She would clean up the kitchen first, then settle down and listen to him properly. She needed time to catch her breath first.

She washed the dishes, then decided to dry them rather than stack them on the draining board. And since she'd dried them, she might as well put them away. She replaced the spices, and refilled an empty bottle before wiping all the counters.

She made herself a cup of coffee in the plunger, heated herself some milk on the stove, then opened the double doors and carried the phone out to the stoep. She dialled, fumbled the number, then dialled again more carefully. It went straight to voice-mail. She couldn't say she was sorry.

'Hi Mike, sorry I missed your call. I hope you were calling to say you'd mollified Mandy's family. I'm sure you did. You were always good at that, although where you got it from . . . not from your mother, that's for sure. But I mean that fondly, as you know.

'What a pity she didn't live to see Mandy being so independent, holding down a responsible job overseas. It's natural there should be hiccups, but we ought to be proud. She's really out there, Mike. Just like any normal kid taking her gap year . . .'

The message came to an end before she was able to say her goodbyes. As she disconnected, she remembered something and hesitated, then dialled again.

'Sorry, the message cut off. I hope you reminded them she did that au pairing course, and her CPR certificate too. She didn't do at all badly either. You must impress on them that she's more than qualified for the job.

'I know you're a worrier, Mike, but don't worry too much. What's the worst that can happen? If they really don't cope with her, the agency can always find her another family.

'Still hot as hell here. Waiting for rain, of course. I hope you're getting some decent . . .'

The message ran out again. This time she didn't call back. Opening her computer, she read her mails, feeling guilty as she did so. She hadn't yet replied to Melissa, and she wasn't precisely sure why.

Partly, of course, it was hard to sound chirpy after your best friend had fucked off to the other end of the world. And then there was her burglary. She didn't like to emphasise that – although it was hardly likely they would turn around and come back, now was it?

At least it was over now. She could finally put the burglary behind her and forget all about it. The big Captain had found her things, and there seemed to be no more bad news from London, so perhaps she could say that things were beginning to look up at last.

'Hey Liss,' she began, then paused. The trick was not to think too deeply or be stalled by the words that sprang unbidden to her fingers. They weren't rational. Melissa had a right to move wherever she pleased. As long as she was happy, a true friend ought to be pleased for her. Yes, the trick was just to keep it light for the moment. Just until she could control her fingers.

'My new shrink says it's psychologically unhealthy to be living in Australia. She says you must move back immediately, or suffer irreparable harm.

'I hope I haven't missed you already. I know you said something about cycling through Vietnam, but I'm not sure when. Or why, for that matter. You never even liked Asian food. Anyway, I hope I manage to catch you before you go.

'I'm feeling bad that I didn't get to answer this before and I know I haven't thanked you properly for your care package. Yes, I am still glad I made the move, you don't have to keep asking. But I promise I'll use your package and do the things we always loved.

'It is amazing that Mandy's actually out in the world. It's like a great weight has been lifted, but you're wrong about the other thing. I dumped the man. He went back to France. The fact that Mandy's left home doesn't change anything. He'll be taking arty pictures of some chic Parisienne by now, with no stretch marks and certainly no baggage. And I'm perfectly fine with that. I'm well and truly over him.

'Anyway Liss, I'll write more when you're back. I hate you as much as always.

Oxx (I'm going to stop ending like this now that I'm in cow country.)'

*Melissa and Gareth will be away till Oct15th while our transfer comes through. Please don't leave messages here. I will only check my mail sporadically, if at all. If there's anything urgent, please phone Damon. We'll be checking in with him regularly.*

It had been a weekend away, that was all. Nothing dramatic or cosmic. She and Patrick had walked among the rust-tinted rocks that sprouted from the grassland in fantastical forms, she spotting the dragons and dinosaurs and whales among them, Patrick photographing surfaces, shapes and wild flower clusters. And Odette.

She didn't look at them any more, but somewhere in her computer was a Patrick file, and within that, Magaliesberg: Odette climbing, Odette laughing, head thrown back. Odette leaping, resting in the shade of an acacia, fanning her face with the hat that Patrick had laughed at. ('You look like an Englishwoman on her Grand Tour.')

There were only one or two of Patrick, when she managed to wrest the camera from him, sheepish at finding himself on the other side of the lens. If she scrolled down, she would reach the second day, when they had climbed to a rock pool in the depths of a ravine. Dragonflies hovered over the water. Directly above, a Martial Eagle spanned their narrow cliff trajectory. A baboon barked.

Patrick had photographed the rock lichen and the designs formed by water flowing over rocks. And Odette. He took pictures as she skinny-dipped; the ripples caused by her sinking body and the spray when her head emerged, and he said she looked like a mermaid, or a seal.

And then there were no more pictures. They had dozed, curled on the same towel. She swam again then stretched her body, cool from the water, over his hot belly and clasped her arms around his back. He leant against a rock and entered her in the dappled light and she felt heavy with the weight of all that she felt.

When they finally scrambled out of the ravine, the sun was disappearing behind the hills and they realised they'd miscalculated. Landmarks had vanished in the dusk that rushed in on them. They could see no lights, except for the flicker of a farmhouse in a distant valley. A cold wind nipped at their shirts, and she began to shiver, chilled from her last swim.

Patrick found a wind-breaker in his camera bag and insisted she wear it. Holding her hand hard, he said they should discuss things, not panic. He asked what she thought they should do, and he listened. He didn't bully and he didn't blame. They agreed on a direction and stuck to it – climbing, so they would have some height to look out for lights.

That was all. It really was nothing dramatic. For a while they'd thought themselves lost. But then they found themselves, and became giddy and euphoric with the danger past. They giggled and kissed, and Patrick popped the cork of the Veuve she hadn't known he'd brought.

That wasn't quite the end of it. When he dropped her home, he came in for a while and she was relieved. She hadn't wanted it to end just like that. She was used to the way her life panned out from day to day, but after a weekend like that, depression could drop as suddenly as the dusk.

When Melissa brought Mandy home, Patrick made them omelettes, then handed each of them a package from the tiny shop beside the guesthouse reception. To Odette he gave a seal, small and sleek and sewn from sheepskin, with a card that said: 'To remember'.

To Mandy he gave a rhino. Trained to observe, he had noticed her fluffy collection, and also that a rhino was the one animal she didn't yet have. Odette still kept her seal among her underwear. That was the way it went. Some memories were good to keep, as long as you didn't expect them to last.

# Chapter 16

*I'm not supposed to lift my pen but if I glance towards the commonage I can see wheeling clouds of what I think are Amur Falcons. That's what the bird book told me, named after a river in Siberia. I might be wrong of course. It's early for them ... I'd prefer not to find out for sure though. It sounds so romantic, and if they turn out to be some lesser more prosaic bird it will only disappoint me.*

*How did that happen? I was once the eternal optimist – the girl who expected only good outcomes. I inherited that from my oupa. Now things begin hopefully enough, but then I envisage a bad ending. I can't help it. I picture myself walking down stairs and falling, cracking my head open. I walk past thorns, and imagine them piercing an eyeball.*

*At least I dealt with my shit, though. I played every hand I was dealt and I've moved on. That's something to be grateful for, although I do wonder how I managed to lose Oupa so completely along the way. I didn't become my mother though. At least I never did that.*

*Another day and I still haven't heard from Mike. It can only be a good sign, surely. I'm relieved he's back and forth this year. He has that skill for smoothing things over. Much better than I would be.*

*I really quite enjoy this ritual, now I've got used to it. Not that I do it every day, but it helps me sort things out in my head. All those priorities and stray thoughts that buzz around aimlessly.*

*Just a quick glance at the clock. (I have to, Heather, even you wouldn't want Captain Fitz finding me here in my pyjamas.) Perfect. Just enough time to slip to the café for milk before the big Captain arrives.*

*I haven't asked which of my things he's managed to retrieve. Now that it's certain, I don't want to speculate. I want to be happy, whatever he brings. I'm determined not to be disappointed.*

'You feel sorry for my burglars? Don't tell me that.'

George had seen her turning into De Wet with her milk and biscuits. He came across when she drew level with his house, brushing off his enormous hands. To his credit, he didn't say 'I told you so'. Too busy shaking with laughter.

He laughed until droplets formed at the outer edge of his eyes, and slowly trickled across his temples. Odette waited for him to scrabble for a hankie and wipe his face.

'What's to be sorry for? It's the lowest of the low to burgle your neighbours.'

'I see it like this. Before, there was always place for people like them. They could work for the railways at least. Now they have nothing. No place and no people.'

'They do have people. They have a church.'

George sucked a click off his teeth. 'Ai, they're just charity cases. That church gives them second-hand clothes, but last I heard, they went and sold them in the location.'

His body shuddered like a jelly. 'They drink in the tavern down by the location side too. It's cheaper. And the whites won't have them.'

'The one where there was a stabbing?'

'Eish, Saturday night stabbing. Nothing serious. The old *madala* and his boy come there to drink most days. Maybe they needed the cash – the tavern only serves if you've got money in the hand.'

There was a flurry of dust as Penis Dog and his gang raced at George's terrier twins, who were sniffing a polystyrene take-away container beside the watercourse. A brief scrap followed before the terriers tore free with a chorus of yelps, making a break for their bakkie. George seemed unperturbed.

'Sometimes I give them a few coins when they've got nothing.' He shrugged and looked back at his yard. 'I can spare it.'

Penis Dog's gang sauntered off to torment old Boer. He flung himself against the gate, which creaked and shuddered beneath his rage.

'Not very streetwise, your two.' She gestured at two just visible noses, one dripping little spatters of blood.

George shrugged. 'They must learn to fight or run away quicker.'

'Poor mites. Or join them, I suppose. But there'll be big trouble if that old Boerboel ever gets out.'

'He's strong, that one. But the others are many, so you never know.'

It was hazy with red dust and dried grass fragments. They were leaning on her gate again, scene of the Captain's greatest triumph (in her eyes, if not in his.) Another police van had just jolted over the potholes, carting the old man off to join Willie in jail. Captain Fitz had come from Ou Stella.

'She's not exactly a friend of the police, so she kept quiet at first. But when I told her we already know, she started to talk. My tip-off fee doesn't harm either. She's done quite well out of this in the end.'

'She did see them though?'

'She saw them all right. That boy leads the old man by the nose. She saw them wheeling your fridge away in a wheelbarrow. Waste of a white skin, if you ask me.'

Odette avoided his eye, but didn't respond. It always went like that. Someone jumped the post office queue and, sure as hell, you'd draw allies on prejudice rather than principle.

'The good thing is, now we have a witness. Which means we can push them to plead guilty so you probably won't have to give evidence.'

He opened the cornucopia of his van and...out came her chair. Her pots and pans and plates; her kettle and small coffee machine. Even her egg timer. And those bloody caps, of course, which would be packed off to Patrick forthwith.

The only things he hadn't found were her good pair of speakers and her TV. 'Straight to KZN on a taxi, I should think. Anyway, now at least you can feel safe again in our town.'

'Thank you Captain. No more strange neighbours.'

'Yes, I don't think they'll trouble you again. This'll teach them a lesson they won't forget in a hurry.'

'Talking of strange neighbours, I've been meaning to ask. There's this weird guy I've seen. Does odd jobs for Mohamed...'

'Wolfie, you mean? No, don't worry about him, he won't hurt you.'

'I'm not worried. I just wondered about him, that's all.'

'If he bothers you, I'll have a word in his ear so fast...'

A car rutted over the potholes behind them. Fitz waited till it had passed and the dust settled about them. 'You shouldn't bother with people like that. I feel sorry for him, but what can you do?'

'Why, what did he do?'

'Not so much him. The whole family's no good. Ag no, it's not a nice story. He's the son of his own great-grandfather.'

'Oh my God. He's the child of incest?'

'I told you it wasn't nice. She was always a bit forward for her own good, that one. Everyone knew she'd get into trouble. Only twelve when she had her first.'

146

'From her grandfather? What about the parents?'

'Dead by then. Didn't stop there either. Wolfie's her second.'

'Why didn't anyone help her? It wasn't her fault. She was only . . .'

'Who, his mother? No, I don't know. People didn't think like that then. Dead now, anyway.'

A stray cow found its path blocked by the police van. Crossing the road, it busied itself with a daisy bush. Penis Dog and his mates approached warily, but decided it was too large to take on.

'What happened to the older child?'

'Set off one day and didn't come back. Went off with a truck driver. No better than she should be either. I hear she's a prostitute down Durban way.'

'But, even if no one helped her then, it's not Wolfie's fault whose child he is.'

'Now don't you go feeling sorry for everyone. That'll just get you into trouble in a place like this. Adriaan did – or rather his missus, and look where that got them.'

'What do you mean?'

'They gave him a job on the farm and he stole the missus's pretty bits and pieces. You can't trust people like that, it's just the way they're made.'

The heat was like a great weight across her body. She felt as though she were being ironed. A chained dog howled its despair into the night. She would never sleep.

And yet she must have dozed, because suddenly she was awake again. It was pitch-dark and there was a great roaring noise. It was raining.

Thunder tumbled from the sky and exploded over their puny houses. The rain was like sheet metal. It was a weapon, a battering ram, set on crushing them back into the earth, where they had come from.

She rose and gazed from the window. Lightning jagged across the sky. Red dust turned to mud. The smell of it rose musty, like roots uncovered, like a living thing that had crawled from the earth.

And then it was gone. Turned off, leaving her garden under-water, leaves and small branches afloat over her new vegetable patch. She put a hand out of the window. Not a drop fell. Yet strangely, she could still hear water – drenching, pouring water – and it sounded as though it were in her house.

Stumbling through the lounge, she found her kitchen as far underwater as her vegetable patch. The rain had stopped, yet water was soaking through the collapsing ceiling. The geyser had burst.

She hadn't heard it because of the rain. Or maybe she had, but hadn't placed it. Perhaps that had been the source of her anxiety as the rain hammered on her corrugated iron roof. She had suppressed it (it was only rain, for goodness sake). Yet it had felt as though her house, and she within it, might disappear beneath such a deluge.

Without thinking, or considering consequences, she phoned Adriaan. She knew he would help, that was all. He arrived within twenty minutes and set them both to work. She switched off the electricity while he turned the water off at the mains.

He looked scruffier than usual. His hair was rumpled and his shirt hung from his shorts, misbuttoned and loose enough to show a patch of dark hair, silvered by threads of grey. Asking for her ladder, he disappeared through the manhole into the roof while she gazed anxiously upward.

'All done,' he said when he reappeared. Oddly, he seemed different, more light-hearted, than she'd ever seen him anyway. 'As much as we can do tonight anyway. You can call the plumber in the morning.'

Entirely without thinking, she stepped forward and tip-toed to kiss him. A thank-you kiss. But suddenly his unshaven cheek was scouring her face. His hand was under her tracksuit top and the icy edge of the sink was pressing into the small of her back.

Within her belly, she felt a chafe, like salt and sunburn on holiday skin. After Patrick, she had cut off all feeling. She had forgotten. But now it was all she could feel. It was all she was aware of, all she could focus on, while water sloshed about their feet and his tongue was hot and heavy on hers.

She took him to her bed. They waded through the kitchen and up the step to her lounge where they sloshed red polish and water onto her new carpet and she didn't care.

When they reached the bedroom, they could scarcely rip the clothes from their bodies. Both their hands shook. He placed large hands around her ribs, just below her breasts and crushed her to the soft hairs of his chest.

His belly slid on hers, slipping in their sweat. It felt, just then, as though he might be able to fill the great hollow within her.

He wasn't gentle and she wanted it like that. He took her without apology and without the courtesies of modern sex between almost strangers. He didn't ask if she'd come. She hadn't, but she felt satisfied in a different way. And besides, they could do it again. Or not, as the case may be.

She had no idea what would happen after and she didn't care. It wasn't love. She knew it was need, both his and hers. But who the hell could quarrel with that?

They must have slept, restless with sheets and duvet. They twisted in the sweat of each other's arms, murmuring and half-waking to caress or bite. Odette woke to find him entering her again, pressing her legs apart with his knee. She only half heard the telephone. His tongue smoothed her eyes closed, reached into her ear.

'Answer it,' he said, his breath cold on its wet surface. She shook her head, but he insisted. 'Answer it. I want you to.'

She half-rolled to reach the receiver and he thrust deeper, his tongue in her other ear. 'Hello.' She cleared her throat and tried again.

'It's Mike.'

'Mike? What the hell...?'

'Sorry to wake you.' He was breathing hard. His voice shook. 'Oh God, Odette. What the fuck have we done?'

Adriaan's cock thrust up and through her. She wanted it out of her. It made her feel ill. She pushed at him, and at first he resisted. She shoved his throat with both hands and he withdrew, rolled off her and stumbled to the bathroom.

'What are you talking... What's happened?'

'The baby's dead. Mandy was baby-sitting, Odette. The baby's fucking dead. Just like...' He didn't finish. But she did, in her head. Just like her brother. And, as only she knew, just like Mandy could so easily have been.

# Chapter 17

MANDY POINTED AND GRUNTED before she learned to speak. Mike made jokes about the child who didn't speak for twelve years (because she didn't have anything to complain about before – ha ha).

It infuriated Odette because she was terrified that Mandy didn't speak. Sylvia said that Odette didn't talk to her enough.

'When did you begin speaking, Odette? Michael was putting two words together by a year. But then I suppose your mother didn't read to you.'

Funny that. Mike didn't turn out the most verbal man in the world. Odette wasn't sure when she had learned to speak. By the time she was old enough to ask, her mother was in no state to tell her.

Sylvia was partially right. It's hard to speak to a dervish. As soon as she could balance on her two pins, Mandy spun or ran in tightening circles until Odette grabbed her and pinioned her arms.

Mandy still couldn't stand to be touched. Her skin crawled if you brushed a hand over her shoulders or head. It drove her into a shrieking ball, mouth flecked with foam. Odette must have discovered this through pure desperation: if you held her firmly, preferably with her arms pinioned, she quietened and, often as not, fell asleep.

Odette joined a mother's group, but they said Mandy was disruptive. She took Mandy to the local library, but they were asked to leave. She did plan to read to her, but once she held her sufficiently pinioned, Mandy passed out and Odette ended up reading to herself, hoping some subliminal language skill would filter through while she slept.

The house felt so silent that Odette chatted away to herself, while Mandy spun or slept. Sometimes she promised herself she wouldn't look at a watch until at least an hour had passed. Then she would and it was ten minutes since her last glance.

One silver lining: Mandy's toddler years taught Odette everything she needed for her present career. She really absorbed those afternoon soaps. They were her only real company.

Sylvia did approve of her decision not to go back into PR. Odette didn't tell her it was less of a decision than the realisation that she couldn't leave Mandy with anyone. They would phone within fifteen minutes to say she was sitting quite calmly, bashing her head against the floor. Odette got used to it, if one ever does truly grow used to self-harm.

At first it had horrified her and certainly it horrified her rare guests. Most of them stopped coming after a time. Except for Melissa, bless her.

Okay, there were moments she cherished. Her favourite photo was one of Mandy as a toddler, standing over the baby of one of Mike's friends. Her two hands were on its head and she was stroking.

As other perfect children were being told: 'No Justin, you're hurting the bunny', her imperfect Mandy stroked with a gentle palm and crooned. She stepped over the ants on their front stoep. She found a nest of rat babies after Mike had put down poison. She fed them with her dolls' bottle and whispered to them.

When they died, one pink, wriggling death after another, she bashed her head against the floor for an afternoon without ceasing. When she thought about it, the only person Odette ever saw Mandy hurt was herself.

The call went straight through to voice-mail, but she disconnected, feeling unprepared for what she wanted to say. She waited a second, then rang again.

'Mike, I'm sorry not to get you . . . Look, I'm really sorry to hear about the baby. Really I am. Cot deaths are tragic, but they're nobody's fault. They shouldn't make her feel responsible. You must make very sure of that. It shouldn't affect her confidence.

'And another thing: I don't see why she should have to leave. The other child knows and loves her already – surely they'll need her more than ever. Obviously they're in shock now, but in time . . . you can raise it when the time's right. Anyway, let me know how it's going.'

She disconnected and her phone rang again immediately, making her jump.

'Odette? Can you hear me? It's Adriaan. Are you okay?'

'Oh, it's you . . . Yes, of course. You?'

'No, I just wondered . . . the phonecall. Was everything all right? You wanted me to leave in such . . .'

'Oh, that. Ag no, sorry. False alarm.'

'I was just a bit worried, that's all. Daughter okay?'

'Oh fine. As always.' She forced a little laugh. 'Always fine.'

'Are you sure you're okay? You sound . . . a bit odd.'

'Why wouldn't I be? I didn't get a chance to thank you, by the way. For the geyser, I mean.'

'No man, it's nothing. All sorted now? I phoned Danie this morning . . .'

'The plumber? Yes, thanks for that. He turned up without my even having to phone.'

'Okay then. Can I entice you to dinner? Any night. You choose. I'll cook if you like?'

Did she want to go? She didn't much feel like conversation. But then, did she really feel like being alone?

'This is Mandy Evans. Leave a message.'

'Mandy, give me a ring when you get this please? I just want to see how you're doing. I don't want you to worry too much. Just remember, it's not your fault.'

She dialled Mike, but the phone just rang. Oh for heaven's sake. Pick up, Mike. Pick up. She sent him a text instead. She knew him. He often found it easier to tap out a message – even something quite detailed – than to verbalise.

*No news? I left you a voice-mail. How r they all bearing up? M coping ok?*

A couple of seconds later, her phone tolled: *Will let u know. Can't talk now. Everyone being questioned.*

It was starting to look like spring. The commonage had turned miraculously green. Pavements lush with grass seeds leapt with hoppers. She wooed a sheep grazing on the wide pavement, but it trotted out of reach, nimble for so ungainly a creature.

Sunlight struck glancing blows against the church. Clouds massed, submerging the street in a greenish unreality, as though the entire town had sunk below the ocean. She thought she caught a glimpse of the strange man – Wolfie – straggles of hair bouncing about his long face. Before she could be sure, the figure disappeared into the shadows on the verge of town.

'You're early.' Adriaan had a dish-towel over his shoulder. He was smiling, and she was pleased she'd come. A friendly face, dinner cooked, a DVD to watch: that's all she wanted right now. And things went well – before dinner anyway. He was making cottage pie. Not her favourite, but she was hungrier than she'd realised. She couldn't remember when she'd last had a meal. She had foraged in the fridge, but not what you'd call eaten.

The furniture was modern, almost utilitarian. He must have

left the farmhouse intact when he came here. New start, clean lines, she supposed. It stormed while she was making the salad, and they couldn't hear themselves speak. The lightning was near, and ominous. They laughed at their brief show of lip-reading and then fell silent, waiting for it to pass.

He opened a Chardonnay, but she said she'd save hers for the meal. He didn't have any sparkling water so she drank tap. It was one of those days when it tasted slightly mouldy.

'Have you been okay?' He gave a laugh. 'It's . . . you seemed not quite yourself.'

'No I'm fine. Just stuff, you know: deadlines, expectations . . . You must be relieved about the rain.'

'Of course. We want to be planting by mid-month. It's just . . . I hope the forecasts aren't too accurate.'

'Mealies?'

'They say we're in for a helluva lot of rain . . . Ja, mealies . . . Just so long as we can get the tractors into the fields. Anyway, you're not interested in this, and I, for one, would prefer not to spend another evening worrying about the maize planting.'

They chatted about whether they'd be ready for the World Cup. Not that it meant much for Nagelaten, but she told him about the construction work in Jo'burg. Hardly a highway or main thoroughfare where traffic wasn't detoured or delayed in some way.

'Hard to believe it'll all be finished by next year. But who knows. Maybe we can pull finger when we have to.'

'Will your daughter be back?'

'Mandy? We don't know yet. She may just stay on for another year.'

'But surely she's keen to come back for it?'

'She's not that crazy about football.'

'No, but still. That's not really the point, is it?'

She grabbed a fistful of cutlery from the drying rack and began setting the small table in the kitchen, but he shook his head and pointed to the door. He'd already laid the dining table. And there were candles. A tremor passed briefly across her shoulders. More expectations.

'Why did she decide to go all that way? She's still so young. Do you have family there?'

'No, why? And I certainly didn't push her, if that's what you think. She wanted to go and she's more than capable. She even did an au pairing course. Did really well in it too.'

'Not at all. I just . . .'

'I saw no reason to hold her back. All the kids were taking gap years. She wanted to show . . .'

'No, no, Odette.' He laid both hands on her shoulders and brought his nose briefly to touch hers. 'I was implying nothing of the sort. I just wondered why she chose London, that's all. Come, supper's ready. Let's go through.'

The lounge was spartan. Couch, chair, worn leather pouffe with a *Farmer's Weekly* folded open on it. She supposed he hadn't lived here long enough to develop clutter.

'Any case, Mike's got some deal in London. He's back and forth just about every month. It's not like she can't come back if she wants. No one's forcing her.'

'That much okay for you? And help yourself to salad. I outsourced that to a truly expert salad maker.'

He poured her a glass of Chardonnay and she took a larger gulp than she'd intended. She should leave it now or it wouldn't last the meal.

Adriaan had bought a painting. A local artist; someone she hadn't heard of. 'But look how well he caught the Bonsmara in the sunlight.' Few people would be drawn to buy a painting because he did cattle well. She thought it endearing. Her oupa would have approved.

They watched one of that class of movie where the taciturn man wanders off into the desert (metaphoric or otherwise), disillusioned by life and love. She could have done without it. She didn't like to think that's what they always did, one way or another.

She wasn't sure how the argument started. Or why she got so upset. Perhaps it was when she mentioned seeing Wolfie. Yes that was it. She said she felt sorry for the guy and Adriaan made a guttural sound and clattered the plates he was clearing.

She felt a rush of fury. More than that. A rush of cold through the veins, as though she'd mainlined it. It was followed by a tingling light-headedness.

'Where do you get off, you fucking Nagelatens. How dare you!'

'Hey, come on now. No call for ... Look, I just think you shouldn't get too ...'

'No, you listen. You're the people who stood by and watched while his mother was abused. She was just a child. Just a bloody child.'

'I know that, Odette. I wasn't here then.'

'Why wasn't she protected? Why didn't anyone watch over her, take her side? What must she have felt like, abused and then still accused by the community?'

She gathered up wine glasses and moved to the sink. She felt a roaring in her ears. It was as though reality had receded and she was whirling, all alone, within her rage.

She slammed the glasses into the sink and they shattered, both of them. The whirling stopped. She watched the blood gather and pool in the sink and felt the room return. Muscles tightened around the tumour of unvoiced sobs that hardened in her throat.

The life he'd been given. The lonely life that his mother had handed him like a gift. A rotten gift full of misery. How must that have made her feel. She'd been able to do nothing to make it easier, not one thing to lighten his load.

And then Adriaan, sweet man that he was, put his arms around her from behind. He didn't ask what the hell had come over her. She would have. Tutting over her hand, he found a first aid kit, led her to a chair, cleaned and plastered it.

'I wasn't here when all that was happening,' he said, glancing up from plastering.

'I know, I'm sorry. I don't know what ...'

157

'Leave it, it doesn't matter. But just so you know, my antipathy isn't a result of his birth. I'm not a Neanderthal, even though I am a...' He glanced into her eyes and smiled, '...a fucking Nagelaten.'

She winced and opened her mouth to apologise again, but he spoke before she could. 'I did give him a chance, you know. But he got a thing about my wife. Followed her everywhere. At first it was sweet, but then... not so sweet. Especially considering what happened.'

'But he surely...'

'No, I didn't then and I don't now. I told Fitz at the time, I don't think he's capable of real violence. Still don't. No, I still think it was a common or garden farm murder.'

'Farmers are easy game, I suppose. Always guns and cash.'

'Wolfie started by just following, watching. Then he started taking little keepsakes. A scarf once, then bits of jewellery, when he was painting the house.'

He was silent. She didn't know what to say. He finished with her hand and turned to repack the first aid box.

'Anyway, what does it matter now? All her jewellery was taken by the robbers in the end. Makes you think about what's important, doesn't it?'

You know, this might not be love, but it could be enough for her. She wouldn't ask for more. Nothing big or glamorous. No great loves. Just this.

# Chapter 18

WHAT WOULD RENO AND Rochelle do? What should they do for the best? It was always so hard. No one understood how hard it was to make the right choices.

When the phone rang, she was confused, as though Mandy, far away in England, was the fiction, rather than the other way around.

'Do you understand what I said?' It was Mike. 'The police were here, Odette. They took her laptop and her Ritalin. Of course, I got straight on the phone...'

'It's just ridiculous, all this. What's the matter with them? It was a cot death.'

'Luckily I found a solicitor pretty smartly. Mate of Grant's, my auditor friend. He asked if they were going to arrest her and they said we could bring her in voluntarily.'

'Oh but...I mean, surely they just want to ask her what happened? Aren't you being a bit dramatic? They have to ask, even if it is just a cot death.'

'For God's sake, Odette. Get real. They suspect that it wasn't.'

'Oh they always make out like they suspect. Even my mother. They have to, just to show they're investigating.'

'The detective asked me what the Ritalin was for. He made lots of notes, like Attention Deficit was hugely significant. He acted like it was a dangerous narcotic.'

'Well, she was medicated so strictly speaking, she didn't have attention problems. She functioned completely normally. And hell, half the world's on Ritalin.'

'I'm just telling you what they said.'

'If everyone who struggled to concentrate at school was stopped from teaching or ... or from having kids, just about the whole world would be barred ...'

'The solicitor told me not to say any more, so I didn't. Amelia's beside herself, naturally. She's turned on me, which is a pity.'

'Some of the most capable people in the world had trouble at school. Even Bill Gates struggles with social cues. It doesn't mean you can't be brilliant at what you're good at.'

Odette's coffee had turned cold. She fiddled with her teaspoon, slopping it over the rusk in her saucer. It disintegrated, crumbs clinging to each other like pale, desperate ants.

'I have to just say, Odette, I told you at the time she wasn't ready.' His breathing laboured, drowning the London street noises beyond him.

'Oh that's just ... Even Mrs Brink said she could do anything she set her mind to. She needed to be given the chance. We couldn't mollycoddle her forever.'

'Anyway, this is no time for recriminations. Amelia's telling them all sorts of things and they're lapping it up. She didn't wash her hair, she froze when they shouted ...'

'None of that affects her childcare.'

'Amelia yelled at me. Screamed. Said she should have seen there was something wrong because her beady little eyes never met theirs.'

'She can't help her fucking eyes.'

Mike breathed. She couldn't listen. The sound hurt her ears. She couldn't look at her rusk. It made her want to vomit. She gazed out of the window. Her refuge, her new home. Cows grazed as though nothing had changed. As though Rochelle wasn't having second thoughts about keeping the baby. As though Reno wasn't

160

full of blame, as though it weren't all Rochelle's fault, as though she hadn't caused all this harm to those she loved most . . .

It made her feel a little insane. It was the only thing she could focus on: Reno and bloody Rochelle. She couldn't seem to think squarely about Mandy. She could only allow Mandy to nibble at the peripheries.

'Do you want me to come?'

It was clouding over, though it wasn't yet noon. The heat was oppressive, weighing her down. If it stormed, perhaps there'd be relief. Storms were supposed to do that.

'Let me find out what's going to happen here. By the time you get here, it may all be over. Let's just see when we take her down to the station, okay? I'll let you know.'

She felt a flash of relief. Mike was the one to deal with this. He would sort it all out. People from his kind of family could do that. They could talk to each other, make things go away.

But if they kept her there . . . the thought flashed quick as a minnow, before she could bash it to death. An unforgivable thought, one that she could never justify, even to herself. If they did – just if – then it wouldn't be her fault. Mandy would stay there and it would all be beyond her control.

'Is she all right, Mike? She must be frightened.'

'It's inexplicable. Something I've never understood. I found her quite calm. She asked if she'd done the right thing, calling the ambulance when she did. I told her she did.'

'Does she understand?'

'On a rational level, of course. She's not completely stupid, Odette. But she's blank. I heard the police commenting on her lack of emotion. Oh Jesus.' She could hear him breathing.

'It doesn't mean she doesn't feel it. Did you explain that to them?'

'They weren't talking to me. They didn't see me there.'

'Did she say anything to them?'

'The solicitor told us she shouldn't say anything. But even before that . . . I don't know. She just closed down. Wouldn't say a word.'

'Perhaps that's for the best.'
'Perhaps it is.'

*[Scene details]*
*Rochelle has woken in the night. She wanders into the kitchen to make a cup of milk and honey. She is clearly distressed. Alerted by her activity, Lettie comes through, begs her to say what she's feeling. Rochelle finally bursts out: She's not sure she did the right thing, cancelling the abortion. For Lettie things are clear. No sister of hers should kill God's creature. Things aren't so clear for Rochelle. She fears she won't be up to the task. All she can offer this child is a difficult life, full of hardship. She fears she won't be able to give it any happiness. And when it matters, when life gets hard, she fears her own powerlessness to help at all.*

She got up to make a second coffee. Then she would just send the thing. She couldn't bear to look at it one more time.

'Hello? Mandy? Mandy, are you there? I'm glad you switched your phone back on. I've been trying to reach you. Are you okay?'
'I'm fine.'
'How...? I'm thinking of you, Sweetpea. How're you coping?'
'Okay.'
'Look, I know this is hard, but luckily your dad's there. He'll sort everything out.'
'I know.'
There was silence. She could hear Mandy breathing, like her father, but faster, lighter. Something kept niggling at her. She couldn't get a grip on the thought, but couldn't rid herself of the feeling either.
'Have you met the lawyer yet? Is he nice to you?'

'It's fine. He's fine.'

Then it reached out and grabbed her. Had she known? That's what had been niggling at her. Had she? When she blithely sent Mandy off overseas, had she any inkling that it might all be too much for her? Or that, in the middle of the night, if the baby cried too much, there might be two of her? Two forces that warred with each other?

'Well don't let it get to you. Just remember, you didn't do anything wrong.'

Had she prepared Mandy for that? For the feelings that come in the night?

'Mandy, you didn't... There isn't anything you'd like to tell me, is there?'

'About what?'

'No, don't worry. It doesn't matter.'

They knew something wasn't quite right. Or rather she knew, and Sylvia told her not to wish things on her child. Mandy's differences were just so subtle that everything could be explained.

'My dear, all babies scream. And not all babies speak at the same time. Life would be very dreary, wouldn't it, if we were all... although on our side, I must say, we tended to be early.'

The bottom line was that Mandy would catch up. There was nothing abnormal about her. Nothing at all. You took what you got with babies. She was a bad mother even to suspect there might be more to it.

Mandy struggled with toilet training. It wasn't that Mandy didn't know what to do if Odette sat her on the loo. She just didn't seem to notice when she needed to go. Sylvia was reassuring. Although Michael had been early, she did know a cousin who had still been in nappies at nursery school.

Eventually, she just feared and wished in silence. The year before diagnosis, Mandy went for all the tests: IQ, psych, performance

... You name it, she had it. They scanned her brain and tested her blood. Dr Prescott took his time. Didn't want to make a diagnosis lightly, he said later. He interviewed Odette several times, asking the same questions over and over.

'Tell me about this head-banging business. And why do you say she lacks restraint? More than other toddlers? Why didn't you seek advice on that?'

She told him again. And then again. She shook her head, ashamed.

'You reported that Mandy has to be told things six times. Is this an exaggeration? Do you find that Mandy learns from her mistakes? And did it still not occur to you to seek...?'

She shook her head. Of course not. Why should it? She'd never had a baby before.

'You say she masturbates? As comfort behaviour? Would you regard it as excessive? And this didn't lead you to...?'

No. For fuck's sake, no. Lots of toddlers masturbated. She didn't want to see it. She didn't want to believe there was anything wrong. He tilted his head at her quizzically, eyes a watery blue over his reading glasses. She detested his thin smile. Did he really think it dispassionate?

How did Mandy behave? How did she learn? He asked about uncles, aunts and cousins; their great-grandparents, themselves and their life together. He asked Mandy questions, then he asked them again. He got her to draw pictures, made her do puzzles. He shuffled through psychological evaluations, reports on co-ordination.

He harped on about their flaws and family traits, clearly enjoying himself. She and Mandy shape-shifted from human beings to subjects for research; fields of study. He despised them – wasn't it obvious? He felt superior, behind his desk blotter and his Mont Blanc pen.

Odette got a call quite late. It was a Monday. She remembered because Mike phoned his mother. Or rather, he was impatient when the call came through because Sylvia would be waiting.

'Odette? Dr Prescott.' Funny how they did that, doctors. They called you by your first name, but denied you the intimacy of their own.

'Can you pop in tomorrow? Around two? There's something I'd like to ... urm ...'

In that moment, Odette realised that she had always known. She knew people said that in hindsight and it sounded all new-agey and mystical. But she wasn't like that. She didn't believe mothers sensed things. Yet, despite not wanting to, she had known.

Mike slept fine. No, that was unfair. She didn't know that he slept fine. Maybe he just lay still and didn't feel like speaking. The morning was interminable. Mike was at the office, but popped back punctually at one and they dropped Mandy with his mom.

He kept them waiting, the bastard. He told them two, but made them hold out, in a waiting room stuffy with temperatures and snotty noses, till twenty past.

He remained safely behind the desk portrait of his blonde wife and two perfect daughters, his eyes fixed on a journal article, but when they sat, he looked up, all business.

Uh-hrum. What they had here was a genetic condition. It was an unfortunate twist of fate, in his opinion, and that was the way they should look at it.

'There's no purpose served by hashing and rehashing origins with conditions like this.' He glanced between them. 'Or trying to apportion blame. Deal with the present, that's my advice.'

He showed them a grainy picture to the side of the journal article. It was a grotesque picture, nothing like Mandy. Nothing at all. The picture was bad, but it was the sound it made when named, when spoken aloud. It had a shape. It formed a bubble, which grew and grew until it filled all the space in your brain.

He couldn't tell them clearly what it would mean. It was impossible to say which features she might have, and to what degree she'd be affected. They would discover that for themselves, 'rather like a voyage of discovery'. He gave an uncomfortable bark of laughter.

She would more than likely improve as she gained in maturity. Some behaviours, like head-banging for example, would subside. And she should progress well with the right remediation.

You could teach people to be less impulsive, apparently. You could impress upon them appropriate sexual behaviour. Social skills could be coached: 'Look at me. My wife says I had none when she met me, but she's coached me well enough.'

When it struck him that no one was about to join in, his laugh collapsed into a small uh-hrum. (Perhaps a little more work required, Mrs Prescott.)

'You're lucky. Her IQ is well within the normal range. Look, she may not . . . perhaps you shouldn't expect her to get her PhD, but then many people live happy, useful lives . . .'

Odette stopped listening. There was a buzzing in her head. She caught snippets: 'No reason, with good remedial input, that she shouldn't be absolutely average.'

Average. What parent hopes for their child to be average. Why did he think that would make them feel better? Fuck him. Mandy would bloody well be more than average. Odette would drill her. Bully her. Fight her. Fight the school system, fight anyone who got in her way.

'. . . very manageable. Yes, an extremely manageable condition. If you put in the effort, she could very well end up living a completely normal life. See for yourselves. You can hardly tell.'

If you didn't know, yes. If you didn't know. But now they did, and they could never not know again. She thought of her child, of the button eyes that she'd thought were a legacy of a great-aunt, barely remembered. Never again could her features be the eccentricities of two families bonded, two dynasties moulded into one individual. They were dysmorphic. They were nothing but symptoms.

Odette changed paeds after that day. She couldn't bear to look at Dr Prescott ever again. Didn't want to meet his eyes, as long as she lived.

During the unpleasant part, when the thought flickered through her brain, she thought Mike might glance her way.

Would it not have been better for all of them, perhaps, if Odette had gone ahead? If Mike had never come round to dissuade her. If Mandy had never . . . It was a despicable thought. She touched his hand. He didn't respond. She didn't blame him. She probably wouldn't have touched her either, given the choice.

She genuinely hadn't heard. Mike breathed heavily, then asked why she insisted on making him repeat it, when she knew very well what he'd said.

'You must know. We've all been expecting this. Please don't be disingenuous.' She was bewildered. What had they known? She never seemed to know anything for sure.

'They arrested her. Actually arrested her. To carry out their inquiries. They didn't mention a charge yet, but the custody sergeant told her . . .'

'Surely they're just wanting to ask her what happened.'

'The custody sergeant told her they suspect she may be involved in the death of little Daisy.'

'That is . . .' She cleared her throat, tried again. 'That is such utter bull . . .'

'They cautioned her formally. All that stuff from TV that you never think you'll hear in real life. About the right to remain silent, about harming your defence.'

'I'd better come. I should be there.'

'There was a reporter outside. I managed to block his view of Mandy. I didn't want him to take some picture that would make her look . . .'

'But surely they can't use pictures of her.'

'Not at this stage, but later they might. Anyway, Ridley asked the custody sergeant not to put her in a cell because of her age. But the interview rooms were all busy. Anyway, she only spent an hour in a cell.'

'By herself? Jesus Mike.'

'I'm doing what I can, Odette. Anyway, it was only an hour.'

'I know, I know. But I should be there.'

'Ridley told the custody sergeant he'd instructed her to say nothing. Which was probably lucky because she seems to have gone into this total trance...I think you should just hold your horses, Odette. You need a visa nowadays and by the time you get through all that, I may just...'

'So you do still think it'll all be okay.'

'I don't know about "okay". But at least she hasn't been charged. Not yet anyway. At this stage she's just bailed as a suspect.'

She resisted sex. Not so much refused as lay rigid enough to withstand all but the most resolute of suitors. And Adriaan was not that. She curled into a ball on her side. She could feel his flanks, radiating heat into her cold bum. It was still chilly at night, especially after a storm.

She must have fallen asleep eventually because she awoke with fear pounding in her chest. She thought she had leapt and cried out, but perhaps she hadn't. Adriaan was still breathing evenly, a small snore, like a growl, in his throat.

It was pitch dark, the moon just a splinter, the stars shards of light in the darkness. That was one of the things she'd had to get used to. In Jo'burg, yellowish light always seeped through, not quite repelled by curtains.

It was cold in the room, but she was sweating. She tried to control her breathing, not wanting to wake Adriaan. Her scalp froze over.

What had she done? What had she wished for? Even secretly. Even as the most furtive thought before she could trap and crush it. She hadn't meant it. She hadn't. Please God, she didn't mean it. Her child could barely cope with life. How would she cope with jail? She would never get the social cues. She wouldn't know how to behave in order to survive.

Nothing else mattered. Never mind this new life she was trying so hard to build. She would trade anything; anything at all. She had given Mandy precious little life of her own. Let her not have been responsible for snatching what little remained.

# Chapter 19

ANOTHER GUSTY SPRING MORNING. It ought to be exciting. She was picking up the espresso machine from its previous owner, an Italian barista whose business wasn't doing well.

Trudie was beside herself with anticipation. She had asked three times about starting her lessons as soon as Odette returned with the machine. Odette reckoned she would have to, if Trudie were to be up to speed by their launch date. They had put so much into it. All that time and enthusiasm, which now felt vaguely naive.

The market square was already alive with people. Women sat on blankets, selling old clothes, overripe tomatoes and eggs encrusted with chicken shit and feathers. Crawling from their mother's blankets, toddlers snatched at plastic bottles and chip packets. People rubbed grit from their eyes. Babies cried, damp cheeks crusting in the heat.

Flies settled in iridescent clouds at its verge where a swollen dog lay reeking. It had been dragged against the sandstone façade of a shop building. If you were able to ignore the dog, it would be a beautiful shop, square blocks carved from yellow stone, with wooden sills and frames.

The journey took forever. Consumed by fumes and the growl of diesel motors, she found it hard to focus on her usual landmarks. She registered the church spire in its valley and usually she managed to see it just like that, as it appeared from the main road, with sunlight glancing off distant windows. But today she couldn't hold it steady.

Her mind's eye slipped its leash and raced across the plain like a dog after carrion. She couldn't just leave it be. She had to worry at it, and what she knew it had become.

It was a ghostly place now, infused with the despair left by its deserters, and the disrepair it took from its appropriators. The old villagers had drifted away, while the new lacked the means to visualise it as anything more than just immediate shelter. But what the hell. Were any of their attempts at a hold on life here any less precarious?

'Unlike you to be late.' Heather buzzed her through the gate and waited for her at the door.

'Sorry. Had to pick up my Wega. I just made the final payment, so Lucky Bean's set to go.'

'That's exciting. Isn't it? Isn't this what you've been waiting for? You're not having second thoughts, are you?'

'Yes. No, I'm happy.'

'You don't look it. What's the matter? Problems in rural paradise?'

'No, not at all, not with me anyway. It'll all be okay though. It'll sort out.'

Someone's gardener was mowing, probably next door. She had always found it comforting, the sound of normal families, where things were ordered and set in their ways, and the gardener came once a week without fail.

'Is it Mandy? Not serious I hope?'

'No, not Mandy either. It's the family. The baby, it died. A cot death.'

'How awful. How's she coping?' Heather passed her a cup, keeping her eyes on Odette's. 'Is Mike still over there? He'll bring her home, no doubt.'

'I'm not sure that would be good. The family will need someone surely...Or if they don't, the agency could find her another family.'

'Would that be best? Isn't she upset? Wouldn't it be better for her just to come home?'

'Far worse to make her feel like it's her fault, I would have thought. Or that she didn't cope. Jesus, I can't believe you even think that's a good idea.'

'Okay, Odette. Take a moment.'

'I don't need a bloody moment. I think it's a stupid idea, that's all. I'm just saying.'

'Okay, I can see that you're angry, but I'd like you to try and express it. Tell me how this makes you feel?'

Odette shrugged, impatient with her. She wanted to be out of there, doing...something, anything, rather than all this endless bloody talk. What good did it do?

'I'm not bloody angry. It's not like it's anybody's fault. I was just impatient, that's all. I've got a lot on my mind.'

Heather was silent. Did she have no other strategies? All she had to do was clam up and the traffic did her work for her, building into a tsunami of sound until you were forced to speak, just to stop it from engulfing you.

'Look Heather, I'm upset about it, naturally. Who wouldn't be? It's hard on her and I can't get there in time to be any help. That's all there is to it.'

Heather still sat watching her. The lawnmower began again. It was such a tangible sound of homes and gardens that she focused on it, as though it could pull her back from the abyss and make their lives as ordinary as the sound. She took a breath. It was only an hour. Less than an hour. She could hold it together that long.

Odette forced herself to smile. She sipped her tea and carefully replaced the cup. 'The worry just makes me a bit snappy, that's all. Sorry.'

Heather shook her head and flipped her hands. 'It's not that, Odette. I just want us to look at why...'

'I'm not that concerned, really. It's not like she's in any danger. Mike'll sort it all out. He's good at that.'

They were silent again. Heather sipped her tea, contemplating her over the rim of her teacup. Odette glanced at the clock. Heather caught her at it, but didn't comment.

'So it sounds like you and Mike are managing to share the decisions on this. What does he think?'

Odette gave a laugh. 'Me and Mike? Share?'

'I see. That's a pity. Is this something that happened during your relationship, or is it a result of your separation?'

'Hell, I don't know. It's no one's fault. He's...'

'He's...what?'

'I was going to say he's a not a bad man...oh I don't know. It's not so very strange, is it? Many couples end up like that.'

'Not at all, Odette. Relax. I know it takes time to build up trust, but I've told you before, you can tell me anything.'

Odette rose, but felt awkward standing. Unsure what to do with herself, she carried her cup over to the teapot. It was cold. The lawnmower stopped. Heather's room was south-facing. Outside, you could see the kind of buzzing sunlight that made you yearn for school to be out. Not much longer to go.

'Well, how can I remember?' she said, sitting again. 'Perhaps we just lost the ability to talk without blaming each other.'

'For what, exactly?'

'Life, I suppose. Disappointments. I don't know. We were so young. And Mandy wasn't exactly the easiest child. She just wasn't. She was a tough adolescent.'

'That's a hard feeling to have. Especially if you blamed each other.'

'Mike and I didn't part from hatred, Heather. We just ran out of other things to say. Banal really.'

Giovanni helped her load the Wega, and asked if she'd like him to throw in the red-checked tablecloths. Same price. She wondered if Giovanni were his real name, or whether he'd adopted it to make his trattoria more authentic. His accent was pure Jo'burg boytjie: a fast-talking boy from the rough side of town who had made good – and then lost it all again.

He didn't say so, but he must have bought here when everyone still thought this would be the next, best trendy destination.

'Considered holding out till the World Cup, but I've got some other deals going down. There'll be a boom, no doubt about it, specially here. It's a good time to buy. Give you a good deal if you're interested.'

Odette smiled and shook her head. In the evening it might be cosy, but at midday it smelled of damp and decades of olive oil that had seeped into the walls. He buzzed her back out through the steel gate that had kept its patrons alive, at least while they were inside.

She cut through town, but hadn't bargained on the new bus routes. Running down the centre of the one-ways, they made a foreign city of familiar old streets. She found herself in a left lane when she wanted to turn right, cut off by a concrete barrier just too high to drive comfortably across.

Constant hooting made her jump and twist in her seat. A taxi came to a sudden halt in front of her. She slammed on brakes and felt the shock course through her legs. The driver slapped the flat of his hand on the outside of his door and yelled from his window.

She only really panicked when she reached the next intersection. She had planned to cut past the buses into the right-hand lane. But a thousand taxis had the same idea – despite the gridlocked intersection. Cars pushed and revved against them long after the light had turned.

When the robot changed again, she found herself marooned, the only driver in the universe who appeared to care, or have noticed at all.

Hooters blared and men swore, making obscene gestures through open windows. Battered taxis shoved their way through the turmoil, while between them all, a constant stream of pedestrians flowed, like ants to a sugar bowl.

She couldn't breathe. She couldn't expel the air from her lungs. She needed to breathe out. She couldn't take a breath if she couldn't breathe out. She had to concentrate. She had to push the air out.

Desperate puffs. Just little puffs. Exhaust fumes dried out her mouth. Her fingers began to tingle. Her body was about to shut down. Darkness edged from the periphery of her vision.

The robot changed again. She put her foot down, fighting the steel tide, ramping the concrete barrier. She thought she caught some bumper a glancing blow. She thought she was pursued because of it, but she could have been mistaken.

She cut down a side street, then another. She lost direction in the one-way streets. And suddenly it was quiet, like being carried over a waterfall, battering over the rapids, then finding yourself in a pool of calm.

She pulled to the side of the road outside the Civic Theatre, to catch her breath and stop shaking. Across the road, a giant digital clock told her it was 269 days until the World Cup.

'You're very quiet today,' Margie said, and everyone's attention was suddenly fixed on her. 'You haven't said what you think.'

Odette had managed no more than a glance at Palesa's scenes. She would have to wing it. 'Well, actually I like it. Especially the . . . the church intervention? It's very funny.' Palesa shot her a smile.

'Oh come on,' said Chevonne. She was spinning her pen in the air and catching it. 'It sounded good in theory, but it stretches belief, don't you think? This whole church mobilising over some poor gay boy?'

Lex sucked at his biscuit. 'I just wonder if we want all these people praying all over the place.'

'Okay, I get that his mom goes all churchy and freaky.' Chevonne chucked her pen again. 'But in this day and age, isn't the dominee's reaction a bit over the top?'

Any other day, Odette would have introduced them to Outer Mongolia just ninety minutes away. But what would it prove? Everyone knew stories from life that would stretch anyone's credibility.

'What do you think, Odette?' Jesus, why did Margie keep picking on her? She attempted deeply contemplative, as though she had thought of nothing else for days.

'I think the dominee believes he has total say over everyone's lives. And I think he would totally think he can cure the poor guy.'

In the end, if she remembered rightly, the church intervention stayed, but the dominee's reaction was toned down a bit. Lex's sucked fingers were giving her a morning-sick quease. She took their notes on her storyline without a peep. Just wrote it all down. She would worry about it later.

'But what happens next?' asked Chevonne. 'I find it all a little weird. She's cancelled the abortion, but then starts having doubts about keeping the ankle-biter?' She thought she might murder Chevonne if she didn't stop flinging that bloody pen in the air.

'It means Reno's still teetering: does he have to tell his wife or not? If she keeps the child, it'll come crashing down on their relationship like a ton of bricks. So that's the dramatic imperative.'

Lex licked another biscuit. 'Ja, but I'm with Chevonne. What's the motivation?'

'I thought I showed that, Lex. Bringing the child home will change Rochelle's life utterly. Nothing will ever be the same.'

'But she must know no one's going to adopt a baby like that?' Chevonne again, font of all genetic wisdom.

'It would make an adoption harder, you're right. Although Down's children do have a huge range of IQ and ability...'

Chevonne caught her pen with one hand. What was Odette thinking? They weren't interested, and she just wanted to get home.

'It's part of the fantasy. It's the dream of this not being permanent. That this one slip won't somehow shape the whole rest of her life.'

'And when they realise they're going to be stuck with it forever, it's too late for an abortion. I like it,' Lex added, waving a disgusting biscuit stump in the air.

Nausea was coming in waves, each raising sweat in the nape of her neck. It was all she could do just to clamp it down. Perhaps it was a twenty-four-hour virus.

Then Chevonne dropped her pen. In the silence, they heard it bounce and roll away, coming to rest somewhere between Palesa and Odette. Palesa slithered beneath the table and emerged waggling her head. Odette could see this was aimed at her, but she couldn't fathom what she was on about. She just wanted it to be over.

Palesa widened her eyes, nodding in the direction of Lex and Margie. Finally, she gave a loud click, fumbled in her purse and produced a crumpled fifty rand note. The best Odette could manage was a weak acknowledging smile. She couldn't even enjoy her triumph.

Driving seemed to calm her stomach. She was speeding on the secondary road, which she shouldn't be doing. The potholes had deepened and it was hard to see them in this light.

She was trying to beat the storm. Concentrating on something made you forget the nausea. The wind was bawling about the car, lifting dust devils and whipping long grass strands across the road. The light was a sickly grey. The sky felt like a too-low ceiling in a sunless room.

It came when she only had twenty ks to go. It began with such violence that it rocked the car and blinded her. No windscreen wipers could withstand that rain, if you could use so inadequate a word. She felt herself disappear, sucked into its depths.

She couldn't see a metre in front of the car. She was crawling, fearing that some idiot in a truck might ram her from behind. Or that she would come up suddenly behind a truck and ram it. She couldn't see the centre line. What if she hit something head-on? She wanted to stop, but couldn't see enough to pull off the road.

A moment or two of straining and she saw the ragged verge. It had broken away, creating a considerable drop from tar to gravel. She made it, pulling as far as she could into the long grass. Rain enclosed her in a solid capsule, but at least she felt safer. Relief came in a rush that forced a laugh from somewhere high in her throat.

Her phone rang. She had to yell to make herself heard.

'It's Mike. Odette, can you hear me? What? Where the fuck are you?' She could tell from his voice that he was breathing heavily.

'Never mind. Listen, I'm going to tell you this quickly. We'll discuss it more when I'm back.'

The car rocked, buffeted by wind and the dead weight of water. 'You're coming back already? Mike, you need to settle it first.'

'Jesus. Where are you living? What planet? For Christ sake, I told you she's a suspect.'

'Yes, but . . . it's ridiculous. Everyone must know that. You know it's rubbish. I don't want her to feel like she's failed.'

'The press is saying they're close to a formal charge. The *Daily Mail* said the police were holding someone for questioning. The police wouldn't have leaked that if . . .'

'Charge her? Actually charge her? With what?' Her coldest fear. Her guiltiest thought. Her fault. Oh God, her fault.

'Murder, Odette. Or if we're lucky, manslaughter. That's the least we can hope for. Okay sorry, I just . . . it's hard, and you don't seem to have any clue.'

'No, what? What are you saying?'

'Look, I'll explain when we're back. In the meantime, the custody sergeant's agreed to bail and I'm allowed to bring her home.'

She couldn't hear what he said next. The wind was wailing about the car, as though it were baying for blood. 'There's things to arrange naturally, but we'll be leaving within the week.' His voice faded again.

'I'm . . . I don't know what to say. Listen, I'll come for a few days, when she's back in Jo'burg.'

'What are you talking about?'

'Well, she can't sit around for the rest of the year. Maybe she could study something, do a course, so she needs to be somewhere she can . . .'

'Odette. Odette.'

'They can't really believe that junk, if they're letting her come home. But she'll need to be in familiar surroundings to regroup and recover. She'll enjoy being around you guys, with Lindy about to pop. And she'll be a huge help . . .'

'Odette, are you insane? We can't have her in the house with a newborn.'

# Part Two

# Chapter 20

*I CAN TELL FROM the light that it's incredibly early. I'm not sure what roused me, but it was a relief. One minute I was deep in horror, the next acutely conscious.*

*The calf next door is still crying for its mother. Cows have motherhood all worked out. No tug of war, just resignation. Release the hopes and desires. Breathe them out. This is all there is now, so just accept. Deal with it, one step at a time.*

*I wish I could cultivate some of that. I might even succeed if only I could sleep. Just one night of deep and dreamless sleep, that's all I ask. I could hear a baby crying last night. It went on and on, a dreadful sound. It reverberated in my brain and sliced through my gut.*

*I searched for it, to make it stop. I had to make it shut up or I'd go mad. I rushed from room to empty room . . . I woke up then and went to the bathroom, but as soon as I lay down again, I was back there, searching. This time, though, I found it. Oh the exquisite relief. But that feeling only lasted an instant. As soon as I snatched it up, I saw that it had no eyes. Still, I tried to shush it, but I found that it had no mouth. Then I saw that it was dead. I had killed it, but I wasn't sure how. I hadn't meant to. I hadn't meant it any harm.*

*My breath feels trapped. It's like a bubble in my throat that I can't swallow... Can't analyse it either. The commonage is still covered in a layer of mist. Quite eerie against the dark hillside, especially when figures appear suddenly through it. A herdboy leading his cows...*

*I don't feel like doing this, but it gives me some focus. Something to concentrate on. When I write like this, I find that random words appear before me, demanding to be written. Like anguish. I like that word. It's a rushing word, like water. It sounds as though you could give in to it, allow it to carry you away. Angst is a harder word, like a stone. Angst.*

*Angst is different from fear, which would mean a material threat. Mandy couldn't be regarded as a material threat. Except... Unless... but that's not something I can deal with right now.*

*Angst means the fear of what is strange, so angst wouldn't be the right word for any normal family homecoming. But perhaps it might do for one like ours. Heather once said that growing up means learning to accept our imperfect mothers. I managed that more easily with Mike's mom. Couldn't stand her when we were first married, but eventually I suppose I learned to see her, rather than the image I cast through my own insecurities. Funnily enough, I miss her now.*

*Sylvia took care of herself. She didn't smoke and never stretched to more than a glass or two of wine and a sherry now and again. How unfair that she should be struck down in the middle of her bridge game. She was dead before she could win the round. She would have hated that.*

*And then my own mother, whose liver should never have survived a week past her fiftieth, is probably still annoying hell out of retirement villagers in Plett.*

*I read somewhere that Kierkegaard saw angst as a profound spiritual condition of despair. Animals are slave to their instincts, but the freedom granted humans leaves them in constant fear of failing their responsibilities.*

*He meant to God though.*

'What is it, Mandy? Are you okay? Is something...?'

'My shelves are different. I don't have the same cupboards.'

Mike shifted. He looked dreadful: bruised patches under his eyes and hair that was lank and greasy.

'They're a bit different, Mandy. Did you bring the stuff from your dad's? Your bears and your animal collection? Look, once they're on your shelves, it won't be much different.'

'I don't want them like this. I want them to look like they did before.'

She hunched in on herself, pacing the kitchen like an impatient troll. Mike rubbed a hand over his eyes. Odette knew the feeling. If Mandy were different all the time it would be one thing. But she could be so nearly, so very nearly, like everyone else. It lulled you. You grew to expect... then it always came as a shock.

'Look, it's a different house. A new town. This room faces a different way, so it won't be exactly the same, but once you have your own things...'

'I want it the same.' She continued to pace, up and down, up and down.

'It's a nicer room, Mandy. This one faces north. It's sunny and you can watch the herdboys bring their cows to graze.'

'I don't want to. I want my old room.'

Mike slammed his cup to the counter, sloshing hot tea over his hand. He shook it and brought it to his face. Odette threw him a tea-towel.

'Mandy, this is it,' he snapped. 'Go and unpack. Now, do you hear me? I won't hear another word.'

Odette tried to catch his eye, to shake her head. Lindy had obviously been lecturing him about limits again. As if Odette hadn't tried that.

'No, no, no no.' Mandy's voice rose and she paced, back and forth, back and forth.

Odette could've told him that would happen. It only made things worse. Mandy had worked herself into a terror. She struggled with change at the best of times, and this could scarcely qualify as one of those.

Odette tried not to see Mandy's rage as personal, as an accusation. She was supposed to be the adult, after all. She knew that mothers always saw the very worst of their own children. Mandy could hold things together out there, but when she came home, she could let it all go. It was a safe place to allow herself to be rushed away by it. Anguish, as opposed to angst.

Odette's breath had formed a stone in her chest. Rage was easy to walk away from. 'Come,' she said to Mike. 'Let's get out of here. We can't talk and Mandy won't get over this while we're both here to rant at. It could go on for hours.'

'No, Mom, no.' Mandy gulped for air, hands jerking and panicked. Not so easy to walk away from.

Odette wrapped her arms around Mandy's stiff body and squeezed. It took Mandy by surprise. She didn't bend or soften into it. It wasn't an embrace. It was all she could think of, an instinct that reached back to Mandy's infancy.

'Mandy, the shelves are different, but we are the same. It'll be fine once you've put your things up.'

Mandy wrenched herself free, flailed her arms and flung herself against the wall. 'I hate you. I hate you.'

Rage. That was easy to walk away from.

It would get chilly when the sun dropped behind the hills, but she didn't want to risk going back for something warmer.

'I knew you should've waited before moving away,' Mike muttered.

'She wasn't behaving like this before she left. She hasn't done this for years. Obviously it's because of what happened over there.'

'Yes, and who . . . Oh never mind. Let's not get into that.'

Odette stopped walking. Mike's flat hair appeared vulnerable to her. He was proud of his hair. She felt like touching it, to acknowledge . . . but they'd lost that way back in the marriage.

'She's just reverting, Mike. And it's understandable if you think about it. It wasn't her fault, but even so, everything's fallen apart. It's frightening. She feels powerless.'

She felt the need to explain Mandy to him. Perhaps it stemmed from the same impulse. He needed that. He needed there to be a reason for her oddness. They didn't speak again until they reached Die Ou Waenhuis. It was too early for other patrons. The restaurant was dark and silent, heavy drapes sombre. It smelt of dust and dead flowers.

She led Mike through to the connecting bar – also empty, aside from a couple of bleary drunks in the corner. It would fill up in an hour or so when the farmers had dropped their workers in the township.

Mike ordered a Bell's and a Grapetiser on the side. Odette shook her head. The wall-mounted TV showed two men in soundless discussion. They were replaced by a stripey team failing to score a try against a hulking blue team.

'Highlights,' said Mike. He walked over and switched it to the football. 'Qualifiers,' he said by way of explanation. She felt a rush of irritation. What did he think? They would hunker down companionably to discuss the World Cup line-up? Jesus.

Arranging two stools to face the set, he turned the sound way down and then she understood. He would find it easier to talk if he didn't have to face her directly. He folded his arms, grasping the glass in the crook of his arm. It was smudged with fingerprints. Any other time, he would have sent it back.

'Letting her come home was a good sign, surely?'

He glanced at her, then back at the screen. 'She's bailed to return in sixteen weeks. They can get her back easily enough when they're ready to charge her.'

'"If" surely. Not "when".'

'Look Odette,' still without looking at her. 'You're going to have to prepare yourself. They think she did it. Ridley's working on the assumption they've only told us the tip of the iceberg.'

'Why didn't they charge her then?'

He didn't answer immediately. On the screen, a dark-haired guy in white blasted the ball into the net.

'We've got Sally Clark to thank for that. Whoa, Lampard you beauty.' He said it under his breath, without altering his expression.

'Is she one of the lawyers?'

He didn't answer during the replay. It was a penalty shot. The goalie dived, but it zipped past him. 'Capello's had a good run with this team.'

'Go on about this Clark woman? I asked . . .'

'She's not a lawyer. She's dead actually, but Ridley thinks she's the only reason they haven't actually charged Mandy yet. Barman?'

He gestured at his glass with a middle finger. 'Single . . . Better give me a pack of that biltong too. Got to drive. Sally Clark was jailed for murdering both her children.'

He thrust a handful of biltong slices into his mouth and worked his jaws rapidly. Just to get it down, it seemed to her. He couldn't be tasting it.

'She was exonerated later. Devastating embarrassment for the prosecution, apparently. I mean, how is it possible that one doctor can quite categorically see petichiae . . .'

'See what?'

'Burst veins in the baby's eyes. Shows smothering. But the other one saw signs of shaking.'

'In Sally Clark's case, or Mandy's?'

'No, that's the thing. They're not telling us the pathology results.

And we can't send in our own medical experts because she hasn't been officially charged. Yet anyway.'

He stopped and swallowed hard. 'God, I'm going to need . . . got any antacids at home?'

She nodded and waited. From years of dealing with Mandy, she'd learned patience. On screen, the Croatian goalie dived to the right and caught the ball.

'It's relevant because Sally Clark became such a national scandal. The doctors disagreed, but she was convicted anyway, because some idiot expert claimed two cot deaths in one family was like . . .' He paused to drain his Grapetiser.

'Like lightning striking?'

'You get the picture. He's completely discredited now. Apparently cot deaths can be genetic, but they didn't know that then.'

'That's good, right? And if the doctors can't agree that's surely even better.'

'We don't know that in Mandy's case. We don't know what they've found, except for what's been in the *Daily Mail.*'

'Why the hell are they so interested in one small case like this?'

'It's sensational, Odette. Obviously. They don't have a murder every half hour over there. Anyway, let's not get into that. Ridley thinks the *Daily Mail*'s got a contact in the police.'

He swallowed the last of the biltong. She waited while he washed it down with Scotch. Mike swallowed again and winced.

'He wrote a speculative piece, quoting "sources".' Mike sketched the inverted commas with his free hand. 'He reckons they're getting their ducks in a row first – with the medical experts specially. They don't want to make a false move, considering how devastating the Clark case was.'

The bar was filling up. So far, Odette was the only woman. She wondered if it was that, or the fact that Mike was a stranger, which drew the looks.

Despite the evening chill, all but one of the regulars wore shorts, cut square across their thighs. The shirts were khaki, or the two-tone variety from the co-op. She saw, rather than heard, one of them ask about the two of them, gesturing with a flip of his head. The barman shrugged and handed him a couple of Castles and what looked like Klippies, with a Coke on the side.

The one in longs was at the door, handing a Coke out to an obese child whose cheeks had swollen his eyes nearly closed.

'For God's sake, Odette, keep your eyes off those gorillas. I thought we came here to talk.'

Three men stepped into Mike's field of vision just as England headed the ball into the net. He bent to see past them, but they were too obviously blocking the screen. They turned, grinning, and the screen once more showed two men, now discussing last week's Currie Cup game at full volume.

'Hey, I was watching that,' Mike said, his voice rising.

The men were already walking away. Without bothering even to look back, one of them spoke: 'Here . . . we watch rugby.'

And that was that. It was a call to arms, of course. Mike stiffened. Odette placed a hand on his arm and shook her head. Too many, too big. She didn't voice it, lest he feel obliged to prove her wrong.

'Let's go,' she said. 'I'm a bit worried about Mandy.'

As they left the heat and stale beer of the bar, she could smell chilled soil and coal smoke. They were high enough to see over the rooftops at the wrong end of town. Wisps of mist garlanded the commonage. Mike breathed in puffs of condensation.

'Mike, do you think she . . . ?'

'You're not seriously going to ask me that question, are you? This is the situation. Let's deal with it in practical terms. The best you can hope is that Sally Clark goes on haunting them. Jesus, I so wish I hadn't listened to you.'

'Me? Are you going to blame this all on me?'

'Okay, enough said. I allowed you to persuade me. I suppose I must live with at least some of the responsibility.'

Children like Mandy are not made for schools. Or rather, schools are not fashioned to accommodate children like she was. She upset the equilibrium. She annoyed the teachers.

It's hard to explain what she did to make herself so utterly friendless. Odette wasn't there and Mandy never told her much, except that she wanted to be home. The teachers said she spun herself dizzy or ran in circles, unable to stop. Odette said she only did that when she was feeling overwhelmed. So if they would only make her feel comfortable . . .

When they put on music, she put her hands over her ears and shrieked. So? Couldn't they just turn the music down?

If they tried to interest her in something, she would slip away and run in circles again. Well, obviously, they should fetch her . . .

And if they sat her back down, she slid to the floor and banged her head rhythmically against the floor. Oh yes, well there was that.

Odette held this image of herself sidling through the school gate with Mandy clinging to her legs. She always walked her in, helped place her bag, all the things mothers did.

She didn't join the other mothers with their school gate chatter about play dates. They didn't have play dates. And none of the other mothers struggled to breathe when the time came to say goodbye.

'Home, home, home.' Mandy clutched at fabric, flesh, anything she could get a grip on. Odette had a deadline. She always had a deadline. Hell, they needed the money. They always needed the money.

'I'm going now, Mandy. I'm sorry, you can't come till home-time. Why don't you start playing before I leave. Won't that make it easier?'

'Home, home.' Mandy's panic fed directly into her own. 'Mandy home. Mandy home.'

Panic transmuted too easily to fury. For doing this, day after fucking day. For making them so conspicuously bad at this utterly normal thing. Mothers raised their heads like thoroughbred horses, sniffed the air and bolted in their dainty brogues. No one wants to be a part of someone else's misery.

Eventually a teacher would come out to prise Mandy's fingers loose, wet with anxiety and the exertion of screaming. Oh the exquisite relief. She should not look back. She should not. The child had to go to nursery school. She needed to catch up. She had to learn. What decent school would take her if she hadn't the grounding...

When she did look back, Mandy's upper lip had become vein-blue, etched in white. Her hands clung like starfish to the fence, as her teacher tore her free. And as Odette continued to walk away.

# Chapter 21

MANDY WOKE AT 10 a.m. There was no particular rush and Odette had learned to pick her battles. Once she was up, Mandy sat another hour, rumpled and sleep-eyed, staring at the place where the TV would be, if Odette still had one.

'Have you kept up your sketching? Doesn't this view make you feel like breaking out your sketchbook?'

Mandy shrugged. Odette had woken with a dull ache of resigned . . . what? Probably sadness. And somewhere she couldn't identify, a flutter of panic. She suppressed it fiercely.

The night before, Mike and she had found a tear-stained Mandy fast asleep on her new bed. Mike had left without saying goodbye; they both recognised the advantage of letting sleeping Mandy lie.

Odette had poured a glass of wine and wrestled with her rage. It appeared to be focused on the Neanderthals in the pub, but even she, who struggled to face bad feelings head-on, understood that her fantasy of returning to Die Ou Waenhuis with a shotgun was somewhat displaced.

She'd spent all night trying not to fast-forward into the future. There was no use in it. Mandy had some artistic talent, it was true. Perhaps a little dark for most people's taste, but good nonetheless, combining a swirling blend of realism with scary, dreamlike images. What could you do with that though? Her real talent lay with kids, and now . . .

She shouldn't be doing this. She should just concentrate on getting through today. One day at a time, that was more than enough. Perhaps Mandy's future would be out of their hands . . . but that she could not even think about.

She left Mandy where she was to help Trudie set up for the opening, then raced home with barely time to change and chivvy. Mandy was still lying on the couch, twirling her hair with one hand, rubbing at her genitals with the other. Odette hadn't seen her do that since she was a very little girl.

It shocked her. But then she supposed her lounge didn't really count as 'public'. It just looked absurdly indecent through her teddy-bear pyjamas. She took a deep breath. Remember she'd been through a traumatic time. Pick your issues, Odette. Just pick your issues.

Odette waited till Mandy raised her eyes to somewhere just above her left shoulder. 'Uh listen, Sweetpea, when you meet these women, I just think . . . it may be better not to mention what happened in England.'

'Okay.'

'Say you came home because you were homesick. I'm not saying . . . not because . . . it's not because of you. I just think it would be better.'

Mandy shrugged. 'Okay.'

They found Lucky Bean nearly full. The room hummed with the high-pitched tone of a party. Bless Trudie. They'd all come on account of her, and perhaps out of a certain curiosity.

'Hell Trudie, if we have this crowd every day, we'll both be on duty all the time. Do you think we can cope?'

'They won't mind. I told them we were practising on them. Sorry my lamb, I didn't see you there. You must be Mandy. Your mom told me you came home.'

'She got homesick, didn't you Mandy?'

Odette spotted Marta somewhere towards the back. Beefy and generically coiffed as the best of them, she was nonetheless impossible to miss.

Odette had met a few of the other women, but she was too distracted to place them out of context. In which shop or bank or butcher had she greeted them? She was as bad as Mandy, unable to recognise people having once met them. This was meant to be the highlight, the culmination, of their venture and it was all different now. Everything had changed.

She watched Mandy carefully, ready to jump in if she blurted something inappropriate. God knows, first impressions mattered and Mandy was here ... maybe not for good, but at least for the foreseeable future. She didn't want them to find her odd. Not again.

A few of Trudie's particular friends rose to exclaim over Mandy, like a flutter of pigeons. In Jo'burg, people's eyes always seemed to measure her up. Odette was sure this was at the heart of her London troubles. Blame the unattractive girl, who lacked the charm to make herself personable. It wasn't easy for a lumpy girl to come across fragile and sympathetic.

Here, she didn't seem quite as out of place. Or, perhaps they were just more hospitable than city people. Odette needn't have worried about Mandy standing too near – the women clustered closely about them both – and if she didn't quite look them in the eye, she shook hands with a slight smile.

'Shame man, she's shy. Leave the poor child be,' exclaimed Trudie, and they returned to their tables.

Since Mandy's troubles, Odette had lost much of her excitement over Lucky Bean, but she looked about now and felt proud. Sun streamed through her outlandish French doors on to their artfully mismatched chairs and odd pieces of salvaged china. The women exclaimed over everything, although someone did worry that the sun would fade the napkins.

Trudie asked if Mandy would like to serve, but Odette made a quick excuse. It wasn't that Mandy couldn't have done it easily enough, but she was clearly still in a bit of a state, and Odette didn't want her forgetting orders or dropping hot coffee on someone.

'Co-ordination's not the best,' she muttered to Trudie. 'Learning difficulties at school. Just fine motor skills and stuff, but it does affect their dexterity.'

'Oh ja those,' said Trudie. 'We don't go in for those problems so much on the platteland. Sometimes I wonder if those city doctors don't just make them up so you must pay more to get them fixed.'

'She's absolutely fine now, of course. It's just that it's her first day back and ...'

'Ag I know, it's fine. Let her relax. We must get her together with the other young people in town.'

Odette watched Trudie prepare the first few coffees, ready to step in if necessary. It had taken Odette a full six weeks, but Trudie had been forced to learn everything in just a couple. Trudie's hand shook slightly, but she dosed the coffee into the portafilter, tamped and flushed the group head with no problem at all.

Mandy had spotted a pram in the corner. Odette kept the corner of an eye on her as Trudie set four cups ready. She held her breath ... and four almost perfect mouse tails trailed into the cups. It was good practice for Trudie so Odette served, handing out scones and koeksisters. One or two of these women had probably baked them for Trudie's shop, but they didn't let on.

The baby's mother chatted to friends, completely unconcerned. Odette kept a covert eye on them. Just in case. Mandy lifted the niggling baby and jiggled it against her shoulder. Odette returned for two more. Mandy stroked its head and crooned. Trudie hadn't managed fern-leaf patterns on her cappuccinos, but it was doubtful anyone would care.

For Mandy, holding a baby was transformative. Her face – to Odette anyway – took on the serenity of an angel. All uncertainty left her. She no longer looked sly. Or clumsy or ... Odette stopped between orders and watched her rock back and forth on her heels to gentle the infant.

'She's wonderful with him. She must come baby-sit sometime,' the mother called and Odette nodded and smiled. Perhaps it wouldn't come up again. She hoped it wouldn't. Because she couldn't exactly say no, could she? Not without giving a reason.

Once they'd all been served, the noise level mounted with much cross-table laughter and teasing remarks that were hard to follow if you didn't know them. These were hard-working farm women who probably didn't get out much – not for events like this – so they made a party of it.

Eventually the baby slept and Mandy returned it to the pram without waking it, which was more than Odette had ever managed.

'Where were you before?' the baby's mother asked Mandy. 'In Jo'burg? Were you working?'

'No, au pairing in England. I was meant to be there for a year, but I came home.'

She needn't have volunteered that, but it was okay. Odette saw old Marta perk up in the corner. There always appeared to be an element of malice to her curiosity, but perhaps that was Odette's own prejudice.

Mandy went to stand beside Trudie, watching her flush the group head. 'You're wonderful with children,' said Trudie. 'They must've loved you.'

'Not really. In the end they didn't.'

'Typical English,' Odette interjected, laughing. 'I'm sure they did really, they just don't show it.'

'Of course. It's always hard, dealing with people who aren't your own. So you were unhappy?'

'Not really,' said Mandy. 'But the baby...'

'She was homesick,' Odette said, nausea rising.

'The baby died and they thought I killed it.'

She expected utter silence. To her relief, no one else appeared to have heard. She caught Marta's eye without meaning to. Marta knew something was up, probably from Trudie's expression, and she managed to look both thrilled and malevolent, as though she were already anticipating an I-told-you-so.

Trudie clattered the cup, spilling a little into the saucer as she handed it to Odette. Well, she needn't have worried about the baby-sitting. And that should pretty much put pay to being set up with the young people too.

'Are you angry with me?'

Odette didn't answer immediately. Whatever she said felt inadequate. Or inappropriate. She shrugged instead; more and more like Mandy herself. They were walking home and the smell of loam and dung rose from the commonage. Above the twisting wetland, hadedas cried.

Odette had been more than complicit, no one was more conscious of it than she, but even so, Mike had agreed to it. And it wasn't as though she had pushed and shoved while Mandy kicked and screamed. All the kids at school had been planning gap years and Mandy had raged at Odette for holding her back; for making her feel different by her very hesitation. ('Why can't you ever believe in me?' Why indeed.)

'You're my child, Mandy. Sometimes I get cross. Everyone gets cross now and again, but that doesn't mean . . . I do always . . .'

'I can see you're angry with me.'

'No. Ah Mandy, it doesn't matter now. What's done is done. But I just wish . . . I mean, bloody hell, if the kids were stressing you, couldn't you just have said something? Okay, okay, never mind. You don't have to answer that.'

Mandy didn't. Just nodded. Sometimes you forgot how literal she was. Odette sighed. 'Are you glad to be home? Here, I mean?'

Mandy shrugged, and Odette couldn't fault her for it. 'I'm happy you're home.' She smiled, trying to catch Mandy's eye, but Mandy was concentrating on the road. Perhaps it came out strained.

'Mandy, this has been really hard on all of us, most of all you, but I think we do need to talk about England. Could you try, maybe?'

There were few cars on the roads. They had stayed to clear up, and the women had all gone home to serve supper to hungry husbands and sons. Clouds clotted about their heads, but no rain fell.

Mandy shrugged. 'What d'you want to hear about? The tube can be really hard to manage sometimes. Everyone crushes into you and then no one says a word to each other. Sometimes I had to push on with Emily and Daisy in the pushchair...'

'I know what you mean.' Odette gave a companionable laugh, only slightly forced. 'And I do want to hear all of that. I want to hear all your adventures, but...Look, I know it was traumatic, but shouldn't we talk about the baby? About what happened, I mean?'

'I am talking about Daisy. I'm telling you about them both.' She raised her face and, for once, met Odette's eyes.

Odette struggled to compose something that would sound clearer. What could you say: Did you do it, Mandy? Did she scream and scream until you smothered her? Did you press a pillow over her tiny nose? Did you shake her till her neck...?

Oh Jesus, not now. She couldn't do it now. She was positive it wasn't true. It couldn't be. And if – just if – well, they needn't face it right now, did they? It was just too hard, for Mandy to express, and for Odette to hear.

'So did you find it hard to learn the tube routes?'

'It wasn't so bad. Me and Emily usually just walked to the park. Sometimes we went on the tube. I know you think I'm no good at maps, but I'm not that bad, and it's quite easy really because of the colours. Sometimes we ended up going in the wrong direction, but then you just have to get out again. And Dad said everyone does that sometimes. I had to change a couple of times to go meet him. He was staying at this really nice hotel...'

'The one in Kensington?'

'Ja, Kensington. If I was there, that's where I'd like to live. It's really old and all the windows were these really long sash windows. You would've liked them. I remember when we had windows like that when I was little, not such long ones though, and Dad wanted to take them out and put in doors, you wouldn't let him. I told him you should be staying there, not him, because he didn't even like old places, but he didn't answer that.'

'What did you...?'

'It was much nicer than the Hopes' place. I know it's a hotel, but it's quite a small one and it seems like a house. I suppose it used to be a house and even inside, you don't feel like you're in a hotel. I know their place is bigger, and it's much fancier, but I still like it more. I'm not sure if Dad does though, because he said it's hard to get a nice place, what with the exchange rate...'

When Mandy was past her head-banging stage, it was never immediately clear to her teachers why they should make allowances for her.

'She has ability,' Miss Andrews said. 'She just doesn't try. She doesn't listen. If I've told her once, I've told her a million times...'

That was it, though. It was hard to understand, hard not to get angry at her. She wasn't stupid, not by any means. So why the hell couldn't she remember an instruction? Why did she blather on and on and on about nothing? Why did she forget her locker combination every single, bloody day?

'Mandy, for goodness sake, Miss Andrews is talking to you,' Odette felt the prickle of sweat at her armpits. 'Look at her. Look her in the eyes.'

Mandy stepped in too close, yet still somehow failed to meet her teacher's eyes. After a while, she reached a hand out and patted gingerly at her teacher's middle-aged girth.

'Do you have a baby in your tummy, Miss?'

The trouble was that another child, as innocent as she, might appear cute. Mandy only managed to look sly. It was something to do with the eyes.

'I'm so sorry, Miss Andrews,' Odette babbled, while Miss Andrews rose abruptly and shoved Mandy from her personal space – a little too hard, but with a quick glance at Odette to see if she'd noticed.

'Miss Andrews.' Oh, but she had. In those days, she would snatch at any small advantage. 'It's your responsibility to make things easier for Mandy at school. I can't be here all the time. For goodness sake, why not just give her lists, if she can't remember? Then she can keep track and tick things off?'

It was a relief to feel angry at someone else. The day before, she had double-parked outside the Spar and asked Mandy to run in for a newspaper, milk and bread. Mandy had come back with milk and *The Star*. Irritating, but not deeply meaningful. Anyone could forget one item, couldn't they? She'd done it herself enough times.

'Where's the change, Mandy?'

'Change?'

'Yes, the change. I gave you a hundred rand. You only bought the milk and newspaper. Where's the rest?'

'A woman asked me for money.'

'What, all of it?'

'She said she needed it. You didn't tell me I must bring it all back.'

It was more satisfying to aim her fury at Miss Andrews. It was an easier battle. She could wrestle the school to make lists, copy notes, turn the music down, explain to the kids that Mandy sometimes stood too close or said tactless things.

So she did. She fought this battle. She had to. Who else could equip Mandy for life? Before the time came for her to leave home, Mandy had to be as normal as anyone else. If she had to batter it into Mandy's head, she would make bloody sure of it.

# Chapter 22

'WHAT'S FOR SUPPER?' MANDY asked suddenly. Odette tensed. Adriaan merely smiled, having no experience of how that one simple question might escalate.

'Why? What're you hoping for, young lady?'

Mandy shrugged. Her eyes slid by him and settled somewhere above his left shoulder. His smile became fixed. Oh Lord, how many times had she drummed it into her? Just maintain the eye contact. And he? What was wrong with him? He was the adult. How hard was it to grasp that it was just her manner?

'It's curry, which reminds me, it needs a stir.'

'I don't like...' Mercifully, she was in the kitchen before she could hear the rest.

When it was served, Mandy ate it meekly enough. She might not be that good at reading expressions, but Odette's expression must have underlined her meaning tonight, probably in bold.

'Little duck, little duck, it's just your luck...' Mandy burst into her ditty just as they were finishing supper. Apropos nothing. Adriaan looked startled and Mandy laughed. 'It's what I used to sing to Emily in the bath. I made it up.'

'Oh well, that's uh...'

'I often made up songs. Children are very receptive to music. They can learn much more if you sing it to them, did you know that? I read an article about it. Shall I sing you the one I made up about the rhinoceros?'

'If you like.'

During supper, she had regaled him with a perceptively argued account of child-rearing in the UK. It wasn't all anecdotal either. She backed it up with a Radio 4 discussion and 'something I read'.

By now he was bemused. It would be followed by intense scrutiny – let's just say Odette knew the process, and Adriaan's expressions weren't exactly opaque. Okay, his face said, so she wasn't stupid. But there was something...not quite right. Something strange...

'Mandy, I don't think Adriaan really...' It was excruciating. Funny, you never could see your child as a separate being, no matter how old they were. Their social humiliation always punched you right in the gut.

'Emily had never seen a rhinoceros. That's why I made up the song. We read an article about poaching, but she didn't know what it looked like. She thought it was a joke animal. Well, if you've never seen one, I suppose it sounds like that, doesn't it? That weird horn.'

'I suppose so. And it may soon be a kind of mythical beast, if we don't control the poaching.'

'Rhinoceros...Preposterous...you were born...with only one horn...'

Adriaan shifted, drawing back in his chair, as though she were dangling some putrid corpse of normality before his nose. He must have heard by now, surely, especially in a place like this. Odette wondered why he didn't say anything. But if he didn't, she sure as hell wasn't going to raise it.

'Mandy.' She sounded sharper than she'd intended. Both she and Adriaan fell silent and looked at her. 'Come help me make the coffee.'

'But I'm talking.'

'You can talk when it's made.'

'Are you angry with me?' she asked as they closed the door. Odette sighed. She was already exhausted, and Mandy had only been home a couple of days.

'No Mandy, I'm...'

'Because I'm doing what you always tell me. I'm making conversation.'

'I know. And that's good. Really. It's just that I'm not sure Adriaan wants to hear...Can't you...?'

'What?'

'Well, maybe you could try to listen more. Hear what people are talking about and try and fit in with that. It just sounds a little inappropriate when you break in with a song.'

'No one was saying anything so there was nothing to fit in with.'

Odette was being over-critical and mean, but for heaven's sake, Mandy was bright enough. Not a genius, but who needed that? Why couldn't she ever bloody show it? Why did she always show her oddest aspects?

They returned to find Adriaan rising, patting his pocket for keys. She couldn't say she was sorry.

'Must go, I'm afraid. Farmer's life and all that. We're shearing tomorrow, before the planting.'

'Coffee's hot though.'

'No thanks. Long day. I'm sure you and Mandy have lots to catch up on. I know what it's like with mothers and daughters.'

The thought of hunkering down with Mandy to share filial secrets was so absurd that she gave a little laugh. 'Yes, it's probably better. I'll see you...'

'Yes, soon. I'll...I'll give you a ring, shall I?'

Even at the age of six or seven, Mandy's days were freighted with sadness. There was a heaviness to her waking ritual, a reluctance that slipped into resistance. Passive at first, limp and slippery as Odette wrenched a shirt over boneless limbs; active later, when it came to breakfast.

Ah, the fight over food. How it had dogged their relationship ever since. 'Shall I make you some toast?'

'I don't want toast.'

'What's wrong with toast, suddenly.'

'I never liked toast.'

'You love...'

'No, I don't. I never, ever did. You just...'

'Well, what do you want?'

'Don't know. What is there?'

By this stage, Odette was breathing shallowly, glancing at her watch. Mike appeared in the doorway, shaking his head. A moment or two later, she heard the gate close behind him. He never ate breakfast. Perhaps he would have, had the scene in the kitchen not been so gothic.

'Well, there's cereal. Or porridge. Wouldn't you like some nice, hot porridge?'

'I don't like porridge.'

They were going to be late. And it wasn't as though they arrived quietly. The principal always watched with folded arms as Odette rushed in, misbuttoned and unbrushed. She seldom commented any more. Sometimes she would raise her left wrist to eye level, as though Odette were a recalcitrant pupil.

'Well, you can have toast then.'

'I don't like toast.' Mandy gave a wail. 'There's nothing to eat on toast.'

'Well, if you told me what you like on toast, Mandy, I could buy it. But right now, that's all there is.'

'I don't like any of it.' Mandy was damp and snotty by now, one shoe left optimistically beside her, so she could slip it on while Odette was busy making her toast. Yeah right.

'Well then you'll have nothing. We're late anyway.'

The wail broke into heart-rending sobs. 'I'm so hungry. And Miss said I can't concentrate if I don't eat.'

Ah yes, Miss would have said that, as though she wilfully deprived her child of food. She knew when she was beaten.

Mandy's hot breath came in foetid puffs. Odette had reminded her to brush her teeth, but she had probably forgotten again. Odette held the rigid body, creasing whatever she'd managed to tug over her head.

When Mandy cried, the verb didn't do her justice. She keened, she wailed, her whole body broke out in a sweat. 'Okay Mandy, okay. What shall I make you?'

'What is there?'

'I told you. Just choose someth...'

'Tell me again. I can't remember.'

'One more time, Mandy, and that's it. Okay? There's porridge...'

'Don't like.'

'And cereal.'

'You know I don't like it.'

'Then there's nothing, Mandy. Absolutely nothing. You can bloody go hungry and Miss Andrews...'

Was this a genetic imperative? Other people's kids irritated, but one's own child's sobs sliced through arteries, embedded themselves in entrails, and then still twisted in the wound.

*If only I hadn't been side-tracked by Patrick... Had my head turned... got carried away with my own hopes and possibilities when I should have been paying attention. I should have tried harder, kept my eye on the ball.*

*She keeps asking if I'm angry. And I am. Of course I am, though I can't admit that to her. I can't admit it to anyone. I'm angry that she doesn't try harder. That she doesn't remember what I tell her a thousand times. I'm consumed by such awful rage. What kind of mother am I?*

*When she was diagnosed, I thought: Social skills? Sounds like Mike, and I've managed to train him. Just watch me, I'll take her parts and glue them together – a little cracked maybe, but I'll make her whole.*

*I created her. Surely I should have been able to fix her, this broken child ... And maybe I could have, if I hadn't started thinking I might have my own life. I failed. I was so sure I could do it, but at this one, most important thing, I have failed so fucking completely.*

*I'm not going to do this fucking writing any more.*

'What are you doing? Come back to bed.'

'Writing.'

'What are you writing at this ungodly hour? Let me see.'

'It would seem to me that anyone insane enough to wake before a farmer to scribble secretly in the dark is not going to share it. I'm finished, anyway.'

'So will you come back here?'

'I'll make coffee. Then maybe you should get going. Shearing remember?'

'Aw plea-ease? Pretty please?' Perhaps he thought the boyish wheedle would make her laugh. Surely that was it. She left the room before she could say something she regretted.

She didn't want to ruin it, not yet anyway. This was sweet. He was sweet, and he was just teasing. It was her own fault: she was brittle. He couldn't know that she had enough to take care of without a great faux adolescent. She should allow the man a little fallibility. Last night at least she had found him endearing, when he'd appeared unexpectedly at her window.

'Thought I'd sneak back. A bit exciting, like being teenagers again. I'll leave before she wakes.'

'She's a grown woman, Adriaan.'

'I know, but I feel ...'

'I know. Never mind. It won't be hard to leave before she wakes, I promise.'

In contrast to his manner, Adriaan's lovemaking had been best suited to the sexual discovery stage of a relationship. He liked to overcome. But perhaps she just hadn't been in the mood.

# Chapter 23

'Did you come in on the M2?' Heather warmed the pot and added a couple of spoons of loose leaf. 'We were in the Midlands for the weekend. That road...'

'I know, it's a mess.'

'We took the wrong turn coming back. The signs are down and the construction makes it all look unfamiliar. Can't see how they'll get it done by the World Cup, and you?' Heather passed her a cup. 'You look tired Odette. Are you sleeping? Tell me what's happening?'

'Sleep? What a strange concept. It's end of the month and there's this shebeen across the road, as I told you.'

'Not picturesque any more?' Why had she never noticed before what an unattractive smile Heather had: long on gum and short on teeth.

'Nothing's picturesque at two in the morning.'

'Even small lives have their disappointments, then.'

On Heather's planet, Odette supposed that passed for humour. She concentrated on her tea till the irritation subsided. When she looked up, Heather was watching her.

'Tell me what's happening with Mike and Mandy. Still battling it out?'

'He brought her home.'

'She's home? With you? In Nagelaten?'

'Yes, with me. Why's that such a big deal?'

'Wow, Odette. I'm just amazed you didn't mention that straight off. So she decided not to try for another family?'

'She was upset about the baby dying, that's all. It made her homesick. It's not so weird.'

'Not at all. In fact, I thought it might. It's just that last time...'

'I was concerned about what was best for her, as I think I explained. And since she was homesick anyway, that turned out to be bringing her back.'

'Okay. I just wondered why you didn't say anything when you came in. I mean, your child coming home...'

'I told you now, didn't I? We were making tea and stuff. I had no reason to blurt it out. I don't see why you think it's so strange that she should be homesick. She just came home, that's all.'

'Tell me what's troubling you.'

Odette no longer seemed to have a crunchie poised on her saucer. She reached for another.

'Why do you assume I'm troubled?'

'You've just told me three times that Mandy was homesick, yet you don't seem the least bit happy or relieved. That she's home, I mean.'

'It's nothing, Heather. Well, it's a bit of a worry, isn't it?'

'Does it disappoint you that she didn't tough it out? Did you want her to so badly?'

'Oh for God's sake, of course I didn't. It's not about me. It's just... well, if your child comes home early, it's kind of a portent, don't you think? For how they'll cope in the future?'

'Oh, I wouldn't say that, especially under the circumstances. It wasn't exactly her fault.'

'No, of course it wasn't. No one said it was. I certainly wasn't implying...'

'Lots of kids come back early from gap year. They're still young. They move on to other things.'

Other kids. Other kids come back and it's not a big deal. They move on to other things and it's not a big deal at all. Other parents don't see it as a portent when their children come home.

Heather was looking at her expectantly. 'I asked if you were hungry. You've just wolfed down four crunchies.'

'Sorry. I'll replace them.'

'Oh for goodness sake. It's just not like you. I want to understand why it makes you so concerned. I know you mentioned that she had a difficult adolescence...'

'Mandy has a genetic condition, Heather.'

Heather placed her cup down without breaking eye contact. Old trees shushed outside her window. A grey loerie whooped.

'You've never mentioned that before.'

'Well, it's not like we've been seeing each other very long. And mostly I hardly think of it. It's very manageable.'

'What kind of condition? How does it manifest?'

'Oh nothing drastic. Learning difficulties mainly. Nothing a million other kids don't also have.'

'And how does that make you feel?'

She shrugged. The loerie whooped again. If she sat up very straight, she could just see its crest bobbing. In her peripheral vision, Heather crossed her legs at the ankles. Waiting.

She shrugged again. 'It's not a big deal. I mean, she was coping so well. She'd left home, got a job... She was getting on with her life.'

'Do you acknowledge that enough? You should still feel proud of that, shouldn't you? Rather than using her early return as a stick to beat yourself. You are human. You can only do so much.'

Her limbs felt jerky, as though they longed to be moving. She knew all this. She had dealt with it a million years ago. It was ancient history. How did she allow herself to be drawn back into it now?

'You don't blame yourself for her learning difficulties, do you? It's just that I remember you telling me you and Mike ended up blaming each other.'

'Of course not. That would be irrational. I'm not one of your ignorant patients who sees it as a punishment from God.' She snatched at one of Heather's tissues and blew her nose. 'Hay fever, sorry.'

Heather nodded. 'So there's nothing you'd like to . . .'

'Jesus, Heather. I'm sorry I mentioned it. You act like you want it to be a problem.'

The other thing that worried her, of course, was Wolfie. But she wasn't sure how to voice that without sounding like everyone else in Nagelaten. When he wasn't delivering coal, Wolfie was only ever to be seen in the shadows, flitting down deserted side streets to his lair.

When she'd left for Jo'burg, though, he'd been standing right out in the open, diagonally across from her house at George's place. He had seemed to be waiting for something, tracing a pattern in the dust with his toe. She wondered if George knew he was there. Or why.

She had bothered herself half to death about leaving Mandy, without having it compounded. Please God, let Mandy be settled on the back stoep with her sketchpad, as she'd suggested.

She had no idea how long she'd been silent. Heather was still watching her. She glanced at the clock. Since he was on her mind, she told Heather about Wolfie; his provenance, not her concerns. The story seemed genuinely to upset her.

'That poor child. Only twelve and saddled . . .'

'With babies. I know.'

'I meant with that shame. And it wasn't even her shame to bear.'

'I know, but isn't that slightly easier than knowing it is? Although I suppose she may not have known that.'

'Is that your experience, Odette? You bear a shame that you feel is deserved?'

'It was an observation, Heather. Not anecdotal. I was being philosophical.'

'It's not how people respond to Mandy's condition, is it? You don't feel some shame – even if, as you say, it's irrational. It wouldn't be unusual.'

'Of course not. Jesus, it's not the dark ages.'

She couldn't hear the loerie any more. Outside the narrow window, a Yesterday Today and Tomorrow wafted the scent of sunshine through the bars.

She felt a sudden yearning nostalgia...for something...she couldn't place it. More a consciousness than a memory. A desire to escape some dark room. Was it school, home? On the other side of the window lay childhood. But it was the childhood of stories, where birds laughed in the trees and sunshine smelt like honey on the skin. Not far. Just outside.

'You haven't told me how you and Mandy are rubbing along. How does it feel to have her home?'

'Come on, how do you think? She's my child.'

'My shrink's intuition tells me you didn't answer my question.'

'Doesn't deserve an answer. What kind of mother would I be if I wasn't happy to have her home?'

'I don't know, Odette. You tell me.'

All the robots were out on the way to pick up the week's coffee beans. Students streamed from campus. In her day, only a few had jolted around in jalopies. Now brash red Tatas and shiny 4 x 4s crammed the intersection, with licence plates reading: 'Dadluvsme' or 'Lindis landi'.

She stopped for a coffee and a ciabatta before loading the beans. Surely she would feel less shaky if she ate something. It must be her blood sugar. By the time she had negotiated the obligatory discussion of grind and blends and battled her way back through the traffic, she was the last to arrive at Venezia.

It had all been so exciting, this coffee business. Now, collecting the beans felt like another burden. The whole venture didn't seem quite real, as though she were playing shop. Her new life was receding as her old life hounded her like one of those Pacman creatures.

Palesa was whispering something. She leant closer to hear. 'I said, fifty bucks on Lex never leaving his wife for Margie.'

Odette smiled, relieved to be drawn out of her own head. 'You only ever bet on a sure thing, don't you. But happily, I'm not afraid of an outside chance.'

'You romantic fool, you.'

At that moment, her chances didn't seem great. Margie looked near to tears. Lex was beside himself. Apparently someone (read Margie) had forgotten to bring biscuits. After all these years as Lex's local, Venezia still never stocked the kind he liked. Margie glanced over at the owner, but he seemed intent upon a hissed dispute with his daughter over some loserbilly who schnarfed in the loo. If she were young, with less on her mind, she would take notes. It made for great dialogue.

'Oh dear, won't someone run down to the Spar?' Margie trailed off. Palesa stared her down. Margie's gaze rested briefly on Chevonne, whose eyes were on the pen she was chucking in the air. Palesa shot Margie an avid glance that said: Oh do try. Go on, I dare you.

'She's chickening,' Palesa muttered. With a sigh, Margie awkwardly shifted past Lex, who was rocking on his chair.

'Oh,' said Chevonne, suddenly aware of Margie moving to the door. Odette and Palesa both stared. Surely, she wasn't going to offer... 'Get me a pack of Stimorol while you're there, Margie?'

Palesa choked on her cappuccino. Chevonne leaned back in her chair and muttered, to no one in particular: 'She really shouldn't wear those pants. Someone should tell her she's a pear.'

It didn't end up being their best session ever. Once the mayor's wife gets over her attempts to pray the gay out of her son, she tries her best to accept him. That opens the way for all kinds of comic possibilities: mother gets ghastly makeover from son's new date; grandmother (whom everyone believes has no idea) asks when he'll find a nice Afrikaans boy to bring home.

The town has won its initial battle to host the post-World Cup charity event. The small-time baddie has been caught, salting away the funding for non-existent consultants. This opens the way for the big-time baddies to enter play. All pretty straightforward. It was Odette's storyline, as usual, that elicited the most comment.

'So we're actually going to have this baby? Like born and on set and all?'

'I thought you wanted drama, Lex? Can you imagine what it's like for Rochelle to have the baby home?'

'Talk us through it then,' said Lex. 'I'm not sure I get all this emotional stuff.' Palesa sniggered.

'Look, Rochelle fears the future, of course, which is where the story conflict lies. And the suspense. But we can still kill him off. Down's babies can have complications.'

'Complications are what we like,' said Lex. 'Go on then. At least I can tell them it'll probably die soon.'

'I just don't get this other stuff, though,' said Chevonne. 'How can any normal person feel angry at a newborn? It's hardly the baby's fault it can't suck harder.'

And then everyone was talking at once. Well, they could just get on with it. She couldn't get a word in, even if she tried. Poor Rochelle, starting from scratch with that tiny baby. She might fear it, but she could have no real conception of how relentless it would be, nor how it would define the rest of her life. Other people might bemoan their empty nests, but deep down they were grateful. Children grew up and moved on. It was the natural order of things.

'Quiet!' yelled Lex.

'You're an idiot Chevonne,' hissed Palesa, who could never resist the last word. 'Any fool can see it's not really the baby she's angry at. Ever heard of displacement?'

Chevonne made a face at her. Lex made a stop sign with his hand. 'Quiet. Margie, what were you saying about adoption?'

Odette felt an ancient rage stirring and for once she was in no doubt of its origin. She'd written such fine, understated storylines. And now, these dolts, these emotional retards ... all they wanted was stereotype. They were going to dispute Rochelle's renewed fight to have him adopted. She wasn't sure she could bear it.

'Odette? What the fuck's the matter with her? Odette.' Lex's voice finally got through to her.

Margie had her perplexed look on. Fool. 'My dear, just motivate this for me. Rochelle's not a desperate teenager. She's not a bad person. What kind of mother wouldn't want to keep her child once she's held him?'

She wondered if she could be bothered to answer. She took a very deep breath. 'A good mother.'

Her throat constricted. They were all staring at her. She gulped at ice-cold coffee. 'A good fucking mother would give her child to someone who might do a better job.'

If Sylvia were alive, she would probably invite her to stay.

The idea sprang into her head and she realised how much she still missed the old battle-axe. It was probably the thought of arriving home in the dark. Little chance Mandy would have given supper a moment's consideration.

Once Sylvia and she had grown used to each other, they had rubbed along pretty well. She still said: 'Well our side of the family ...' and 'Michael was very quick ...' Odette just didn't take it to heart any more.

Odette wasn't what Sylvia would have chosen for her son, but she'd say this for her, she made the best of it. In those few years before she died, Odette came to rely on her more than she liked to admit.

Close on lunchtime, she would inevitably find herself still in pyjamas. Mandy was a toddler by then – she no longer had the excuse of a newborn. Most of her friends had fallen away, except Melissa, of course, but she was doing her work experience overseas, as they had once planned to do together, in another lifetime.

Mandy couldn't be left for an instant. If Odette went to the loo, she would tug drawers from their sockets, drop the forks in the dustbin, fill the dishwasher with sand from the sandpit. And there, like an angel of mercy, would be Sylvia, standing at the door with a quiche for lunch.

Sylvia got pretty good at pinning Mandy to her lap and spooning her lunch in. Perhaps too good. Mandy never lost that need for instant gratification. But the main thing was, Sylvia was calm, never shaking and fearful.

What had Odette been so frightened of? Her own child? It had seemed so real at the time, yet hard to reconstruct now. She remembered how desperate she'd been for Sylvia to stay. How terrified she was to be left alone with Mandy. She feared . . . those feelings, of course. It was the 3 a.m. feelings she dreaded. She feared what she might do, should she grow desperate enough.

Her cell rang as she was about to pass. Ah well, perhaps it was a good thing. Visibility wasn't great and the tar had collapsed into cavernous valleys from too many heavy tyres.

'Ja hello. Odette?

'Captain Fitz? Is that you? Oh please don't tell me . . .'

'No, no, nothing bad. I just wanted to tell you we've come to an agreement that your neighbours will do community service.'

'For burglary?'

'Hell, I know. Their own neighbour. It's terrible. But I think they've learnt their lesson and it's better in the long run not to put them in with hardened criminals.'

'Aren't they . . . isn't Willie a hardened criminal? He's no baby.'

'Yes, but the jail . . .'

They spoke for another couple of moments while he danced about the words he could no longer say. Green? No, not that one. Red? The jails were too red for them? She took pity on him eventually and cut him off. What did it matter anyway?

The streetlights in De La Rey were off again – probably to save electricity. No one seemed bothered, as long as they stayed on during the World Cup. (What would the world think of us?) It did make it hard to negotiate the potholes though.

She was parking when she became aware of a shadow. Just a thickened area of darkness, where night had congealed in the corner of the stoep. Her scalp pricked. Oh God, Mandy. She had left her alone in this strange town.

The figure slipped from the stoep and loped off. Wolfie. She thought of Adriaan's wife and his obsession for her. She would kill him. Never mind how the town had treated him, she would rip him limb from limb.

# Chapter 24

'MANDY! WHERE ARE YOU? Are you okay?'

'Why wouldn't I be?' She was sprawled on the couch where Odette had left her that morning.

'There was a man . . . did he . . . did you see him?'

'You mean Wolfie?'

Odette visualised her heart. She pictured herself smoothing it back down where it belonged. 'You didn't let him in, did you?'

She concentrated on her breath; forced herself to sit. A wine glass stood on the floor beside her. No . . . two. Two wine glasses. Both beside the couch.

'Why wouldn't I?'

A bottle stood on the mantelpiece. Fetching another glass gave her legitimate reason to pace, at least to the kitchen and back. She poured the glass she'd been so looking forward to. It worried her sick when Mandy drank. Luckily, she had never seemed to like the taste much. But she was suggestible and he . . . Of course, he would be a drinker.

'What did he want?' The wine burned her throat, not unpleasantly.

'I invited him.'

'What would possess you to ask a stranger into our home?'

'He's not a stranger. I met him when I went for a walk. Do you know there's a whole lot of children in that little house down below? I thought maybe I could help them.'

'I don't think the squatters will require baby-sitting. And never mind them for now. This man, he's not your friend. You've only just met him.'

'He is my friend. What would you know? He was nice to me.'

'Of course he was nice to you, Mandy. He wants...oh, for God's sake.' Mike would never forgive her. Not in the midst of all they had to deal with.

'You said I should get some exercise.'

'But Mandy, he's...I'm sure you can't have much in common. I don't think he's very bright.'

'Well, most people think I'm stupid when they meet me, so we have that in common.'

'Yes, but you're not. It's just ignorant people who don't understand.'

'Well I'm weird anyway. And so is he. You're always telling me to be sociable and make friends. And when I do, you moan at me.'

'Yes, but not...Listen Mandy, you don't know about his family.'

'If you mean about his father, it's not exactly his fault, is it? Children can't help what their parents do before they're even born.'

Pain irradiated her chest as though her heart might literally break. She pressed at it with a hand till it subsided. 'No, it's not,' she said, more quietly. 'It's not his fault. We should be nice to him. But that doesn't mean...'

Odette finished the glass far too quickly. Now she would have to face the remains of this ghastly evening with none. Mandy reached over to the coffee table and drew her sketchbook onto her knees, as though the matter were closed. But then she added: 'Actually, he's not as stupid as you think.'

Mandy began flipping through her book. Odette glimpsed the river, but she had transformed a few plastic bags, left by the last rains, into evil-looking fruit trailing from riverine branches.

She paused over a minuscule figure menaced by the oversized buildings of De La Rey Street. Wolfie. He was easy enough to recognise. Mandy had caught his lupine gait, weaving between a monstrous church and bank which appeared to be closing in on him.

Mandy flipped. Wolfie again, this time close up, with a gaping wound in his chest, showing a perfectly detailed heart and lungs. Mandy paused, glancing at them critically. Was it insolence? Defiance? No, of course not. It just wouldn't occur to her. Mandy had no deviousness. It wasn't part of her being.

'And actually,' she said, as though there had been no pause, 'I wasn't thinking about baby-sitting. I thought I could teach them. I've learned lots of children's activities now; ones that are good for development. I decided that's what I'd like to do. I'd like to be a nursery school teacher.'

Odette nodded, unable to speak. There had still been no news. There was nothing to be done. Nothing at all but submit to this thing hanging over their heads. And for just as long as it felt like hanging there, like a dead cat nailed to the door frame.

'By the way Trudie. I've been wanting to thank you.'

'Ag no man, we always knew I'd do most of the serving. I'm here anyway for the shop.'

'No, I mean...'

'I've got Lindiwe for the dishes. It's nice if you pop in when you can. Gives me a chance to practise. And if it gets really busy, we'll take turns like we agreed.'

Odette was forced to spell it out. 'No, I meant: Thank you for not telling people. About what Mandy told you.'

Trudie paused. Her hand shook slightly, smudging the heart she was fashioning in the foam. 'O *magtig*. Now, we'll just have to drink another couple.'

'Terrible hardship. I mean it, Trudie. It's not easy to keep something secret in a small town.'

'No man, it's nothing. I know with my brother... he sometimes used to blurt out stuff.' She looked up. 'Not that... I know she's not the same as Hendrik, but I could see there was something...'

Trudie put the cup down and reached a damp hand to cover hers. Odette allowed it to remain there as Trudie continued. 'The child needs a new chance. I would've wanted that for Hendrik. Will she be okay though? Hendrik's heart...'

Odette swallowed. She noticed their hands were clasped. She gave Trudie's a squeeze and gently withdrew hers. 'Yes, no her health is fine and you're right. She's not like Hendrik. She'll be completely fine, as long as they just leave her be.'

'I'm sure it wasn't her fault, or they wouldn't have let her come home.'

Odette changed the subject. Lucky Bean was empty, but Trudie assured her there had been a modest rush for their muffin breakfast. It was a novelty in Nagelaten, having breakfast out. 'Even Marta came with poor old Gerrie.'

'Marta spent actual money here?'

'Counted it all out in coppers.' Trudie nodded. 'She brought it in an old sock.'

'You're not serious.'

They laughed until Trudie covered her face and crossed her legs. That set them off again. Odette scrabbled for a tissue.

'The old witch. I'm sure she must've pressed you a bit too. About Mandy, I mean. I saw her watching.'

'I put her off, don't worry. Only thing...' Trudie began steaming the milk again.

Odette waited, but Trudie side-tracked herself: 'Nice to *kuier* a bit like this, isn't it? A good old *skinner* when there's no one here.'

'Only thing, what?'

She watched Trudie pour, executing a passable fern leaf this time. 'Thing is, you never know with Marta, when she's telling the truth.'

Trudie slurped at the cup, giving herself a foam moustache before scooping the rest of the milk into a bucket. Above the noise of the steam nozzle and, without looking at her, Trudie said: 'Marta said you and Adriaan...you know...that he's been staying over.'

Odette was completely taken aback. She felt like a schoolgirl caught snogging at her matric dance. 'Trudie, it's not serious or anything.'

Then she was angry at herself for being defensive, as though she were ashamed of him. Actually, she was more stunned than hurt. For a moment there, she had let herself believe that she and Trudie...

'But Trudie, we're both free. There's no reason we shouldn't see each other.'

Trudie lifted her forearm to wipe at her upper lip. 'You've just come from the city. You don't even know what we're like yet. You hardly know him.'

'Oh for God's sake, I know I'm not exactly one of you, but I don't see why that matters so much.'

'It's not that. I'm thinking of you. Surely you don't want to be tied down? Just give yourself time.'

'I am giving myself time. We're just friends, okay?'

Trudie smudged her fern leaf and clattered the jug to the counter. '*O genade.*'

Odette walked home briskly. It did no good to agonise. Perhaps she should just accept it at face value. Trudie had known Adriaan since childhood. It was natural she would hate to see him hurt, particularly after all he'd been through. It was stupid to take it to heart.

She was just angry with herself. It made her uncomfortable to allow anyone too close. Why the hell had she allowed it with Trudie, especially when they had so little in common? In future she would just trust her instincts.

She speeded up, seeing George and his dogs on the pavement, surveying an old kombi that listed tiredly to one side. He waved, while the dogs made a dissonant dart in her direction. George shooed them under his bakkie with a good-natured '*Voetsêk*', then he grinned, closing one eye against the light.

'It's what I like to see. Good watch-dogs.'

'Yes, I was surprised they didn't make more fuss the other day.

I saw Wolfie hanging round outside here. Did you see him? That weird-looking guy who lives down by the coalyard?'

'I told the boy he could do a bit of work for me when I'm busy.'

'Is he capable?'

'He's quite handy with the motors. Doesn't argue. No complaints. Doesn't ask for much either. Why? He doesn't bother you, does he?'

'No, no, I just wondered.'

The dogs crept out from under the bakkie and sniffed her feet.

'And I see he's made a friend.' George's chin quivered as he gestured behind her. She turned. Mandy was returning from the shops, lugging a bag in either hand. 'Your daughter, right?'

'Mandy, yes. I can't understand how they met, though. He never seems to talk to anyone.'

'I called her over to greet. Saw her in the street and wondered who she was. She made friends with my dogs and that's when they started talking.'

'I'm not really that happy...'

'You're a good person. I thought that the first time we greeted. Not many whites would have him in their home. Or blacks for that matter. Not in this town.'

It was time to start on supper, but her storyline was due and she was finding it hard to concentrate. Somewhere out in the darkness, a dog howled.

Rochelle's mother is telling her to grieve. This makes Reno angry, but her ma tells him in no uncertain terms that he hasn't told his wife yet, so he has no say in the matter.

He retaliates by saying that Rochelle chose to call off the abortion. She chose to let the child live so she has no right to grieve.

The dog howled. She had no hope of locating him in the dark, but tomorrow she might see if she could find him. She wished

Melissa was still here ... but in the end it was her problem. She had created it. She should deal with it.

She couldn't bring herself to write it all down in an email. It made it so permanent. So indelible. She couldn't even face her Morning Journal right now. Her hand kept drawing her back to things that were dead and buried and surely it couldn't be healthy to exhume them.

She lifted her cell, then replaced it. If there'd been more to tell, surely Mike would have phoned. He was becoming increasingly curt. 'No news,' he'd said that morning. She had phoned just as she emerged from the shower – when she knew he'd be awake, but not yet in the traffic.

'But isn't it possible – what with the Sally Clark debacle – surely it's possible she can still get out from under this thing? Surely they don't want to make idiots of themselves again?'

She had heard the wheedle in her tone and wondered who she thought she was pleading with. What did she think Mike could do? Not even his name was any use to them in this. It must be strange to feel so powerless.

'I think you should resign yourself to the fact that she won't ever be completely free of it.' Mike didn't plead. He grew more abrupt each time she phoned, as though this were entirely her doing.

'But if they don't have enough to charge her?'

'Don't bank on it. They've good policing over there. And even if they don't find enough evidence, it'll still hang over her. People will always know what she did.'

Rochelle ... In a minute, she would yell for Mandy to start the vegetables. Or perhaps it was better just to leave her be until she finished writing. She never quite knew what to do for the best.

Rochelle's ma is the wise one. Of course you can mourn for someone who's still alive, she says. You're not mourning the actual child. You're grieving for what you imagined he would be. You're grieving for the imagined child.

The dog's disembodied wail reverberated through the silent town, setting off all the yappers and barkers. Neither Rochelle nor her ma knew it, of course, but they were lucky. Rochelle could allow herself to grieve. Other people would understand; sympathise even.

If his condition were less obvious it would seem an indulgence. No one would make allowances, least of all herself. She'd be too busy making sure he was normal; bullying him into it. If the possibility existed, that is.

'Can I see?' Adriaan reached for Mandy's sketchbook. Odette stiffened. He opened to a self-portrait. Mandy had exaggerated her small eyes till they were no more than pinpricks in her face.

Adriaan had turned up with take-away burgers just as they were starting on the veggies. She was grateful. She was. It was just tiredness, that's all. She wanted to relax, not stand between Mandy and the world, her cosmic mediator. Oh, to hell with it, she might as well get used to it again.

'Well, this is interesting.'

'She's good, isn't she? Quite dark at times.' Odette gave a little laugh, glancing over at Mandy, who was curled on the couch, a blanket tucked over her teddy bear pyjamas.

The evenings were still chilly and, to tell the truth, she was relieved not to make a drama of sending her for a dressing gown. Mandy didn't always notice things like that.

When he reached the drawings of Wolfie, he paused and looked up. 'Do you think this is wise?'

Odette shrugged, framing the words, working out how much to say with Mandy still in the room. Adriaan must have thought she chose not to answer.

'Just because you don't approve of the way we've treated the man, must you make a project of him? With your own bloody daughter?'

He had spoken softly, but she'd never heard him swear before. And suddenly she was furious. What was she, a miracle worker?

People were always expecting her to achieve such wonders. Make Mandy do this. Not let her do that.

'As you know, Adriaan,' her tongue felt thick and slow, yet she'd had no more than the glass he'd poured when he arrived, 'I'm not constantly home. And as I shouldn't have to point out, Mandy is an adult.'

'Yes, but clearly she's . . .'

'That's enough. Not another word. Mandy, I'd be grateful if you'd pick up the plates and take them to the kitchen.'

'Why do I have to?'

'Never mind the plates. Please just go to your room, just for a while, so I can have a little privacy with Adriaan.'

'I'm not a baby. You don't have to get rid of me.'

They'd been careful not to raise their voices, so she couldn't expect Mandy to take the hint. Strained expressions went right over her head. They could have spent dinner glaring at each other and she would have asked Adriaan for the salt. Naturally, it would confirm all his preconceptions.

'Mandy.' She took a breath. 'It's not about you and I'm not trying to get rid of you. Adriaan and I just have something to deal with quickly.'

Mandy didn't move. Odette strode across the room and plucked the blanket off her, largely to avoid ripping her head off. And of course . . . She should have noticed that Mandy was twirling her hair with the hand she could see. She felt an overwhelming urge to burst into hysterical laughter.

Perhaps that's what Adriaan reacted to, she didn't know. He stood abruptly, grabbed Odette's wrist and pulled her after him into the kitchen. She just laughed; couldn't stop herself.

'Stop it.'

The more she laughed, the more rigid he became. And the more she laughed. She couldn't take his outrage seriously. He was always telling her he wasn't a Neanderthal. But perhaps his was the normal reaction. Perhaps she was just habituated to weirdness. That just made her laugh all the more.

'Stop it. Stop laughing. It's not funny.'

'Okay,' she said. 'Okay sorry, I will now. Really I will.'

She switched on the coffee machine. They might as well have some while they were about it. 'It's better to laugh than cry isn't it?'

'Why the hell didn't you stop her?'

Then she did stop laughing. 'What did you expect me to do?'

'I'm a guest in your house. And you let her disrespect . . .'

'Jeez Adriaan. It isn't all about you. She hasn't done that since she was a tiny thing. Clearly it's because she's all stressed out.'

'You should have stopped her. Sex isn't just . . .'

'Isn't just what?' The conversation was making her uncomfortable.

'No coffee for me. Sex isn't just about urges and you don't have to look at me in that superior way.'

'I'm not. I just don't understand what you're getting at.'

'How can you let her . . . in public. No wonder . . .'

'It was me who pulled the blanket off, remember? So don't start with "No wonder". What did Marta tell you, anyway? She knows nothing. Absolutely nothing. The child had a few learning difficulties, that's all. No more than millions of other perfectly normal . . .'

Odette continued adding milk, aware that it wasn't quite hot enough. He'd fucking well drink it, if she had to pour it down his throat.

'Is that how you see sex?' he asked.

She slammed a mug down, sloshing most of the coffee over the counter, but still he went on: 'An itch to be scratched? Animal sensation, without consequence? To anyone? Without caring about the damage caused . . .'

She stared at him. She was very good at nuance. This wasn't about her and Mandy at all. Her anger drained. Just soaked away, like a rain shower in drought.

She still couldn't deal with him though. Another woman might reach up and ask how he'd been hurt. But she had only so much sympathy to go around.

'Maybe you should just leave.'

Odette had once harboured the fantasy that she would find a man who could cope with them, Mandy and her. And for a split second there, she had believed that she had.

She had imagined Patrick taking her part, but not to the point that it raised her protective ire. He would get Mandy, but not enough to permit her total liberty with Odette's feelings. He wouldn't blame Odette. Or Mandy.

She had seen them, in her mind's eye, shaking their heads, laughing ruefully at things other people could never understand. Who had she been kidding? At least she'd realised before he had.

Oh well. Another one bites the dust. Perhaps it was for the best.

# Chapter 25

SHE THOUGHT SHE KNEW all the dogs in the neighbourhood. It couldn't be old Boer. He never howled. It wasn't those small ratdogs either. Too full-throated.

Eventually, she found him at the house behind the shebeen. Poor Howling Dog. He'd wrapped his chain around the stake he'd been fastened to. His head was tangled and a frantic paw had tipped his water bowl. He was fierce with fear and despair, but not vicious. When he was untangled, he nuzzled his nose into her belly. She refilled his water from the garden tap. It was a nice feeling, being able to make him feel better.

Her detour made her late to open Lucky Bean. Captain Fitz and his sidekick were already waiting for their coffees. 'Sorry I'm a bit late. Sit a minute while I make them?'

'No worries.' He folded himself into a neat stack of muscle. Sidekick stood by the door, arms folded, as though he weren't really there at all. 'Coffee, Laaitie?'

Laaitie nodded unhappily, but kept his eyes fixed heavenward. Imagine what Laaitie's drinking buddies would say if they saw him in this hang-out of moffies and women. He'd be dead in this town.

'I wanted to tell you, Willie and the old man will be dropped by the prison van this afternoon. If they give you any trouble...' Mercifully, the grinder muffled his words.

'Take-away or drink it here?'

'I think we better get out and catch some crooks, hey Laaitie?' Laaitie nodded, lips pursed. 'They'll be starting their community service next week.'

She nodded. What the hell. 'Cake or muffin to go?' He shook his head, patting his belly with a rueful tug of the mouth. 'I wanted to ask you something else though, Captain, just before you go: is there an SPCA in town?'

'Nearest in Standerton. You can report animal stuff to the police though. And isn't it lucky that you has the police right here in your shop.'

She laughed. He was all muscle and twinkle. Not much good it did her, though. 'Oh no. I thought you wanted to complain about the donkeys. Now that's a problem, those donkey carts. Kept as a guard dog, I suppose. Can't do much about that. Ja, three sugars. *Dankie.* Don't tell the other Captain.'

'Don't tell the other Captain what?' Trudie entered in a flurry of floral. Incongruously, she dropped her head and raised her eyes as she addressed him.

'Trudie, it's your morning off. Go enjoy yourself.'

'No man, I just saw the van as I was passing. Thought it might be the Captain. Can't I pop in for a chat?' And with her girlish giggle: 'Thought I'd be your customer today.'

'Must be off in a minute,' Fitz said. 'I was just telling your friend here she shouldn't get too sentimental. She can't save all the dogs in town.'

'Oh I didn't even think ... but of course you should have a dog. It would be protection too.'

'No, it wasn't ... I can't. I go back and forth too much.'

'*Nonsens,*' said the Captain, opening the lid and blowing gingerly at his coffee. 'Adriaan tells me his Jack Russell's about to have pups.'

Odette started to shake her head, but Trudie was gazing at him with an expression she couldn't read. 'Do you think that's a good idea?'

'A dog, Trudie. What's wrong with getting a dog? Ag, I don't have time for these woman things. Morning ladies.'

After he left, they chose millionaire's shortbreads and mini milk tarts from the home-industry to display in Lucky Bean: for this market, the sweeter the better.

'Koeksisters, do you think?' Trudie asked.

'Why not. Everyone likes them. What did you mean, by the way?'

'About the koeksisters?'

'No, about not getting a dog from Adriaan. Not that it matters, anyway. It's not very likely now.'

'Rather use a paper doilie. They leak everywhere. And cover them.'

'I was going to. Flies are terrible today.'

'Mm, it's the cows. I just...I don't know, really. Why do you say it doesn't matter?'

'I don't think Adriaan and I will be seeing each other any more.'

Trudie said nothing. Not a word. No matter how she worried about him and disapproved of their friendship, Odette would have thought that at least she could have spared a quick sorry for a friend.

Rochelle is having a stand-up fight with the social worker. The woman is self-righteous. She explains that it'll be very hard to place baby Ricky in a loving home, especially since he has a mother who is perfectly placed to keep him. She tells Rochelle that Down's babies bring a lot of joy.

They wrangle and the social worker is insulting. Is Rochelle an unnatural mother? Does she feel nothing for this child? Is she ashamed of him?

In the next scene, Reno comes over. He's in a foul mood, struggling with whether to tell his wife or not. If Rochelle keeps the baby, his wife is bound to find out. It's a small town. They talk at cross purposes. He's maundering on about Corinne. Rochelle is obsessing about what the social worker said to her.

'She thinks I don't love Ricky.'

'Sooner or later, someone will tell her, Rochelle.'

'But if Ricky's with someone else; if he's somewhere else . . .'

'Well maybe that would be for the best.'

'If he's in another place, with other people, I can still see him in my mind's eye.'

'That's what I've been saying, haven't I?'

'I'll see him learning to play. I'll imagine him having a life. And in my heart it'll be the life he should have. The life he deserves.'

She gave herself a break at 11 a.m. If she bought Howling Dog a blanket, she might come upon Mandy perambulating the town. That's what she hoped Mandy was doing anyway. Odette hadn't seen her since her second coffee.

Wolfie was a ghost, always in her peripheral vision yet never really there. She saw signs of him everywhere: in a swiftly washed cup, a glass forgotten alongside the couch, a sketch rapidly flipped past.

She caught sight of Mandy outside the post office, but then the girl turned and Odette saw that she was nothing like her. She had an open face that broke easily into a smile as she was joined by a friend.

Pep Store was packed. She was jostled by mothers with babies on their backs and young girls trying on sunglasses. Winter camphor creams were being shifted to higher shelves, making way for summer sunscreens, but she found a blanket easily enough. Winter was still tardy at night and shacks were cold.

When she took it to him, Howling Dog nuzzled her middle, grateful for the attention. She rubbed his ears, hating to leave him, confined to his half-life. Even the squatter dogs were better off. They weren't overfed, but at least they were free.

She tried not to think of him on the way home. At least he would be warmer, and perhaps she might even get some sleep. She hurried when she saw George slam the door of his bakkie, open the flap for his dogs, and head into his workshop.

'George? Is Wolf... Have you perhaps seen Mandy? I can't find her.'

He lifted a pan of old engine oil and joined her on the pavement. Positioning his feet further apart, he bent to place it carefully alongside him. How did you dispose of that gloop? She'd have to ask him.

'Your girl?' He stretched an arm out, fingers up. 'Went for a walk with the boy. Not far, I don't think. Ja, there they come now. I was finished with him for the day.'

As she glanced towards the commonage, Wolfie detached himself from Mandy's side and melted up the side street that led to his house. Diagonally across from them, Willie and the old man closed their gate and set off up the street. Willie glanced behind him and, seeing Mandy, nudged Fanie. They stopped as if to wait for her.

'On their way to the churchyard,' said George, gesturing with his chin. 'Community service.'

'I wish they'd just been kept in jail.'

'It makes a good joke though: two white garden boys.'

'Glad to be the indirect cause of so much enjoyment. What do they want with Mandy now?' They were in plain sight. She didn't want to rush over like a crazy person, but still.

As Mandy reached them, each adopted an absurdly subservient pose. Mandy reached into her pocket for her purse.

'Mandy, no.' She seemed not to hear. Counting out a couple of coins, she placed them carefully in each of their palms. They backed away, bobbing their thanks.

The old crooks. They knew they were being watched. As they set off again, Willie glanced back, lifting his head at them. Was it triumph? Defiance? Or just a greeting? Probably all three.

George was quivering with laughter, his stomach advancing on his shirt buttons. He reached for a hankie to wipe his damp forehead, still trying to control his amusement in the face of Odette's patent lack of humour. 'Hey, hey, hey,' he said at last. 'She gave me money too, you know.'

'What? When?'

'First day we greeted. I went up to her, so maybe she thought I was going to ask for money.' When Odette still looked uncomprehending, he added: 'Because I'm black.'

'Oh my God, I'm so very sorry, George. She doesn't always get...'

Lifting the pan of engine oil in one quick movement, he emptied it into the storm water ditch. The sludge began its long slide to the commonage, and from there to the river. Well, that answered her question. She wondered if she should say something...But no, of course she couldn't. Particularly now. He raised his head again with a grin.

'No, no, really. I didn't give it back because I didn't want to hurt her feelings. It was kind of her. She's a good girl. You should be proud.'

Mandy was in the bathroom when Odette followed her back into the house. Her sketchbook lay on the kitchen counter. Feeling like a sneak, Odette paged rapidly past those she'd already seen.

She came to Wolfie on the riverbank, a vicious-looking hadeda at his left shoulder. He looked dishevelled but, thank the Lord, fully clothed. Closing it quietly, she noticed a smaller book beneath. It appeared to be an earlier workbook. There were a few recognisably English scenes, a bus, a park, the elder of her charges...

Oh dear God. She felt the hair pricking at her forehead. Thank God, oh thank the Lord they hadn't found this when they searched her room. The last sketch in the book showed Mandy and the little girl, side by side. Both their eyes were on the baby, the inert baby, whom Mandy was placing in a pram.

There was something about the baby's attitude . . . no, it wasn't the baby. The baby looked peaceful. It could easily be asleep. It was the way Mandy held her away from her body, as though in distaste.

It couldn't be, surely. It could be any time she'd put the sleeping baby down while the child looked on. One of Mandy's hands was beneath her back, the other under her neck, as though she were offering her to someone on a platter.

Up to now it had all been about themselves: how it affected Mandy and her life; Odette and hers. Those nice English children had barely entered her consciousness, but now the sight of them brought the bile to her throat.

She had sent them a child not yet ripe or properly formed. And why? Because Mandy had wanted to go? Yes of course, and because Odette hadn't wanted to tell her she might not cope. But also – there was no way she could escape this – because she had so badly wanted her to go.

She had wanted a break, that's all. She had wanted her life back. And she had wanted to picture her there: laughing with friends, taking the kids to the park, making a life for herself in the real world.

That baby's inert body lay on her own hands as much as Mandy's.

'What are you doing?' Mandy emerged, shaking damp hands. Odette looked up slowly, feeling the flesh drawing itself back from her mouth. Mandy watched her for a moment in silence, then spoke.

'That's mine. It's my private book. You shouldn't be looking at it.'

# Chapter 26

IT HAD BEEN OVERCAST in Nagelaten, but it was pissing down in Jo'burg. Odette collected the coffee beans and still somehow managed to be early. Heather was busy with another client so she waited on the stoep, splashes of water making her feet damp.

When she was growing up, summer had followed an invariable pattern: hot day, spectacular storm between four and five, followed by a warm, still evening. How effectively they had messed up the environment in just twenty years or so. Bad choices. Just like her life: twenty years ago, she'd also been warm and sunny, with stormy patches.

'Weather for ducks, hey?' Heather opened the security gate, buzzing her other client through a side door. Odette laid out the millionaire's shortbreads, slightly gooey from the drive. Heather chose one, but Odette could see it was to be polite. Then she settled herself fastidiously and looked expectant. Sometimes Odette could murder her for that expectant look.

She was well-prepared though, and with a story that couldn't make anyone think badly of her. Satisfyingly, Heather tutted and frowned through a good few moments of Howling Dog. Everyone likes a mistreated animal story.

'Why is it you feel so responsible for Howling Dog?'

'Responsible? Jesus, Heather. Wouldn't anyone?'

'We're not talking about anyone. You chose to open our session with the confinement of this poor dog and your need to save him.'

'So much for making conversation. I thought you were supposed to be my friend.'

'No, Odette. I'm your psychologist. Friends are the things you're making in your new town. Aren't you?'

Odette got up to pour more tea. She clattered Heather's delicate china teapot, feeling childish.

'I'm tired, that's all. It's been a long week. Sometimes I wonder why I put myself through this, racing to Jo'burg to spend an hour drinking tea with you.'

'And? Do you have an answer?' Heather gave her gummy smile.

'I don't know, Heather, maybe I like you. But only when you're not being so bloody patronising. Don't push me, okay?'

Odette took her seat again. Somehow, she had managed to slosh tea into her saucer. How come Heather never so much as sullied an edge of hers? Right now she was nibbling gingerly at the corner of her millionaire's shortbread.

'Bloody hell, eat the stupid thing, can't you? Or throw it in the dustbin. Don't gnaw at it distastefully just for my sake.'

'It's how I like to eat. I savour my biscuits. How are you getting on with Mandy? Is she coping with her feelings about the baby?'

'I guess. Not that she says much. She just hangs about. Nothing for her to do there, of course. I wish she had something to keep her busy.'

'Perhaps she should look for a job. Does she know what she wants to do next year?'

'No, not really. Not yet, anyway. She has ... ideas. It's just ... We don't know what's going to happen next year.'

'Well, this move was unexpected, so it's natural she'd need time to catch her breath. Does it still worry you that she came home?'

'No. No, she'll be fine, I'm sure she will. Eventually. When ...'

'When what?'

'Nothing. When she settles down, I mean. It's just ... There was a bit of bother before she left. But I'm sure it'll soon be forgotten. It's best forgotten.'

'What kind of bother? Where, in England?'

'Ag, it was just rubbish. There was some suspicion – just a suggestion really – that it might not be a cot death. But nothing's come of it.'

'Goodness, they didn't suspect...No, but they let her come home, of course they didn't. I can see why you were so ambivalent, though. How did it...?'

'It didn't make me feel anything at all, Heather, because it was rubbish. And I didn't mention it because, to my mind, the sooner it's forgotten, the better.'

'I understand that, but it's still tough. I know you feel you have to shoulder everything, Odette, but this is the kind of thing you can share with me.'

'It's nothing though. Sometimes I think they just have to show they're investigating. It's the new witch-hunt, isn't it? Child abuse?'

'Perhaps preferable to the alternative – look at that poor boy in your town – but yes, I agree. They can be a little over-zealous. Those poor parents.' When Odette didn't respond, she added: 'How is Mandy taking it all?'

'Just like normal, it seems to me. She resents everything I say, sleeps all day, mixes with unsavoury people and doesn't help around the house.'

'Goodness, she sounds like a perfectly healthy teenager. You must be an excellent mother.'

Odette smiled, but it was an effort. She could hear the rain pattering on concrete, competing with the hollow roar of the M1. She glanced at the clock. From the corner of her eye, she watched Heather pick a non-existent crumb from her lap and smooth her skirt.

'So who saves you, Odette? When things are difficult. Who do you have to untangle your chain?'

'Are you still on about that bloody dog? I thought you'd be interested, that's all.'

'I'm just interested in who you can talk to at times like this. I know you're an only child, but you never speak about family.'

'No, and sorry to disappoint you, it's only because I don't have any.'

'Your parents...?'

'I hardly remember my father. I was crazy about my oupa though. So, yes, I do have a good model for my relationships.'

Heather smiled. 'And women? You never mention your mother.'

'My mother was an alcoholic.'

'Oh, so she's also deceased. I'm sorry.'

'Lots of people have alcoholic parents, though, so please don't go making a big deal out of it.'

'Did you get the chance to make peace with her? Do you still blame her?'

'What, for my idyllic childhood? It's hardly unique.'

'It's a hard feeling to have though.'

Odette rolled her eyes. Heather acted like she hadn't seen. Really though, it drove her mad when Heather said things like that. How were you supposed to answer?

'I dealt with it. Ticked it off and moved along.'

It made her claustrophobic to be put in this position, which was exactly why she had always made a habit of avoiding subjects like this.

'Do you blame her for your difficulties with relationships?'

'What difficulties?'

Odette got up and peered out of the window. 'You can't actually see the M1 from here, can you? Funny how much like a forest it looks from the ridge. Must be great when the jacarandas are in bloom.'

'How's it going with Adriaan? Is he someone you might confide in?'

'We broke up.'

'Oh? I thought you were just friends.'

'Friends can break up too. It's not a big deal, and probably for the best anyway. I've quite enough on my plate, with Mandy home.'

A pair of loeries was romancing in the jacaranda that shadowed Heather's window. Probably the same two she'd seen last time.

238

Their crests bobbed and nuzzled at each other. It gave her a funny feeling.

Heather waited while she took her seat again. 'Look, I can understand that you don't have space for a relationship. After all, you're still on the rebound from Patrick. But the timing . . . was it connected to Mandy coming home?'

'Not at all, I'm just a natural introvert, that's all. I don't easily form close relationships. We all have things we can't tell people, but I just happen to find that more stressful than other people.'

'Can't? What can't you tell people?'

'Nothing. Forget I said it. I don't know what I meant.'

'About you or . . . surely not Mandy? Learning difficulties are nothing to write home about these days. Even I spent a couple of years on Ritalin. It's not shameful.'

'No. For fuck's sake, no, of course it isn't.'

Her bloody tea was cold again. She should move to the coast, where no one knew her and the boiling point was higher.

She couldn't tell whether Margie had been crying, or whether she had a cold. You could never judge these things by Lex's demeanour.

'Shit, what kind of weather is this?' Palesa crashed the door of Venezia open with the wheel of her bike. She parked it against the wall and began stripping off her rain gear. 'I nearly fell in a pothole the size of the Kimberley hole. Why don't we talk about that in the soap, by the way?'

Lex was paging through his notes, studiously ignoring everyone around him. Margie was blowing her nose, already red from dabbing.

'Lex? Hey Lex? Why don't we work the state of the roads into a storyline. Maybe that'll get their arses into gear and get them fixed before the World Cup.'

Lex acted as though she hadn't spoken. He sucked on a biscuit, then brought his notes towards Margie, muttering something about 'unrealistic dialogue'.

Margie turned her head aside and snivelled, trying to find a dry patch on her sodden tissue. Not a cold then. Palesa caught Odette's eye and rubbed her hands together ostentatiously. Odette didn't have the heart to speculate.

'How's your cat, Margie?' she asked. Margie broke into sobs. Odette flipped her hands for Palesa's benefit – good call. Nothing to do with Lex.

'I'm sorry Margie. Lex? Shouldn't we maybe just get on with this? Margie's obviously not feeling great.'

Lex turned, rearing slightly, as though he had only this minute noticed that she was weeping. 'Okay. Okay then. Let's get on. Where's Chevonne?'

'Here, okay? I was here. I just went to the loo. How do you like my nails, guys?'

She held them under Margie's nose, while Margie tried vainly to turn her head away, guarding with her tissue. Odette wondered if Chevonne had gone to the same sensitivity school as Lex.

Most of the notes were for Palesa. Lex didn't find the gay story funny. Lex was the kind of guy who said: 'Oh yes, that's a joke. I knew that.'

She was aware that she owed Palesa more support, particularly since she'd blown her off for drinks again. It couldn't be helped though. She couldn't do more than she could do. Couldn't keep her eye on the page either. A couple of times she completely lost the thread...

'...don't get why she loses her friends.' Like there. Lex had moved on to Rochelle without her even being aware of it.

'Me too.' Margie was making an effort, hiccupping slightly, but determined to stand by her man. 'Surely her friends would be her greatest support.'

'My girlfriends would so be there for me,' added Chevonne, forming an unlikely alliance. 'In my culture, we stick by people.'

She turned her fingers and blew on the nails. The half moons had been painted white. It made her look ill.

'Okay,' said Palesa, lifting her palms in surrender. 'We all know you're so, like, *ubuntu*. Let's just hear what the poor white girl has to say.'

'Bad things make other people feel superior... No, that's the wrong word. More like virtuous. No one wants to believe these things are random. Random's much too scary.'

'Ah I get it,' said Palesa. 'Like, if it could happen to anyone, then it could happen to me.' It was nice of her, especially after Odette had been so little help to her. She tapped Palesa's hand with her pencil and pushed on.

'So after a while, they start to think this person must have done something to deserve it. It makes them feel better to have someone to blame so they end up feeling justified in avoiding them.'

'Oh rubbish,' Chevonne didn't look up from her nails. 'Do you really think people would be so weird about it? She'll end up with no one to talk to and she'll turn into this weird recluse.'

'Don't really care,' said Lex through a mouth full of biscuit. 'It's dramatic. That's all I care about. Anyway, we won't have much chance to see it. That baby will soon be as dead as our chances in the World Cup.'

She was awake. There was a noise, a scratching sound. Her window. It was at her window.

Panic was without words, without thought. It was ice-cold and viscous, squeezing at the heart, swelling in the throat, shutting it down.

'Odette? Are you awake?'

'Oh for fuck's sake, it's you. Of course I'm not bloody awake. You scared me half to death.'

Adriaan laughed. Bloody well laughed. 'This isn't Jo'burg, you know.'

'I nearly passed out. Now shut up before you wake Mandy. What do you want?'

'Can't I...?'

'I suppose you'd better come in.'

She hadn't seen Adriaan in a week. Not a word, apology or otherwise. Not a bloody word.

She tugged on her gown and wrenched at the curtain. Her hands were still shaking. She struggled with the French door, which was stuck from the rain. He tried to embrace her, but she pushed him away. She could smell alcohol. It reminded her of far too many childhood goodnights.

'Your hands are cold. What do you want?'

'Now that's a helluva way to greet a long-lost...'

'Cut it, Adriaan. You've been drinking so... what? You suddenly think of me?' Despite herself, she became aware of how she must look, with her puffy eyes and flat hair. She resented the self-consciousness, yet was unable to banish it.

'No,' he said, jocularity gone. 'No, that's not it. I had an idea.'

'And it couldn't wait till morning?'

'Can I at least sit down?' He perched on the bed. It was only a week, yet he seemed out of place. She had grown reconciled to the inevitability of her solitary bed.

'I'm sorry, my *skat.*' He had never used an endearment before. 'I know I behaved like an ox.'

'And it's not just Jo'burg, by the way.' He looked uncomprehending. 'The fear. I'd have thought you'd be the first...'

She had wanted to hurt him, but his face changed and she regretted it. 'Okay, okay. I accept your apology.' Odette wondered if he'd come in the middle of the night to be certain of avoiding Mandy.

'I'm not going to sleep with you.' She sounded severe. He had his back to her, fiddling with the French door, checking for its sticking point. When he turned he was smiling, a bit rueful. No, not rueful. Reproachful.

'I didn't come for that. And I wasn't *drinking*. I had a couple with poor old Gerrie, that's all. I've been thinking about you all week, but I couldn't . . . I didn't know what to say.'

'"Sorry" may have helped.' Her hands still shook. Adriaan stepped forward, lifted one and kissed it. His lips were cold.

'I know. I started to drive home and . . . I just missed you. It seemed stupid to waste a whole 'nother night.' He leaned forward and she could no longer smell the alcohol. He rubbed his nose to hers, like an Eskimo. 'So that's what I came for, suspicious woman.'

'Did you get the shearing done?'

He nodded. 'Pray we don't have another cold front. Well, since you're not going to take pity on me, I'd better be going. Picking my guys up at five.'

'Planting?'

He glanced at the window viciously and shook his head. 'Ground's too sodden.'

'As they say: "It never rains . . ."'

'And we're going to need a helluva crop, with America flooding the market. I'll see you tomorrow.'

'What was the idea, by the way?'

'Coming here? I told you.'

'No, you said you had an idea.'

'Oh yes. Are you intending to use that bottom room? The one that leads off the kitchen?

'No, why? It's half-in, half-out. It's got the washing machine, but it's so huge . . .'

'I've got a use for it. You'll see tomorrow.'

'Ah hell, Adriaan, just tell me. I hate surprises.'

'You'll like this one though, I promise.'

# Chapter 27

SHE HEARD THE BAKKIE from about De La Rey. The morning was silent, rain gone for now. A gentle heat buzzed in the undergrowth, with hoppers rising in clouds each time you placed a foot.

'How's this for an idea?' Voice raised in excitement, Adriaan spoke long before Odette could wrench the door from its damp frame. He sounded like a kid. Oh Lord, what had he thought of now?

And there she was again, expecting disappointment from every good intention. What was wrong with her? Shamed, she didn't question his instruction to open the farm gate and ran ahead of the bakkie to unlock the sticky kitchen door.

He had brought one of his workers. When she caught up to them, they were carrying school desks into the covered courtyard behind her kitchen. Six of them, the old-fashioned kind, with a hole for an inkwell and an ancient blackboard.

'*Dankie* Piet,' Adriaan said as they placed the last of them. 'Look, it'll be freezing in winter, but it's a long time till then.'

'Where did you find them, though? Doesn't someone else need them?'

'No man, they were piled in a barn, doing no one any good. From the days of the old farm schools when our workers still lived on the farm.'

Mandy appeared, dishevelled from sleep. She didn't speak, but walked between them, touching seats and lifting desk lids.

'Your girl might as well use them for some good.' He joined Odette and dropped his voice. 'She'll have something to show for her time here. Maybe she'll decide to become a teacher for real.'

Odette wondered briefly if that was his real purpose, to urge Mandy from the nest again, then felt guilty for doubting his intentions. Unable to contain himself, he dogged Mandy's steps, pointing things out, showing her the old blackboard.

Mandy raised her face and Odette saw that it was pink. It glowed. For once, her awkward child looked . . . Oh hell, she was beautiful.

Odette walked to Adriaan and raised her arms. 'Thank you.' She wanted to say more, but couldn't form the words.

Adriaan left at some ungodly hour for the stock auction in Standerton. She had taken him to Die Ou Waenhuis as a thank you. Mandy had cried off, unwilling to be dragged from her makeshift classroom and Odette hadn't pushed it.

She couldn't sleep again and it was too early to phone Mike. Sometimes she missed the stupid Morning Journal. It gave her something to do with her hands, at least. The downside was that it did less than nothing for the rest of her.

When she finally admitted defeat and went through to switch on the coffee, she saw two cups in the lounge. The couch was tousled, as though it had been doing something indecent. Two wine glasses perched, a little too close, on the small table. Mandy's bed was empty. Slept in (by one or two?) but empty.

'Oh there you are. I was worried.' Mandy was in her classroom, walking through the desks, trailing a hand, lifting lids.

'They're a bit dirty. I'll have to clean them. Why?'

'You're never up this early.'

'I am if I've got stuff to do.'

Odette found a bowl, wondering how to broach the Wolfie issue. 'This boy you seem to like...' She filled it with warm water and Handy Andy and found them each a cloth. 'Here, you start at the top and I'll do this side.'

'What about him?'

'Mandy, I'd really rather... I just worry. He doesn't look clean.'

'He washes as much as you do.'

'Leave the lid up for a while, so it can dry. Look, you're a grown woman. Just about anyway. I just hope you're sensible enough to use a condom.'

Mandy stopped wiping and looked at her. One eye still wandered, usually when she was stressed or tired. 'He's never done that.'

'I'm relieved, but sooner or later he'll try.'

'No, he's never done it. With a girl. Anyone.'

'Oh sure. And what is he? Twenty-three? Oh Mandy, don't believe everything a man says.'

Mandy threw her cloth down and crossed her arms across her chest. 'He's never had a girlfriend. No one likes him here.'

'Yes, but there are other...'

'And besides, he doesn't like it. He told me.'

There was something deeply disgusting in this desk. Odette scrubbed at it vigorously, hoping it was vegetable rather than animal.

'His mom used to cry when his big-oupa was with her, but he was too little to help her. I think he felt...' Her eyes wandered the room as she searched for the word. 'He told me he hates how men can behave... so I suppose he felt ashamed.'

And so did Odette. She stopped scrubbing. 'Well, perhaps I'd better meet him properly. Mandy, are you okay about... I mean, that old man should have gone to jail for what he did.'

'I know that.'

'Okay well, why don't you bring him during daylight. Or for supper. Why must he always skulk about in the darkness when I won't bump into him?'

'You mean like Adriaan does?'

Two horses with speckled flanks cantered across the commonage. Halting beside the weeping willow, they were joined by a mare and her foal, black silvered by sunlight.

The horses grazed, ignoring the cows lumbering through the trees from the township. The foal skittered as the herdboy swung his stick in wide arcs, flinging it into the air and catching it.

The air was languid with heat and lush with jasmine. Her garden, a dustbowl just weeks ago, was profuse with shrubs and blossoms. The orchard rustled with birds.

The landline was ringing. 'Yes. Hello? Mike?' No one else rang her on the home number.

'Is that Mrs Evans?'

'Well, I . . . who is this?'

'Are you Mrs Evans?'

'I don't use that name.'

'I'm sorry. But you are the wife of . . .'

'Ex-wife.'

'Apologies. You're the mother of Mandy Evans though?'

'Who is this?'

'This is William Ash from the *Daily Mail* in London. I wondered if I could speak to you for a minute.'

Way, way across the river, two hadedas burst through the bluegums at the foot of the rocky koppie. Keening across the sky, they startled the horses, who reared and raised dust before galloping away.

'I don't have anything to say. How did you get my number?' Odette caught herself covering her breasts, as though he could see her. Ridiculous.

'I'm afraid I can't reveal that. But I would like to get your family's side of the story.'

She'd been working in her pyjamas for an hour or so. She tried to relax her arms, but still felt exposed. She sat in her desk chair, raising her knees to her chin. 'We have absolutely nothing to say. To you or anyone else.'

'Would it be possible to have a word with your daughter?'

'Absolutely not. And if you dare...'

'Look. The Hopes are speaking freely. We just wanted to give you the chance to give your side before she's officially charged. At this stage, we can't write anything that would jeopardise her trial. We can't even identify her.'

'If. If she's officially fucking charged. Not when.'

'But once she's charged, there'll be a bunfight. At this stage, only we know who she is so you can be sure of getting a good hearing. From the Hopes' side, she isn't cutting a very sympathetic figure.'

Odette couldn't speak. She could find no words to answer this fast-talking man. Excitement lifted his sentences as though this were a game. As though it were fun for him.

'Hello? Hello? Are you there? Mrs ah...' She wouldn't give him her name. She would not be named by him. She would never give him that power.

'I don't like the way you just assume there will be a trial. Or that she will be charged.'

'Well look, I'm sorry, um...Ma'am, but my sources tell me, off the record, they're confident they'll soon be charging her for the death of baby Daisy. They're preparing to interview the other child...'

Her hair follicles pricked. She heard a rushing in her ears. Jagged shards of ice filled her brain.

'...Emily. She's very young of course, so it's slow going. There has to be a social worker present. Anyway, I understand the police are very confident they'll soon have enough to make a case...'

Odette replaced the receiver, very slowly and carefully. Then she unplugged it at the wall.

Mike's phone was off when she tried him on his cell. She supposed he took the view that he could always turn it on when he had something to tell her. It clearly didn't occur to him that she might have something that he needed to hear.

She found Mandy in the kitchen, dressed and buttering toast. She looked different, as though someone had placed a tiny torch in her mouth, glowing pink through her cheeks.

'Can Wolfie come for supper tonight? I thought I could make supper for once. You know that pasta with the bacon? I think I could make that and you like it too, don't you?'

'Not tonight, Mandy.'

'But you said . . .' Her eyes slipped away, mouth dragging into the thin line it so often took with her.

'Yes, I did. But not tonight. I think you and I had better talk.'

'I don't want . . .'

Odette's phone tolled like a bell. 'Look, I'll take you to the Waenhuis. You can have a burger if you like. I know I said they're not good for you, but just for a treat, okay? We really do need to talk.'

'Is Adriaan coming?'

'No he's not. Just you and me. Adriaan's in Standerton for a few days, anyway.'

'Well, why can't I ask Wolfie? Can't he come with us?'

'Not this time. Another . . . any time. How about tomorrow?'

Odette retrieved the SMS. Mike: *Lindy in labour. Still no news.* She dialled swiftly, but he had turned off again.

'Your stepmom's in labour, Sweetpea. By this evening, you may have a new brother or sister.'

A scrap of joy fluttered to her face, lifting her eyes, unscrewing her mouth. 'Do you still have my bunny plates?'

'Of course. They're yours.' She meant the Royal Doulton she had received as a birth present from her grandmother. Thankfully, they'd been returned with the rest of the stolen goods, and without a chip.

'Can I give them to my new brother or sister?'

Odette looked at her. Mandy loved that set, still used the bowl upon occasion, when she felt vulnerable or sad.

'Are you sure? I thought they reminded you of your gran.'

'Yes, no they do but I'm sure. I'm too grown-up for them now. I'd like the baby to have something from its big sister.'

Ou Stella must have had the same idea as Odette. She found the old woman peeping through the door at Mandy and the kids. It was hot, but clouds were massing for a full-on assault.

'Miesies,' she said, unsmiling, with a nod of her head.

'Afternoon Stella.'

'What does the *klein miesies* want to teach them after the school?' She frowned, suspicious old witch.

'From what she told me, Stella, I think she's going to do activities that help them learn and develop. And probably a bit of English. She'll help them read more easily and count.'

'At the school they learn in English.'

'Yes, but it's not their home language so it will help them to have a little coaching.'

'Why does the *klein miesies* do this?'

'She likes kids, Stella. She enjoys teaching. And . . . maybe this is a way we can thank you. For telling the police what you saw.'

'Will you give them food?'

'Well yes, I suppose we can. If you want.'

'If they must come here, you must give them.'

The matter settled, Stella turned and left without another word. Odette stood a little longer, watching. Mandy was flushed with the importance of what she was doing.

'Look Janet, look. See how John runs.' It flung Odette right back to Miss Malan, who whacked their fingers with the metal edge of a ruler and humiliated her for having a mother who smelt of booze at the parent-teacher meeting.

Mandy and she had found the mouldering reading books in one of the desks. God knows how long they'd been there. By the time Mandy started school, they had accumulated more appropriate reading matter.

'Very good, Bongi,' Mandy told the smallest girl with the largest eyes. 'Let's give Bongi a clap. Yay for Bongi.'

Odette felt an unfamiliar emotion. She realised it was pride.

# Chapter 28

'*DIS DIE ENGELSE*,' THE octogenarian called as Mandy and she entered, either unconcerned about their hearing or deaf as a post.

'You're quite right,' Odette said with a smile. 'It is the English. Now the English wants to know: if I order by the glass, does it come from a box or a bottle?'

'Box. Order a bottle.'

'I only want one glass.'

'Take it home. I'll give you the cork. We have a nice Chateau Lib.'

'And?'

She shrugged 'And nothing. That's the wine.'

Mandy ordered a mango juice. Odette was relieved. Die Ou Waenhuis was filling up. At the next table, four plump children drank lurid milk shakes. Their slip-slops lay under the table as their bare feet kicked each other in a tangle of scarred flesh.

'Boet, *moenie*.' their mother said tiredly, before concentrating on the heavy drape of the curtained window. Their father ate stolidly, looking down at his steak.

A black couple entered, flustered and dripping from the storm. They looked to be in their late thirties, early forties. She wondered if they were local government. Their clothing didn't come from Pep and he was swinging a car key that spoke of German engineering.

More likely just passing through. Jo'burg people, washed up in another universe.

Odette held her breath. The octogenarian greeted the couple scrupulously, showing them to the table between them and the plump children. All four ceased sucking and kicking.

'Boet, Leandri.'

She waited till their burgers arrived and the octogenarian retreated. 'Mandy, I...look, I think we need to talk about what's going on with the investigation. Just so you know what's happening.'

Mandy nodded, but continued removing the onion and scraping tomato sauce from her patty.

'I understand they're questioning the elder child...'

'Emily.' Mandy put down her knife, but remained focused on her plate. Odette couldn't read her expression.

'They're going to ask her... I'll pour my own wine,' she snapped, as the octogenarian appeared at her shoulder.

'I hope they don't frighten her,' Mandy said.

'No, but how do you feel about it from your point of view? When you found...when the baby died...surely Emily was asleep. Wasn't she?'

Mandy glanced past her towards the door. Odette twisted her head, but there was no one there. The rain battered on the tin roof. She leaned forward to hear, but Mandy still didn't speak.

'Where was Emily?'

'She was in the room.'

'In the baby's room?'

Mandy nodded, then began eating again. At the next table, Boet was donnering his sister. The younger boy was staring open-mouthed at the black couple. 'Boet, Klein-Jan, *moenie.*'

Odette put her knife and fork down. 'Did she see?'

'Did she see what?'

'Anything. Could she see anything from where she stood?'

'Of course. We tried to wake her, but she wouldn't wake up. That's when I ran out to call the ambulance.'

It was only the next morning that Odette finally reached Mike. She'd been trying since she awoke, not caring how early it was. She tried again while washing, not really expecting it to be answered.

'You woke me.'

'Yes, but Mike, I needed to talk to you.'

'Is Mandy there?'

'Yes ... no, she's still asleep. Look, I got a call from the *Daily Mail.*'

'Ja, they got me last night. Luckily, he's the only one who seems to have our numbers. Ridley said the police must be going insane trying to plug that leak.'

'The thing is, though ...'

'Thank God he's being scrupulous about not identifying her. He hasn't mentioned her nationality so, for the moment we're safe from the local rags. Small mercies, I suppose.'

'But the thing is, he said ...'

'I know. They questioned the child yesterday and it appears she wasn't even in the room, thank the Lord. That's really good news. In some ways, that guy's been a godsend. At least it gives us some inkling of what's going on.'

'She wasn't ...? No Mike, no.'

'What's the matter with you? This is good news. She wasn't in the room. She was asleep, so she can't ...'

'But Mike, she was.'

'She can't testify to what she didn't see. Don't you understand?'

'But Mandy says she was.' Odette stared at her ghostly face in the mirror, half-smeared with cleanser.

Silence. 'She must have ... she must be telling you ... Jesus, Odette, that's not what she said in her original statement.'

'I know. That's why ... Please don't shout.'

She scrubbed at her face with a tissue, as though it were somehow at fault. 'I suppose ... there can only be one reason, can't there? For her to tell them the child wasn't there?'

'A bit idiotic though. Surely she knows they'll find out? The child's young. She won't hold that secret for long.'

'Why would the child . . . Do you think Emily's trying to protect Mandy?'

'I think it's far more likely she's blanked it out. Too painful probably.'

Only when she replaced the receiver did she remember that she hadn't asked about the baby. His, that is. She didn't tell Mandy he'd called, regretting that she was unable to give her more news. Mandy tried him when she awoke, but his phone was off. Probably still in labour, Odette told her. Sometimes it could go on for a couple of days.

Teaching seemed to take her mind off him, as did the preparations for Wolfie's meal. She didn't have the heart to retract her promise, and at least it gave them both something else to concentrate on. Odette went with her to buy the spaghetti and bacon. They found a neglected tin of tomatoes in the cupboard and luckily, she'd brought olives from Jo'burg. Not much call in Nagelaten.

Odette left her during the afternoon to take a turn at Lucky Bean. Trudie's younger son had an appointment for his acne. Mercifully, there were only a few ladies in for tea. Unable to summon the energy to focus on any one of them, she bustled about asking generic family questions. It was after five when she was able to relax her painful jaw.

Reaching her front door at last, she heard animated voices. It wasn't yet dark, and the jasmine climbing the front stoep was overpowering. It had rained, but now the air was still and heavy with fragrance. The voices ceased abruptly as she made her way to the kitchen, steamy with Mandy's efforts.

'How do you do. Wolfie, I presume.' Odette was formal, adding to Wolfie's patent discomfort. She caught an exchanged glance and was shamed, unsure of her motives.

'You seem nearly ready. It looks brilliant. Anything I should do?' She sat across from Wolfie at the kitchen table. He smelt of wood fire. Wielding a dangerous-looking screwdriver, he was stabbing at Odette's expired snackwich maker.

'You can grate cheese,' Mandy said. 'And pour your glass of wine, the food's coming in a minute. Wolfie said he'd fix that for us. He's really good at fixing appliances, aren't you, Wolf?'

Both Wolfie's eyes wandered outward, like errant dogs when a gate is left open. He blinked firmly, squeezing his lids together. When he opened them again, they were under control.

Odette noticed that she had grated a veritable mountain. She rose to pour her wine. 'I thought that snackwich was brain dead. Do you think it can be saved?'

'We're losing her.' Mandy swung the colander of spaghetti on to the table with a clatter. 'Asystole. Defib. Defib. Stat. Pass the paddles and . . . clear.'

Odette laughed. Mandy was crazy about medical dramas. Now why couldn't she have been this vivacious when Adriaan was here? She was more relaxed now, of course. Less likely to miss the social cues.

'Shall I be mother tonight?'

'I await the day,' said Odette. 'I should only live so long. Though not too soon, please.'

They both laughed. Odette couldn't remember when they'd accomplished the mother-daughter thing with such ease. If ever. Perhaps Mandy was finally . . . Then she sobered. She pictured another baby, and another future altogether.

Mandy served and Wolfie placed the snackwich to one side. He treated her to a smile. His teeth were as bedraggled as his hair, but it was a sweet smile nonetheless.

'My mom liked spaghetti.' He struggled with his English and spoke deliberately. 'She could eat it every night. Ice cream too.'

As he spoke, Odette developed a reluctant picture of his mother: Eternal child; perpetual granddaughter; adult before her time. She didn't want it. She had enough sad pictures of her own.

'She liked ... she played tricks. Sometimes she put salt in the sugar and my ... my ...'

She took pity on him. 'Your dad? Did he get cross? Here Wolfie, maybe you want a spoon as well.' He was struggling with his spaghetti, slurping so that it snapped back, spattering tomato acne over his face and neck.

'No, it's okay. He screamed at us. But I never had done it. He take the wooden spoon and ... *jaag?*'

'Chase. He chased her?'

'He chase her outside.' His shoulders heaved and Odette realised he was laughing. Perhaps that was a skill he had learned – silent laughter, silent tears.

'You were close to Adriaan's wife, weren't you?' She shouldn't. She really shouldn't go there.

'What do you want to know about her for?' A hint of Mandy's filial asperity returned. 'Have some more, Wolfie. We won't finish it.'

'Just curious.' And she was. Not just about Liesl herself, but to her surprise, Odette realised she was genuinely interested in his sense of her. When you got past the disastrous first impressions, there was something ingenuous and candid about him.

'Missie Liesl?' Wolfie looked up. His eyes were behaving again. 'She was nice. She also liked to laugh, like my ma. I didn't like it when she cried.'

'What do you mean? Why did she cry?'

'I don't know. She said life made her sad sometimes.'

'Sounds like maybe she got depressed. Finished, Wolfie? Have you had enough?'

'Ja thanks. Full.' He placed a hand over his belly, then surprised her by rising and collecting the plates. 'She said she wished she has a nice boy of her own, like me.'

'Maybe she wanted a baby. Maybe that's what made her so sad. Don't worry with the dishes. We can do them.'

'She told me stories from when she was young on the farm. Once she give me a stone on a chain. A real jewel from her jewel box. They thought I stole it, but she gave it because I liked the colour. She said it's to remember her by.'

To remember her by. How weird. As though she were about to leave. As if she had felt some presentiment.

They were preparing for bed when the phone rang. Mandy got there first.

'Mandy speaking, oh, hi Dad.' Odette switched the kettle off, so she could eavesdrop.

'So I'm not an only child any more.' She sounded animated. Good. Something to take her mind off the other thing. 'But I am a big sister . . . yes, yes I know . . . I know it's only half, but she's still my baby sister.'

'Okay, I'll tell Mom. What's her name?'

'Yes, I like that. It's a good name. Uh Dad? When can I come see her?'

'Oh. Oh okay . . . You mean when she comes out of hospital?'

'Oh.'

'Well, how long does it take . . . to be accustomed to a baby?'

'No, but how long? About. I mean like . . . before she goes to school?'

'No, I'm not being funny, I just want to know.'

'Oh. So will you tell me? When the right time comes. Will you let me know? So I can at least come see her?'

'Okay, bye.'

Mandy came through to the kitchen. Their eyes almost met, but Mandy's swerved aside at the last minute. It was obvious Odette had been listening. Besides the hurt, it must be humiliating. Odette stepped forward, but Mandy had never enjoyed being touched. She was rigid and Odette's arms fell away.

Mandy moved to the cupboard, and she heard the perilous sound of porcelain being shoved and shifted. Odette saw what she was after. Her Bunnykins set: cup, bowl and porridge plate.

Gathering them in her two hands, she placed them carefully beside the sink.

Odette lifted her hands and then dropped them again. She had nothing to say. She couldn't stand between the world and this child. Never had been able to.

Mandy turned then and met her eyes. 'Give them away. Give them to the kids down below . . . or to anyone. I don't care. I don't need them any more.'

# Chapter 29

ODETTE SHOOK HER HEAD at Heather's dry little offerings. Despite having left so early, she still felt unable to stomach a thing.

'I said we were seeing each other again. I didn't say it was a relationship. I mean, obviously it's as much a relationship as any friendship...'

She petered out. Heather waited. She didn't have the energy. She glanced at the clock. Oh Lord.

'He's not Patrick though, is he?'

'Why do you always bring up Patrick? Okay, you're right. Adriaan and I have very little in common: he's a farmer with a dead wife and a church. But in a funny way, he does get Mandy.'

'Why do you make that sound so unusual? I thought her problems had mostly to do with school work?'

'I mean for a childless man.'

'Okay, although she really is more of an adult now, isn't she? So I assume that lingering unpleasantness has dispersed?'

Odette launched into a description of Adriaan arriving in his bakkie with the desks, which Heather seemed to take as tacit assent. In the end, it swallowed a good fifteen minutes, since one thing led to another and they ended up discussing teaching programmes, places to study, working with kids.

When the subject was exhausted, there was silence again. Heather waited. Odette felt herself being sucked into the vacuum Heather probably hoped it would become.

'I'm not doing that Morning Journal any more, by the way. Complete waste of time that was. It just ended up as a writing exercise, that's all.'

'Then why did you stop so abruptly? Why couldn't it continue to serve that purpose?'

Irritation caused a restlessness in her limbs. Heather couldn't take a thing at face value. Not one bloody thing. She got up and busied herself placing a cup on its saucer, then changed her mind and sat again.

'In case you haven't noticed, I don't have endless time for scribbling idly on bits of paper. Or for chatting idly about my day.'

'What does that mean? Sit, Odette. We've still got a few minutes.'

'I don't know. I'm just wondering if our sessions haven't run their course. It's not like I really need you, is it? You were always an indulgence. Just someone to drink tea with in Jo'burg once a week.'

Chevonne had a new set that she'd ordered off the Internet. It included a small cup on a stick for pushing back her cuticles and Odette found herself fascinated in the way people are by alien lives exposed on TV.

'And it looks like we're going to have to kill off that baby, after all.' Lex had been droning on, but now his voice penetrated the fog that surrounded her.

'What?'

'What have I just being saying, Odette?' Lex appeared to have more authority than usual. 'I've been talking about the economic downturn ... for the benefit of those with better things to do.'

He waved his biscuit at Chevonne and then Odette. Chevonne appeared to be rubbing at the surface of her nails with a rough pad, then turning it around to smooth them into a sheen.

'I thought it was only the SABC shows that weren't getting paid?' Chevonne asked her left hand quietly.

'They're in trouble, but we're all caught in the crunch. We can't be stupid. We're going to have to write to keep production costs down.'

'Well, not with my baby, you're not. You're not going to sacrifice him because it's easy. Find your own bloody scapegoat.'

'I grant you we've been getting a little lax with new sets. We're all going to have to keep to existing sets for a while, but this is a material saving we can make. The baby must go.'

Odette felt a moment of relief for Rochelle. Then the pang hit. It was unexpected, but it whacked her in the side like a stitch.

'How can you be so stupid? Can't you see this is the most emotional story in the series?'

'Well, that's another thing.' Lex paused. She wasn't sure if he was waiting for the espresso machine to subside or just for effect. 'We have to remind ourselves how close the screening of these stories will be to the actual World Cup.'

'I've got the mayor's son designing matching Bafana Bafana T-shirts,' said Palesa. She blew on her cappuccino and was freckled by specks of foam and chocolate powder.

'Sure Palesa, all of that helps, but I'm also saying... I mean, what does this Mongol child...'

'Baby with Down's,' whispered Margie, with a meaningful look.

'... have to do with the World Cup?'

Odette kept feeling as though she were from a different planet today. She glanced around the table. Palesa was trying to pick chocolate powder from watering eyes. Chevonne was gently stroking on an undercoat.

'You can't just kill him because he's in the way. Why is he always your most obvious target?'

'Look, last week's ARs were okay, but not great.'

'Although I must say,' Margie placed a proprietorial hand on Lex's wrist, 'we did beat *Temptations* in the "All Adults" category.'

Lex's arm twitched and she drew her hand away, as though she'd always intended it to rest there only for an instant.

'Different LSMs,' he muttered. 'The advertisers would prefer a few more of the 9 and 10s.'

'I think we should all give Lex a little hand for that.' Margie burst into a patter of applause, but gave it up when no one joined her.

'And us. What about applauding us?' said Chevonne, looking around for the first time. She shook her bottle of nail polish vigorously so that it gave a small ting-ting.

'You know very well those ARs are for the stories we wrote six months ago,' Odette said, hearing the strain in her voice. 'Before she even had her amnio. There was no baby. And certainly no Down's baby.'

'Goodness,' said Margie. 'You are spirited in defence of this baby. I'm just wondering if you're not taking it . . .'

'And why the hell shouldn't I be? I've got a really strong story-line. And maybe, just maybe, other members of the team are feeling the pressure.'

There was uproar, as she'd expected, she supposed. They were all talking at once. Chevonne poked her nail polish brush at her in a threatening way. Only Palesa looked amused.

'This is a small town we're writing about.' Lex had the loudest voice. 'There's intense excitement. Come on, Odette. You should be able to give us some idea of the feeling in places like that. Flags, pennants. Those helmet things. What're they called again?'

The owner's daughter came in looking like a drowned rat. It was going to be hell getting home. And she had driven all the way for this.

She took a breath. 'Must I remind you the Down's child on *East Enders* drew the highest ARs they'd ever had? Just give him a chance. A proper chance, that's all he needs, I promise you.'

'My question remains,' said Lex, throwing his arms out and swinging on his chair. 'What does this all have to do with a small town preparing for a World Cup charity event?'

'You're being incredibly short-sighted.'

'We're in the middle of an economic downturn . . .'

'Yes, and what happens when the whole World Cup thing's over and done? Do you want to be cancelled? Come on Lex, see it this way. Like diamonds, genetic conditions are forever.'

Odette was taking an inordinate amount of time preparing for bed. The drive had been exhausting, headachy with fumes and too dark to see the road clearly, yet she couldn't settle while Mandy was still shuffling around. She was brushing her teeth when Mandy appeared in the doorway.

'Adriaan phoned by the way. Before you got back. I forgot to tell you.'

Odette straightened, watching Mandy in the mirror. 'Oh yes? Listen Mandy, perhaps we should sit down and talk about your dad. I think Lindy's just being...'

'Nothing to talk about.' She had lost form, a figurine moulded from dough and crushed too hard by an unthinking child.

'So what did Adriaan want?'

'He said he'd be back tomorrow and asked us for a braai at his farm Friday. I said "okay".'

'Oh good, that should be fun? Something to look forward to?'

Sometimes she could make herself cringe. She moved into the bedroom and began undressing. She didn't want to look at Mandy. Beyond the windows she could hear Howling Dog. Eerie, disembodied; yet another tragedy she could do nothing about.

'Also ... Patrick phoned.'

Odette whirled. 'What did he want?'

'He wanted you. He said he got the caps, whatever that means.'

'Yes, but did he give you some idea...?'

'He said he was back in the country. He wanted to know how you were. I said you were fine.'

'How did he find our home number? I switched cell providers ... he must have gone to so much trouble.'

Mandy shrugged. 'Maybe he just phoned 1023.'

'So was that all? Did he ... Did you tell him anything else? You didn't tell him why you were back...?'

'I told him you've got a new boyfriend.'

# Chapter 30

AFTER THE NIGHT'S RAIN, the commonage looked fresh, despite the chip packets and polystyrene containers washed down from the market square. If you raised your eyes, you hardly noticed them. Hardly at all.

Mandy and she were walking. It was unusual for Mandy to agree and Odette was hoping she'd get a kick out of it, so they might find the space to talk. Perhaps even make a habit . . . but she shouldn't jump ahead of herself. It was just a walk.

She waved to George. His terriers lolloped about them as far as the big gate on to the commonage, when George whistled and they raced back. Mandy turned a couple of times, perhaps to catch sight of Wolfie. He didn't appear.

They strolled in silence as far as the river. Odette didn't want to spoil things. The air rippled with warblers and the waa-aark of tick-birds strutting the backs of cows. Crystalline drops clung to the long grass and spangled the spiders' nests in the undergrowth.

Calves pranced while cows stood their stolid ground or gazed warily at their approach. On the riverbank, they startled a rainbird skulking in the undergrowth in search of its breakfast.

They clambered down beneath the weeping willow, garlanded in plastic bags carried downstream by the rain. Odette raised her eyes so as not to see them, just as the rainbird took off in a descending scale of displeasure. The crossing was muddied and trampled by cattle. Their feet squelched into what she hoped was mainly mud.

'Oh by the way, just so you know, Emily told the police she wasn't in the room when the baby...'

Mandy nodded. They saved their breath to climb the other bank. Odette brushed past a bush that covered her pants in blackjacks. She bent to tug them free in small barbed clusters. It was slow going.

'So how...I mean, I suppose you're relieved. I certainly am.'

'I hope that's the end now.'

'I'm sure you do.' Odette found more blackjacks on her socks and picked at them.

'I just don't want them scaring her more.'

'Mandy you must think about yourself a bit too.' It was a stupid thing to say. What could Mandy do anyway? Nothing but hope they didn't question the child further. Mike was right, a child of that age wouldn't hold out very long.

The smell struck them as they rose out of the river bed on the other side. A sickly scent; the smell of death. It was hard to ignore. Hard to raise your senses above or beyond it.

It grew stronger as they pushed through the trees to the koppie beyond. A cow lay dead against a stump, abdomen bloated and ready to burst. Flies swarmed in a buzzing cloud. A white-necked raven, disturbed in the process of pecking an eye, lifted its wings and flapped almost insolently away.

'So, how was the auction?'

Adriaan shrugged. Patrick would have had stories. Wherever he went, he would come back with anecdotes of people he'd encountered. But then Patrick was a photographer. A trained observer. Adriaan was a farmer. It was an unfair comparison.

'Was it the usual auction – the one in Standerton? I just wondered why you were away so long.'

'Why? Did you miss me?" Adriaan turned the chops over perfectly glowing coals. That was one thing he could do better than
Patrick. She smiled and shrugged. She didn't want the irritation to
crawl in beneath her defences. It was Patrick's fault, for phoning.
He should have left well alone.

'I went over Fouriesburg way after Standerton, that's why I was
a bit longer. Heard of a farmer selling up.'

'Gone under?' Perhaps she did prefer her grandfather's more
quixotic view of cows, but this was Adriaan's life, after all.

'Converting to game, like half the province. Says he's going to
open a lodge. I got some good buys.'

She was past irritation at what Mandy had told Patrick. She
was resigned. Mandy's mouth just repeated whatever popped
through her brain. She couldn't help it.

'...cows and calves. Bonsmara mainly. Great condition. Not
the cheapest, but good breeders.'

And to be fair, she wasn't wrong. What was Adriaan? Chopped
liver? Why should Odette find it so upsetting to have a former
partner find out she was seeing someone?'

'...seller's market, of course, with the maize price so low, but
he wants a quick sale and the cows were still thin from calving.'

Patrick would have turned the auction into an adventure. He
would have made her laugh. But then to be fair, it was hardly
durable. She had never expected him to settle on the bottom rim
of Africa for long, when he could live anywhere, with anyone.
Anyone who didn't have baggage like an albatross about her neck.

'Needed some new breeding stock. And in six months, those
calves will be worth...Now I'm telling you all the fascinating
details of my cattle auction and I could swear you weren't even
listening.'

'I'm listening. You said you needed new breeding stock and you
got some nice Bonsmara. Pretty cows those. Red, aren't they?'

'Good girl. We'll make a farmer of you yet.'

What the hell. It was for the best. It was all for the best, even
Mandy using the word 'boyfriend', a term Patrick would find
amusing, and that he would probably think she got from Odette.

Adriaan laid the braai tongs on the low wall of the stoep and reached out to refill her glass. She held her hand over it.

'Move,' he said. 'It's a very nice Shiraz, which I brought back specially for you. If you don't move, I'll trickle it through your fingers.' He was grinning, but this wasn't Odette's favourite joke.

'Come on,' he wheedled. 'Let your hair down for once.'

'Don't be a bully, Adriaan.'

He jerked his arm back and clanked the bottle on the wall with an ominous grating sound. Leaning away from the eddying smoke, he shifted around the braai till his back was to her.

She sighed. It was a beautiful evening. They were on the westerly side of the wrap-around stoep of the old farmhouse. Beneath a sky daubed with pink and shades of blue, the land lay spread-eagled, hazy with evening light. To their left a barn hunkered beside a rock-strewn koppie. And beyond it a dam glistened, milky as a moonstone.

Stepping from the shadow of the barn surrounded by goats, Mandy seemed part of a rural idyll. She bent to the spindly kids nuzzling and butting to suck her hands and the last rays of sunlight caught her in a web of fleeting happiness.

'Are you going to be angry with me now?' she asked.

'I'm not angry.'

'I can see you're angry. Tell you what, I'll go and find the loo and when I come back, perhaps you'll have forgiven me?' As she stepped inside, a jackal cried in the koppies behind the farm. It sounded like a lost lamb.

The floor creaked and she stepped quickly into the lounge where a floral rug covered the wide floorboards. The furniture was old, rather than antique, ball and claw and flowered linens. Against one wall, a doilie spread itself protectively over a nest of tables and, on a second, a glass cabinet held a collection of thimbles and small porcelain dogs.

It felt like a parental home. But of course, that's what it was: a parental home preserved in time. Adriaan no longer lived here, although . . . it had been someone else's home. Adriaan's wife must have enjoyed the same tastes, or perhaps she had just been too sensitive to redecorate once the old lady died.

There was no rug in the hall. The floor was bare, slightly darkened near the door. It was at that point she realised she could be standing on the spot Liesl had bled to death.

Had she let them in? Or had they unlatched one of those old sash windows? This wooden floor may have been the last thing she saw. Did she cry? Call for Adriaan? Or was she stoical to the end, suffering the lot of farmers since Voortrekker days?

They shouldn't have come. He shouldn't have suggested showing her the old homestead. Perhaps he had felt that he was opening his life to her. His life and his past. But it was too much: for her, and certainly for him. Of course it was. That was why he was edgy.

Here they were braaiing, laughing and teasing each other when just beyond the door . . . What unimaginable horror must he feel each time he opened the great front door and his mind recreated how he had found her?

She stepped behind Adriaan and placed her arms around his waist. He had a slight tummy, which she found endearing. His muscles flexed as he reached out with the braai tongs.

'Come on, Adriaan, it's just a small idiosyncrasy. My ma was an alcoholic. It scares me a bit, if you must know. It's not such a big deal.'

He turned at last, wielding the braai tongs in one hand, a bit like a weapon. 'I'm not a bully.'

'As long as you don't attack me with those tongs. No, seriously Adriaan, is that what's bothering you?'

'I was teasing. It was a game. I'm not a bully. I'm not that kind of man and I don't like . . .'

'Okay, okay.' She raised her hands defensively. 'I'm sorry I used the word. Really. Come on, forgive me.'

'Okay.' He planted a clumsy kiss on her forehead. 'If you pass me that torch. Can't see this bloody wors at all.'

She yelled for Mandy before it became too dark for her to make her way back. The night was pitch, or perhaps it just seemed so, beyond the pale light of the stoep.

Anyone could lurk just beyond the house. They could watch and wait, unseen and still, until the householders were at their most vulnerable... Okay, enough! They should just enjoy the braai as far as they were able and then get out of there.

'Well, here she is,' Adriaan said heartily.

Mandy was pink, animated by the goats' attention. 'They're so sweet, Ma. You should've come down. They suck your hands.'

'They can suck really, really hard, can't they?' said Adriaan, who was trying really, really hard. He was a kind man, for all his idiosyncrasies. And who didn't have those by this age?

Saying he had one more surprise, he led them into the kitchen where his Jack Russell lay in her basket, surrounded by four blind, nuzzling pups. 'Willem, my farm manager, was looking after them while I was away. But since I'm on the farm every day, I thought I could keep a better eye on them here.'

Mandy could manage only an expelled 'oo-ooh'. She was undone by anything helpless.

'Be careful she doesn't snap.'

But Mandy couldn't hear and he needn't have worried. She laid her stumpy hand over the dog's head, as though blessing her. She fondled her ears till the dog crooned. With a finger, she stroked each of the puppies while they curled hairless bodies in bliss and nestled closer to their mother's belly.

'Come,' Adriaan said. 'The food's nearly ready.'

Mandy fixed Odette with an imploring gaze. Her one eye wandered slightly. It hardly ever did that any more. Odette shook her head. 'I don't think so. We don't know what's going to happen, or where you'll be...'

Mandy nodded, but her eyes shut down, a translucent membrane closing her off from the world.

'You still have time to think,' said Adriaan. 'They're very young.' Mandy's face soaked animation from the hope he fed her. Odette didn't contradict him.

Adriaan served them chops, crispy round the edges, and succulent boerewors. Never mind cows, auctions or French doors, this was the man's real talent. After supper, Adriaan proposed that he and Mandy check first on the puppies and then the goats, while Odette washed up and ladled out a Coke bottle of milk to take home. He had clearly decided that Mandy couldn't be avoided. Well . . . she'd have to see how long it would last.

Carrying the dishes through, she filled the sink. Mandy crooned at the puppies and then set off with Adriaan for the barn.

Odette knew she shouldn't. It wouldn't make her feel any better. But she had grown intensely curious about Liesl, who was kind, but sometimes cried. Why was that? It was hard to be born with an inability to feel happiness. It was the kind of life she feared for Mandy.

She found the bedroom at the far end of the musty passage. Perhaps it was macabre, but Odette needed to find out more: what she'd looked like perhaps, or worn; the kind of things she had liked.

She opened the cupboards. If she'd expected a shrine, or at least a life preserved, she was disappointed. She opened cupboard after cupboard, bedside drawers, small cabinets. She found odd remnants of Adriaan: a few old batteries, coppers, a worn wallet, a single cufflink and a James McClure novel with its pages coming loose.

On the other side of the bed . . . nothing. On one side of the cupboard, she found a lone belt, a couple of flannel shirts – the Chinese kind from the local outfitters – and a greasy overall crumpled at its foot. On the other, nothing.

The dressing table, shaped like a kidney and glass-covered, was coated in a fine dust. The shallow drawer was sticky to pull out – and completely empty. It smelt of face powder and a perfume that was vaguely familiar. Wrestling it back into place, something caught her eye. It was the cracked cover of a lipstick. She retrieved it, overcome by the poignancy of its bright red traces.

It was strange how differently people dealt with grief. Perhaps it was because Adriaan came back here on a daily basis. Maybe he popped into the bedroom when he needed his overall, or it became chilly enough for a flannel shirt. Perhaps he just hadn't been able to deal with the pain, but Liesl was nowhere to be seen.

Not a picture or a lacy petticoat remained to remind him of happier times. Not a perfume that brought her to mind, a book she had read, a face cream used every night before bed. She had been utterly expunged.

Adriaan dropped them back and she hesitated. It seemed churlish not to invite him in for a coffee, but she knew what that meant and she wasn't sure she was ready. She didn't want to compare him to Patrick there as well. That would be the end.

Adriaan might have sensed something of this, or perhaps he also struggled with comparisons. 'I'm up very early tomorrow. Have to get the bakkie serviced.'

'Me too. Up early, I mean.'

Mandy leapt from the double cab with a mumbled explanation about hot chocolate. Odette didn't presume she had read the social cues. She was sure she just felt like hot chocolate.

'I like your puppies. And your kids,' she said, as Odette handed her the keys and the bottle of milk. It was Mandy's way of saying thank you. When you had children, such things could fill you with gratitude and joy.

'Are you taking it to George? Your bakkie? He's a nice guy, do you know him?'

'The backyard mechanic? Seems nice enough. No, not this time. I need a full service and you . . .' He ruffled her hair. 'You just like everyone. You don't take enough care.'

'But he is nice. There's nothing . . .'

'No, I didn't mean just with him. And I will give him a try sometime. As long as he doesn't get big for his boots and raise his prices.'

'What d'you mean, big for his boots?'

'He's not a fully qualified mechanic – what did you think I meant? No, he seems competent enough. He just shouldn't charge what Theuns does or he won't get business.'

He pulled the key from the ignition. Leaning over, he draped an arm about her. She felt like a teenager at the drive-in. 'So, I didn't get the chance to ask what's been happening in your life while I've been away.'

'Nothing much . . . oh, I meant to tell you, we had Wolfie over. When you get past his appearance, he's not an unsweet boy. One of life's innocents.'

'Not such an innocent.' His voice hardened. 'I told you, you don't take enough care. Just watch your stuff, particularly anything shiny. Don't say I didn't warn you.'

'There's one thing I wanted to ask you, though. He told me Liesl actually gave him that piece of jewellery. Don't you think she might have given him some little piece, out of kindness?'

He jerked his arm back and shifted upright. 'He spoke about that? He had the cheek to bring it up?'

'Look, not that I'd blame anyone for thinking him capable, the way he looks.'

'It was not some little piece. It was a Charles Greig I ordered in Johannesburg. For our anniversary. She was hardly likely to give it to him a few weeks later, now was she?' Adriaan jabbed the key back in the ignition and started the bakkie.

'Okay sorry. I didn't realise.'

'No, and neither did she. She didn't suspect. She thought she'd somehow managed to lose it.'

He got out and came around to open her door. 'I know you're trying to be kind, but I told you before, it's best not to encourage him. And he's certainly not the best companion for Mandy.'

# Chapter 31

ODETTE WAS MAKING HERSELF some lunch and taking the opportunity to slap together the peanut butter sarmies and soup for the squatter kids. There had been no further word from Patrick. And why should there be? He was probably just checking that she hadn't topped herself.

She hadn't been able to bring herself to phone Mike. The very thought of him filled her with a rage too intense to contain, yet she would probably have avoided speaking to him anyway. It was pure superstition. She was desperate for the interview with Emily to be the end of it. Asked and answered: couldn't they leave it at that?

Mandy should have been making the bloody sandwiches. Odette had relented when Wolfie arrived out of the blue, with a puppy-like enthusiasm she hadn't seen before. Something about a surprise, and wanting to take Mandy for a walk to show her something.

Look, she was wary. It was true, Liesl would never have handed over the designer jewellery her husband had just given her. But she'd seen no signs of aggression and, if he couldn't resist shiny things, well, he wouldn't find much shiny and precious in their house.

He was odd. No doubt about that. The thing was though, when she saw the two of them pottering off, side by side, she hadn't the heart to put the brakes on that friendship.

It had been springtime when Mandy had started at yet another school. Odette remembered the morning sun slanting across the classroom of miniature desks, one of which she'd been forced to sit on.

Miss Pienaar sat on the edge of her desk, legs neatly crossed, looking down at her. The jasmine had drifted from the playground on the slight breeze.

'We moved her here because we were told you didn't put up with bullying.'

'I think perhaps Mrs Brink didn't understand quite the extent of her problems.'

She stood abruptly and strode to the window. It was break. Little girls in blue sat about in groups. They looked more grown-up than Mandy, more substantial somehow.

'I get the feeling she just doesn't try. She could at least make some effort to join in. Same goes for her handwriting. Plain slovenly. Shouldn't she be having occupational therapy?'

There at the far end of the field, Odette could see her. She wasn't alone. She was walking beside a smallish boy, who was dressed in ordinary clothes.

'Once a week in the afternoon. Who's that boy Mandy's walking with?'

'Well, I hesitate to criticise a professional, but I must show you their planet projects. The girls didn't even want her on their teams, she makes such a mess of everything, it's as if she just doesn't care.'

'I said, who's that boy Mandy's walking with?' They looked like an ancient couple, out for their constitutional. Hands behind their backs, they leant forward in earnest discussion.

'Oh, don't tell me he's there again. It's most inappropriate. The groundsman's son. Government schools are on holiday this week. I'm sorry about that. Mrs Brink did tell Lucas his son was not to mix with our girls...'

'No.'

'I don't know why he and Mandy...he's not really...it's keeping her from making an effort with the girls.'

Round and round the field they ambled, nodding gravely to each other.

'I said no. Leave them alone. Let them be friends. Please. Just let her have that.'

The landline rang. Odette couldn't find the handset, rummaging through the lounge with the hand that wasn't peanut-buttered. She found it slipped down between the cushions of the couch.

Mike. She found it hard even to greet him, but it scarcely mattered. He spoke enough for two, desperate to justify himself. 'Lindy's understandably nervous. It's her first child. Surely you can see that.'

She clamped the receiver between shoulder and ear. Best get on with doing something. (Preferably something that involved a sharp knife.)

'Even you must be able to sympathise. I mean, you weren't exactly the most maternal...okay, no need to go into all that, but even you must understand the need to protect...'

'And surely you can see what that did to her?'

'Perhaps she should have thought of that before... Look, I can't believe you're even questioning this. She needs to come when I'm home so I can keep an eye on her. At this stage, I think it should just be a brief visit.'

Odette felt herself grow limp. She couldn't fight this thing. It had rained during the night. Sunlight glistened in drops suspended from leaves and on the tracery of a spiderweb in the bougainvillea.

'Well, make sure you do that soon. Because I can't cope with her expectations. Or her disappointment.'

'I'll arrange it as soon as I can, okay?'

There was silence, a chasm they both feared to breach. She put the knife down and sat. 'Have you heard any more? Do you know if that last interview was the end?'

'Ridley was contacted by that *Daily Mail* guy again.' She waited, packing the sandwiches into a neat pile, screwing the top on the peanut butter.

'His sources tell him the police shrink is going to have another go. They're not satisfied yet. They think the child knows more than she said.'

The droplets were drying already. Without them, the spiderweb was tatty, torn on one side, abandoned by its previous inhabitant.

'Ridley says not to worry too much though. If the child changes her story, he'll have a lot of fuel for his cross.'

'His . . . "cross"?' Absurdly, she pictured Mandy spread-eagled, crucified.

'Cross-examination.' Impatient with her, he put his hand over the receiver and said something indistinct. Unmuffled again, he added: 'He can argue "suggestion". That she started giving answers she thought would please them.'

'You mean, in court?'

'In Mandy's trial. If the child changes her story, which I fully expect her to do, it seems fairly certain Mandy will be officially charged. Most probably with murder.'

Odette heard rather than saw Mandy and Wolfie return by the chatter of children who wrapped themselves around her legs and clung to her waist. She would wait to tell Mandy. That was one thing she could do for her now. She could carry the worry alone for a while.

Mandy was pink with the exertion of lifting and dragging the small creatures who clucked and chattered, clung to her legs and hitched rides on her feet. Odette carried mugs of soup, sandwiches and apples into the utility room and they disengaged, surrounding the food in a voracious swarm.

Wolfie began his awkward goodbyes. Mandy was still pink – from more than the exertion, it appeared. She had her hand to her throat, an unusual mannerism. Wolfie was grinning, pleased with himself.

Then she dropped her hand and Odette saw a silver chain on which was suspended a rectangle. In one corner, a small red stone glinted. The piece was too simple to be anything but extortionately expensive. It wasn't the kind of thing you would find in Nagelaten.

'Where did you . . .?'

'Look what Wolfie gave me, Ma.'

Odette turned to look at him. No sign of guilt. No shame that she could discern. His eyes were steady, behaving themselves for once. She struggled to keep her voice calm, so as not to spook him. 'Wolfie, look at me now. Where did you get that?'

'It was Missie Liesl's.' The follicles at her hairline prickled. 'But she wouldn't . . . she would like for me to give it to Mandy. She wouldn't mind. I promise.'

Locust-like, the children had finished every speck of food and were now swarming back to Mandy.

'Come,' said Odette, placing a vice-like hand on his wrist. 'Come outside with me. Mandy? You carry on. Give . . .' But she didn't have the heart, not for the moment. Let her wear it for one afternoon.

When she closed the door, she turned to him. 'Wolfie? This isn't the stone you said Missie Liesl gave you?'

'No, I gave that to my ma, but they took it back anyway.'

'So where did you get it? The jewellery was all stolen when . . .'

'I found it in the veld.'

Behind his head, she saw Willie and Fanie returning from their community service. There was so much else going on in her life that she'd lost the will to hate them.

'You saw it in the veld! Just lying there.' If, by some remote chance, the robbers had tossed a valuable piece of jewellery, or dropped it even, what were the chances he would come upon it on some random piece of veld?

'Wolfie? Tell me the truth now, please. It's important. Did you get this while she was alive?' Please, please, let her have been alive. Let this just be a petty theft.

'I got it . . .'

'What? What did you say?' She struggled to hear him above a chorus of children's voices from inside.

'I say no. I found it in the veld. When . . . after she was late.'

# Chapter 32

SHE GOT LOST SOMEWHERE after *''n vrou is 'n pêrel...'* Weren't good women usually compared to rubies? The dominee spoke fast and, as she tried to summon the exact 'rubies' quote, she missed a few sentences of his 'pearl' metaphor. Her Afrikaans wasn't good enough to pick things up in the middle.

'Why did you bring us here?' she muttered. 'You could just have strangled me at home.'

Adriaan lifted a hand from the table. He didn't look at her until the dominee wound things up. She missed the punchline, but laughed and joined the smattering of applause. There was a general shuffling and clearing of throats. People shifted and exchanged a word or two. Some of the women rose to help with the lunch. (They might be pearls, but that didn't absolve them from serving their menfolk.)

Only then did Adriaan turn to her. 'You shouldn't have agreed to come if you disapproved.' A tiny gobbet of spittle struck her on the cheek.

'Ah come on man, I was teasing. But I must say, it does surprise me you wanted to come.'

'It surprises you? I'm one of the few members of my community who doesn't regularly attend church.'

'So?' Surreptitiously rubbing the back of a hand across her cheek, she returned to picking at the dry arrangement on the table. The colour of dust, it exuded the faint odour of dead leaves.

'Is it so strange that I should want the acceptance of the community I grew up in? Is it so outlandish to want their for- giveness?'

His voice was hoarse and it struck her that he wasn't just being vehement. Could he be angry? But what about, for God's sake?

'Forgiveness for what? For going away? For not going to church?'

Trudie and the other women from their table were handing out plates. The men had opened the side door and stood just outside in the muddied yard. It had clouded over during the speech and a fine drizzle misted the air. She couldn't hear what they were laughing about, but it sounded like rugby. Probably rugby. A couple of them were smoking. Odette hadn't smoked in years, but she had a sudden longing to inhale deeply on something unhealthy.

Adriaan and she were the only two left sitting. She ought to join the women, but now she'd started something she wasn't sure how to finish.

'Oh forget it,' said Adriaan, glancing over her head with an approximation of his bellowed laugh. She followed his gaze to the dominee, who was making a beeline for them. 'I thought it might amuse you, that's all. And I don't want people thinking I've grown so citified and *volks-vreemd* that I can't even join them for the odd function.'

Perhaps she was mistaken about the anger. He probably thought she was being snooty, but his mood would make it difficult to raise Wolfie now. And she couldn't say he hadn't warned her. Why did she always have to know better?

'I can understand that, Adriaan. I'm sorry if I . . .'

But the dominee was upon them. Dominee Prinsloo, thanking them for joining the Women's Lunch. He was a desperate-looking chap, not as old as a dominee ought to look, but quite as fraught.

She judged him to be somewhere in his thirties. He was thin and pale, flesh drawn taut across his skull, eyes a white-washed blue.

Odette asked why they didn't hold the lunch on Women's Day – especially since it was a public holiday these days. They both looked at her absently. She hoped the dominee wouldn't notice the hillock of dried leaf fragments in front of her.

'Well,' said the dominee at last, 'This is a traditional day for our people...'

'It's always been in Spring,' added Adriaan, 'as long as I can remember.'

'More of a local celebration really. Started by the Vroue Federasie. For the women of the Great Trek who founded the town.'

Of course, of course. Women's Day was different. Quite different. It was a new-fangled holiday, to commemorate other women, and another struggle altogether.

She excused herself to join the women in the kitchen adjoining the hall. They stopped talking as she entered. Okay, she was being paranoid. Perhaps it was only because they tried to switch to English. She had begged them not to; sworn that she could understand every word; but that always succeeded in bringing an abrupt hush to the room.

They worked in silence, bar the odd comment about Saar's koeksisters and whether Liesbet had brought her bredie. Trudie was tossing salads and shaking a lump of coleslaw from Tupperware to bowl. Odette busied herself removing cling wrap from chicken à la king and a bobotie so that Anna could warm them in the microwave.

It was probably the silence. She could never bear a vacuum. And you couldn't tell her they never skinnered about the dominee when no one else was around.

'So, what's up with the dominee?' Another coleslaw slopped into its bowl. Knives clattered. 'I mean, here he is officiating at the Women's Lunch – with no woman by his side? Why hasn't some mother snapped him up for her daughter?'

The microwave hummed gently to itself. Cling wrap crackled.

'Does no one want him? I know he's a little . . .'

'Dominee Prinsloo is divorced.' Just that, from the woman who ran the outfitters where everything was Chinese. She was cutting slices of government bread.

'Now that I never guessed. Isn't that a little shocking for a dominee?'

She could hear the swish-swish of a knife on margarine.

'Oh, don't tell me. He's not gay, is he?'

Smash. Trudie caught her sleeve on the cupboard door and dropped one of the coleslaws – as luck would have it, right at Odette's feet. Her bare legs were dripping with milky liquid, in which squirmed fat cabbage tadpoles and wormy bits of carrot.

'Ag sorry man. Come, let's go clean you up.' The rest of the women busied themselves with their tasks. 'You're even bleeding a bit. Let's go to the toilet.'

It was a relief to leave the room, which smelt of disapproval and a perfume that caught in the throat and made breathing difficult.

'Ag Odette.' Trudie was leaning over with a paper towel and at first Odette thought she was shaking her head over the state of her legs.

'Can't you ever leave well alone?' So it wasn't her legs. Somehow she'd managed to put her foot in it again.

'What did I say? I was just messing about, Trudie, surely no one took me seriously. Half the world's divorced, for God's sake. I'm divorced.'

A toilet flushed. Marta appeared and made her way to the basin. She looked faintly thrilled, as though her I-told-you-so moment had finally arrived.

'For us, these things are different,' said Trudie, dabbing at the cut on Odette's calf. 'We don't like to talk of it.'

'Ag Trudie, if she wants to know, tell her,' said Marta, whirling to face them. There was something malevolent mixed in with her pleasure. 'You want to know about this town? I'll tell you about this town.'

'But I just don't understand why it's so terrible.'

'Sylvie, that was Dominee Prinsloo's wife,' Marta shook her hands dry, 'came from Pretoria.'

'Oh I see, an outsider.' Odette crouched to help, but Trudie shoved her hands away and continued dashing at her legs with wet paper towel.

'No, you don't see. As the dominee's wife, we owed her our respect, and we gave it.'

'Marta, I don't think this is right.' Trudie shook her head, trying, but failing, to get in the way of Marta the bulldozer.

'We accepted her. Gave her our love even, speaking for myself and my friends.'

It was cold in the bathroom. It smelt of damp concrete and Jeyes Fluid. And the sickly smell of pink soap that dripped from its dispenser into the basin.

'So when she ran away with someone, he followed her and brought her back.'

'Oh my God, he chased her down. And what? Forced her to come back?'

Trudie made an abrupt shushing motion with the paper towel. 'It was right, Odette. Maybe it's not your way, but she owed us. She was our dominee's wife. The mother of our community and she treated us...'

Both women fell silent. Odette let the silence hang. Eventually Trudie rose again, hands to her knees as though they hurt her.

She leant over the basin, clutching its sides, damp paper towel in each hand. Seeing her from the back, matronly dress stretched over the indent of her bra, Trudie seemed... old. Old and tired and it took her by surprise. She couldn't possibly be old. Trudie wasn't much older than she was.

'Before the service that Sunday, Dominee Prinsloo called her to the front,' Marta continued, arms folded, feet astride. 'She stood before the congregation and she said she was sorry: for her behaviour and for the way she'd treated us.'

'Poor woman. How humiliating. What happened to her after that? Where did she...?'

'No one kept in touch with her,' said Trudie. 'Come. We must go back in.' Odette glanced down. A carrot fragment still clung to the side of her knee.

'And the man?' she asked 'What happened to him? Did he also come back?'

'Odette, come we must go. Marta, let's just . . .' Trudie grabbed her arm and dragged her from the bathroom. All the way back to the hall, she could hear Marta coughing, like a starter motor that never caught.

Just before re-entering the hall, she tugged at Trudie and whispered: 'So was he married? The man. Sylvie's . . .'

'Oh Odette. Maybe now you'll understand why we have such strong feelings about these things. It wasn't a man.'

*[Scene details]*
*Reno and Rochelle are in the bedroom. She is re-applying make-up. He is buttoning his shirt. Reno says he hasn't told Corinne – about his affair, or the baby – but he has told his mother. Ricky is her grandchild, after all. She'll keep the confidence. Rochelle isn't bothered about whether she keeps the confidence. She's trying to persuade Reno to go to the heart specialist with her. Reno is really uncomfortable talking about his child's health issues.*

She got up for a second coffee, but really to check up and down the road for Mandy. She had walked off to the Chinese shop close on two hours ago to buy a cover for her cellphone. Of course, she didn't really need to check on Mandy. She kept forgetting she'd been living overseas. It was just habit.

Until the age of about fifteen, she hadn't been able to let Mandy out of her sight. Mandy would start conversations with drug dealers on corners. She would tell tuckshop moms she'd walked in on her dad having sex. She would give graphic details of her mother's pathetic love life to anyone who would listen.

When she was twelve, Odette had once leapt from an idling car to stop Mandy going home with an older man who had offered her a new set of charcoals and pastels. In Jo'burg. It was a miracle the car was still there when she'd retrieved her, followed by the sleazy old guy protesting his innocence and threatening legal action if Odette suggested otherwise.

Social skills could be learned. To an extent. And you could batter someone into being less impulsive, thank God.

The sun was out today, but the ground squelched beneath her feet. Peach blossoms oozed the smell of spring. She leant over the gate to absorb the sunshine and watch the world go by. She needed a little break from Rochelle.

Odette hadn't mentioned her encounter with Trudie and Marta. Whatever it was she had with Adriaan, she thought perhaps it was best left well alone. It wasn't like her but then, as she had just observed, some things could be learned.

Adriaan had come in with her after the church-do. Dreading more confrontation, she hadn't wanted to make an issue of it and she'd been relieved to find that Wolfie was nowhere in sight. Mandy had remained closeted in her room.

She had managed to pour a few espressos down him before bed, since he'd been forced to drink all but one glass of his Shiraz by himself. He had made a valiant attempt to offer it around, but most families had brought Coke or fruit nectar. One or two of the men had bottles of brandy or cooler boxes filled with beer.

She would probably have sent him home had they not been at the point where it would have seemed a more significant rejection than intended. Instead, she had turned her face into his neck and tried to ignore the miasma of alcohol. Aah, the heady smell of childhood.

Adriaan hadn't seemed to notice the unavailability of her mouth. He'd made brisk and vehement advances before turning over abruptly and falling asleep.

That had once been her favourite time. She would lie curled against Patrick and they would tell each other all the funny or

286

nonsensical things that had happened during the day. They had rituals, like ten kisses before sleep. Sometimes he would tease her with nine, but she would wrestle him until she had won the tenth. Funny what you could make do with, when push came to shove.

The sun was getting too hot, but it was a relief after the overcast days. Willie and Fanie bobbed past, on their way to the churchyard. They greeted her with a grin and a toss that spoke of a certain defiant pride.

She didn't hate them any more. But she didn't greet them back. In her world, you didn't burgle your next-door neighbour and then shake yourself like a dog happy with its own fleas.

*[Scene details]*
*Rochelle is making a cup of tea for Reno's mom, Renata, who is sitting at the kitchen table. Renata says doctors are wrong all the time. Especially that rubbish about genetics. She says Rochelle must enjoy this time and shouldn't long for her life back. The child will be grown-up and gone soon enough. Rochelle breaks down and says: Can't you understand? There's only two options for us. Either I'll never have my life back – Ricky will never be completely 'grown-up and gone'. Or else, he won't survive at all. What kind of choice is that?*

# Chapter 33

'HAVE YOU SEEN THE puppies yet?' asked Captain Fitz, ducking through the doorway for his morning fix.

It brought a spurt of irritation, but she turned and smiled. 'I'm not sure I want the added responsibility of a dog. Americano, Kaptein?'

'*Sommer* a coffee. Strong.' She had so wanted half an hour to reset the grinder and orient herself. She'd had visions of testing the setting on a large cappuccino, just for herself.

'It's a good companion, a dog.'

'Yes, and I don't have enough demands on my emotional energy.' But she muttered it, and the grinder was on.

'Come again? Jack Russells is good little watch-dogs, you know.'

Oh hell, he was just being protective. But now he was going to stand and watch her and, if she didn't do this now, she wouldn't get a chance. Trudie might ruminate over the rain's effect on planting or the calving, but she wouldn't give a thought to how it changed the coffee's consistency.

'How's business, Captain? Catching crooks?'

He shrugged. 'Luckily we don't have the problems Standerton does. We have the burglaries, of course ...'

She flushed the group head and fitted the portafilter. Ah yes. A perfect mouse-tail. What a pity the Captain would be entirely unaware he'd just been served the perfect cup.

'But you do have some violent crime. I mean, you have had one or two farm murders.' She added water and steamed a full jug of milk. She might as well join him.

'It's a general problem. I reckon those okies come from far afield. They look for isolated farms, hit and retreat. If it was local guys, I'll know about it, believe me.'

She amused herself fashioning a heart in the foam. Cheered her up no end. Sad, but true.

'No, they're based somewhere they can get their heads down. Big location, most likely Gauteng. That's where most of the attacks still happen. I think I'll have one more quickly, and one of these...'

'Millionaire's shortbread. Help yourself.'

'They could just as well slip into Lesotho, for that matter. Or they could even be Zimbos.'

'If someone here was involved in that kind of robbery, you think you'd know?'

'Hundred per cent. It's not such a big township and I've got informants for Africa. Pay them well enough. Believe me, I'll know.'

'So...' Odette busied herself foaming her second cup. 'If, just say, someone here... someone like Wolfie, for a completely wild example...'

'A-ag no, Odette. I can see... Look, I sure as hell wouldn't be happy if my daughter was seeing the man.'

'Who told you that? Adriaan?'

Fitz consumed his millionaire's shortbread in two swallows then shrugged, brushing the crumbs from his hands. 'He was concerned, that's all. But hell, not for anything like that.'

'So you don't think he's violent?'

'I've known that boy since he was born. Look, you wouldn't take him for a white man and I wouldn't put it past him to pilfer a thing or two. But robbery...'

She took a breath, but expelled it again. She didn't have the will, or the strength, to take on that battle. She had not the slightest clue what to do about Mandy and Wolfie and, right now, her first priority was to hear him out. 'So you don't . . .'

'No man. If it was an isolated robbery, it would be a different matter. You know the statistics. Every two days a farmer is murdered. It's organised, this thing. Black on white. In the two weeks after Adriaan's farm, there was another couple near Newcastle and then one near Bergville.'

He shook his head and swallowed the rest of his coffee in silence. Abruptly, with a 'Have a good day further,' he left, no doubt terrified she'd start bothering him with more suspects of her own.

Trudie arrived just as the van roared off. 'Did he only have one cup today? How could he have finished so quickly?'

'No, two. But I opened early.'

'Early? But why?' The colour in her cheeks deepened. 'I mean . . . not that it . . . Of course he can get his coffee any time he . . .'

'Hell Trudie, here was I worrying about trivial things like coffee quality when I should've been concerned with the bigger picture.'

Odette started to laugh and after a moment Trudie joined her, pink and slightly shame-faced, but a whole-hearted trill at her own expense. 'Not that . . . you know it's nothing.'

'Oh I know that, Trudie. Millions wouldn't. Nah, I know he's just your excitement for the day. Look what I've done, by the way. I reset the grinder. Can I pour you a cup?'

'Please. I must just unpack these carrot cakes. Piet dropped them off for Yolandi when he came through to pick up his workers. You can still talk. I can hear you from here.'

'So do you have to keep farmers' hours too? I thought you just packed Willem off and stayed in bed. Here, I'll help you. There's no one in here.'

'No . . . ag Odette, you do make me laugh. He dropped them on my stoep. He comes through before five.'

They packed cakes on shelves in companionable silence. Or perhaps it wasn't so companionable. Trudie glanced sideways at Odette. A couple of times she took a breath, then let it go.

'What is it you want to say, Trudie?' She couldn't bear it any more. 'If you want to tell me off, feel free. I'm used to it. I know I put my foot in it the other day and I've already said sorry.'

Trudie stopped and pushed the tendrils of hair from her forehead. It was going to be a hot day. 'I'm not...why do you think I'm going to tell you off? I just wanted to ask...but it's none of my business.'

She felt a surge of hurt. 'Hey, how should I know? I'm just seeing the man. I have no idea where it's going, okay? Does it matter so much to you?' She continued arranging cakes, but in a way that spelled danger for carrot cakes everywhere.

'I just was worried, that's all.'

'I know I'm an outsider, but I'm not about to drag him away, or alienate him from the community.'

'It's not him.'

'Am I not good enough for precious Adriaan? I'm not trying to replace the saintly Liesl.'

'Odette, stop it. Leave those cakes. They're all about to topple. And come to that matter, Liesl was not so very saintly.'

'I can't stop being the dreaded English, but I do try...what did you say?'

'I said, Liesl was no saint.' Trudie took a breath and looked at Odette, pursing her mouth.

'You mean...' Trudie nodded. 'Did Adriaan know?'

'Of course he knew. Everyone knew.'

Odette reached convulsively for a cake but, nervous of dropping it, set it down again.

'If we didn't know before, we all knew when Sylvie apologised to the congregation. Then, everyone knew.'

'What are you saying?'

'Now maybe you can understand our feelings about that kind of thing. Maybe it's okay for the big city, but we know how much hurt it can cause, and how it can damage a community.'

'Why didn't you tell me, Trudie? Didn't you think I should know?'

'I tried, man. There's just such deep hurts here, I didn't want to burden you with all our old history.'

'And Adriaan? When did he find out?'

'Adriaan was there in church to hear it, along with everyone else. Liesl too. She didn't look left or right. Neither did he. But they both sat there and listened while Sylvie told us all what they had done.'

Odette felt disloyal. Not just disloyal. She felt guilty, as though she were sneaking behind people's backs doing something dishonourable. But she had to know.

Her car would never have managed the farm tracks and, for a while, it had seemed impossible. She'd been relieved. But then she'd thought of George, the only soul of her acquaintance here who wouldn't cross-examine her. The only person she knew (besides Ou Stella) who would have no inkling of the dramas playing out in the local Dutch Reformed. And who owned a bakkie.

She hadn't planned this. She'd been driving home from the coffee shop when she'd seen Wolfie loping across to George's. She had stopped on impulse to ask him where exactly he'd found the pendant.

It had been worrying her since he'd told her. He seemed so utterly without guile that, instinctively, she believed him. But she had to clear him completely, in her own mind at least. And if it had been dropped by robbers, the place might give an important clue to the direction they'd taken. Captain Fitz might be instrumental in tracking a gang that was murdering farmers across the Free State. Gauteng even.

George handed over his keys without a qualm, and watched Wolfie leave with her with no more than an inquiring look. He offered the dogs too ('for protection'). Kind, but impractical. She didn't want them raising the alarm.

'Where exactly, Wolfie? Which direction?'

'I can show . . . just drive for now.'

Most of Adriaan's workers were on the far side of the farm, nearest the main road, taking advantage of the clear day to cut the Oulandsgras and bail it for the next winter. They hadn't seen her turn onto the farm road. Mandy would be teaching, which was just as well. She still tended to blurt things out when you least expected it.

'Won't someone see us?'

Wolfie shrugged. For God's sake, why was she asking him? This was her responsibility. Her decision. And she was perfectly entitled to be doing this. It wasn't as though she were doing anything wrong.

It would just have been stupid to raise the matter with Adriaan before she had something concrete to report. And it was surely better to make a quick recce while he was in Standerton. He was there for the weekly auction, selling *uitskot* cows for meat: the ones that had been barren for two years running.

She should have realised it might be on the farm itself. So why did she still not tell Adriaan when she found that it was? He was away, that's why. It wasn't the kind of call he could easily deal with while auctioning cows. Second of all, it was a painful subject. Liesl had died before he could forgive her and now he never would. That was worse, far worse, than having someone die on you when you were at peace with them.

Not that she had managed to forgive people who were still alive. Perhaps she never would, but at least she still had the choice.

'Go this way. Follow the track. Ja, it goes by the dam. Here. Ja, okay stop.' Just as well. The dam was full and the track mushy. The last thing she needed was to get George's bakkie stuck on Adriaan's farm. How would she ever explain that?

It was clouding over again, a Pierneef sky that was heavy and dank, broken by eyelets of light. Elongated beams shone through them, creating tapered spotlights for the side of a rocky koppie, the far end of the dam, a field of cows on the horizon.

It turned out Wolfie came to the dam quite regularly, and not only when Liesl had been alive. He often hitched a ride along the main road to fish in the farm dams. Most farmers probably turned a blind eye – if they even knew. There was always the weekly auction day, if you were clever.

He had told her all this so openly, and brought her here so unerringly, that she didn't doubt him. Yet something still didn't sit right. Would they escape over the land like this? It was slow going. Wouldn't they make for the main road as fast as possible?

'Wolfie?' He stood staring at the water. 'Where exactly did you find it? Show me.'

He pointed at the dam. 'What d'you mean? You said you found it in the veld.'

He nodded and pointed again. 'Ja, I said ... there it was.'

'In the dam? But how did you find it then?'

'Before the rains, it was veld then. But now the dam is full.'

Dummy that she was, it only now occurred to her what he'd been saying. And she also realised that Liesl had been murdered in summer. Mid-summer. The dam would have been full then too.

She had imagined it falling as they ran. Why would they fling a valuable piece into the dam? It didn't make sense.

'I was still asleep, Odette. What is it?' Mike was barely audible. Oh, how she remembered that – the whispering and tip-toeing around the transitory silence of a sleeping baby.

'I just wanted to know if there was any news. I have to drive to Jo'burg. Thought I'd check in before I left.'

'Obviously I'll tell you when there's news. We were up half the night with the baby. I really don't need to be woken ...'

'I just can't bear the waiting. I'm going out of my mind. When exactly are they going to question the child?'

'We don't know. But perhaps you should just put it out of your head and enjoy this time.'

'How can I? What do you mean?'

'Exactly that. Live for the day. While things are still in limbo. Before they've squeezed the truth from the child and the shit really hits the fan. The trial, the publicity, the sentencing...It's not going to be pretty, Odette.'

# Chapter 34

HER MIND FELT LIKE an electrical board that you overload and over-load until it shorts out. She remembered nothing of the drive. All she knew was that she'd left very late, yet still made it to Heather with two minutes to spare.

'What is it, Odette? You look completely rattled.'

'I thought I was late, that's all. I had a fight with Mandy this morning. It held me up.'

'Well, catch your breath. I made Earl Grey. Oh, and by the way,' Heather said it with a smile, slightly arch, 'I'm happy you decided to come back.'

Odette opened her mouth, but could think of nothing to say. She had forgotten she'd ever threatened to quit or, if truth be told, that she'd even had an alternative this morning. Her car had taken over, bringing her here of its own volition.

She took a breath and poured. This was not how she liked Heather to see her, because it wasn't the real her. She was never like this. There was an absurdity in there somewhere; it didn't entirely escape her, but she wasn't in the mood to pursue it.

Heather only had rusks. From a box. How rural she'd become, expecting home-baked goodies from farm kitchens.

'Go on then. Tell me about the fight with Mandy.'

'Don't miss a thing, do you? You're like the neighbour's dog with a compost rat.' She needed time to breathe, that was all, then she would be all right.

'I know you, Odette. You're playing for time. You have a real problem with relinquishing control, don't you?'

She felt a surge of fury. What did Heather know? What did she really know about anything, with her powder-blue walls, her Earl Grey tea and dry rusks.

'Jesus Heather, surely holding your life together is the healthy alternative. It can ruin lives, losing control. It only takes once, and wham, your life is never the same.'

'Tell me what you mean by that. Have you experienced a loss of control that changed your life?'

Odette took a sip and felt the flesh on the roof of her mouth scald. It felt good.

'I was speaking hypothetically, but it's true. Let go just once and you could crash a car or have unprotected sex with someone with HIV . . . And before you ask, I haven't done either. As you pointed out yourself, I have the opposite problem.'

'Did you lose control with Mandy this morning?'

'No. Would've liked to, though.'

She had hoped to avoid speaking of that. Not that it was particularly remarkable, just distasteful. And it didn't reflect well. In any case, there was nothing Heather could say that she hadn't already told herself.

She was the adult, she ought to have retained . . . yes, absolutely . . . Had she exercised more control over the situation, it would never have escalated. It would never have happened at all had she just taken the bloody pendant immediately, as she had known at the time. Somehow she always tried to please and ended up making things worse.

'Go on.'

'Oh I don't know. It was the usual sort of fight. I'm the worst mother in the world, apparently, intent on ruining her life. Stupid to get into it now.'

'You mean, everything wrong in the world is your fault? You can tell me, Odette. You're not alone. I have a client whose child failed university and he said it was all his mother's fault.'

'Except that, in my case, she'd be right.' She slurped again and felt a burnt flap of skin loosen on the roof of her mouth.

'Do you believe that?' Heather had lost her jocular tone. 'Why is it all your fault?'

Odette shrugged, worrying at the burnt place with her tongue, pushing at it, feeling it bubble. 'Isn't that the universal sign of motherhood? Don't all mothers think everything is their fault?'

'I don't know, you tell me.' Irritation flared again. Did shrinks really believe that worked?

'How's the weather been here? I hope we won't have days and days of rain this summer. Do you think that's climate change?'

Heather laughed. 'Okay, okay . . . I'll pander to you this once. But just to catch your breath, mind? And so long as you don't feel guilty about the weather too.'

'Well shouldn't we? Isn't it our responsibility?'

Heather crossed her legs carefully. Clearly she thought nothing could faze her. Odette would like to see her expression if someone really did expose their full ugly truth. Would she maintain that look of neutral interest, or would she forget herself for once and show some good old, genuine disgust?

'. . . you haven't mentioned your small-town swain. You are entitled to a life, Odette, even with Mandy home. She's a grown woman.'

'But not like other . . . not entirely.'

'Well, she's still young. And children with learning difficulties mature later, it's true. But as you said, Adriaan really does seem to accept Mandy. The way he brought those desks . . .'

'Patrick phoned, by the way.'

'Oh, so I suppose that's thrown you into a quandary.'

'Not at all, it's over and done. I didn't even speak to him and he didn't bother to phone back.'

'So why didn't you phone him?'

Odette stared at her. Heather quietly filled the pot from the vacuum jug, swirled and refilled Odette's cup. Heather waited for her to scald her mouth again.

'Are you sleeping okay?'

Odette shrugged, unwilling to say anything that might alert Heather to her dream-riven nights. But she did want the spotlight off Patrick and Mandy, and there were still a good fifteen minutes to go. Then she remembered that absurd old dream. Nothing too bad. Just one of those idiotic dreams that recurred from childhood.

'Go on, then.'

'It sounds stupid when you tell it. But when you're a child, some things seem imbued ... They seem scary when they're really nothing.'

'And this dream retains that menace for you?'

'I suppose, perhaps because it was real first. Before it was a dream, I mean. At least, I think it was. I've dreamt it so many times, it's hard to remember exactly.'

'So tell me the real incident, as you remember it.'

'Okay, but it's really stupid.'

'It doesn't matter. Just tell me what you remember seeing and hearing.'

'Well, my oupa hadn't been staying with us for long and he didn't know the town well. He'd invited some second cousin over, who was visiting from England.'

The bubbling flesh on the roof of her mouth bothered her. She longed to worry at it with a finger.

'Was this cousin coming to stay?'

'No, for supper. She was just passing through. Anyway, she didn't arrive and didn't arrive. It got darker and later ... Of course, this was way before cellphones.'

'Yes, it's sometimes hard to remember what that was like.'

'Eventually, she must have found a tickey-box because I remember Oupa saying to my mother: "The child is lost, Vonnie. Help her, can't you? She can't find her way". Naturally, my mother was completely incapable of doing anything.'

'So did she ever get there?'

'Eventually. But I was scared because my oupa was nearly in tears. My mother had passed out in the lounge and he kept railing at her to pull herself together because the child was lost.'

'Did you meet her eventually?'

'Not properly. I was out of my mind with exhaustion, I suppose. She was the palest girl I'd ever seen, almost translucent, and dressed all in black. I'd never seen anything like that. She looked like she'd come back from the dead or something. Ag, this sounds stupid.'

'You were a child. You didn't know what was going on.'

'I suppose there was so much worry flying around I just caught some. I remember asking: "Are you the lost child?" Then Oupa sent me to bed. He forgot I hadn't eaten but I didn't care. I was too worried about her.

'In the morning, I didn't ask Oupa because I'd heard him say he couldn't help her; only my mother could do that. So I asked my mother if the child was still lost and she said: "What child?" It was then that I knew she'd be lost forever.'

'So you dream of the pale child, floating out there somewhere, lost forever in a forbidding universe?'

'Like a soul in limbo. I told you it was stupid.'

'So Odette, who is the lost child? Is she you or Mandy?'

Odette drove down Munro Drive. The city rolled out like a purple carpet at her feet. It was days like this, when the jacarandas were blooming, that made you wonder why on Earth anyone left Jo'burg.

Lately, she'd been trying to remember what exactly she'd been hoping to leave behind. It was the new grail – the new, inverse grail – not to stay; not to grow old here. If only you could get out of Jo'burg, you felt you could walk away from all that was venal and cruel and violent in the world.

You couldn't though, could you? You carried the world like a shell upon your back. Whatever had given her the idea that she could simply walk away? Or that, by leaving, you could somehow ditch accountability for what you helped create? These things were part of you. The very worst of the world was part of you. You could never walk away from yourself.

She was early for the storyline meeting. Or perhaps everyone else was simply late. It was summery and it seemed a crime to hurry. People were shopping in their sundresses. There were greetings, shared laughter with the man who carried shopping from the fruit shop for a two-rand coin. Funny how the whole mood of the country lifted as soon as the jasmine bloomed. Even the broom sellers seemed less intrusive.

She sat outside, watching Rita, from Zimbabwe, try to sell her hand-embroidered tablecloths in laughing exchanges with people who no longer seemed so harried.

'But Rita, how many tablecloths can a person have?'

'For a gift perhaps?'

'But how many gifts can a person give, Rita?'

She turned and peered through the door of Venezia. It was all set up for them, but the owner and his daughter were arguing again. The daughter made some retort that Odette couldn't hear, shoved at the door and stalked off down the road. He followed shortly after, scrabbling for a pack of Camels.

'Daughters,' he said, lighting and sucking. 'Fucking daughters.' He spoke through a held breath as though it were a joint. Odette didn't say anything.

'All I said was that it was hot and she could take off her bloody cardigan, couldn't she? But she can't take anything at face value. Suddenly now I never trust her just because I'd like to see her arms now and again.'

Why was he pouring this out to her? They had never shared more than a 'Cappuccino please. Hold the chocolate sprinkles'. She wasn't that impressed with his coffee either. He never bothered to flush the group head.

'I mean, I haven't been the most together man myself. And it's true, I still enjoy the odd spliff. Who doesn't?' Did it show, is that what it was? Could he sniff out the signs of failed parenthood?

'Now she says I'm a fuck-up and a hypocrite and it's all my fault. But I told her I've never been so stupid as to cut myself. Who would do that to themselves, you tell me?'

He gave a shudder of laughter, like a dog shaking itself.

She nodded vaguely, watching the breeze rustle the purple cloud of jacarandas in the yard diagonally across.

'It probably is. Jesus Christ, you're made a certain way, then you have a laaitie and all of a sudden you're expected to be some kind of saint. And she's probably fucking right. I'm probably the worst fucking father. Do you think we do this to our kids?'

'Hell, don't ask me. What do I know?'

She could see Lex and Margie meandering along the road. They were in no hurry. She'd be driving home in the dark, but what did they care.

'I'm Paul, by the way. I see you every week, but I'm not sure we've ever really...'

'Odette.'

'Hey! Like the Resistance heroine. My ma was mad about that book.'

'Mine too. She was reading it when she was pregnant, which is why I was cursed with the name. How is one supposed to live up to that expectation of heroism?'

'Jeez, sometimes I think getting through each day is pretty heroic. Maybe that's all she did. The original Odette, I mean. Got through the days. Only her days were different from ours.'

Odette laughed. 'Just an ordinary day having your toenails pulled out. You could look at it that way, I suppose.'

Lex and Margie had met up with Palesa, who was rushing from the fruit shop. Margie was fingering the Zimbabwean linen and looking sidelong at Lex. Unlikely. The last time Lex caught a hint was when someone sledge-hammered him.

'Anyway, maybe it's genetic,' Paul said. 'My daughter, I mean. Maybe it's not my fault she slices her arms to pieces.'

'Oh don't you worry. There's always room to blame yourself if you've a mind to. Either you did something wrong, or you bred without paying attention.'

'But either way, you can just as easily blame your parents, can't you?'

'What can you blame your parents for?' Lex asked bluffly. He had a sprig of jasmine behind one prominent ear. Margie, no doubt. They crowded about Odette and Paul. She wished they hadn't heard.

'For the way your kids turn out,' Paul said. 'Surely it's all because of what your kids inherited, or how your parents dragged you up.'

'But then you have to look at their parents for how they turned out, ad nauseum,' added Margie. 'How far back are you going to blame?'

'Good question,' said Palesa. 'And if we don't start this storyline meeting quite snappily, I'm going to blame you, big time.'

'Good news everyone,' said Lex. 'Our contract's been extended for another year. So we'll be taking *Trophies* beyond the World Cup. Paul, doesn't that mean you should stand us all a cappuccino?'

'Jesus Christ, it's not my good news.'

'And Odette, that beloved Mongol of yours gets to live – for a while, anyway. The audience is responding well to the pregnancy apparently. So maybe you should stand us all to a cappuccino.'

'It's not his fault,' said Paul. 'He's a baby boomer. They're all stingy. It's their parents' fault, they lived through the depression.'

Hell, he wasn't such a bad guy after all, that Paul.

# Chapter 35

IT FEELS STRANGE DOING this after so long. I'm not sure what I'm going to write about. Maybe just the day. Let's stick to that for now, then see how it goes. I know I'm lucky to be living here. I can sit up in bed and see the horses exercising on the commonage. They look wild, like I imagine they would on the Camargue or somewhere, except they're not white, like they were in the poem.

I awoke with the smell of spring. There's a texture, a feel to the air when spring comes. In winter it's sharp, cutting. It splits your knuckles and lips. In spring, it feels like moss. Soft enough to sink into, like musty soil.

It's odd I should be thinking like this. It's almost nostalgic, as though I were looking back on it, or as though I might not have it for very long. But perhaps it's good to appreciate something even if you see it every morning. It's something my mother used to say . . . funny. I normally credit Oupa with the whimsical or romantic comments, but it's not so strange. She is his daughter.

It must have been seeing Heather yesterday, but I couldn't get my mother out of my head and it gave me the urge to write again. It *started all these thoughts churning in my head and, in the end, I had to find some way of ordering them.*

*She was a terrible mother. It's just that I can't really remember how she was before Lucien died. Did she drink then? Or was it only after?*

*I wonder how much she blamed her parents for the rotten parent she was? Because . . . is this a new insight, or have I known this all along? I don't hate my mother for the childhood I had. I can cope with that. I hate her for the rotten parent I became. All this time, I thought I'd come to terms with my guilt. Dealt with it. And all this time, I've been passing it all over to my mother.*

*In fact, I haven't even started. I haven't got to the entry point of this particular funfair. And another thing I suppose I'll have to consider: rotten as my mother was, as drunk and pathetic and incapable, she never inflicted the kind of damage that I did.*

She dosed and groomed the coffee grounds, trying not to talk to Trudie. It wasn't Trudie's fault. She had to order her thoughts, push them into different compartments, or she'd go mad. She had phoned Mike before leaving the house. Still no news. He'd said she wasn't to phone again until he phoned her, so there was nothing to do now but obsess.

It was seeing the Captain that brought the other thing back. Not that it was something you would forget in the normal course of events, but when so much was going on, something had to give. Some kind of priority formed without your even realising it. And somehow, Liesl's murder had dropped down her list.

'You've been doing that for half an hour, Odette. Surely it's ready for Fitz's coffee?'

'Sorry, yes. Americano, Kaptein?'

'S*ommer 'n koffie, dankie.'*

'Don't tell me,' he said, as she handed him the cup. 'You've found me more suspects. What crime will you solve this week? I have a burglary that is still not solved.'

He was bluff and she smiled, but without much humour. Trudie giggled. 'Ag Fitz man, you need a bit of something to keep you going. Let me go find something.'

'*Dankie* Trudie. One of those whatchamacallits...'

'Millionaire's shortbread,' Odette said. Trudie disappeared into the back to unpack the perfect chocolate confection to lay before him. Around here, food equated love.

'Actually, I did want to ask you something.' As if she didn't have enough to worry about. But now that he'd brought it to mind, she had to know. She had to put this in its compartment so she could worry about everything else on her shopping list of anxieties.

'I know you said you never suspected Wolfie of robbery. But what if Liesl's death wasn't a robbery at all?'

She was thinking as she went along. It was a bit like free writing. She could feel her mouth leading her brain, and into territories she wasn't at all certain her brain was content to follow.

'Did you never consider that it might just have been a murder? Like a crime of passion or something, and nothing to do with robbery?'

The Captain put his cup down carefully in his saucer. Trudie came back bearing her offering. She stopped in the entrance, glanced from Odette to the Captain, then quietly deposited it beside him. Poor Trudie. Again she'd ruined the romance of it all.

'You see, Wolfie found pieces of jewellery on Adriaan's farm. I think they'd been thrown in the dam.'

Trudie turned and shook her head at her, but she couldn't stop. 'Why would robbers throw the stuff away, and why would they escape over the farm rather than the main road?'

The Captain hadn't touched his coffee or his millionaire's shortbread. He was staring at her. Something clicked in her brain.

It must have shown in her expression because he stood abruptly, unbalancing the cup, which clattered to the newly tiled floor and smashed.

He crashed his fist into the table. His face appeared to swell, suffused with blood.

'You've been working towards this all the time, haven't you? With your talk of Wolfie and the location. This is what you were really thinking.'

'No, I haven't. This has only just been occurring to me now. I was just trying to make sense . . .'

'You are a stranger here,' he roared. 'You are not one of us. But still you must know the number of farm murders. We are under siege here.'

'Look, I'm sorry, I just need to . . .'

'You need what? We took you in here. We treated you with . . . with . . .'

'I know that.'

Trudie had dropped into a chair and placed her fingertips against her temples, as though her head ached. She lifted her eyes, but still Odette couldn't stop.

'I'm not exactly sure what I'm saying, just that it's strange . . .'

'God almighty, she finds it strange. And do you find it strange that a farmer is killed every second day in this country? That we are slowly being picked off one at a time? We are being decimated.'

'I know all that. About the figures, I mean.'

'We are in a deadly struggle for survival. And still, you want me to turn on my own people. Never mind there are such obvious culprits out there, you still want me to investigate my own?'

'It's not what I want . . .'

'Maybe you want me interrogate the dominee? Or Dr Van der Westhuizen perhaps? How about Meneer Scholtz from the pharmacy, or Dr Bester, the vet? Would that make you happy?'

'I just know you're a good policeman, that's all. You told me once that you never discount anything. So I thought . . .'

'And why, Missie? Why would I start looking at my own community?'

'I don't know. Maybe just to rule out the idea that anyone here was involved.'

'I didn't need to, that's why. I have no need to throw good money after bad. I know these people. I know what they're capable of, and everyone knows who's responsible.'

'So you didn't even consider the possibility?'

'Or would you only be satisfied if I tortured them one by one till I found some scapegoat among our own people. And for something that's systematically being done against us. I'm sorry, Trudie, but I can't sit here . . .'

He looked down as though realising for the first time that he was already standing. He strode to the door. Trudie stayed where she was, hands folded on the table in front of her. The Captain turned in the doorway, silhouetted by the bright day outside.

He jabbed a finger at Odette. 'You! You have been shown nothing but kindness. We accepted you in our midst. Some of us . . . one in particular . . . would have given you his love . . .' He appeared to choke, then shook his head and left.

Odette felt suddenly bereft. She truly had not seen it coming. She hadn't spotted the realisation her words had been edging towards until it was too late. She had simply been trying to work out an answer that made sense.

She hadn't expected this, though. She hadn't expected the roof to come crashing in or the walls of her life in this town to collapse.

'Ag Odette. Why do you always have to push and shove at what is none of your business?' As though she could undo what had been done, unsay what she'd said, and not think the unthinkable.

'Do you know?' Odette felt sick. 'Do you know who murdered her? Please tell me you don't know for sure, Trudie.'

'Of course not. How could you think such a thing, Odette? How could we possibly know that and not say anything. We're a God-fearing community. Any case, how could we know who did it? It was a farm murder.'

'But the circumstances are so weird. Didn't it make you wonder? You must've known it didn't make sense.'

'I know nothing of the kind and neither does anyone else in this town. Fitz thinks it's Gauteng blacks. Who are we to argue with that?'

'Just like the old days, right? Do what you're told. Don't question a thing. My God, Trudie, I thought you said the community had changed.'

Trudie pulled back her head as though Odette had struck her. She was very pink. 'We are a community pushed beyond our tether. You couldn't possibly understand. You are not one of us. But Fitz is right: we are under siege. We must *maar* stick together or we will not survive.'

'I thought you were my friend, Trudie.' Odette leant against the counter, which she had planned and built for her new future, here in this small-town haven, away from all that was venal and cruel and violent in the world.

'I was . . . I am your friend. But you just wouldn't listen, would you? If you only listened to me, none of this would've happened.'

Odette moved forward and stood in front of Trudie. Two women appeared at the door, but saw Odette's face, or perhaps they heard the intensity of her tone, and retreated.

'*Alles reg*, Trudie?' came a disembodied voice from outside.

'*Ja, ja, alles* okay,' Trudie called back, but her voice was strained.

'But you suspected, didn't you? You suspected who it was or you would never have tried to warn me off him.'

'Are you mad? I told you, we're a God-fearing community. I suspected nothing of the kind. I warned you because you're a stranger here. You get the wrong ideas.'

'No. You warned me because you were worried about me. Because you were trying to be a friend to me.'

'It's hardly likely, is it? A white man from a good family? But even if I did . . . which I don't. But just say I did, the whole thing would *maar* have been such a tragedy. The circumstances would never, ever repeat themselves.'

'Does that make it okay?'

'No, of course not. And if we really thought for one moment . . . No, Fitz said it's a farm murder, and he should know. You said yourself he's a good detective. In any case, you of all people . . .'

'What do you mean: "you of all people"?'

'Don't lean over me. I mean with your daughter. What happened overseas. You understand how . . . tragedies can happen. And you understand the need to protect your own.'

Odette walked without looking where she was going. She had burnt her bridges, made her bed, and all those other things you do when you've nowhere else to go. She had sold her house in Jo'burg. She had put all her savings into this coffee shop.

Now what? She could go on, she supposed. She could avert her eyes like everyone else in the village. Shut up and say nothing. Pretend she hadn't seen what she had seen. And why not? Wasn't Trudie right? Wasn't this what she had always done herself?

All her life, she had done no more and no less than these people were doing. She had looked the other way; kept her mouth closed. Because who did it harm, after all? Weren't such things better locked firmly away? Trudie was right. She had no right to comment. In her own dreadful silence, she was no better than they were.

She found herself at the commonage. The horses had been retrieved by the stud farmer. The cows had the place to themselves. They and the tick-birds, gorging themselves on their backs. The only sound was their hoarse wa-aark.

The river was full, but the rains had brought more trash. Packets and cartons festooned the river's edge and hung brightly in the bushes. The entry point to the river crossing had been trampled by many hoofs into a mash of mud and dung and indescribable animal and vegetable remains.

The wind was blowing the other way. She came upon the dead cow before she remembered it was there. The abdomen had burst, entrails exposed, gnawed on by dogs, set upon by flies.

She blundered back into the trees, back towards the river. They weren't indigenous, those trees. Bluegums for the most part. They probably didn't belong there. But since winter, awkwardly sheered stumps stood sharp-edged and stark. Other trees had been stripped of their bark, fodder for still more cooking fires. It made her sad, yet who had the right to say people ought not to be warm and fed.

In a couple of years, there would be no more trees here. It would be stripped of all that had not originally been part of this place.

# Chapter 36

HOW DO YOU BREAK *the silence of a lifetime? How do you tell a child something like this? There ought to be a best-practice handbook for mothers to explain how they came to ruin their children's lives.*

*It sounds so stark when stated baldly. So harsh and unforgiving. I wish I could rather show her a young girl, not very much older than herself. I would like her to see... to feel... that young girl's loneliness. One mistake, that's all. One evening, out of a lifetime of evenings, when that young girl reached out for the only thing she'd learned would always be there for her, and in so doing, destroyed a life.*

*In that I am no different, no better, than anyone in this town. I can face that now. But I can do one thing differently. If I choose to. I can break the silence. I can use this awful truth to some good.*

*No matter what she has done, Mandy is still my child. I want to save her the pain of it. She wasn't ready, and it wasn't her fault. I want to give that to her now, my tainted gift, so that she will have someone else to blame. I can carry her guilt for her. I'm used to it.*

*This is why I have to tell her before the formal charges. Before the whole awful thing lumbers to its inevitable conclusion. I so wish*

*I could rewind that young woman's life, so that my child can feel what it was like. I don't want to have to say it. I'm not sure I can form the words.*

*Because besides all that, I suppose, I still long for her forgiveness.*

Odette slipped out early to find boxes for packing. When she returned, Adriaan was lounging over her gate. He tried to look at ease, but his fingers drummed on the metal.

'What do you want, Adriaan?'

'Who the fuck are you, woman? What kind? You let me ... we made love, for God's sake. Then you go and make accusations?'

'I wasn't making accusations. I just couldn't understand why Fitz didn't investigate, that's all, if only to eliminate any lingering doubt ... Let me pass, Adriaan.'

It's a strange feeling when you begin to fear the person you thought you might grow close to. She wasn't fearful of what he would do, out here in the street. It was the coldness she feared. The icy neutrality of his expression that made him a stranger.

'That's the difference between us. That's what you could never understand about us; why people here find community so important.'

'Look Adriaan, I was just trying to work out why robbers would fling Liesl's jewellery ...'

'Because in the end it's your own people who stick by you. They don't need to eliminate doubt, because they believe in each other.'

She looked at him now, this stranger, this man she had made love with. This alien being whom she had once, so very long ago, thought might be enough for her, in a life that was small and manageable, and that she had chosen.

'Let me pass.'

'So that's it then. I thought we had something special. I really did. I'd just like you to think about this for a moment. I'd like to know ...'

She tried to walk on. She would walk around the block if necessary. But his hand shot out; the capable hand that she had once admired.

'I'd like to know where you get off. You people think you're better, but you're no different from the likes of us.'

She began to walk to the front door so she wouldn't have to push past him through the yard gate.

'With that murdering freak of a daughter.'

She stopped. Slowly she turned to face him. She wanted to say that she knew. Up to that moment, she had not been certain, but now she knew exactly who, and what, he was. She wanted to tell him that, as long as he lived, he would know that she knew. She hoped it burnt a hole in his life. She hoped it shrivelled his soul. She hoped he would be driven mad by it.

Instead she said nothing.

*Once upon a time there was a young girl who expected good outcomes. No. This is something I have to face now. If I can't face it on paper, how will I be able to explain it to Mandy.*

*Once upon a time there was a young girl who expected good outcomes. And that young girl was me. I met a young boy with an open face and blond hair that flopped down over his forehead. I was the young girl who envied his ease, the way he could fling a cardigan over his shoulders and small-talk his way through any company.*

*And it was I who slept with him and thought myself in love. I thought I wanted him, but really I wanted his life. I wanted his family and their Friday night roast.*

*The young girl, the person I used to be, didn't mean to fall pregnant. But she stayed over one night and she forgot her birth control pills.*

*She forgot them through the next day until, the following evening, she saw that the pill she was about to take was labelled 'Tuesday', instead of 'Wednesday'.*

'It's not what we would have chosen for you, son,' his mother told him. The young girl was listening, of course, hoping his family might overlook the shotgun this one time. She hoped they could overlook the family, the neighbourhood and the school. Because... she was part of their family now, wasn't she? Nothing could make them happier because she made their boy so happy?

But he didn't sound happy at all. He sounded... trapped. So she fought him. She battered at him from the depths of her hurt and fear.

'That evil bitch thinks she's better than me. Whether she likes it or not, I am the mother of her grandchild.'

He fought her back as hard as she'd fought him. 'You were listening? That just shows how little decency you really have. My mother was right. In the end, class shows.'

'You can't stand to have a baby with someone like me, can you?' she screamed. 'So what do you want? Do you want to be rid of it? Will that make you happy? I bet you wish you'd never set eyes on me.'

'If you must know, yes.'

The young girl believed him. No. I can't do this any more. I can't treat it as if it all happened to different people, in a different life-time. It was me. I did this. Not some young girl. Me.

I believed him, and that was the end of it. After the weekend I would book my abortion and I would never set eyes on Mike again, *with his skew smile and his mild eyes. I would never become part of the sibling squabbles over a Friday joint, where there was never more than an elegant sufficiency of food or wine.*

*I drove home. No. I intended to drive home. Instead I drove to the bottle store. I rushed into the arms of the lover I had learned would always be there for me. That was the lesson I'd taken from my mother. It was her legacy to me.*

*On the Sunday, Mike came looking for me, because he was a decent young man. He was a good person, who had been given too much to bear. He came to say sorry. He came to say that I shouldn't have an abortion. It wasn't the right thing to do. He had a duty here and he would do it.*

*And he found me, all right. Not some other young girl in someone else's life. He found me, exactly as I was, where I had passed out, a bottle of gin dribbling its last dregs on to the carpet. I was sticky with sweat, vomit in my hair and blood on my teeth. He was kind. He unpeeled Friday's clothes and ran me a bath.*

*'I drank though . . . the baby . . .'*

*'You're hardly pregnant. And it was only this one time. It can't possibly matter.'*

*Through all the nights of that pregnancy, I swear that I never touched another drop. It was only that one time.*

So this is the woman who grew out of the young girl who could only see good outcomes. If I'm to get through this in one piece, and still be strong for Mandy's sake, I'm going to have to do this now.

I'm going to have to face this other woman – the one I became, and that I am now.

I lied to Mandy this morning. I swore to tell the truth, yet I lied once again, because I wanted to get us out of there without incident. I wanted to be on our way. Hopefully it will be the last lie that I tell her.

'But I've got used to the house now. What about the children? I'm teaching them. And Wolfie...'

'We'll come back later. Maybe to stay, you never know. We have to come back to get our stuff anyway.'

I took her round to Wolfie to say her goodbyes. They both wept and I hated to tear her way. I told him that, when we were settled, wherever that was, he could come and stay. That much was the truth. That much I really meant.

When we got back to the house, Stella was waiting. I don't know how she knew, but why was I surprised? The old witch probably knew everything that went on in that town.

'Miesies?' she said. 'Go well, Miesies, and the *klein* Miesies too.' And then she smiled, showing the yellowed stumps of her teeth.

I packed as much as I could in the car. I'd worry about the rest later. George appeared while we were packing, with oil for the Toyota. I didn't know what to give him so in the end, I gave him the meat from my freezer. I think he liked it better than some useless token anyway.

I couldn't face Trudie. Not yet. I would drop a note off about the Lucky Bean. Maybe one of her church friends would buy me out. Later on, I would send her a letter. A longer letter, saying everything that should decently be said. She had been a friend after all. She had tried to protect me, but I hadn't listened. As usual, I hadn't paid enough heed.

And when we were on our way, first thing tomorrow, I would break this destructive silence once and for all. I would do what this town had never managed and probably never would. When we were on the road, we would stop somewhere for a picnic, just the two of us, and I would tell her.

*The young girl – that optimistic girl – had a baby of her own, something she had longed for. She had wanted the chance to be a mother unlike her own. She would never forget a birthday. She would never pass out before bedtime. But instead she became a different person.*

*She knew something was wrong. She didn't want to think it, yet she knew it before she was told. And deep down she also knew that she was to blame.*

*Her golden young man knew it too, and over time, he forgot his part in it all. It slipped his mind that once, when she had needed him most, he had turned his back on her in his disappointment and despair. So he turned from her again, this time in disgust.*

*She had a comrade in arms, who tried her best to share it as she'd once shared her Barbies, her LPs and her friends. But the young girl couldn't loosen her grip on it. She couldn't allow anyone to help her bear it. Perhaps it was true that it might have happened to either of them. But it hadn't, had it? It happened to her. It happened to her child. In this thing, she knew she was alone.*

*In the end, her comrade left too, when the responsibility of having lived here and of her parents and grandparents having lived here before her and the consequences of living here still, became too heavy to bear.*

*In the last resort, the young girl had to bear it alone, this burden. This shame. It was her responsibility. Not another soul on Earth would ever be able to look at her – or her child – with love, with friendship, with anything but revulsion, if ever they knew what she had done.*

*That is what I believed. And that is the woman I have become.*

*I had a baby who couldn't bear to be held, who bashed her head on the floor. A child who screamed through the night and seemed not to want love.*

*It was a Monday when Dr Prescott called. I remember because Mike was waiting to phone his mother.*

*I remember every detail of that day. I remember every word he spoke. I can recite it all still, word for word. He kept us waiting, the bastard. He told us two, but he made us wait till twenty past.*

*He remained safely behind the desk portrait of his blonde wife and his two perfect daughters as he showed us a grainy picture to the side of a journal article. It was a grotesque picture, nothing like my baby. Nothing at all. The picture was bad, but it was the sound it made when named, when spoken aloud. It had a shape. It formed a bubble, which grew and grew until it filled all the space in my brain.*

*'Alcohol-related neurodevelopmental disorder.'*

*'But I thought you said it was a genetic condition.' I remember being surprised at the sound of my own voice. It was strange to me.*

*Glancing between us then, he smashed my last hope of retaining anything at all of the young girl I once was. 'It is genetic in that the alcohol affected her genetic make-up. It's not inherited though, if that's what you mean.'*

*'But how bad?' I asked him. 'What will it mean? What kind of life will she live?'*

319

'At this stage, it's impossible to say precisely to what degree she'll be affected. You'll have to find out for yourselves. Rather like a voyage of discovery.' And then he laughed, a short laugh, as though he had made a clever joke.

He told us her condition should improve as she matured. Some behaviours, like her head-banging, would subside. And she would more than likely progress well with the right remediation.

He yammered on. She showed few clinical signs, that was why he had taken so long with a diagnosis. At least, he said, she didn't have full-blown Foetal Alcohol Syndrome. She was just part of the spectrum. As if that made it any better.

'She'll more than likely show some delays in milestones, as you've seen already with her speech. Her concentration could well be diminished, or problems with memory and executive function.'

He talked about a 'cocktail personality', whatever the fuck that was. I couldn't take it in. She might relate more easily to younger people, apparently, and react oddly to change.

'But don't forget, you can do a great deal, now that you know what you're dealing with. You can teach people to be less impulsive. In time, I believe you can impress upon her appropriate sexual behaviour. Even social skills can be coached.'

He made some stupid joke that made me want to leap over his desk and gouge his supercilious eyes out.

Finally, he told us how lucky we were that her IQ was in the normal range and that many people lived happy, useful lives . . .

*I stopped listening. There was a buzzing in my head. Ice formed in my mouth and my ears. I felt it hardening in the hairs of my nose. I caught snippets: 'No reason, with good remedial input, that she shouldn't be absolutely average.'*

*Fuck him. Why did he think that would make me feel better? I would show him. She would bloody well be more than average. I had broken her, it was my responsibility to fix her. I would make sure she had no disadvantage. I would drill her. I would wrestle this child of mine and everyone who stood in her way. I would bully her into being normal.*

*'If you put in the effort, she could very well end up living a completely normal life. See for yourselves. You can hardly tell.'*

*If you didn't know, yes. If we didn't know. But now we did. And we could never not know again. Her features would never again be the eccentricities of two families bonded, two dynasties moulded into one. They were symptoms, that's all. Dysmorphic signs. Features.*

*'How is this possible?' I remember asking. 'It's such a devastating punishment for one transgression.' I was begging, bargaining, as though he were God; as though he could give us our lives back. And as though he could return our perfect child, the one we had imagined.*

*'I know you must wish you could take it back and do it all again,' he said. 'But this is the reality now. You're going to have to deal with it.'*

*'But one weekend. Jesus.'*

*'Believe me, that's all it takes. You may not have eaten much, and ... look at you, you don't weigh that much either.'*

'We just didn't know though,' said Mike. He hadn't spoken until then. He hadn't looked at me either. 'It's not fair. I thought that only happened . . .'

'To the indigent. Yes, I'm afraid many people make that mistake.'

During the unpleasant part, when the unforgiveable thought flickered through my head, Mike, who had been brought up with decency, never glanced my way.

Briefly I wondered if the same unforgiveable thought might not have crossed his . . . and I reached out and touched his hand, to make him feel better. He didn't respond. I didn't blame him. I probably wouldn't have touched me either, given a choice.

We left at first light and I pulled over before the end of the secondary road because I saw a weeping willow. We had to scramble through a fence and down an embankment to a small river. The willow provided a bit of shade, but we had to perch awkwardly on coarse tufts of grass.

Now was the time. No more excuses. Mandy had to know before the phone rang. Before her life was destroyed, she had to know whose fault it really was.

This was the one thing still within my power that I could do for her. It was the only way I could make myself different from the village I was leaving behind.

'Where're we going, anyway?' Mandy's face was still puffy from weeping.

'We're going to your ouma for a while.'

'But she's dead.

'No, that was Gran. Your other ouma. My mother. We're going to get to know her, just while we catch our breath and decide what to do.'

Mandy reached for a sandwich. Bacon and peanut butter. Her favourite. But not crunchy peanut butter, because she couldn't stand the texture. Since she was a baby, she hadn't been able to bear a mix of smooth and grainy. It made her sick. I couldn't eat. Not yet. Not till I told her.

'Why haven't I met her before?'

'I was angry with her.'

'So aren't you angry any more?'

'I don't know. Perhaps I still am. Or maybe I realised it was myself I was angry at all along. I suppose she did the best she could, in her way.'

Mandy nodded. My phone rang. Oh no, not yet. Not now. It was too soon. I was prepared to ignore it, just for a little while longer, but its insistence broke into my thoughts. I could no longer remember how I'd planned to begin.

'Mike? Please don't tell me...'

I listened. I didn't interrupt. There was no need. I took a sandwich. An egg mayonnaise with chives from the garden. It tasted delicious. Mike cut the connection and I laid the phone between us.

'Don't you want to know what your dad said?'

Mandy shrugged.

'He says you're free.' She sat looking at me, sandwich in hand.

'Do you understand? There's no charge. Nothing. You're free of that nightmare.'

Still Mandy said nothing. 'Can you hear what I'm saying, Mandy? Do you understand? Your dad says the little girl finally broke down and told them what really happened.'

Mandy laid the sandwich down and dusted her hands carefully.

'It turns out she was the one who hurt the baby.'

'I know. She dropped Daisy.'

'You knew? But why didn't you say?'

She shrugged again. 'I went to the loo after I put Daisy down. I thought Emily was asleep. I even checked on her after putting Daisy's light out, but she said something woke her – maybe it was me checking on her. Anyway, when she couldn't find me, she went in to play with Daisy. She just meant to sing her a lullaby. She didn't mean to hurt her.'

'I didn't know, but apparently dropping a baby produces symptoms that can easily be confused with shaking. That's what they're saying, anyway.'

'She took her out of her pram and sat with her on the bed. Daisy just slipped off her lap. She couldn't help it.'

I laid my sandwich down. 'You protected her.'

She shrugged. 'I promised. She was scared.'

'But you? You must also have been scared. Yet you did that. You protected her.'

After Mandy was born, I only saw bad outcomes. I imagined the worst. Always the worst. And it was no more than I deserved. I couldn't expect good outcomes, not after what I had done. They were for other people, not for me.

But this was a good outcome. Oh yes, this could not be denied. It was a very good outcome. The best, in fact.

'Why are you smiling?'

'I don't know. I suppose I'm just so proud of you.'

It was a novel feeling, but it was real and true. Never mind all those fucking perfect children, doing what they were meant to do. Here was my damaged child, my less-than-perfect masterpiece, and she had done something braver than all of them put together.

'What were you going to tell me?' she asked.

'Before we talk, I'm going up that hill over there to make two phonecalls. I thought I'd phone Melissa, if she's back from Vietnam.'

'Will you tell her about Daisy and Emily?'

'I'm going to tell her about you. She tried so hard to share the bad times, I want to tell her something good for once. It's not bad to let people in, you know, Mandy?'

'I could've told you that.'

She looked so earnest that I laughed. 'Why didn't you tell me then?'

She shrugged, her face serious. 'You never asked me. Who's the other one to?'

'The other phonecall? I'm going to phone Patrick, just to see how he's doing.'

She nodded. 'And after that, when you come back, then will you tell me?'

I took a breath. 'Yes I will. Everything.'


*THE END*

# Acknowledgements

WHEN I TOLD MY mother I was making Odette's mother an alcoholic, she sighed and said: 'Oh dear, now the book club will start hiding the sherry.'

So, for the sake of the Port Elizabeth book club, let me make it clear that, to my intense disappointment, neither of my parents drank to excess. Nor did they abuse or neglect me. In fact, they were inconsiderate enough to be great parents. How was I supposed to become a writer, I ask you? I was forced to resort to fiction which, as everyone knows, doesn't sell as well as non-fiction accounts of hardship and misfortune.

As it happened, my mother became ill while I was finishing this book. I spent much of three days reading it aloud to her, some of it in a chemo centre, and she still managed a chuckle and a comment or two. My dad, from whom I inherited my love for this strange country, died before he could see this book come out. So this book is dedicated to both my parents.

The idea for this book was originally sparked by reading Lionel Shriver's *We need to talk about Kevin,* in which a mother struggles to form an emotional connection with a very troubled child. I believe that all mothers experience some difficult feelings towards their offspring, but these are seldom expressed or even admitted to. I became fascinated by the idea of rummaging about in feelings that were difficult to explore, then extrapolated these to a situation likely to produce extremes of ambivalence and guilt.

For my research, I am indebted to parents everywhere, but particularly those I discovered through the South African Inherited Disorders Association and the International Genetics Alliance. I have shamelessly plundered their deepest fears and darkest feelings, as well as their guilts, the heaviness of their responsibilities and their joys.

Thanks to Professor Denis Viljoen, who runs the Foetal Alcohol Syndrome (FAS) programme in South Africa and Professor Arnold Christianson, head of the Department of Human Genetics at Wits University, who helped and supported my efforts.

Most of all, huge and grateful thanks to my friend, Sister Merlyn Glass, genetic counsellor extraordinaire, who selflessly sacrificed herself by reading two drafts of this book to check my facts.

I'm deeply grateful to Liz de Bruyn, her husband Paul and son, Paul junior, for schooling me in matters agricultural, and in the esoterics of different churches in a small Free State town.

I'm thankful for all the people and characters of Vrede, where my partner Fred and I spent several weekends over a few years. They provided me with inspiration, although none of them actually appears in this book. (Except perhaps our neighbours, who really did burgle us, and who were genuinely caught as a result of a Blue Bulls cap.)

In many ways, it was a serendipitous burglary – one of those weird small-town occurrences that is too strange to make up, yet fitted so perfectly into the structure and narrative of the story I was writing.

Thanks also to Herman Botha, local attorney, for his friendship and hospitality, and for giving me loads of local Free State colour.

I was moved by the story of Sally Clark, after reading news reports about her shortly after her premature death. I have used information I found in those, as well as her judgment in the Court of Appeal (Criminal Justice Division) before Lord Justice Henry, Mrs Justice Bracewell and Mr Justice Richards.

I also drew on her case history, poignantly compiled by her father, Frank Lockyer, on www.sallyclark.org.uk.

Figures on farm murders were drawn from the Institute for Security Studies Africa, quoted widely in reports and articles on the subject. Thank you to English solicitor, Jim Nichol, for assisting me with details of an English arrest and the granting of bail.

Judith Ancer, who is my friend, despite being a clinical psychologist, was my first port of call for information on therapy. She is adamant that all mothers wish their children dead at some stage, and gives a talk on this natural, but unattractive urge, entitled: 'Why some animals eat their young'.

Sports details, as usual, were extracted from brilliant journalist and dear friend, Archie Henderson, who has helped me appear to be a rugby and football expert in the past. Two other extraordinary journalists, Peter Sullivan and Mike Cadman, educated me on birds and wetlands. It's the price of friendship with me.

As usual, I bothered Norman Manoim and expected him to be available whenever I needed his vast store of legal and other knowledge, despite his extremely demanding job as head of the Competitions Tribunal.

I successfully persuaded a couple of impressionable journalism students to look up facts and figures for me. Thank you Samir Areff and Jan Bornman. Now where exactly did you get the idea this job would improve your marks?

Jennifer Cohen once told me her tombstone would read: 'Here lies Jennifer, who read my third book six times, one more time than she read *To Kill a Mockingbird,* her favourite book ever'. This time, I interrupted her idyllic new life on a Karoo mountain-top to make her give her cogent, sometimes strict, comments on various drafts of this book.

Dr Jenny Newman, author and lecturer at John Moores University in Liverpool, whom I met at the Time of the Writer Festival in 2008, and who became a dear friend, gave me endless support, talked me off ledges and gave me extremely coherent and constructive comments.

My other faithful readers were Colin McGee (in Westbrooke, Maine), renaissance man Doug Band (in Cape Town), who has supported me throughout my writing career, and Vicky Unwin (in London), who used to be my agent, but is happily still my friend.

Andrea Nattrass, Publisher at Pan Macmillan, was a constant support through my editing process. She built me up when I collapsed in a heap and was endlessly patient with my oversensitivity. I'm deeply grateful for her sensitive comments and constant availability. As she was for my last book, Professor Ashleigh Harris was a tough, but very knowledgeable editor.

My boss in the Journalism Department at Wits, Professor Anton Harber, supported my application for a sabbatical on the basis that I would produce (shock, horror) a creative work, rather than a journal article, and who told me, each time we spoke: 'Write, write, write'. Also great thanks for the support I received from my Head of School, Professor Libby Meintjes, and head of Creative Writing, Dr Bronwyn Law Viljoen.

Endless thanks to Richard Beynon, who provided details about soaps and storylines, helped me brainstorm when I got stuck and gave me tough, but constructive notes on a good two drafts.

This book is also for my lovely partner, non-fiction writer Fred de Vries, who is not my greatest critic. (Too traumatic.) But he supports me and offers clever ideas when I'm lost.

While we were both rushing to finish drafts, we spent several idyllic weeks in the village of Kasouga in the Eastern Cape, where we wrote, wrote, wrote, and went for walks on endless beaches. Thank you Sarah Sephton and Monty Roodt for the house.

Lastly, thanks to my two brilliant children, Emma and Josh, who generally roll their eyes at my projects, but in an affectionate way. I consulted them both on subjects as diverse as psychology and the esoterics of Pokémon. Having kids can be a lottery, so I'm thankful that Mandy is based on neither of my children, and deeply grateful that they're both successfully launched on their life paths.

The following books provided inspiration at various points on my writing journey for this book:

*The Challenge of Fetal Alcohol Syndrome: Overcoming Secondary Disabilities.* Edited by Ann Streissguth and Jonathan Kanter (University of Washington Press).

*Fetal Alcohol Syndrome: A Guide for Families and Communities* by Ann Streissguth (Paul H Brookes Publishing Co.).

*The Broken Cord* by Michael Dorris (Harper Perennial).

*Fetal Alcohol Syndrome: A Parent's Guide to Caring for a Child Diagnosed with FAS* (Wake Forest University School of Medicine).

*Breed Brochure.* Issued by the Cattle Breeders Association of South Africa.

*The Abundant Herds: A Celebration of the Nguni Cattle of the Zulu People* by Marguerite Poland and David Hammond-Tooke (Fernwood Press).